At Play
and other stories

At Play
and other stories

Amita Basu

Bridge House

British Library Cataloguing in Publication Data
A Record of this Publication is available from the British
Library

ISBN 978-1-914199-98-1

This edition published 2025 by Bridge House Publishing
Manchester, England

To Anna: writer, friend, critique partner, and role-model.

Contents

FISH

April 15th, 2020. Day 24 of Lockdown.

I'm walking to the fish shop. Saleem has phoned to say he's received fresh *rahu*. Juhi and I have been conserving groceries for weeks, and yesterday Modi extended the Lockdown till May 3rd. Juhi's Goan-style fish curry will fortify us for two more weeks of this nightmare. At midmorning it's already sweltering, but Covid has made the streets startlingly dust-free.

Up ahead, a line of families straggles down the main road with cloth bundles and toddlers too tired for mischief. Bangalore is opening its pores and releasing, drop by sweaty drop, its millions of migrant labourers. These families, heading towards Nagasandra, must be going home to the villages around Tumkur. Some of them look like they've been walking for days, from Vellore, perhaps. A bulge-bellied man in khaki stands, arms akimbo, wooden *lathi* protruding like a slender electroshocked tail. A masked old man approaches cautiously, mewling, brandishing before him the white flag of a doctor's prescription. The policeman waves him on and resumes his scowling scrutiny of the migrant beeline.

It is not, I remind myself, so bad for us. Normally, Juhi and I would be working all year in different cities, meeting at Holi, Dussehra, and Christmas. Now we work across from each other at the desk all day, then relocate to the sofa for Swiggy home-delivery dinners over true-crime documentaries. For us Covid's been a long holiday.

As I approach the fish shop, a couple in ice-blue jeans, FabIndia *kurtas*, and sunhats turn to glare at me. I retreat to await my turn outside the fish shop. Fingering their PM-95 masks to check for good seal, the couple scan me for signs of disease.

Outside Saleem's shop there are no squares chalked on the pavement, six feet apart, to remind customers to socially distance while queueing. Outside this shop there's no pavement. There's unpaved earth and the back alleys leading to tin-roofed hovels.

The couple is inside the fish shop now, still looking over their shoulders occasionally to glare at me. They don't know me, but I know them. Every morning in Nike Airs and high-tech tracksuits they trot their two snorting pugs beside the lake. Everyone knows Utkarsh and Nikita Sharma.

"*Basa*, you have?" says Utkarsh, simplifying his English – for Saleem the fish-shop-owner is illiterate – and shouting, though Saleem isn't deaf. Maybe it's to project through his own double-masked face that Utkarsh is shouting.

"Yes, fresh *basa*!" From the small cooler, Saleem produces a lissom, pink-finned beauty. Its scales glitter million-silver in a sunbeam breaking through a hole in the tin roof.

"One kilo. Bengali cut," says Utkarsh, "no backpieces!" For the dorsal side of the fish bristles with hair-thin bones.

"Backpieces hard to eat," Nikita explains more mildly, half to me, half to Saleem.

Saleem nods. This shop is poor but this neighbourhood has gentrified. Saleem's intimate with the whims of the wealthy. He passes the fish to his sons at the worktable.

Eleven-year-old Hasan scales the fish with a broad-faced nail-studded wooden brush, sending scales flying towards the walls, which are brown with congealed fish blood. Then fifteen-year-old Ali guts, cleans, and slices the fish.

"Bengali cut," repeats Utkarsh, raising himself on his toes ten feet away, keeping on this side of the invisible fence he's built. Ali nods.

9

I'm standing in line outside the shop. Over Utkarsh's shoulders, beneath the counter, I see a cat. White, with adult proportions, but stunted and emaciated. Belly-up on the grey stone floor, she plays with Saleem's black rubber slippers.

She looks starving. How is she just lying there playing? Maybe the slippers chew like food. Or maybe they're her pacifier, her hunger-killing opium.

This cat is new here. She must be a migrant too. Perhaps she used to haunt another, bigger fish shop. With so many shops shut, streets empty, and rubbish dumps picked clean, millions of street cats and street dogs have been displaced too.

"Shop open all day?" Nikita interrogates Khadija.

Behind the counter Khadija, Saleem's leather-faced wife, looks up from her basket-weaving, which provides the Abduls with a side income. Alone in the family, manning the cash drawer, Khadija keeps her hands fish-free.

"No mam. Four hours only," says Khadija. "We follow government orders."

"Bet they do," Utkarsh mutters to Nikita, "with nobody to enforce them!"

"You *should* follow government orders," insists Nikita, speaking slowly, as if Saleem were a three-year-old. "Shop open four hours only, yes? Everyone should come morning only. Like us. Then you close. Then everyone safe!"

Khadija nods. Hands and eyes busy with her basket-weaving, she says, "After Their Majesties have transacted their business, everyone should shut up shop and go starve so that Their Majesties stay safe." She speaks in Kannada, her tone casual as if discussing the wholesale rate for *basa*.

Saleem smiles affably at Utkarsh and Nikita. The Sharmas, who speak only English, smile back. Saleem disappears into the back room.

The cadaverous white cat rises, stretches, and follows. Behind half-drawn dingy curtains, four cots lie pushed together under motley, dingy bedsheets. Here, under the hot tin roof, the family eat and sleep.

An old man shuffles up the empty road. He's wearing a *kurta* and *dhoti* which were once white. His eyes are bloodshot. His left hand unsteadily grips a crooked walking-stick. His right arm is extended palm-up. Seeing us, he frantically jingles the heap of small change on his palm.

"Why can't they put beggars somewhere inside," Nikita mutters, "and feed them? Look at him just walking around, spreading disease. This is why Lockdown had to be extended. Here!" She flings a coin at him from twenty feet away. The beggar is alone on the street but he crumples in a panic and gropes in the dust. He drops some of the coins he already has, then makes a fist of his hand and uses his thumb to recover the runaways. His eyes bulge with panic and he gnashes his teeth at an imaginary rival scrambling for his coins. Then he rises slowly to his feet, his knees wobbling, his mouth working with the pain of stiff joints tested, his hand fisted around coins and dust.

When he reaches me, I hand him the two packets of Parle-G biscuits I carry for street dogs. Even in Bangalore, where beggars never were as numerous as in Delhi or Bombay, beggars have become more numerous, now, than street dogs. The Sharmas' disapproving gaze pierces me.

"He's not even wearing a mask," Nikita calls out at me from her sanctum inside the shop.

"Surely he can afford one?" Utkarsh reasons with me. "Those cheap black ones? How much can those cost? Ten, twenty rupees?"

Disregarding them, I finally enter the fish shop – there's room enough – and approach the fish cooler and select my *rahu*. The Sharmas edge as far away from me as they can without brushing against the blue walls splotched brown with fish blood.

"Utkarsh," Nikita mutters, "let's find another shop. These Muslims," – she eyes me, checking if *I'm* Muslim too – "everyone's saying they spread Covid deliberately, congregating in mosques. And just look how they live! Guaranteed to spread disease."

I watch Ali gutting the Sharmas' *basa* in one dexterous motion. Hasan is scaling my *rahu*. Saleem re-emerges from the bedroom, milk bottle in right hand, infant on left arm. He catches me staring.

"My sister's," he explains. "She's in the hospital... What a time to be born, eh!" He laughs at the cat, who's hunting his trouser hems. "This unfortunate has also newly entered our lives."

The cat battles with his hem. Has hunger driven her mad? She sinks her teeth into the fabric, gets them stuck, then panics with frantic claws and manic eyes to get free.

"Enough, Monkey," murmurs Saleem.

The cat ceases and desists, and sits back and meows, her eyes blue saucers.

"I'll feed you soon," Saleem tells her. "Have this, meanwhile." His foot nudges out a cracked and dented aluminium bowl from under the bench where, in better times, customers waited to be served. He squirts some milk into the bowl. The cat drinks.

Ali sets aside the *basa*'s backpieces and plastic bags the rest for the Sharmas. Will the backpieces go discounted to another customer, I wonder, or into the Abduls' lunch?

Saleem weighs the *basa*. "240 rupees, sir."

"Google Pay?" asks Utkarsh, brandishing his iPhone.

"Cash only."

Grumbling, Utkarsh counts out the notes to Khadija, receives his change with the tips of plastic-gloved fingers, and sprays with sanitiser the notes that've come out of the cash drawer. Khadija snaps the hundred-rupee notes straight as the Sharmas leave the shop.

Whistling, Ali tosses a slice of rejected *rahu* backpiece. There's a flash of white and then the cat retreats under the bench to enjoy her lunch.

"Selfish idiots," I mutter, watching Utkarsh and Nikita stroll away through the heat-shimmering noon.

Khadija laughs. "There's a saying, mam," she says in Kannada. "'People are as stupid as life lets them be.' When there are floods, potatoes get pricier. But rich people don't notice. They don't eat potatoes. They eat kiwi fruit from Australia. If a neighbour moves, or dies, they don't notice. It's not like their neighbour used to babysit for them, or steal from them. *We* notice because we have to."

Waiting for my *rahu*, I watch the migrant white cat eat. Emaciated but unhurried, she picks her way around the deadly bones.

NIGHT

Vikesh wonders how Simran felt, signing the attendance-sheet then sneaking out of her hostel before curfew. To avert suspicion she wore her homeliest clothes – *salwar* calf-long and two sizes too big, *dupatta* drawn up to chin – and avoided the guards' eyes. But they never stopped her. For Simran's got an angel face. What an innocent she was when she came to him, that first night in the hotel room he'd booked. He coaxed her open, showed her what he liked, and got her – as a man does – to show him what she liked. Their nocturnal education notwithstanding, her face still is like this full moon in the murky autumn sky. His blood churns in his heart and throbs in his groin.

The boys' hostel has no curfew, so he decides to embark tonight instead of waiting until morning. Who knows what'll happen to him tomorrow: but he's doing the right thing, and he must keep looking the world in the eye.

As he approaches the hostel-gate, the guards bid him good evening as usual. He returns their greeting, nodding graciously. His trepidation retreats, making room for other feelings. God, if his own hair ever got as thin as this old man's, he'd know better than to oil it flat. These poor men don't seem to care what face they turn to the world. No proper pride.

"That's the cousin of the student body president," he hears the long-time security guard murmuring to a new colleague. "His cousin controls contracts worth crores of rupees, yet Vikesh sir" – that's how the 45-year-old secondary-school graduate speaks of the 21-year-old months away from getting his B.A. – "is as modest and affable as my five-year-old."

Vikesh pretends not to hear but, mounting his Royal Enfield outside, he pulls himself up straight. In their eyes

14

he's still the man: if something goes wrong they might be useful. God willing, nothing will go wrong on his last date as a free man with the love of his life.

He rides down Bank Road lined with hostels. Show your money and take your pick: private hostels and public, old buildings and new, red-brick and cement-and-glass, five-to-a-room and one-to-a-room, air-conditioned and hot-tin-roofed. At 9 p.m. the November smog is settling, smudging the yellow streetlights into halos. The smog is at streetlight height: hasn't yet descended to the asphalt. How wide the streets look, traffic-free, night homogenising the potholes and dung-stains that give a street its features but steal its spaciousness.

The fragrance of *shiuli* turns his head this way and that, seeking the inconspicuous bush that perfumes late monsoon and early winter lemon-vanilla. Can't see the bush – must be behind a wall. He remembers the *shiuli* bush in Simran's hostel garden. He'd stand waiting at her gate, his nostrils flaring and narrowing to draw in the fragrance from the small cream-petalled, orange-stemmed flowers, which the girls gathered for evening puja in the shrines in their rooms, with tiny idols and flashing lights.

Simran doesn't go in for that old-fashioned nonsense. Sometimes she cradles a few flowers in her handkerchief – shielded from body-heat, keeping their freshness – and sniffs them when they're riding down a particularly rubbishy or cow-dungy street on their Allahabad tours. She sits pillion on his Royal Enfield, face dupatta-veiled against the dust, arm lightly circling his waist, cream-coloured legs in thigh-shorts resting against his hips. Under her oversized *salwar-kameez* Simran wears these party outfits, disrobing at her friend Ishita's. But she bares her skin only when Vikesh is there to protect her.

15

He's never had to ask her. Simran's a feminist, but sensible.

It would've been awkward having to ask her. It's alright when you can tell people to do things. But Simran's never been the kind of girlfriend you tell – at best, with trepidation, you ask her, and watch for the lip-pursing that's her only indication she's displeased. Alone among his friends Vikesh has a girlfriend who has her own mind. He'd never admit this to his chauvinist-pig friends, but he's proud of Simran's mind. For a pole cannot lean on a creeper. His chin rises into the descending smog, and his heart surges thinking of the treasure he's won.

The road runs between campus scrubland and Company Garden's flowering trees. Stripped of their flame-coloured flowers and fan-shaped leaves, the gulmohars' branches are a? lifeless taupe under the white streetlights. The amla trees flaunt their silver-green foliage and pale-green clusters of super-sour fruit, bleached in the artificial light. Here amid greenery the smog falls early and thick; here the smog's sulphur nausea is dispelled by amla's earthy freshness: for feasting squirrels have left the fallen fruit, half-eaten, to scent the air. Vikesh slows and sniffs. For weeks he's looked forward to tomorrow. Now his heart aches with all that he's giving up. Never has the amla smelled so delectable, nor the smog-blanketed city looked so cosy.

The headlight of an approaching motorbike looms disembodied, rocking as wheels sink into potholes and roll over the speedbumps that fight a losing battle against Allahabad's traffic. Vikesh remembers the lantern-bearing ghost – out on a foggy night, approaching the man whose hour had come – with which his grandmother frightened him on demand as a child. Emerging briefly from the smog, the motorbike passes by. Vikesh smiles, remembering what silly things used to scare him, then purses his lips as he realises nobody warned him about life's real dangers.

He draws up outside Simran's hostel, facing the university's Science Faculty campus. The light's on in her first-storey room. Has she already returned from the mess, or is she cooking her own dinner? She's a good cook, producing traditional recipes with remarkable consistency and gentle twists: *aloo jeera* with *saunf* as well as *jeera*, *baigan bharta* with capsicum instead of eggplant. She's made lunch for him all year. They eat her cooking out of his tiffin-carrier on the lawn, under the peepul that murmurs its wisdom patiently to the flighty winds. They watch their peers straggle down the History Department's wide stone corridors, cool even in June. The university's buildings date from the British Raj. So does its syllabus.

Staring up, Vikesh wonders if Simran's convection heater is on. It's not cold enough for her to need the heat, but perhaps she's cooking on it. Cheap to buy, costly to run, electric coils naked, blazing orange-red, these little monsters electrocute a few people every winter. But they're cheap, and in this city of students they sell like hotcakes. One of them disfigured Simran's cousin as a child. Still Simran refused to let Vikesh buy her an induction cooker and a sensible space heater.

"This is what I've grown up with," she said. "Just have to be careful. I keep my eyes open – I'd never have an accident."

"Then think about the electricity bill," said Vikesh. "These things suck up electricity like, uh, like something into a black hole." Picturing Simran crouching cooking over a death trap upset him too much to conjure a proper simile.

Simran tossed her head. "The hostel pays the electricity bill. Besides, everyone else has one."

"By that logic," said Vikesh, "you should get an AC unit too. You're always complaining how hot your room gets in summer."

"Oh, coolers are good enough for me. That's what I've..."

"...Grown up with," Vikesh supplied, and a laugh ended the argument.

But she perplexes him: a one-in-a-thousand woman whose favourite phrase is "good enough for me", an intelligent woman who's convention-bound. Vikesh knows now that "good enough for me" is Simran's way of refusing to argue. As for convention – after tomorrow she will have to think for herself. He's giving up his own freedom to set her free.

Engine idling, rolling down against the chill the carefully folded-up sleeves of his blue-and-white-checked, Superdry button-up – he remembers how she'd fast all day before she came to him: self-conscious about bloat and food-babies. God bless women, inventing things to worry about. She hadn't been as innocent as she looked, not even that first night, when she yielded to him after eleven months of coaxing. When applying for an overnight pass she told her hostel warden it was to visit her local guardian. And she'd meet him only once a fortnight: any oftener and they'd suspect, she said. Vikesh didn't argue: he understood she was projecting her own guilt, and it saddened him that she felt guilty. His own conscience was clear: they weren't violating ethics, only hostel rules set by sex-starved wardens.

A jamun tree insinuates a sturdy primary branch towards Simran's second-floor balcony. On the nights she wouldn't go to him, he could've come to her. The hostel's boundary wall is fifteen feet tall, but the plaster's coming off, providing footholds, and there's no barbed wire on top. Drop into the garden, clap to scare off snakes, scale the jamun tree that pelts the earth all July with large-stoned, God-fleshed purple fruit, and crawl along the branch to Simran's balcony. He suggested this scheme to Simran in February.

Her head whirled to him and her brows knit in that childlike wonder he loves to earn. "How did you know all that? Does being related to the president mean the guards let you into the women's hostel compound also?"

Vikesh grinned. "I despise people who use their status to get privileges... No, I just keep my eyes open. You can see all this from the gate... So? May I come? We'll be quiet, and your cooler's fan will cover up any noise. I can come to you, and you can stop complaining about running the gauntlet of the security guards' eyes."

"No," said Simran. Someone would find out. One of her neighbours, her bosom friends would expose her. She'd lose her hostel room, her reputation, and probably her life: for the hostel warden would write home and her parents would ask her, "Have you gone there to study or to fuck?" and then they'd kill her.

"Hmm." Busy considering logistics, Vikesh hadn't considered consequences. So all year he's made do with her rare visits. After tonight there'll be no worry about logistics.

Vikesh turns off his engine. All his first year of undergrad, before she said yes, he haunted this road. He didn't stop haunting it afterwards, still alone most nights. Here he came to watch the moon rise and set, listening to the night's yawning silence, to its sudden sharp noises like the choking snores of sleep apnoea. Sometimes they spoke on the phone, Simran staying inside her room; but mostly she was busy studying, her phone switched off. He'd stay here till he got pleasantly drowsy; then he'd return to his room and leaf through textbooks in bed till he drifted asleep.

19

Leaning on his handlebars, he closes his eyes and smells her lying beside him on the hotel bed, jasmine perfume mingling with musky nether odour. She learned fast. Her nervous giggles ceded to the same grave interest with which she regards textbooks, civil-service exam-prep books, their lecturers, and everything else she's decided is important. As a teenager, Vikesh taught his younger brothers cricket and football. They still play fervently; Vikesh now only dabbles. But it was Simran who really taught him how to teach: how to communicate the most intimate things one person can to another. Gratefully he spent hours showing her the city and the state, discussing his plans for their future. They'd move far away from this cultural backwater, and surround themselves with progressives: that'd make it easier for him to act right, for of course he knew the patriarchy had tainted him too. She looked and listened. But when he asked her what she'd do after graduation, or how she liked this banyan that was its own forest, she only tilted her head and pouted her lips.

Sometimes her passivity annoyed him. But he reminded himself she'd grown up beautiful. It'd been enough for her to arch her brow, to make her breasts shift under her T-shirt. She hadn't had to plan and opine. Nor, he reflects, drawing up his collar against the cold, had she had to become brave. That's why they're doing it this way.

After two years sneaking out of hostel to meet him, she told him last month that her parents had arranged her marriage to a 25-year-old Brahmin software engineer. After he recovered from his shock, Vikesh rode to Chandigarh to scout his rival. He brought Simran back an accurate picture: flabby, only ever goes to work, boring car. Simran listened attentively, for she wouldn't meet the man herself till the engagement. Then she shrugged. "A man doesn't need to be interesting, only kind."

Vikesh begged her to tell her parents about himself, to tell them it was him she wanted to marry. "They'll behead me," she said, "if they know I'm not a virgin. And they'll hunt you down and strangle you and toss your corpse into the Ganga. When people fish you up, your own mother won't recognise you."

"They wouldn't hurt us," Vikesh protested. "We're in love; it's right for us to be together. We just have to do the right thing; God will look after the rest." Exigency had made Vikesh religious.

"Maybe if you'd been a Brahmin too, I might've dared tell them," she said. "You know I don't believe in that caste nonsense myself, but... D'you want to get us both killed?" Her coal-black, fire-bright eyes beseeched him to see sense. He could see only the blank of a future without her.

That's why they're doing it this way. When the alarm is raised, please God, they'll be where nothing else can hurt them. Filling his eyes one last time with her window's square of light, stark behind the jamun branch, he rides off.

It's 11:21 on Vikesh's Titan Black Dial, the readout dim behind the streetlamp's yellow glare. He speeds across the city, taking turns without slowing down, picturing himself as he'd look to someone peering through the curtains of a third-storey window, his wheels at an acute angle, the asphalt grazing his calves. Of course he isn't really going that fast – impossible on these streets – but playacting never hurt.

They call Naini Bridge the rocking bridge – but really it just trembles under the weight of the eighteen-wheeler trucks that'll be allowed into the city after 11 p.m. On the Ganga's slothful surface this windless night, the yellow moon fractures into big clean shards. One night he brought Simran here, she leaned over, and the pendant he'd given her broke its slender silver-link chain and dropped 300 meters waterwards. He watched the panic in her eye, her hand snatching at air. He saw himself jumping after the trinket, plunging into the river which, below its slothful surface, hurtles seawards, a million gallons a second. It would've been worth it to calm her panic.

When he was six months old his mother had left him on the table with the cassette player. Playing with the cassette covers he'd dropped one, and pursued it down, racing gravity, earning a head-bump. His family loves recounting this story, laughing at him. But love has made him a child again, eager to dive after the impossible.

"Forget it," he said, taking Simran's wrist, steering himself away from the edge. "I'll buy you another – or a different design, if you prefer it."

"That was my favourite piece of jewellery ever," Simran insisted. Moved, he'd pecked her lips. Pecking was all the PDA she allowed, even on a deserted bridge at dawn.

The lost pendant was a leopard – Simran's favourite animal, he'd discovered. A month before her birthday, this discovery had cost him a maze-like conversation with Ishita, his question buried in the maze's heart – lest Ishita guess his intention, blab to Simran, and spoil his surprise.

Outside Higgins, Roshan's waiting, pacing by his hot pink TV Pep Plus. A female cousin who graduated last year gave it to him, and he doesn't seem embarrassed to use it. But Roshan was raised by women: can't hold him to normal standards. Stamping out his cigarette, Roshan crosses the street to Vikesh, who's leaning on his bike. Roshan smells of green apple and menthol, the most popular flavour of hookah. Hookahs, outdoor dining, and orange chicken are the three sirens beckoning to Higgins people across Allahabad over the Ganga.

"Enjoying yourself?" says Vikesh.

Roshan replies with a shrug studiedly casual. The bad boy look is a motorcycle jacket Roshan's still growing into.

Vikesh remembers Roshan from their first year on campus: a Sociology student, thin and stooping, his face pimple-strewn, in thick eyeglasses and ill-fitting, plaid button-downs picked out by his mother. But no wimp. A student thug sauntering near the teashop knocked down Roshan's books for fun and felt a fist flying into his throat. Only Vikesh's presence saved fifty-kilo Roshan from annihilation in broad daylight. All that first year Roshan pored over his books and resisted his hostel mates hustling him out for a night of fun, viz riding around mildly drunk, wildly whooping, courting the police. He told his hostel mates straight-faced that his widowed mother depended on him to study well and enter the Civil Services.

Now glancing left and right, like a trainee thug himself, Roshan hands Vikesh the package. Brown paper and tape. Slender and flat. Trust Roshan to have the packing skills of a gift-shop clerk. This ordinary-looking package will alter the course of many lives.

"Nobody knows," Roshan assures Vikesh. "A friend's friend had the key. I've covered my tracks."

Vikesh claps Roshan's back, lightly, but Roshan stumbles and his eyes fly open – as if Vikesh were already an outlaw, and contact with him contamination-by-proxy. Briefly Vikesh pictures punching the lights out of this small-town, soft-brain shrinking from him. Vikesh totters on a cliff, ready to fall down either side. He falls into laughter: first gentle, then rising into hysteria. Roshan watches him wide-eyed, waiting for the laughter to explode into a punch.

Vikesh wipes his eyes and sighs breathless. "Aunty would be proud," he says. They're not related, but every civil young person addresses elders as relatives. "You wanted to grow up fast and make your mother proud. Now you have."

Roshan grimaces. Where his hostel mates failed to bring him out of his shell, the big city's charms succeeded. Roshan's found new friends, and they're very friendly indeed, for night after night Roshan loses money at poker, and doesn't see how, and pays unfailingly if grudgingly. Since May it's with Vikesh's pocket-money that Roshan's been paying his poker debts. "Pay me back later, or never," Vikesh told him, long before he had any idea he'd need him – for Vikesh pitied the small-town boy gone astray.

"You haven't told me what it's for," says Roshan, gesturing at the package distantly, eyes averted.

"I told you what it's for," says Vikesh. "Science experiments."

"You're a History student."

"Not a good one!" His smile fades. His hysteria has taken the edge off his feelings. Gazing at the restaurant's yellow-orange lamps, he becomes reflexive. "There's nothing for me back here, nothing I can do with my own efforts I mean. I could get someone to get me a plush job, grow flabby and smug, but that's not my style. If you've got nothing to lose, it's easier taking a risk, eh?"

"Good luck," says Roshan, sincere now that he's out of it. He knows about Simran. Vikesh has told everyone about the love of his life, the woman he's going to start a whole new life with.

The Royal Enfield glides back over the river. The fat lazy water rustles in Vikesh's ears. The water dampens the wind, blunting its blade; but the water chills the wind into a hammer of cold. Going at 70kph, Vikesh's unhelmeted face numbs. To awaken his muscles he grimaces at the moon in the river, shrugs mightily, and jogs his shoulders, all without slowing down.

A good friend deserves loyalty unto death. This thought spasms in Vikesh's heart, pumping out a flood of blood suddenly alive, throbbing alive, pushing into Vikesh's consciousness the fact that all this while he's been terribly lonely. Tears blind him. Midway over the bridge he slows down and wonders: should he jump in? That, too, would solve all his problems. Simran still has enormous qualms about running away.

He can't jump in. When he was a kid, his father told him: "If you get beaten up at school, don't come home till you've beaten the other boy up." What would his mother think, when they found his corpse and showed her her grown son beaten by a girl?

Tomorrow morning at 8:50, when Simran leaves her hostel gate, soft fingers adjusting satchel straps, feet stepping lightly as if nothing's wrong, Vikesh will be waiting. The brown-paper bag ready, the flat bottle inside opened, his arm raised.

Simran said they couldn't be together. Vikesh wept and pleaded and argued. Now he accepts her decision. But if he can't move forward with her, then he must move radically backward without her. If he can't have her, then she must lose something too.

She must lose her parents' approval. Her parents think she's a do-it-all: acquiring a Western education while clinging to her Indian *sanskaar*, preserving her virginity for the man they've chosen for her.

She must lose the life that's been planned for her. A life with that mama's-boy, a flabby virgin who has bought Simran with his upper-caste birth-certificate, and with the plush job that is the reward of a lifetime's mindless grind.

She must lose her beauty, which draws strangers' eyes from across the street – but seldom draws their whistles, for her beauty's babylike, her face an angel's face, protecting her even from street harassment. A woman who flings away her virginity, then flings away unblinking the man to whom she flung it, deserves a face to match her heart, a face to tell the world how to treat her right. The prospect of their parting doesn't seem to trouble her: too late, he's realised she's always considered this a fling, and that he's fallen for a whore.

What will they do to him? It doesn't matter, for he can see no life without Simran. He's told everyone about the woman he loves, the woman he's going to marry, and she's made him lose face, so she must lose hers. Tomorrow at 08:50 Vikesh will be waiting, bottle uncapped, to fling sulphuric acid into Simran's face.

REBIRTH

All day I've struggled not to remember *that* day, but my cramp has been building. Clutching my belly, I confront my dinner, seeking the culprit: another thing to eliminate.

My coffee's decaf – decaf is safest after heart surgery, so it might also help me avoid heart surgery. My coffee's also black – when I was five, I had diarrhoea after a pint of ice-cream; two years ago I realised it was probably because I was lactose-intolerant, and got off dairy. Dinner was decaf instant coffee and white-bread-and-mayo sandwiches. Vegan mayo – Dadi has high cholesterol.

There's nothing left to eliminate. There's nothing on my plate that could've caused my cramps.

All day I've kept my eyes on my work. Now they steal towards Prabhat's ghost: the rectangle of wall paint slightly cleaner than the rest, lighter. We got an old-fashioned studio portrait framed on his first birthday. Now the portrait's gone but it's left behind this ghost.

I'm watching the news on television, and the television is muted – less scary so.

Microwave explosion!

A microwave has exploded in a Munich flat. "…probably an accident," says the reporter in closed captions, "though police are considering the possibility of arson…" The resident had a vengeful ex-boyfriend. He's been spotted lurking in the neighbourhood. Fortunately, the resident left last night on a last-minute work trip. "The property damage is minimal, though the noise frightened neighbours…"

My throat clamps closed. Forcing it open with swallows of sugar-free, milk-free, caffeine-free coffee, I absorb the news. Munich's just 6,000 kilometres away. What if Tarak breaks in and blows up *my* microwave? He still hasn't forgiven me for Prabhat's death.

Time to lock away my microwave. After all, why have I put this off? Dadaji was prescient when he warned us about microwaves. Splashed across every newspaper now is *Cancer!* I confront my Sunday dinner. Yes, I can make do with untoasted bread for my sandwiches and decaf stirred into cold water. I unplug my microwave. I'll Quikr it later. For now, I haul it to my storeroom, which used to be Tarak's office.

It's a small room and it's been a long three years. I push the door half-open. Out spill photo frames, anniversary gifts, and rocks and twigs picked off trails on weekend walks before Prabhat came. I thrust the microwave in. I lock the storeroom door and slump against it, massaging my aching belly.

I'm used to grief cramps – what the doctors call psychosomatic symptomatology. These days I get them only on significant dates. I've locked away the calendars but my gut continues masochistically to mark the time.

Today the pain has sapped my self-control: I've allowed myself to think their names. I swore not to do this to myself. I haul myself up, dry-swallow another paracetamol, and clear away my half-eaten dinner.

I finish my assignment: blueprints for Hyderabad's first Taoist temple. I sign my name: Aarogya L. I seal the blueprints in an envelope. I'll run down to the lobby at dawn, when only the guard's there, nodding under his cap behind the desk, and pop it in the outbox. It's 2023 but my firm still insists on a hard copy: a formality, a backup.

I was good enough at my job that when I became housebound, they kept me on remotely. I can still see a few buildings through my windows, and as many buildings as I want in the books I choose from print catalogues and pick up from downstairs. The internet is a minefield.

Bedtime. Check time. Windows opened a chink – don't

want to suffocate – but just a chink. Last December, in New Jersey, a pair of drunk college students climbed into a flat on a dare and terrorised the old couple with a gun. The gun was unloaded but the old man had a heart attack. Rubbish bin lidded and lifted for the night onto the counter – yesterday, in the lift, a resident was telling her great-grandson about the rats that used to scurry around the bedroom she shared with three brothers. Rat traps set. Power-sockets not on fire.

Check! Time for bed. It's kind of fun narrating your own life always in your head.

I drift in and out of nightmares. The nightmares, too, are abating: now when I awaken, I remember them for a half-second and then they're gone.

Past midnight I awake, gasping. My gut feels like it's slipping out my backside. Convulsions sit me up then double me over. Even gasping hurts. Is it my gut? I ate nothing unusual. Neither does this feel like grief cramps.

Suddenly it's here, jerking me onto my feet. Understanding runs through me, flushing me warm, then draining me cold. I clutch my abdomen with both arms and stumble to the bathroom. My head swims. How can it be? Tarak left weeks after Prabhat died. I've been alone three years.

Perched on the bathtub I lower my pyjama shorts. With a final convulsion my body ejects something. My eyes are squeezed shut but I felt it as it came out, I can picture it now my pants: a puddle, slimy soft. Well, I know what to do. This time, I didn't know I was pregnant. This time, there's only relief. I ease my pants down around my ankles.

I open my eyes. In a puddle of mucous and blood swim two tiny bits of flesh: hairless and squirming, nude and translucent. Just like my miscarriage, only tinier.

What have I given birth to? Another monstrosity, only this time I know it. I picture fleeing the scene. That's what

I should've done three years ago, five years ago: fled this flat, where only guilt lives, bashing its head against empty walls.

I massage my larynx. I take my pants off, white pants against white tiles. I squat. I peer. The two tiny bits of flesh are rat-like creatures, each about an inch long. Their skin is a transparent sac, taut over pink-and-black innards, sealing in the black dots that are their eyes and ears. I'm staring and wondering and my eyes fall on the rat trap on the toilet's flush tank and I realise what I've had.

I sprint out the bathroom door and halfway across the drawing room. I look back. They're not following me. I creep back, clutch the bathroom door, and peer. The night tides of my revulsion ebb, and dawn rises, gentling the waves. Staring, ready to flee, I creep forward.

Does their skin seal in their mouths, too? How will they eat? Squatting five feet away, I offer a fingertip. Breath, tiny but warm, scopes me. Two tiny mouths nudge my fingertip. Toothless gums nibble me. So: the sacs don't seal the mouths. They can eat.

I withdraw my hand and clutch my head and rack my brains. My cramp disappeared the moment I ejected these things. My part is over now. I could flush them down the toilet, incinerate my pants, and go back to my life. I didn't ask for any of this.

Still I'm squatting and staring and my hand is straying back towards the rat-babies. They nose blindly around my fingertip. They whine. I know what they're looking for.

If I were thinking, I'd be paralysed with disgust. I'm no longer thinking. I scoop the tiny things up in a white hand towel, clean them as best I can without squashing them, and carry them in the palm of my hand to the fridge.

Here's the milk carton. I still keep milk, in case a starving street cat sneaks through the window chink and only a milk offering can save me from claws of wrath. In my palm the two morsels wriggle, rearranging themselves, seeking the warmest crannies. How deep to them the hollows between my fingers must be, like a ravine, or a crib. I've got to heat the milk.

I open the storeroom door. The microwave topples into my arms. I microwave the milk one second at a time. It must be warm, I remember, not hot. I'm not used to microwaving a thimbleful of milk. I run the microwave one second at a time. I remember to check the temperature, a single drop on the inside of my wrist, a drop so tiny that it refuses to drop, that I must shake down from my finger.

The rat-babies love to sniff!

I set them down at the saucer. Will they be able to sip from the saucer, or must I finger-feed them? They sniff around blindly, wriggling away from the saucer, but it's sniffing that brings them wriggling back again, and – yes, I notice, disappointed, almost – they can drink by themselves. They drink and drink, their tiny sips making tiny ripples, and as they drink they keep sniffing. They knead the saucer's edge, as if it were rat-teats they were kneading to release milk. Little idiots, reversing cause and effect! Sniffing, snorting, they get milk-soaked. All through this they're fully blind, half-asleep. Afterwards I swaddle them in a fresh hand towel, tucking it around them, leaving their noses free.

Again I confront the storeroom door. For three years I've been half-opening the door, shoving things in. Now I push the door fully open and fight my way inside. Things spill out all around me. I put them down further from the door, not looking, quickly before I can identify what they are, before I can remember. In this blind way, I find Flaxie's crate.

Our yellow lab died peacefully at fifteen after a short

illness: he felt no pain, and I felt no surprise. But his loss, treading on the heels of the others, overwhelmed me. No more pets, I vowed.

I dust Flaxie's crate, bed down inside it my babies, towel-swaddled, and bolt the crate door. Just in case the street cat's on the prowl. Dog crate by my pillow, feeding alarms set for every half-hour, I go back to bed. Perhaps this is just another nightmare. My eyelids close on a Hyderabad dawn, the sky glimmering grey-brown.

The alarm awakens me. I lie, eyes closed, waiting for the nightmares to go, willing them to pass through me tracelessly. Looks like I wasn't having any. Through the grill I check my babies. Under my fingertips two tiny heartbeats race.

All week, the babies' bodies stay pink-skinned, their eyes and ears skin-sealed. All day I watch them sleeping, feeding, mewling, squirming. Checking them repeatedly for abnormalities, I run my finger down their tiny bodies, palpitating, their heartbeats impossibly fast – which, Google reassures me, is normal at that age. Their bones are spongy, like cartilage. Again I count their appendages: four toes, plus one ankle-hoof. Tiny toes, whittled by microscopic elves.

Skilled elves: the babies are perfect and healthy. Can a dried flower come back to life if you sprinkle some water on it? Warm drops of water, right in my nostrils, and I shake them off and draw a sharp breath. And it's safe, now, and here they are, now – my babies. Great.

Under the translucent skin-sacs, their facial features grow. Then they protrude. Into the smooth eye sockets protrude rubbery black raisins. From either side of the skull protrude two tiny black rosebuds. Their eyes and ears are coming.

I try putting my babies in the kitchen, in the sun: but I find myself continually running over to watch them. So now I keep them beside me as I work. I peep at them every minute – but my work's getting done, too. Details which I'd vacillated over for days, back when I had all the time in the world, now fall into place with a straightforwardness that I thought belonged only to other mothers.

Those other mothers told me that "mom brain" was a lie, that what a baby really does is clarify your priorities, show you the quickest way to do things and then make you do them, bypassing the oh, buts, and what ifs. And I thought those other mothers were lying. With Prabhat I never had clarity. He was born with a death certificate and I was never really here. That way, I thought, I could save myself. But he's gone and I've still not been here. Everyone told me you can't escape the pain, you've got to work through it and I thought, you're all wrong and I'll prove it.

I carry my babies around even on bathroom breaks, tucked into my cardigan pockets, lined with paper napkins. This phase, I remember, won't last forever: this half-blind, mewling, total dependence.

They need fresh air. So, at night, instead of closing the windows to a chink, I leave them half-open.

The eighth morning, my final feeding alarm awakens me from a sleep still nightmare-free, but awakens me to panic. Across my bed the early sun's rays fall aslant. My babies have wriggled, out of towel and crate, up against my calf. But what's wrong with them? Why do they lie unmoving where Prabhat lay that morning with that sickening shine? Blood runs through me, making my teeth grit and my hands fist. I feel my eyes glazing and my mind checking out. They're dead, they're gone, I'll flush them down the toilet. Nobody knows about them, nobody will know they've died, nobody will look at me with different eyes. This is not my fault.

I sit up and fumble at them. My eyes adjust to the slanting sun. Now I see what the sick shine is. Fur.

They've begun growing fur: still thin and colourless, already lustrous. I clutch them to my bosom. They wriggle and squirm. Flush them down the toilet, indeed! Only now that the terror has passed do I realise how it shook me. I giggle and shriek and howl. My babies crawl away from my shaking ribs up into the crook of my neck.

At two weeks old, their eyes open, black and sleepy. Their ears pop free of their skulls and nestle, still flat, in their fur. Their fur begins to brown but it's still just a dusting, baby fur just covering their raw pink nakedness.

At three weeks old, they're as long as my index finger. I run my finger down their backs, neck to tail. Springy muscle, and bones no longer spongy, resist my finger now. Life is growing up and against. Still they're babies, still whining with pleasure and squirming into my massaging fingertip.

I watch them constantly. Still, again, their next metamorphosis happens overnight. I bid my half-nude rat-babies goodnight and awaken to find them in full fur coats. They're playing castle between the crenelations of my toes. Sensing I'm awake, they come scurrying, nosing my lips, welcoming me to their new day, unself-conscious of their new beauty.

At four weeks old, their dull brown infant fur differentiates into their colours. One baby is mostly cocoa, the other wheat. They're fully mobile now. I've binned all my rat traps, taped over the ankle-high electric outlets, and if there'd been anything lying around on the floor I'd have taken that up too. I give Cocoa and Wheatie the run of the flat. Hither and thither they scurry and scamper, whiskers quivering, pink noses glistening.

Always their globetrotting expeditions terminate at the Bermuda Triangle: the storeroom door. They rear up, forepaws hanging, raised noses interrogating the air. They turn on me with begging black eyes. I open the storeroom door a smidge and block entry with my foot. If they got in amongst my life's rubbish, I'd never find them again. They peer and sniff.

I go in alone to find playthings. I offer my babies my dusty old self-help books. Cocoa shreds them into ribbons.

I retrieve Flaxie's toys. To a textured rubber chew ball, the size of a tennis ball, Wheatie clings two-handed like a drunken pilot, whiskers wriggling like octopus tentacles. Heart in mouth, I watch her. What if she topples backwards and gets steamrolled by the ball? But dancing awkwardly she stays aloft.

I go storeroom-diving again. Here's the calligraphy set I gave Tarak on his birthday. Tarak had always wanted to try calligraphy, but now he questioned the timing of my gift, told me I was just conjuring distractions, accused me of not caring at all. He never even filled a pen, told me he had no time. And he didn't. He spent all those two years ringing surgeons and pharma companies, taking Prabhat from doctor to doctor.

He took nothing with him when he left, not even his laptop. He had the right idea: start afresh. When did I appoint myself museum curator of our lives?

But his way was wrong, too. He told me that I'd never cared, that I'd been relieved when it finally happened, that I was a monster. And he'd cared but he was a monster too, but, because I didn't care, I didn't tell him that. I let him win and walk away.

I retrieve the calligraphy set from the museum.

"I'm the world's worst museum curator," I tell Cocoa, scratching her neck with a golden nib. "Exhibits all tossed away unlabelled in the backroom." Cocoa's got an idiosyncratic pleasure point just right of centre from where her skull meets her torso. A brief scratch here has saved me many reward-pellets during training. As I scratch, Cocoa's eyes close, hoarding the privacy of her pleasure. Her right hindleg windmills: she thinks she's scratching herself. Little idiot!

When will she learn to tell my scratching finger from her own scratching hindleg? Flaxie never learned. I give Cocoa's torso a squeeze. Her jaws drop the fountainpen and close on my forefinger. Playfully, pressureless – but lightning-fast, her play-soft eyes instantly alert. My babies' non-humanness astonishes me.

Also astonishing: I've remembered what to do.

I thought I'd forgotten. I thought forgetting was my only hope.

On hindlegs, Wheatie spends hours peering out the balcony door, which I've kept locked since the incident of the kite.

First we lost Prabhat, three weeks before his second birthday. Right on time – the doctors had given him two years. He was born and that was it: no more Old Bollywood movie nights for us, no more kitchen disasters or weekend hikes in Ramnagar or Channagiri. One morning I awoke to find Prabhat, as usual, in our bed – he was always crawling out of his special crib into our bed. But that morning he hadn't made it past my calf. We kept his scalp shaved, it was good luck, Ma said, and we tried everything. Sickly his scalp shone in the morning sun. A quiet morning, right on time, and that was that.

Tarak and I sent out our messages, donated Prabhat's things, and went back to work. I thought we were doing fine, not talking, yes, but then there was nothing to talk about. Then Tarak left. Then Flaxie died. Then, one morning, alone in the flat, I awoke shivering at dawn. A cool breeze kept wafting over me, a rush of something. I unplugged my ears and lowered my eye mask just in time to duck. A Brahminy kite was flying across the flat, crashing top speed into the bedroom window, falling, rising and flying top speed again, crashing into the balcony's glass door, falling. The balcony door was ajar. That's how he'd got in and now he couldn't find his way out.

I got myself together and crept out of bed. If I could just sprint across and open the balcony door wider. The bird flew away from me, crashed into the balcony door with a sickening sound, and fell down. It didn't get up. I crept close. I stroked its feathers, so soft. I looked into its eyes, as brown as its feathers. I picked it up, so strong, so light, flying into my life only to drop dead.

At midnight I crept down to deposit the dead bird at the front gate. I got locks installed on the balcony door. And finally I heard the message the universe had been shouting at me: Life is not for you.

My phone's alarm goes off. I shake myself off. It's lunchtime.

I watch Wheatie studying the world through the locked glass door. I prostrate myself behind her, trying to see what she sees. She abandons her studies and climbs into my hair. I give her a hand to wrestle with. She's as big as an adult with the energy of a teenager. She roughs up my hand with her needle-sharp claws; I sit up and signal the end of play. She sits back at once but her mouth pouts sorry and her whole body quivers. I walk to the balcony door. She darts after me and raises herself and scratches at the glass. Cocoa, distracted from her mid-afternoon treasure hunt under the bed, sprints up and joins her.

They've been mobile for six weeks. For six weeks, I've wondered: should I open the balcony door? I've made a series of concessions. I've let them root in the rubbish bin – there's never anything spoiled or sharp in there. I've let them in the bathtub – they seem immune to drowning. But the balcony door terrifies me.

37

Back at work, I watch my babies still scratching at the balcony door. Fully grown, but noses still pink, always quivering. Have I the right to fear, for them, what they don't fear for themselves? Scratching the glass, they look like they're running. Running nowhere, trapped here with me.

If I were thinking, I'd be paralysed with terror. I'm no longer thinking. I cross the drawing room. Hands clasping doorhandle, I brace myself. Look at them, standing back, ready! They've never seen the balcony door open, they've never seen a glass pane moving, but they've seen the front door and the storeroom door and they've generalised. I've got the brightest babies in the world, and no, it's not my braced stance that's cued them in. They jump onto my socked-and-slippered feet and they stand up like meerkats, sniffing the door crack. Craning their necks up at ridiculous angles, they beseech me with galaxy-bright nice! black eyes.

Open!

Air rushes from the world across the balcony into me. I stumble out and steady myself, hands clutching banister. With slow forceful breaths I massage my gut out of its clench. The breeze stirs on my face: sun-warmed, autumn-sharp, bursting with smells fire-engine-red, sulphur-blue, sunshine-yellow. I shut my eyes.

Cautiously, my breathing slow and shallow, my nose sniffs the world's scrambled odour-rainbow, picking out memories. Saptaparni flowers, their pungent odour hovering between intoxicating and nauseating. Biryani, pungent with star anise, grounded by bay leaf. Dry leaves swept together and set on fire, not burning yet, just smouldering.

I used to be able to identify burning leaves by their smell. After the flames envelop them, they all smell the same, but when they're just smoking they smell different. Teak. Coconut. Bamboo. Tarak used to joke that I had a dog's nose. Had I known I'd be hibernating for three years,

38

I would've hoarded up the smells of the world for my long winter.

I open my eyes. The sky's too blue; too bright. I shade my eyes and peer below. The vendor across the street, operating a wheeled cart, is frying *dosas* to order on a cast-iron skillet over a gas-powered flame. *Dosas* made 101 ways, declares his mobile hoarding.

Saptaparni. Dosa. Skillet. Out here is the world, still. In my head are the names for things, still. A tide surges up my throat. Joy, that it's all still here. Sorrow, that I've wasted three years of it.

Squeals at my feet rouse me. My babies are scurrying away. Instinctively I shut the door behind them. Alone on the balcony I turn to face my fate.

Motionless above my head, now in my face, a wingspan wavers, briefly blotting the afternoon sun's indolent gold. A falcon lands on my banister a foot from my face, jolting me awake. Pitch-black eyes, ringed in sunshine-yellow, glare at me. Coal-Gray wings fold away and he stands dapper in his scalloped knickerbockers and yellow socks. He scowls at my babies, who're safe behind glass. He turns his scowl on me.

I stand paralysed, waiting for panic to jolt me into action. But it's something else that comes rising up my throat. I recognise it only when I hear it.

Laughter.

The falcon starts, flaps a bit, then steadies himself and glares in offended majesty. I hoot and howl, clutching my stomach, but my stomach is all loose, there's no holding it in, there's nothing to hold onto anymore.

I wipe my eyes and clap my hands. "Boo!"

The falcon flies away.

I reopen the balcony door. My babies scamper back into the wine-drunk October sunshine and huddle against my ankles. Well, my little explorers? You'll stay near me, now, eh? Maybe they won't always. But they knew to run. The world's full of hiding-places for my babies.

I laugh, not hysterically now, just enough to squeeze the tears out of my eyes, to clear my sight.

ALL CREATURES GREAT AND SMALL

Beyond the glass, sagging city buses and sleek SUVs raise dust clouds and drone like undead bees; in here, there's only the hum of the air-conditioner. From the bedroom-turned-dressing-room, Pugsy barks, excited for playtime. Sukhi is bent over her broom, moving dining chairs out of the way and sweeping around towers of Amazon boxes, empty and full, all stacked together. It was nice sitting home all these months, getting paid without working, but then her joints got stiff, and her conscience heavy, for all her neighbours lost their jobs weeks into Lockdown.

Sukhi straightens up too quickly. The giddiness that's hovered behind her forehead all morning sweeps her up into a storm. She clutches the granite countertop to keep from falling. Inside her sudden darkness, the thunder of an alien rage rumbles. She longs to shred the broom, smash up the kitchen, and fling herself banshee-shrieking through the balcony's glass doors. Mechanically Sukhi reaches for the solution – another slice of white bread heaped with Kissan mixed-fruit jam. She chews quickly, eyes on the door of the dressing-room, where her employers are preparing for their weekend. Her vision clears. Gratefully, sunflower-like, she raises her face to God.

Sukhi has always been famous for two things: sweet tooth and sweet temper. But these black storms are coming often now. What if they cost her her job? She bends slowly over her broom again. Pugsy waddles out, licking his chops. Sana-mam has re-retied the blue-and-white bow around his throat. Sukhi offers the squash-face the remnants of her jam-and-bread. For surely the vet is mistaken: how can Pugsy be allergic to anything when thousands of street dogs thrive on garbage? Pugsy sniffs Sukhi's offering and recoils.

The smell tickles his nose and itches his skull. He shakes his head trying to shake it out. He sneezes and chokes. Look at this woman, trying to choke him to death! He waddles backwards, growling. She laughs at him. How heartless! Just wait till he tells Mom and Dad about his intruder with her sneeze-making poisoned food and her guffawing. He barks for his parents. They don't come. With a final growl over his shoulder he trots back to the morning-room.

"Ammamma!" Titli shrills from the sofa. "Look, tiger!"

Sukhi goes to stand behind the sofa. Her granddaughter likes coming over here, and the Vermas don't mind. On the huge television screen, some villagers are telling the *NDTV* correspondent that droughts and floods and rock-bottom prices drove them out of rice-farming, and now the Forestry Department is driving them out of goat-herding. Sweat streams down the villagers' faces. Their eyes confront the camera, bright and opaque, like the eyes of wolves. Their clay-brown skin is stretched drum-tight over skulls too big for their bodies.

"They showed tiger," Titli insists, appropriating the brown-and-white stuffed rabbit, Sana-mam's childhood companion, now shabby and perching on the side table beside the mauve satin sofa. "Tiger was hungry."

Sukhi pats Titli's head. On weekdays, when she picks Titli up from school and they're alone here, Titli wanders around the Vermas' condo, sounding out the English words on snack packs and video-game cases. Sukhi, who struggles to make out the instructions Sana-mam leaves her in large all-caps on the fridge whiteboard, listens as Titli reads out the English headlines rushing across the television screen. Sukhi swells with pride. She doesn't know that Titli's reading out nonsense, that Titli's English lessons have only got to ABC.

A forest guard defends government policy to the *NDTV* correspondent. It's his job, he says, to keep all encroachers out of the Sunderbans. Next a tiger appears in closeup. Titli squeals and points. The tiger stalks through marshy undergrowth, head lowered, neck flattened, flanks skinny. The camera pans, with dramatic jerks and soap-opera lightning flashes, to a herd of goats. Titli huddles up, clutching the limp rabbit between chest and chin. Sukhi strokes her granddaughter's short silky hair and resumes sweeping.

These emaciated villagers have stirred up the old terror inside Sukhi. She longs to sneak a *motichur laddu* from the red-and-gold box forgotten in the fridge. But Sana-mam emerges and wanders around the living room, dousing her snake-plants and succulents with that stinky new plant medicine that arrived by courier. "ORGANIC", read a label in English, hovering like a lone fly among the spiderwebs of foreign script sprawling crawled all over the box. Sukhi bids her 30-year-old employer good afternoon, then sweeps past her with eyes lowered. What if Sana-mam smells her breath and threatens to lock the fridge, like when she caught Sukhi bolting *rashmalai*? Sukhi decides she'll admit to the white bread but claim it was the super-expensive, sugar-free jam that she lathered on.

She lowers her face to hide her grin. It's like she's seven again, trying to persuade Amma it was a crow that stole the last *Mysore pak*.

Now Varun-sir emerges. Both these young people require hours to prepare for their Saturday, and all three bathrooms, with jars and bottles crowding the basins and stampeding the windowsills. But Sana-mam and Varun-sir always look the same, always in black. Varun-sir ruffles Titli's hair. Titli's watching unblinkingly for the reappearance of her starving tiger.

Varun-sir returns Sukhi's full-toothed smile with his

shy, lopsided grin. You'd never think he was a bigshot law partner: so humble. "Are you sure I can't make you breakfast?" says Sukhi.

"No, thanks," says Varun-sir, as if addressing one of his corporate colleagues. "We're brunching with friends."

He watches Sukhi nod side-to-side. He's watched her sitting down suddenly when she thinks nobody's looking. He's watched her bright eyes dulling year by year, and new planes and angles parsing her once moon-round face. Perhaps, he reflects, her cheerfulness is only the child of folly, of refusing to take seriously problems she thinks she can do nothing about. He admires her cheerfulness nonetheless. "How are you, Aunty? How was your check-up?" He speaks lightly, checking the urge to scold her preemptively.

Sukhi ducks her head. The Vermas earn fifty times her salary, but they call her "Aunty". If they heard about her collapsing on Friday after dinner, and her daughter rushing her to hospital, and the doctor saying her blood sugar was 451, they'd tackle her here and now and give her the injection. Last month, after Sukhi emptied that box of *jalebi* in one morning, Sana-mam said that she'd bought a syringe, and the next time Sukhi sneaked any sweet stuff she'd hold her down and inject her with insulin. Sukhi giggled with terror.

Sana-mam had retorted, "You don't believe me? You want to see the syringe?"

Eyes popping, about to lose bowel control, Sukhi had sworn she'd learned her lesson. She's had three children, and lost many relatives to alcoholism, and she's still always smiling. So nobody takes her blood-and-injection phobia seriously.

"Check-up fine-only, sir," Sukhi answers Varun-sir. Then she begs him to let her sort through the Amazon boxes and bin the empty ones. She grins, proud for so deftly deflecting his attention from her so-called health problems when he, along with everyone else, dismisses her phobia as childish. Then she bites her tongue. She knows he means well. She knows she's being foolish.

"Hmm." Varun-sir scratches his chin. "We'll have to sort through the boxes, first, and decide which ones to save for packing-boxes."

How big his finger-joints look, and how his veins pop out of his arms! Sukhi's grin disappears. The dumbbells and whey-protein-powder jars are piling up in Varun-sir' room, but this boy's getting so skinny. God knows when he'll fade into thin air. He used to be so nice and plump, back in 2010, when she began working for the Vermas in their last flat but two. Sometimes, for no reason, you see someone as if for the first time. What unrequited need, she wonders, drives this boy to chisel his poor flesh into stone?

"So much dust the boxes are getting," she pleads. "Very bad for your asthma!" It's bad enough that her potbellied son and lame middle daughter are always nagging her about her blood sugar. She won't listen to any more of this scarecrow's health warnings.

"We'll do it soon, I promise!" he says.

The Vermas set the air purifier on max, clear a track, and assume their stations to exercise Pugsy: Sana-mam under the kitchen window, Varun-sir at the dining room's far end. He has a frisbee, she has a tennis ball, and they both have beef niblets. Pugsy had a poor appetite through the pandemic. The vet discovered that he's allergic to most foods. Now he's on a diet of free-range organic beef shipped, every week, in an icebox from Kerala, one of the last states where you can slaughter a cow without risking your own neck. Sukhi watches the squash-faced pug waddle back and forth, carrying his toy half-heartedly, dropping it midway to sprint towards his nibble-sized reward. He's already snorting, his eyes flaring as if trying to become auxiliary nostrils, pink eye-membranes sagging.

Varun-sir frowns. "Well, at least he's not wheezing."

"Trust me," says Sana-mam, scratching Pugsy's forehead, "this is better than walking him outside in all that smog."

"Hmm," says Varun-sir.

Did he want a different dog, Sukhi wonders, one of those shapely glossy breeds? She's never understood rich people paying lakhs for defective animals. What her neighbours could do – what she could do – with that kind of money! But this is just how the world works. It's nobody's fault. Her menfolk love getting worked up, ranting over politics till they're frothing at the lips. Much good that does them! When they tell her she's an oblivious fool, she smiles.

Sweeping, bending to reach under cabinets and into corners, Sukhi enters the master bedroom. Here, with the blackout curtains drawn against the sweltering heat, it's dark and close. Her head reels. Clutching the headboard, she squats, and waits till her giddiness passes.

Every month, when Sana-mam draws her up a diet plan, Sukhi nods attentively, spews promises, and mentally hums the latest Tollywood item number, waiting for Sana-mam's lips to stop moving. It's not like she can't afford oats and lettuce – the Vermas pay her generously – she just can't stomach that new-fangled stuff. Sana-mam makes her boil three eggs for breakfast on weekdays, one each for Sana-mam and Varun-sir and Sukhi. "Protein will keep you full," she says. Sukhi feeds her own egg to Titli and rinses both their mouths out afterwards.

Sukhi finishes sweeping under the master bed. She rises too suddenly. Again the giddiness lifts her off her feet. She leans against the window, clutching her head, waiting. Sukhi's son and grandson have developed an appetite for chicken nuggets, but she'd almost rather an injection than flavourless cow-food or bird-flesh.

No use getting worked up, worrying about tomorrow. God will look after her. God got her, injection-free, through three childbirths, including the thirty-two-hour-long birth of Titli's mother. She's sick of popping pills, sick of ignorant people's confident advice, sick of youngsters scolding her, as if her illness has made her everybody's child. She earns the lion's share of the family income. How dare they scold her? The pandemic has confirmed that life is too short to worry. She sweeps the dust heap out of the master bedroom.

In the living room, Pugsy sprawls panting under the AC. Varun-sir has angled the vents away from Pugsy's sensitive eyes. The flat, enclosed in glass, stinks of dog breath and red meat. Struggling not to gag, Sukhi breathes a prayer on the Vermas' behalf for the cow whose death lies at their door. She beams at the pug so infirm, yet still so cheerful.

Sana-mam approaches the sofa. *NDTV* is showing an infographic that contrasts two aerial views of the Sunderbans: all jungle and mangrove in 2001, mostly farmland and pasture in 2023. Both images are grainy and sepia-toned. Sana-mam bends her face close to the child's.

"Wanna watch something else, Titli?"

Titli buries her face in the shabby bunny, hiding from the pretty lady. Sana-mam flips to *National Geographic*. Here's the Serengeti, still lush: from high-definition cameras, from the rains, and from David Attenborough's caramel-brittle voice. Lounging lions with full tummies and benevolent eyes flick their tails at herds of wildebeest cropping golden grass.

"Ha-ah!" Titli gasps at all this magnificence. Abandoning

47

her stuffed rabbit, she slips off the sofa and around the coffee table – heaped with cosy mysteries and advertising books book-marking each other – to settle on the pashmina carpet right under the television.

A car ad interrupts the animals. Titli stares at the car's body, black as a panther, big as an elephant, shiny as a snake. Time halts and opens its maws wide to swallow the world. Titli wishes they had a car like that outside their house, a big flat television on the wall that you could watch from any angle without glare, and animals on all day. But this is not the right way to think about things, Titli knows already, wordlessly. She peeks over her shoulder, catches the pretty lady's eye, and blushes. Life is good. Most days, here, there's nobody but Ammamma and herself. Back home she's always spoiled for choice of companions. *Her* life is good, Titli decides, as time picks up pace again and the jungle comes back on television.

Sana-mam replaces the rabbit on the side-table and stands watching. Attenborough's is a land without time, like the land of *Friends* and *How I Met Your Mother*. In this land, Adam and Eve never discovered sin and the trees never began to shed. It's been a hard week at work, plugging away on the Cola account. This is no weekend for watching news. It's hard enough keeping your head down. Why let bleakness infiltrate your hard-earned weekend? Titli, too, should learn to focus on the good things, should know there are still good things in the world. What was it Jim Dixon says? Nice things are nicer than nastier things.

Sana-mam's Fitbit beeps. Pugsy's break is up. Sprawled on the dining-room's cool uncarpeted floor, his panting has slowed. He looks satiated. But Sana-mam says, "You're getting fat again. We're not done exercising." She walks to her treat-bag on the counter. When she turns around, Pugsy is at her heels, eyes bulging and curled tail wagging, suddenly ready for round two. Sana-mam cocks her brow and looks up at Sukhi.

Sukhi giggles. "So greedy he is! Can't *con*trol himself *at*-all."

The next instant Sukhi is faint again. She grapples along the walls into the dressing room and sweeps behind the cupboard, sweeping away another impending storm. These fits of annoyance are shading increasingly into anger that threatens to break through. Sukhi pictures the *laddu* in the fridge: in the back of the second shelf, supposedly hidden from her, now forgotten by the Vermas themselves, the glistening orange surfaces sprouting black moles. But she can't get at the *laddu*. Not with them about. And, in this impasse, the pattern emerges: her mind finally sees the solution her body has already been implementing.

She just needs a little sugar!

She pictures the cola in the fridge door, also bought months ago, also forgotten. It's expired, she heard Sana-mam telling Varun-sir. But neither of them remembered to bin it. It'll be here till spring-cleaning. The cola is easy to reach and will leave no smell on her fingers. Soon Pugsy will finish exercising, Varun-sir will go to his study to check his computer, and Sana-mam will wander back into the master bedroom, trying on outfit after outfit. Then Sukhi will sneak a sip of Cola. One sip, just to dispel this giddy rage and make her herself again: Sukhi the bread-winner, Sukhi the smiling saint. Already she can taste the sip, picture its blade of optimism scything through this alien darkness. She stands up too quickly, deliberately this time, and giggles through the ensuing joy-ride of giddiness. She sweeps around Varun-sir's piles of barbells and Sana-mam's forest of desiccated cacti.

No mere illness will take her cheerfulness and no whippersnapper will take away her life's chief pleasure.

AUDIENCE

"Screw them both," Prasanna mutters, turning from Kanakapura Main Road into the service road, "I don't need them." All weekend at Victus's country estate, Prasanna was occupied with weed and music, dancing and photoshoots. She didn't catch her third ex-husband and his girlfriend – who's half their age, first of all – laughing at her. Alone, now, looking back, she sees their eye-rollings and lip-clampings, clear as this Sunday afternoon sun in her eyes. She lowers the visor in her fifteen-year-old Maruti 800. How pitiful to laugh at someone who's just enjoying life. She parks near the tender-coconut vendor and half-empties a Wills Light. Her window is rolled down. Two policemen stand yards away, outside Jesus College, chatting with the college security-guards, who are never off duty, even at the weekends. Prasanna focusses, with a child's total focus, on her IndiGo in-flight "NutCase" snack box, where she's crushing her weed, which is half seeds and stems. She studies Annie's WhatsApp message.

"Loved meeting you. You're everything Victus told me and more. Hope we'll see you again *very* soon."

4:11p.m. Annie must've texted just after Prasanna left – the second time. Prasanna had driven down the bumpy dirt road, missed her purse, and driven back. She pictures Annie about to text, and Victus in his gravelly chain-smoker's voice saying, "Not yet," winking as Prasanna bounced back into view.

"It's true," Prasanna mutters between drags, "I always forget something." She's spent the decade since this divorce cooped up; only recently has she resumed going out; nobody's told her she mutters to herself. "So what? Everyone forgets sometimes. But of course he's told her everything bad about me." When Prasanna found her purse, between the jaws of the

50

white lab ensconced in the rainbow of cushions on the divan, she opened it and checked her mobile-phone. It was 4:08 p.m. Yes, Annie knew to wait till Prasanna's second goodbye. She thinks she knows all about Prasanna!

Prasanna saves half her joint for her three-hour drive home and steps out of her flame-orange hatchback. Two stunted construction workers, wearing men's shirts over their *saris* for extra coverage, gape at Prasanna from under the cement-mixer trays they're head-carrying to a tiny construction site wedged between two new private-hostel buildings. Prasanna half-notices them. She learned decades ago, on the runway, to block out people staring. She hitches up her black satin bustier, arranges her magenta ringlets over her bare shoulders, and adjusts her grey asymmetric-hem tulle skirt over her bony thighs. She fashioned this skirt herself: she layered two thrifted skirts of different lengths, sewed the waistbands together, and let the muse guide her scissors. Beautiful, if she does say so herself!

Hope we'll see you again very *soon.* They must think she's a fool. Screw them. And screw these poor gaping illiterates. These are not her people. A lot of big people admire her. Kamal Joglekar himself requested selfies with her, during her latest solo exhibition at Kalashilp, which he'd arranged for her – the camera held up at arm's length, her face turned up like a sunflower. In the photo it looks like Kamal's groping and she's shrinking. Bad angle, that's all. She cropped the best photo for her Facebook profile. The director of Bangalore's oldest art gallery is courting her and this upstart thinks she can laugh at her! Annie's message deserves no reply.

Yes, it was 4:08 p.m. when she left Victus's estate the second time. What Prasanna can't remember is what time it was when she glimpsed a conversation with a "Sid" on Victus's phone. The memory of that glimpse wrenches her

51

heart loose and jumping up her throat. Memory or fantasy, she's still not sure. She got unusually stoned this weekend; the boundaries blurred. Of one thing she's sure: if it *was* Sid, then it's *her* Sid. Victus would never save some other Siddharth or Siddhant or Siddaramaiah on his phone as "Sid". Should she just ask Victus? But if she's wrong he'd laugh at her, sniggering like the devil, to punish her for opening old wounds.

At the tender-coconut stall, clasping one of the bamboo poles that supports the coconut-thatched roof, Prasanna tells the vendor, "A nice big one, Sharmila, with both water and flesh." Even after four decades down south, Prasanna's Hindi remains fluent. Hindi's her mother tongue, though English has been her head-language since her teens. When her chess-game with her Bihari mother reached its climax, ditching Hindi seemed a logical first step.

"OK, may-daam," says Sharmila, staying seated. Prasanna exercises her privilege as a regular customer to make her own selection. She picks, weighs, shakes, and listens to one green coconut after another.

Sharmila mouths Prasanna's words: "*Ek badhiya*, Sharmila, *paani aur goonda waala.*" Rocking gently on her beaten-up plastic stool, its legs uneven on the dirt, Sharmila mouths other words. *Bewakoof.* Is that Hindi or Marathi, where did she hear *bewakoof*? Foreign-language words all sound alike. Whatever language it is, *bewakoof* means fool. This much Sharmila knows.

Speak of the devil! Sharmila's phone buzzes. Her heart jumps as she scrambles to unlock her phone. It's only Piyush-Anna. He's texting to say he's stepping out, and would Sharmila keep an "eye" on Manoj. Well! Sharmila dials her husband's number. She listens to his phone ring. Is it already too late, she wonders. The phone rings on. She wants to cry and she wants to laugh.

Bewakoof paani aur goonda waala! The sentence comes together in Sharmila's panic-jolted brain. This is the sentence she'll fling at Manoj tonight, as she brings him dinner, as he sits in his corner, knees drawn up into chest, eyes lowered, vague and wandering, a lost dog. *You foolish sack of blood and flesh.* Not that he'll understand. Lurking behind the counter, in another man's grocery shop, a lackey at fifty, refusing to learn a word of Hindi or English to transact with the customers who refuse to learn Kannada, a useless lackey, always watching for a chance to sneak out and sneak a drink – what does he know of the world? He sits nursing his sick urge while his woman goes out to do battle with the world.

"Hello, Manoj?" says Sharmila. "Yes, are you buying bottle-gourd for dinner or ridge-gourd? What? You want *me* to buy?" Piyush-Anna has told her not to let Manoj see they're monitoring him. Maybe Manoj has guessed nonetheless. Surely he has guessed, if he's got one percent of the brains left, with which he charmed her in tenth standard. "But didn't you say *you* would shop today? Oh, never mind! Your memory is going to hell." It angers Sharmila to have to lie about why she's calling, to worry over her husband as she never worried over her children. "What am I going to do with you?" She rants on, listening to his sullen Hmms, listening for any change in the soundscape behind him that might signal he's left the shop.

She watches Prasanna-may-daam lifting and shaking coconuts, bony muscle standing out from her arms, fat jiggling underneath. She remembers the day Prasanna-may-daam told her, "Some of these weigh almost a kilo! Tell me, how many 68-year-old 45-kilo women could lift these up so easily? And me a vegetarian!" She's like a special child, Sharmila thinks, kitted out in carnival costumes begging for praise. But as Sharmila continues

53

scolding her husband over the phone, listening to his curt replies, she remembers how, that day, Prasanna-may-daam's eyes, normally vague and wandering too, lit up with pride in her strength. Sharmila's voice grows tender. "OK, fine, I myself will buy."

Manoj grunts, as if to say, "Of course you will."

No, Manoj doesn't deserve her tenderness. "Everything falls on my shoulders!" says Sharmila. "Curse the day I knitted my fate to yours." In her mind it's herself she curses. She knows this isn't what she should be saying to Manoj, to keep him on the phone, to keep him safe. But what should she say – what are the magic words? To think she could've married Piyush-Anna! She'd be lolling in luxury's lap. Piyush-Anna was plain old Piyush once, her besotted classmate. And she was the class belle, beautiful in thick glossy braids down to her butt.

She hears Piyush-Anna's voice on the other end. She winds up and hangs up. She finishes assembling the Hindi sentence she'll fling at Manoj tonight. *Foolish sack of blood and flesh, you trapped me well and good.* Amma did warn her. Manoj is far too handsome, Amma said, far too high-spirited to be any good. Sharmila didn't listen. Manoj is what she deserves. Last night, his eyes were more dog-like than ever, his breath extra stinky from the *paan masala* she allows him.

Prasanna presents her selection. Sharmila beheads it and hands it back with a straw.

In her pleather magenta thigh-highs, Prasanna stumbles down the service road, strewn with potholes, and with rubble-heaps from the little engineering college they demolished last summer. She sits down on a roadside bench. Sucking tender-coconut water, she browses the photos Annie took of her. Every weekend since reconciling with Victus this winter, Prasanna has carried multiple outfits to

54

the estate and got someone to do a few photoshoots. Till this weekend, Victus was the photographer. Whose idea was it, again, that she should meet his girlfriend? Browsing the photos, Prasanna pictures Annie secretly smirking behind the lens. But the photos aren't half bad. Prasanna's new phone has a 64-megapixel, quad-lens camera. As for Prasanna herself – once a model, always a model. Half-noticing the approaching crowd, Prasanna readjusts her bustier.

A dozen final-year BBA students from Jesus College stop at Sharmila's stall. They've finished prepping the main auditorium for tomorrow's panel discussion. Abhilasha and Vidvesh are at the back of the gang of 21-year-olds. Maybe that's by accident. But lately, it seems, Abhilasha thinks, smoothing down her French Connection mini-dress, like Vidvesh has been hiding her. She squeezes Vidvesh's laxening hand around her waist and slowly stands up taller, sucks herself in as they toe the tender-coconut queue.

"So, what're we gonna do, Vidu," she says, her voice high and sweet, "go out or go back?"   ?

Vidvesh shrugs. His eyes are leopard-gold in the afternoon, listlessly scanning their peers. "Sometimes I feel like what's even the point of Sunday. We get one day off, and even that we spend half at college."

"I so-oo get you," says Abhilasha. Jesus's admin, paranoid about what students might get up to over a full weekend, schedule classes Saturday mornings. "I haven't had a proper weekend in years."

Vidvesh is looking here, there, everywhere but at his girlfriend. Abhilasha watches him checking out the other guys' biceps, feels his arm flexing around her waist, watches him lifting his chin till the V of his neck muscles jumps out. He looks kind of ridiculous. She strokes his back. He's in his Calvin Klein muscle t-shirt. It's the same

55

light brown as his skin: you'd think he was topless, but for the embossed design, like a bird's chest feathers, which you don't see at first. She watches him watching as strangers spot him, do a double take, and look again to admire his muscles.

"So, then, d'you wanna go back and finish the assignment?" She pinches his back. Finally he glances at her. They're still doing all their assignments together: that's one small victory for her.

"Ah, what's the use? We could bust our asses but it's not like we'll get the A+. Not," he adds, dropping his voice, "while that Tam-Bram has all the faculty in knots."

Abhilasha glances at their Tamil Brahmin classmate and his girlfriend-of-the-week. Jesus College, chasing higher NAAC compliance grades, enforces a grading rubric that allows only 2% of students to get a mark over 80% on any assessment. Whether it's because the faculty are mostly southerners too, or because the Tam-Bram is turn-a-straight-dude hot, or because he's worked out the ChatGPT equivalent of the no-makeup-makeup trick, he's got a near monopoly on top grades in their batch of 50.

"We could still shoot for an A," says Abhilasha. Sharmila hands them their beheaded coconuts. Abhilasha's already scanning the GPay code. She basks in her own efficiency. Then she wonders why Vidvesh doesn't say, *Thanks, I'll get the next one.* But surely he can't dump her now. Look how he confides in her. This is intimacy. Nobody else knows what he's thinking. Look how he talks about everybody else! "Hey, I know. Let's go check out that new club! Some other guys are going too. It's been aeons since we danced." She spot-dances a little.

Vidvesh glances at her involuntarily, at her tummy, and looks away. "Nah, you're right. We'd better work on the CIA."

Under cover of her coconut, Abhilasha smooths her dress and gropes at her control top to check it's in place. That look of his was a stab in her heart and the blood is spurting up her throat. She sucks hard, gulps sweet-salty tender-coconut water, and swallows her tears. They stroll towards their peers, gathered around two benches along the service road. Clearly Vidvesh wants to be around other people with her: the hot wet mess inside Abhilasha turns to joy. Clearly Vidvesh just doesn't want to be alone with her: the hot wet mess turns to titanium and pulls Abhilasha down towards the centre of the earth.

"It's our final sem," he adds in explanation. "Let's stay focused. One last push and we're out." He rants about this circus of a college. You work your ass off but your grade will just be whatever point is vacant in the normal probability curve of grades that the NAAC requires for every assessment.

Abhilasha listens, nodding, rubbing his back. But Vidvesh still isn't looking at her. Then it comes to her, like a sudden stink hitting you between the eyes when you're strolling down the road: Vidvesh's confidences don't signify intimacy. He's just shooting his load into a sock – thinking aloud, and she happens to be there, and he doesn't care what she thinks of him. She's his sock. They sit down on the corner of a bench.

"Check out Granny," someone whispers. And the 21-year-olds take turns to stare at Prasanna, breasts spilling over her bustier, thumbing through her phone.

Rapidly Prasanna thumbs, identifying bad photos at a glance. Here her tummy's sticking out: that thrifted hot-pink top is too thin. Here her smile looks wrinkly: she needs more reps with her face gym. She demands dozens of photos per shoot. A model knows that's how many it takes to get one good one. She deletes the bad ones immediately, saves nothing she can brood over struggling to fall asleep back home, alone. She selects a photo in her royal-blue sweetheart-neckline dress. It's shot from below, but her throat holds up. Her homemade serum is working. She uploads this photo to her WhatsApp status, her Instagram story, and her Facebook groups: Fabulous Fashionistas and Gorgeous Goths. Her hair absolutely glows in this photo, in the noonday light filtering through the canopy of the red-barked banyan that shades the estate's kitchen with its barbecue station and three fridges.

Prasanna commences her wait for the plaudits to start pouring in from her audience – connoisseurs of true style and beauty scattered all over the world. *Ping! Ping! Ping!* Almost already she can hear them.

"What a Harley Quinn," says Vidvesh, light eyes wide open. "You gotta pity the mentally defective joker she's out to trap."

"She probably immobilises them for sex," says the TamBram, "like a praying mantis, or with some Irene Adler injection shit."

But the young men's voices are soft. They'd be embarrassed if Granny heard them, maybe even ashamed. For Granny is not their audience.

Their batchmates snigger. Ageing is beautiful, they reassure each other, pulling their tight cheeks upwards, but this is disgraceful.

Only Abhilasha isn't laughing. Vidvesh will not look at her but he cannot stop being aware of her. She always was a prude. As if sensing his scrutiny, Abhilasha joins in now, excoriating Granny's boobs sagging over the bustier, her tummy sagging below. But it's all phony talk, Vidvesh can tell: Abhilasha's heart's not in the game. Maybe she feels guilty, not about Granny – that'd make no sense, that's just a harmless game – but about what she did to Vidvesh. She jumped the gun. They were just casually dating but she told both sets of parents they were serious. And now they're engaged. And he can't back out. Their fathers are old friends and now, more than ever, his father needs a friend. She knows what she did! That's where all this touch-feely is coming from, out of the blue. His thighs tremble with rage against hers on the bench.

Under cover of the barrage of whispered insults against Granny, Vidvesh texts the TamBram – TB for short, like Tuberculosis. Tuberculosis is sitting on the other bench, rubbing some chick's neck. "Guess what," Vidvesh texts. "A finally agreed to film a porn. Guess we've run out of stuff to do. Not that we'll post it." He squeezes Abhilasha's knee and feels her jump. "Also I accepted that offer from Siemens. Might as well, right." And he sends TyphoidBelt the screenshot of his offer letter from Siemens. No doctoring required here. Total pay package: 21 lakhs.

Half-hearing the whispers rustling somewhere to her left, stooping over her photos, Prasanna sees her magenta curls with new eyes. She frowns. Everyone loves her hair. Even Annie was effusive. Everyone but Bhikkhuni. Prasanna hasn't visited the Maitreya Buddha temple since last Wednesday. That was when Bhikkhuni drew her aside, as Prasanna was sweeping the courtyard, to request her to dye her hair back. "If you were just a patron, it wouldn't matter," said the shaven-headed head priestess. "But you're a priestess. You must present an image of sobriety." Prasanna pointed incredulously at the dowdy *salwaar-kameez* she always swaddles herself in for temple: a costume, a sacrifice of her birthright of self-expression, a cloak of invisibility as if she were just another old woman. But Bhikkhuni was firm. Dye it back, or goodbye. Prasanna was still gaping when Bhikkhuni was called away.

"She'll come around," Prasanna mutters, thumbing

through Instagram, waiting for the pings. The temple cannot survive without Prasanna. She performs rituals in those becoming robes, helps prepare the evening meal and, since emerging from her decade-long hibernation, she's brought them dozens of wealthy donors. (Old friends. Would it kill them to buy one of Prasanna's paintings? No! Forget it. *She* doesn't need anyone's charity.)

Bhikkhuni will come around. They'll call her back for the big function tomorrow. Bhikkhuni is like her mother. And, unbidden, Mummi jumps into Prasanna's head, Mummi who, just to win their seventeen-year-long chess game, hung herself in her bedroom. Checkmate. It was the night before Prasanna's board exams began, the most important moment of her life. The black queen, knocked down, cast a shadow ten miles long. Prasanna shakes her head violently trying to shake the image out.

Bhikkhuni will come around. Bhikkhuni is her real mother. She's nothing like Mummi. She doesn't hold grudges.

She begins an argument with Bhikkhuni in her head. Buddhists encourage argument. That's what's so great, that's what makes Buddhism not really a religion, makes it something a liberal can openly discuss. "Enlightenment pertains to the spirit, doesn't it," Prasanna mutters, "not to the body?"

"Yes," mutters Bhikkhuni, in Prasanna's head, in Prasanna's voice, weak from Prasanna's lifelong dieting. "But we are creatures of the flesh. Our way out of the flesh must be through the flesh. You must choose between standing out of the crowd or surrendering your will."

On the stone bench, on her bony bottom, Prasanna shifts. The thing about being an artist is that you're open, like a wet quivering wound, to voices antithetical to your own. It's not all a cake-walk!

60

Vidvesh's phone buzzes in the pocket of his Levi's dark-wash jeans. It's TinyBalls, texting back from ten feet away. "Congrats on Siemens! You deserve it, bro."

Vidvesh chokes with rage. To coax his throat muscles back open he sips his tender-coconut water. Trust TeatBlood to patronise him till the end. An insecure son-of-a-bitch. He must've doctored his own offer letter from Phillips.

As if he'd been waiting out his decision period just for this, Vidvesh goes ahead and now accepts Siemens's offer over email. Then he posts the offer letter, which he just sent TaintedBones, all over social media. It's March, two months before final exams. Soon he'll receive the joining letter. He'll post that too. And then, a week before his joining date, he will send Siemens his regrets.

For there will be for Vidvesh no glamorous corporate job. He spent last winter break back home, busting ass in his final internship, stuck in his Audi in traffic that seemed to move backwards, putting in solid water-cooler hours. Dad took him out one evening to Bombay's newest pub. After five whiskey sours Dad told him the family business, into which he'd poured eighteen years and half a crore, had gone bust. Vidvesh listened, stunned. Poor Dad! Nobody else to listen to him now. "We can't tell Mom, not yet," said Dad. "She'd die of shock." Dad looked half-dead himself, shrunk and grey and sagging. Maybe that was just the club's flashing lights. "We've got to prepare her, step by step."

"Look at her," whispers ToyBaboon, "just asking for it. And no, I'm not condoning rape culture. Granny could stalk up and down the streets naked but who would want to fuck her?"

"An auto-wallah?" suggests Abhilasha.

"I don't know," Vidvesh puts in. "She'd probably be up

for anything. That might be kinda fun. Her self-esteem has gotta be, like, the square root of negative infinity."

I'll help you, Vidvesh told Dad, answering the question Dad was unable to ask. I'll join the business and help you salvage whatever we can. Together we'll prepare Mom. The right words came into his mouth. His lips formed them. His ears heard them. What choice had there been? This man, hunched before him, elbows on table, filling him with pity shading into revulsion – he had been for twenty-one years Vidvesh's prince, playmate, and principal role-model. And Mom was innocent, tiny little Mom, with her primping and preening, like a child who is her own doll.

"Yeah, I guess her asshole might still be tight," says TrannyBoy. "Probably doesn't use it much. Probably subsists on diet pills."

Abhilasha crinkles her nose. "Wouldn't that make her shit more?" she says.

"Hmm."

Now, just to get one up over TonsilBooboo, Vidvesh has accepted Siemens's offer letter. He knows he's setting himself up to burn bridges like an idiot. But he's got to think, too, about his short-term reputation. He's spent three years getting owned by ToadyBastard in the classroom, and gym, and bedroom. This is their final round. He had to post a point. With sinking stomach he thinks: what choice did he have?

Suddenly suffocated, Vidvesh rises, winks at his friends, hands Abhilasha his coconut, and strolls towards Prasanna. Fists in pockets, eyes dulled, he circles around Prasanna's bench. He pauses behind her and stares at her phone. His lips fall open.

"Guess what Granny's doing," he whispers, coming back and sitting down, his batchmates crowding around, wriggling with anticipation. "No, not mail. Everyone's grandma is on mail, big deal... No, not Instagram. Well, yeah, that too, but keep guessing... Think big. Tinder. She's on Tinder!"

The collective gasp is loud; they check to make sure Granny hasn't noticed. Vidvesh continues, "She was just swiping, a lot of left swipes, can you believe it... No, I didn't see any old dudes. I dunno, maybe there are no old dudes on Tinder... Yeah. You're right, she must just have set her filters to young dudes. God, how vain can you be?" As his batchmates speculate in sibilant whispers, looking over their shoulders, Vidvesh ponders the limitlessness of women's vanity.

"See? I was right. Clearly she's in mad heat," says ToolBox, massaging, under cover of a backrub, the sides of his girl's firm breasts. "But if she's just lefting, then who *is* she looking for? A toddler?"

"Maybe a BDSM-type guy?" says Abhilasha. "She's practically dressed like a sex slave." She glances at Vidvesh. Vidvesh isn't looking at her. He's sat back down on the other bench and he's staring at his phone.

TurtleBanger has texted him again: "You should go ahead and post your video online. It's not like girls watch porn. Anyway there's billions of porn videos. And my CXO cousin says Google video search is at least two years away. But just to be safe, reverse the image or change the aspect ratio. A will never find it. And hey, welcome to the club, bro! Better late than never." There's a link in the message. A Pornhub video.

I'll open it next time I want to self-flagellate, thinks Vidvesh, and What a homo, sending me a porn of himself, thinks Vidvesh. But he's been scrutinising TarotButt for three years. He's a bastard but he's got no flaws. Vidvesh's fury redirects itself to Abhilasha.

She used to let him grope her through her clothes, back when he even wanted to touch her. And then, at the exact moment, she'd push him away. "Baby," she'd tell him, "everybody else is doing it, being nasty, freaky, dirty. We're better than them. Let's do it only after marriage." And look at her now, shimmying over in those ridiculous heels, straps cutting into flesh, begging him to make room on this bench. He shifts three inches. In private she's all Sita Mata. In public she can't keep her hands off him.

She's sitting beside him again. She's got him back. But she feels his thigh recoiling from hers, feels him crossing his legs so his butt isn't touching hers.

"Maybe she's looking for, like, some guy who's into double anal?" she continues. "Like in that Swedish flick about the porn industry."

Is it because she's got fat, she wonders, that he's wriggling away from her? Is it the lack of sex? Does he even want sex anymore? He seemed kinda into it when she told him that chastity could be their M.O. as a couple. He's been such a gentleman. You should see how the other guys treat their girls! The girls are into it, too. They're playing with fire and they don't know it.

When her girlfriends told Abhilasha about the rumours that Vidvesh has been circulating, among his guy friends, about their wild and kinky sex life, Abhilasha felt flattered. So Vidvesh really wanted to do all those things to her? But she also felt worried. Maybe she's let her fears get in the way. Maybe Vidvesh is frustrated. Maybe those rumours were not flattery but vengeance. After all, Vidvesh is a good guy. Vidvesh would never do to her what Didi's boyfriend did to her. And she needs Vidvesh. She can't lose him. She can't start over.

"I wonder if she's got kids," says Abhilasha suddenly.

"Who'd have kids with her?" says Vidvesh.

"Maybe she does," says Abhilasha. "Maybe she was normal once, and pretty. I mean, she still is skinny."

64

"It's easy to be skinny," says Vidvesh, raising his coconut unnecessarily high, draining the water, flexing all over. How silly he looks, Abhilasha thinks. And TamBram isn't even looking. "What's hard is to be lean. Though, I guess, some females struggle even to be skinny." He stands up and holds out his hand. Abhilasha hands over her coconut, though she's not drained it yet. "You want the flesh?"

"No," says Abhilasha, "you go ahead and have mine too." She waits for him to insist, "No, you should have yours; you haven't eaten all day." He stalks away with the two coconuts. The TamBram follows with two more.

See you again *very* soon. Why did Annie italicise very? Why would Annie want to see her *very* soon? Prasanna's been mulling for an hour and now it tumbles into her mind, like opening your window one fine morning and having a dead squirrel tumble in. A threesome.

Prasanna inhales sibilantly, puts her phone down, and clenches her fists over her elbows. How dare she, the presumptuous chit. Then she notices how big her hands look at the end of her toned arms. She unclenches her fists to admire her bruise-purple nail polish. *Preening and primping, that's all you care about, and getting freaky as you put it. I know very well what that means. You're not fooling anybody.* The letter bomb explodes all over her again. She hugs herself. The afternoon is turning to evening. A cool breeze is blowing. She's sitting again on the stone steps of the estate, reading Sid's letter, over and over. *You want to portray this spiritual image, but all you care about is people lusting after you, like some unattainable goddess.* The breeze cuts through her in ice daggers. Prasanna shivers.

Why blame her alone? Why not blame his father too? It really was Victus's fault, mostly. But Victus was glad to let Prasanna alone stand condemned in their son's eyes. What has she not done for Victus? Look where that's got her.

She saved his life. Victus was at death's door, in the hospital, just last summer, with a perforated colon. His drinking, which had escalated after Sid left, and had finally ended their marriage, had caught up to him at last. The doctors shook their heads. They all thought he was done for. Prasanna begged for ten minutes with him, did reiki for him, and colour therapy: drew circles with her lucky black marker pen, on his thumbs and palms and wrists. Exactly seven days later, he was out of the ICU, walking to the bathroom. Now he's back home, enchanting fresh fools with his eagle's nose and grave eyes, his voice that comes from down in his guts to churn your own guts into mush. And he was grateful then, while he was still in hospital, awake and convalescing. Now he laughs at her and calls it all mumbo-jumbo. Ungrateful man!

Then there's Annie. It was Prasanna who introduced Annie to Victus. Prasanna was at last year's annual alumni meetup, at O&M, where in the '80s Prasanna had pioneered direct marketing. David himself had named her copywriter of the year, and signed her letter of congratulations. David Mather! With his own hands. Prasanna had felt sorry, that's all, for the fat chick, so she'd introduced herself and given her tips and tricks for work. Annie had listened with those unblinking eyes – pretty eyes, though, Prasanna admits. Weeks later, when a mutual friend told Prasanna that Victus was in ICU, and Prasanna's car was in the garage, she rang Annie. "Yes, of course, my pleasure to drive you," said Annie. Prasanna did her God's errand at the hospital and left. Victus had plenty of hangers-on to hold his hands. Half his former students were still in love with him. And Prasanna wasn't looking for some big filmy reconciliation. She was well rid of him and his drunken rages and jealousies. Only this weekend, when she finally met Annie in her new role, did Prasanna picture her, driving back to the hospital alone, getting close to Victus when he was at his nadir. The minx! For months they'd kept it going behind her back.

Prasanna rocks herself. How he must despise me, to go from me to her! She's as big as five "me"s, second of all. How could he go from the sylph who graced *Femina* covers and Satya Paul ramps to this elephant with unblinking eyes who listens, and watches, and gives back nothing? They're moving around inside her, like that toothpick Victus swallowed was moving around inside him in ICU – those words from Sid's letter that went into her like daggers and never came out again. Has he told Annie about that too, she wonders. Maybe he has. Maybe he's painted Prasanna the villain, just like Sid did. But Sid was just a kid. Victus has no shame. No, Annie's text deserves no reply.

The pings are still not pinging. Prasanna thumbs through her conversation with Kamal Joglekar. "You've got to come back and do this every year," he told her. She sits up straight, her 28-inch chest expanding under her bustier. And this guy has been in *India Today*, and he knows Raza, Seema Kohli, and Anjolie Menon! She listened when he talked about them, his arm around her waist, the two of them alone in the gallery. (Even if you're a bigshot, there are always lulls during an exhibition.) She stored up the artists' names, gathered that *they* were bigshots, pretended she'd heard of them. She's as erudite as anyone. She's published novels, too, believe it or not, and she started with zero contacts in publishing. But, as an artist, you've got to protect your individuality, avoid getting too deeply into what other artists are doing.

And this big man begged her for selfies, and he wants her to show at Kalashilp every year! And look, here on Tinder: hundreds of guys half her age are chasing her. Prasanna swipes left, barely looking, left, left.

Her thumb stops. Her heart stops. The boy on her screen

has big chocolate-brown eyes, an eagle's nose, and wheatish skin. And he's thirty-six, too. Sid's age. Ha! She swipes left, left, left. She doesn't want to date someone her age, another fat drunk bald slob most likely; but what're all these young'uns looking for, she wonders, chasing women twice their age? She wishes she'd checked the doppelganger's occupation.

Sid's a lawyer now. Sid did well for himself: got into Yale on a scholarship. That's where he went, after writing that letter. He changed his name. It took them years to track him down. Years after that evening, when Prasanna sat on the steps under the banyan-tree, clutching Sid's letter, outside Sid's room – the sunken cave-like room, cool even in midsummer, a child's paradise – years after the divorce, Prasanna and Victus separately tracked down their only child. Was Sid's doppelganger on Tinder a lawyer too, Prasanna wonders. She swipes on, barely looking, looking for who knows what.

Sharmila sits watching the students. She tallies mentally who's already paid and who hasn't. She tries to guess who is with whom. Most of these kids still have some shame. They keep their hands to themselves. Not that fair-skinned pretty boy, though: he's openly feeling up his girl. And his girl is letting him, too: more fool she. As if getting a guy all worked up were an achievement! Sharmila's contempt struggles with her pity. Pity wins.

Sharmila's ears are pricked, listening for more words. But these kids talk English as fast as foreigners. She can't pick much out. *Beech*, she hears, *beech*. She knows that one: *beech me*, in between. Caught in between the lust of two boys, the plain sensible boy and the handsome daredevil, Sharmila made the wrong choice. She should've kept studying, finished school, at least. She was bright. and Amma would've fought with Appa to keep her in school. But Sharmila was a fool.

Down the service road, a mountainous cow approaches the heap of discarded tender coconuts. She sways side-to-side, the rope that runs through her nostrils tied around her forefoot, hobbling her. The college girls leap from the benches, shrieking, fleeing the fly-flicking shit-encrusted tail. Sharmila feeds the cow three coconut husks then shoos her away. Silly girls, acting scared for the men's benefit. No sensible man would fall for that.

Her phone rings. Again her heart jumps with panic as she pictures Manoj drunk, unconscious, in an ambulance blaring its horn, about to race past her on Kanakapura Main Road. She checks the caller ID. She groans. It's only that poor widow from next door, the one who's always doing dishes, one dish at a time, two dozen times a day, wasting soap and water – just for an excuse to spy on her neighbours out the kitchen window.

"Good afternoon, Aunty," says Sharmila.

"Hell-oo?" shouts the deaf old woman. "Yes, listen!" In garden-path sentences, with tangents and sub-tangents, like pulling your teeth, the widow tells Sharmila that last evening, on his way home, she saw Manoj walking with a certain disreputable character, whose history "everybody knows." This fellow gave Manoj a sip from his Aquafina bottle. "Just casually carrying around water suddenly, it seems, like one of those rich people whose throats are always dry." Manoj took one sip from the fellow's bottle, then another. Then they parted ways. But Manoj never returned the bottle. The bottle was three-quarters full when Manoj slipped into his home, home alone, my poor darling blind daughter. "Hell-oo? Are you still there? Damn these tiny phones."

Sharmila's phone has dropped into her lap. Now she understands why Manoj's eyes were extra vague and wandering last night, why he stank extra-strong of *paan masala*. A mosquito hovers around her ankle. In her stall,

69

in the shadows of tall buildings, moist from tender coconuts and their innards, evening's mosquitoes come early. Sharmila doesn't notice the mosquito needling her big toe. A tear falls down her face, big and fat, navigating wrinkles, lighting up sunspots.

She wipes her eyes. She stands up. She carves up the four drained coconuts the two biceps-bound boys have brought her. Crack-crack! Her iron scythe is ancient but in tip-top shape, glinting sharp. One of the boys has already paid. Well, his girl paid for them both. Maybe he's a loser, like Manoj. The other boy pays now. Both boys move away a little and start munching coconut flesh.

The moment she's alone again, Sharmila texts Piyush-Anna. She doesn't tell him Manoj is drinking again. She cannot be sure. Maybe that was, oh, God grant that was, just water in the bottle. "I'm worried he might start drinking again," she writes. "Just a fear, irrational most likely. But just in case, would you walk him home tonight? Tomorrow onwards I'll walk him, myself, all the way to your shop, and back. You'll just have to hold him back there, somehow, till I arrive."

All this scheming, neighbours watching, not a scrap of privacy left, never a moment's peace. And, after all this, it might already be too late. God damn her folly.

The pretty boy's shameless girl comes up and tells him they're all booking the cabs to Aristo's and is he ready to go? Yes, he says. They're speaking Hindi now. Prasanna can just about follow. She eyes the boy admiringly in spite of herself. His white skin glistens as he eats the coconut flesh. His black eyes shine as they run up and down Prasanna-may-daam's flesh golden in the evening twenty feet away. They move back towards her stall. "Does that old *pagli* come here every day?" he asks Sharmila in accented Hindi.

"Only on Sundays," says Sharmila. "She's crazy alright. She's always dressed this way. Everyone on the street knows her." *Pagli*, she will tell Manoj back home tonight, *pagli* I must've been, despised of God, to knot my *sari* to your *lungi*.

"What a hoot," says the pretty boy's girl. "An absolute *churhail*."

"Ye-es," says Sharmila reluctantly. "Witch" isn't exactly how she'd describe Prasanna-may-daam. "She's strange, it's true. But she's got a good heart. When the tea-shop is open, she buys biscuits, dips them in her tea, and feeds them to the stray dogs."

"It's natural for one stray to sympathise with others," says the boy in the naked shirt. He tells Sharmila about Tinder, explains what Tinder is, and what Prasanna-may-daam is doing on Tinder. Sharmila's eyes open wide. What nonsense are people up to! As if the people around you weren't trouble enough, you have to go looking for trouble on the phone?

Sharmila's phone buzzes. It's Piyush-Anna texting back. "Yes," says Piyush-Anna. "Of course I'll do it. You don't worry." The young people wander away. Sharmila sits down, heavy with relief, on her wonky stool.

Prasanna's phone buzzes. In her haste to unlock it, one thin purple-painted nail scratches the fine skin of her hand – which is already all scratched up, from playing with the eleven rescued dogs that she feeds and houses. About these dogs hardly anyone knows. This is not the kind of thing you brag about. Who's made her phone buzz, who could it be? Who has commented on her new photo?

It's only another text from Annie.

"Sorry I didn't get to attend your show. We had training that weekend. But Victus has told me all about your art. I'd love to visit you and buy a piece."

71

Her first sale! Prasanna's heart hammers against her bustier. A whole weekend fal-lalling about Kalashilp and not a single sale, barely any visitors besides Victus and his former students. And now Annie! But why does Annie want to buy a piece? "Oo-om," says Prasanna to calm herself. She sucks at her straw. Her coconut's drained. She holds up the translucent pink straw and sucks it dry. He's told Annie all about Prasanna's painting, hasn't he? *Painting as if a demon was in you and never mind where your son was.*

"Fuck-all you know about my art, you chit! Gossip, that's all you're after, picking our lives to pieces. I am not the woman Victus has painted to you. I don't need your pity! Komal Joglekar himself calls me his friend. Bhikkhuni herself saw the light in me and made me a priestess." Prasanna puts her phone down and resumes her argument with Bhikkhuni.

"It might be true," Prasanna mutters to herself, "for ordinary people, that the way to the spirit is through the flesh. But what about after someone achieves enlightenment? Surely, once you're free of temptation, then you can indulge yourself without harm?"

"And you put yourself in that category, do you?" replies Prasanna-as-Bhikkhuni. "So it wasn't you who showed up to temple last month with flesh on your breath? And when I asked you, you told me it was only a piece of chicken a friend had offered you, and you had said a prayer over the drumstick, and the chicken was dead anyway, so it was OK? And it isn't you who sprays perfume on your tongue to cover the smell of *ganja* every day, thinking I don't notice?"

"What's all this got to do with dyeing my hair back?" says Prasanna.

But her heart sinks. She realises she cannot win this argument. She's an exhibited artist, a published writer, an

72

award-winning copywriter – and this is how they treat her! Right or wrong, let Bhikkhuni be the one to wave the olive-branch.

Somewhere someone laughs. Off to her left, where she still doesn't hear too well. It's her first husband who punched Prasanna on her ear, back in the '80s. Bhikkhuni recommended forgiveness, explained that Prasanna must've had bad karma with him in a past life. Anger makes you ugly, Bhikkhuni told her. It furrows your brows, lines your chin, and hardens your eyes. Forgive people for your own sake. The doctor recommended hearing-aids. But Prasanna can hear fine! She's no hag to go hobbling around with hearing-aids. Laughter, again. She peers and smiles vaguely at the kids sitting twenty feet away. Young people did always admire her. But why is nobody responding to her photo? It's Sunday afternoon. What's everyone doing? Why hasn't Bhikkhuni called her? She drapes her ringlets over her bare shoulders and hugs herself.

It was just so that she sat on the steps outside Sid's sunken cave-room fourteen years ago. "Five years," said Sid's letter. "Five years it went on and you never noticed. Dad was always busy sleeping off a drunk, or playing cool professor. All his students had a crush on him and he knew it. Or maybe they just pretended to have a crush, to get free weed. Five years it went on and you never noticed. Preening and primping, that's all you care about, and flirting with your guests who bring you truffles and colognes, holding forth about your latest silent retreat so your guests will know you weren't just another airhead materialist, and getting freaky as you put it. I know very well what that means. You're not fooling anybody. He was your friend and you never noticed. He kept on coming, like it was nothing. You kept putting him in my room. What did you know? All the rooms were overflowing. Dad was sicking up in some back bathroom. And you! You were

73

keeping the last person up with you, so you could shake your stuff at him, or invite him to watch you paint, show him another facet of yours, put on an act like the painting demon was in you. Never mind that your son was stuck in his own room with that fat grey rummy drunk."

"But I really didn't know, my darling," Prasanna mutters, rocking on the bench by the road. "It was your Dad's house, my darling, Dad's friend, Dad's parties. Why did you address that letter to me alone? Why d'you hate *me*? You should've told me," Prasanna mutters. "I would've knocked his teeth down his throat."

With fists clenched Prasanna hits out at the air. But it's Kamal she's pushing away, Kamal who's come begging for selfies after she's closed her show. Alone in the gallery, on Sunday evening, visitors peeking in, walking past, moving on to the other rooms, all fifteen of Prasanna's paintings, self-portraits in various styles, hanging where they'd hung all weekend. And he did. He did grope her, all over her bum like a lizard, just like all those guys in her modelling days. His groping is what made her smile look weird in those photos, alone and weary and wrinkled.

Vidvesh sits eating his tender coconut, the decapitated coconut head serving as a plate. Abhilasha sits holding the other heap for him, the flesh from her own coconut. TickleBunny and some others have gone off to Aristo's. The others have wandered off to cafés, malls, and friends' places. Abhilasha's been racking her brain for something to say. Now, almost sorrowfully, she resumes the old topic.

"Isn't there a category for GILFs," says Abhilasha, "on porn sites? Like MILFs but with grannies."

Vidvesh shrugs. "I don't know. I'm not into kink." He pauses. He knows that Abhilasha has heard the rumours he's been circulating about their kinky sex life. "How do *you* know? You're not into that shit, are you?"

74

"Go on, woman. Tell me you know what I've been up to. Tell me I'm no gentleman. Let's call this whole circus off. If I raped you, I'd be in jail. Rightly so. You've trapped me, and I'll be forced to marry you, but nobody will raise a finger for me. How can that be right?"

Vidvesh had been waiting to speak to his father face-to-face, last winter, to tell him they'd have to call off the wedding, that he'd never wanted to marry Abhilasha Sharma. Then his father had told him that his business was going bust, and that Mr. Sharma was one of the last few people left who might be willing to help. And Vidvesh had kept his mouth shut.

"No," says Abhilasha, "I'm not into kink. *She* probably is."

Vidvesh snorts. She'd never let him call their wedding off. She's got nobody else. She's still shitting on that harmless hag just to try to get close to him. Now that they're alone, of course, she's sitting on the other bench, hugging herself, legs crossed. She thinks she's so clever, trapping him. Just wait till she finds out she's married to the son of a bankrupt. He snorts with laughter.

"You sure you're OK?" says Abhilasha. "You've been kinda… quiet."

He shrugs. He could tell her now, of course, and offer to break off their engagement. But, oh, what a payback it'll be to marry her. As with the Siemens offer letter, which he accepted just to post on social media, though he knows he must renege on his acceptance – to this marriage, too, the 21-year-old now sees himself drawn inevitably.

"I'm OK," he drawls. "Just thinking about some things." He always knew he was meant for something special. Turns out he was meant to walk with eyes wide open towards special tragedy.

Thoughtfully he chews his last piece of tender coconut.

And it occurs to him: a way to get back at her, a way to save Dad one ridiculous expense. He has only to keep "playing hard to get" – which is no doubt how she rationalises his aloofness – and then he could propose that they elope. "Darling, I love you, but I've just been thinking, you know how we've always been so much better than everybody else? I've got a rad idea. Why don't we elope? Registrar's office, two witnesses, bing-bang-boom. Don't worry, darling. I'm master of Midjourney. I'll give us a virtual wedding in Belgium, Bahamas, Basti, wherever. You'll have tons of glam photos to flood Instagram with. And it won't cost us a damn thing."

"Thinking about, like, what things?" says Abhilasha.

"Like the wedding, things like that. We should talk after CIAs…" All the GILF talk has got him studying Granny afresh, wondering if she's ever filmed a porn.

"We could talk about it now!" says Abhilasha, edging towards his bench.

"Hmm?" says Vidvesh. Speaking of porn, he's got a brilliant idea. He rises. "C'mon, enough with the coconuts. No, I don't want that one." He dumps the husks and uneaten flesh on the pile of discarded husks by the roadside. "Let's go finish our CIAs?"

"Come to my place," says Abhilasha. "My roommate's out." As they stroll down the road towards her private hostel, she squeezes his butt. He doesn't respond. He knows how much these promissory notes of hers are worth. "Let's get some beers?" she says. He shrugs.

Prasanna's phone buzzes again. But it's not a thumbs-up on her photo. It's another text-message. From Kamal, this time. Her stomach flutters. Maybe he's finally remembered. Maybe this is an offer to buy a painting! Oh, he must just have been busy before. He's a big man.

"Looking luscious, lady," says Kamal, "like a *langda*. I'd like to lick you all over your lush—"

76

She scrolls away, blushing furiously. What a lewd response to an artful photo! Why couldn't he respond on Instagram or Facebook, where she posted the photo, with a heart-eyes or a witty compliment? Why send her this filth in private?

She scrolls back to his message. It's gone. Her head spins. Did she imagine the message? No, look: Message Deleted. He just waited till she'd read it and then he deleted it. Fucking lecher. What does he know about fashion, or art, or beauty! Tears sting Prasanna's eyes, further blurring her poor vision.

The worst part isn't that he groped her. The worst part is that he gave her no discount on renting the gallery, even after last year, even after inviting her for next year; that he brought none of his big-shot friends to review her show or buy a piece; that he bought nothing himself; that he didn't even help her pack up afterwards. She's worse than a whore. She's a whore for free.

She swipes through Tinder, left, left, left. The sense of all she's lost this weekend descends around her in a fog. Bhikkhuni still hasn't called her: she seems to have cut her off. So Prasanna has lost the temple, which has been her real home these ten years, which lifted her out of the abyss that Victus and Sid had dug for her. She's lost Victus once again. She thought they'd become friends again, after her reiki saved his life. But he's been dating this chit behind her back, he's told this chit all about their lives, and now he's set the chit to mocking Prasanna's "artistic attempts". She can just see the air-quotes. And now she's lost Kamal and the whole Kalashilp connection. How can she possibly face Kamal again? Not that those shows did her any good. There was barely a notice or two, a single paragraph, tucked away in the bowels of a couple of no-name newspapers.

She pictures evenings back home, the dusk blue through

the windows of her two-storey house on Mysore Road. High-rise condos have sprung up all around, darkening her narrow windows. She keeps the lights off as much as she can – the tariffs are climbing like mad. Her smelly old reject dogs clip-clop around in the dark, pausing to rest their scarred or half-blind or asymmetrical heads on her knee. She swipes left, left, hoping perhaps that Sid's doppelganger will show up again. Maybe she can ask him: "Could you ever forgive your mother?" Maybe that's the kind of question you can answer only if it's a stranger who's asking.

"I have," Abhilasha realises, as she strokes Vidvesh's back through his naked tee. "I *have* let my fears get in the way. And you hate me. You think I don't want you." She takes his hand, wills her hand to tell his hand, *I do want you. Tonight, in my room. Finally I'm ready. Let's do it.*

She loves him and she needs him. She needs some stability, something achieved. She's bone-tired. She needs a break. You study all day, all year, and it's not enough. You were smarter than everyone at school, but in college you're not even in the top twenty percent. Every year your juniors are smarter than you, more articulate, more savvy. And everything you've ever worked for has ended up in nothing. Mathletes. Theatre. Dance. The Entrepreneurship Incubation Cell at Jesus. Every time, you get just far enough in some endeavour to live for a few mad months in false hope. She cannot let that happen with Vidvesh.

She's been waiting to have sex with him till the sex could be good. But those weight-loss pills aren't doing shit, just making her break out. Maybe she should've tried amphetamines. It's too late now, she realises, squeezing his hand, willing him to squeeze back. She'll do it tonight, whatever she's got to do to keep him. Mom and Dad would like that. They wouldn't want the details – gross! – but they'd want her to do the right thing.

God knows Dad and Mom don't expect much from her, not after what happened with Didi. They just want her to be safe. Mom checks Abhilasha's Insta every day, and two phone-calls a day with Abhilasha aren't enough; she never stops worrying about the child that's left. Never again will Mom be caught napping. Abhilasha will do what she needs to keep Vidu. And Mom will get to plan her wedding, pick everything out, dress her up, splash the photos all over Insta for the whole family to see. Mom deserves that much.

And when they're married, then, finally, she'll have a year or two off, just to look around and feel the ground under her feet. Then she'll work, of course, but maybe she will no longer be so panicked about fucking up her life once her marriage is sorted.

Here's the shop. Let's get you some alcohol, Vidu: it'll be easier for you if you're drunk. Poor boy, she thinks, surveying herself in the merciless mirror of a woman's eyes. But don't get too drunk, darling. What if you can't get it up – how will I know whether that's the alcohol or my spare tires?

Her heart beats fast and shallow, and her hand is sweating into his, as they halt outside an MRP shop milling with students. Vidu will know how much to drink. He is a man.

"Kingfisher OK?" says Vidvesh.

"Kingfisher, Budweiser, Magnum – you choose," says Abhilasha. "I don't like beer anyway."

"Let's get something else, then," says Vidvesh, scrolling through his phone. "No hurry. Take your time."

Vidvesh, pursuing his brilliant idea, is scrolling through Pornhub, looking for a video. A very specific video, a PoV video where the dick looks like it could be his, and where the woman is masked but looks like it could be Abhilasha. And then, when TurpentineBath sends him his own offer letter from Phillips, he will send him, in reply, this link. I did it, uploaded the porn A and I made, here you go, TupperwareBollocks!

Abhilasha frowns through the glass store-front at the tables and racks and fridges, wines and whiskies and coolers. "I'll barely be drinking," she says at last. "You decide."

"Hmm," says Vidvesh, scrolling.

TenderBolus. TackyBitch. He could keep going all night. He's witty, quick, the smartest guy in class. He entered the creative-writing contest in college last year. Just for fun. And he won. He outshone all those Humanities losers. But it's no good. He's got to give Siemens the middle finger and go help Dad, go work on Mom preparing her for the news that life as they know it is over. He was the second-hottest guy in class but it did him no good. He had the luck to sit next to Abhilasha during freshers' orientation, to agree to have coffee with her the following week, and now she's told everyone and he's trapped.

"Vidu!" Abhilasha whines. "You pick. I just wanna get a teeny bit drunk."

"For what?" He looks up into her eyes. She runs her finger down the front of his jeans. "Oh." No jolt of excitement runs up his neck. He snorts. "Let's get a quart of scotch, then." Ten-to-one she'll back out of this at the last minute. Either way, he'll have a drink.

They stand before the window, waiting for the weekend student crowd to thin. Her hands are all over him again. His arms hang by his side. He can't do this sober, not with her anyway. He pictures it, up in her room, on her quilted satin bedsheet. Abhilasha will swear she doesn't need a drink. But she will sure enough. Just a sip, she'll say. But then she'll get so drunk that later she can pretend she wasn't in control, it wasn't her fault. He sees it all, clear as day, as if they've done it a thousand times already. This is to be his life now. He finds a video that looks close enough, amateur enough, and sends himself the link, for later, when TamBram texts again.

He sets his jaw. He takes Abhilasha's hand. They step into the store.

Sharmila sits rocking on her stool, flicking mosquitoes from her ankles, watching a beggar child half-jogging, half-walking up the service-road. A tiny child, five, maybe, two feet tall, naked feet slipping over stones and potholes. If he stops to beg, Sharmila decides, she'll give him a tender coconut instead, best in stock, *badhiya*. She'll hold it for him while he sips, then feed him the flesh with her own fingers. For his fingers are soot-black.

But the child doesn't stop. Thumb in mouth, without noticing Sharmila, the child walks on. Sharmila looks after him with an aching heart.

Her own children are all grown. They've all left home. They never speak to Manoj. That man had it all and squandered it all. Looks, brains, spirits. Not a single soul respects him, and, oh, how does he go on? The beggar child speeds up and catches up with the cow, which is feeding at a rubbish-heap up the service-road. The child reaches up towards the shit-encrusted, fly-flicking, windmilling tail, and giggles, and claps. In the dusk a warmth spreads through Sharmila's chest.

She lights her kerosene lamp and sits down again, sari pulled down over ankles against the mosquitoes. It's easy to be kind to dumb creatures from whom you expect nothing. Maybe, after all, Manoj is one such creature. There is at least no evil in him. He is a child, a cow, her husband at world's end. Poor man! His own children disown him. Their son ran away at sixteen. Their married daughter never visits home. They still take *her* calls, speak to her frequently. All the neighbours laugh at him. And maybe, now, again, the laughing will begin afresh, another round of favours that Sharmila must beg but can never repay, maybe she will find, again, a length of rope hidden under Manoj's mattress. She rises and paces around her tiny stall. She can't catch her breath. She goes outside and rearranges her stack of coconuts, tall and neat.

After all, who's to say she would've been better off with Piyush-Anna? Piyush-Anna owns two buildings, with rooms for rent. He has his son manning a second grocery-store. "We must work," Piyush-Anna says. "It's sinful to sin idle." But his wife is asthmatic, house-bound, sprouting a moustache from her steroid meds. And everybody in the neighbourhood goes to Piyush-Anna for help. He always frowns and scolds, his brows thunderous, his bass earth-shaking. But he always relents. He opens his purse, his home, his heart. In this life, perhaps, you can only ever be either he who helps or he who needs help. Is it, after all, so much worse to be he who's always falling than to be he who's always stopping, sighing, and holding out a hand to those who stumble?

Oh my husband! I forgive you.

Another gang of students approaches her stall. Sharmila straightens her sari, and smooths her hair, still night-black after all her worry. She begins planning a different kind of performance for her husband: a parody of Prasanna-may-daam. There's this old loon, she rehearses – as she smiles at the kids, and assures them her stock is *badhiya*, *paani aur goonda waala* – there's this old loon who comes to my stall, every Sunday, dressed in a toddler's party-clothes. Everybody stares at her. But she stares straight ahead, like some hi-fi model up on a runway in foreign. As the kids queue to scan Sharmila's GPay paycode, she pictures Manoj and herself rolling on the floor, laughing at Prasanna-may-daam, laughing till their tears run. She grins as she hands the kids their decapitated coconuts.

Ping! But it's only another message from Kamal.

Prasanna lifts her lip. You can't delete a message without opening it, without him seeing, from the two blue tick-marks, that you've opened his message. So she does him one better. She deletes the whole conversation. Let the old pervert wait for his blue ticks forever! If he texts again she'll block him. She'll find somewhere else to exhibit. She refreshes her Facebook and Instagram.

Here's her photo. Where are all the thumbs-ups and heart-eyes? Where is everybody this Sunday evening? She pictures her school-mates, college-mates, former colleagues all ensconced amidst their families, warm and cosy. She panics. In the twilight on the unlit street she browses other photos from this weekend, looking for another good one to upload. Oh, look. Here she is in that scarf, that Ritu Kumar silk scarf that Victus gave her when Sid was born. And it's wrapped around her head.

Of course. She looks up and gapes across Sarjapur Road. Why didn't she think of it earlier? She'll just cover her hair at temple until the magenta curls grow out! She's got loads of scarves, all different shapes and sizes, all matching some outfit or another. She pictures tying them on. You've gotta tie each one differently. You've gotta have taste. Nothing else really matters. You can't buy taste. You're born with it or you're not. What about this, Bhikkhuni, will this work? You can't see a single strand of magenta. Oh, say this will work. If not, I'll just lop off my hair. Annie told her she'd look fantastic with short hair, like a pixie. But maybe Annie was just mocking her again.

Ping!

Someone from the Fabulous Fashionistas Facebook group – a new member, a style blogger from Seattle, with two million Twitter followers – says, "Gorgeous shot, Prasanna! Love the shoulder-sweeper, your pose, and the well-chosen background."

"Thanks, Sarah!" Prasanna fires back. "A lot of my stuff is from flea-markets."

"So you're a superstar shopper as well as a fashion icon," Sarah replies at once. "Wow!"

Prasanna hearts the comment. She lets the warmth wash over her.

She rereads Annie's messages. A threesome – how could she think so! Annie's just being nice. Annie wants Prasanna to keep coming over. Annie's not jealous at all, bless her; she just recognises what a special person Prasanna is. She's got good taste, gotta give her that, just like Sarah from Fabulous Fashionistas: she might be a little chubby but she's always well-dressed. And she *wasn't* mocking Prasanna this weekend, wasn't smirking behind the lens. She genuinely admires Prasanna. Look at these gorgeous photos she's taken of her! Young people did always admire her. How kind of her to offer to buy a painting. So what if Victus has set her up to it? Victus always encouraged Prasanna's art, always had good taste, kept offering to introduce her to his artist and art-collector friends. He brought all his friends to Kalashilp when there was nobody else. Victus has paintings all over his walls, absolutely teeming, by European artists and Indian, established and emerging. Prasanna knows exactly which self-portrait she'll sell them, and just where it would go: right between Victus's installation of assorted carnival masks and the shelf full of assorted skull sculptures. Yes: her two-headed golden-skinned wasp-waisted nude, with the rhinestone G-string, would fill that nook perfectly.

Thank God Kamal didn't buy one of her paintings! God knows where he'd have hung it and what he'd be doing with it. She's well rid of Kamal. Who needs him? Now that Kamal's out of the picture Prasanna will take Victus up on his longstanding offer. It was only pride, anyway, the determination to make it on her own in this domain, too, that's kept her from accepting Victus's offers of introduction. She even begged him not to bring his artist friends along! She wanted to see if they'd come unbidden. Silly prideful woman!

Prasanna rises, shakes the pins and needles from her booted feet, and flings her coconut-husk amidst the rubble from the demolished engineering college. She stalks up to the stall, scans Sharmila's paycode, and waits to say goodbye. But Sharmila's busy with the kids.

In the thick blue dusk Prasanna stalks towards her car, her boot-heels unsteady on the potholes. But she barely notices. For she's sure now, sure suddenly, that it wasn't a dream, that it *was* a conversation with Sid she glimpsed on Victus's phone. So! Fourteen years after he went away, Sid has resumed speaking to his Dad. Stop visiting the estate – how could she think so! She'll keep visiting Victus and Annie, show them she's grown. And they'll tell Sid. And Sid will forgive her. Sid has forgiven Dad. Surely, in time, he'll forgive Mom, too, Mom whom he blamed unjustly to begin with. Maybe, this summer, when Sid gets holidays at his law-firm in Chicago, he'll come visit. They'll sit all together under the banyan-tree. Yes, and Annie, too. Annie, the smart, sweet glue-stick of the old family unit.

"Yes, my son," she'll tell Sid. "Yes, I failed you. Just like Mummi failed me. Well, not exactly like that. Mummi wanted to hurt me. Still, I wish Mummi and I could've told each other, I forgive you. I never wanted to hurt you, Siddy. You know I'd never willingly. I'm so sorry, son, sorrier than I can say. Tell me you forgive me."

"Loved meeting you, too," Prasanna texts Annie. "Yes, we must meet again soon. Let me know when you want to come over and look over my stuff and pick something out. I'm free anytime except when I'm at temple."

SHOES

Monday morning after Ganesh puja, the walkways are littered with the soot-stained crimson shells of firecrackers curled up foetally. Overnight, leaves have fallen from the imported maples lining the boundary walls, burying the festival's remains. Asha sweeps standing upright. Only the tip of her broom touches the litter, not gathering it but scattering it. She glances back down her section. Should she redo it? There's no use. September's just begun; these trees have just begun shedding. Asha wipes the sweaty handle of her broom on her blue uniform: washed and mended by Amma, her mother, who made her get this job. Asha glances at her lipstick-red stilettoes. Quite funny, wearing these shoes to work – she giggles – but she's got to break them in. The audition is next week.

Housekeeping have been sweeping since 7am. Asha has watched the software engineers, fresh from gym and shower, board air-conditioned company vans for commutes to suburban tech parks. It's almost 10 now. Asha stretches her neck.

Between the condo complex's ten 22-storey towers, mattress-thick lawns luxuriate under sleepless sprinklers. Odd-shaped, odourless flowers she has seen nowhere else bloom under palm-trees shaped like waving hands. Down the terracotta walkway stroll sleek black-clad housewives and tracksuit-clad entrepreneurs muttering into earpieces. Asha picks out "Yeah" and "Thanks". If only she'd been sent to an English-medium school! Maybe if she'd been a boy, Amma would've found the money. As she gazes after the residents, the dead leaves skitter away from her.

Her broom nudges a leaf pile that the wind has swept against the potted marigolds, and unearths a sanitary napkin. It's coming unrolled, wrinkled, the blood faded

86

yellow-blue, stinking sickly-sweet. Above her, Tower Ecstasy's balconies, encased in tinted glass, wink down. Holding her breath, Asha manoeuvres the pad into her bin.

A young couple pushing a pram emerges from behind Tower Elysium. Asha scrutinises the woman. Levi's Jeans. True Religion tee-shirt. Twenty thousand rupees for common-looking jeans and a boxy slogan top. Asha straightens her uniform and sweeps towards the couple, her bright black eyes glaring.

Instagram is where Asha learned to identify brands. She used to think Instagram was a waste of time. Then she realised that's where the influencers post their outfits. Outfits are crucial on *Dance India Dance*. It was on a model's feed that Asha saw these Mango stilettoes. Funny brand-name, Mango, but these shoes really are luscious. When she went home wearing them, Amma called her "slut", asked God how she's deserved so wanton a daughter, and burst into sobs. Asha wanted to go hug Amma and she wanted to scream at Amma. She stalked away to her room and tried to slam the door. The door stuck, so, feeling silly, she pushed it quietly closed.

Amma never could understand how Asha struggles, defending the fortress of her spirit through the assault this job makes on her spirit from 7am to 7 p.m., how hard she struggles to resist all of life's other temptations: her cousins gossiping whole Sundays away, her own phone trying to seduce her into endlessly ogling mansions, gowns, and vacations abroad. Asha's sweeping slows, then halts. She pictures her lipstick-red shoes flying around her room tonight to the stark percussion and dissonant harmonics of "Sheila ki Jawaani", the item number featuring a singe-hot Katrina Kaif. Please God her roommate, her cousin, won't be home early, offloading another day's drama with her secret boyfriend. Can't Asha get a half-hour alone? She needs privacy: the dance moves are all hip-flinging and bosom-flexing.

"You must get used to an audience," taunts the voice in her head. Fear balls up in her chest like a puppy street-born in December. "The audition's soon," the voice screams. "When will you get used to an audience, never will you, cantevendancebeforeyourcousin. Her shiny red heels totter on the dull red tiles. She hasn't told Amma her dream, but cramped rooms can't keep secrets and it's Amma's voice in her head that taunts her.

The young couple approach. Asha resumes sweeping. When she's got the moves down, then she'll show her cousin. Then her cousin won't laugh. The woman in Levi's and Superdry glances pointedly at the walkway still leaf-strewn. Asha stares back. The woman passes on. She'll never meet Asha's eyes, she'll never wonder who empties her bins or cleans her swimming-pool. She isn't even one of the working ones: she stays home, though her baby's got a nanny. To think, these are the people she used to envy! They could do anything but they're just strolling round and round in unadventurous clothes.

She checks her phone, a tiny Samsung so laggy it often makes her weep with frustration. Yes: the Bangalore audition is still next Thursday. She'll leave home at dawn to beat the queue. Then nothing can stop her. She won't reproach Amma for her unkindnesses. "Goodbye," she'll say, and Amma's lips will move slackly and soundlessly. Success silences the people who try to snatch your dreams away, to hand them down to children still young enough to play.

"It's a slim chance," she mutters to herself, "I know that." She scolds her smile away. It creeps back. The news is brimming with people who clutched their passion close, fought through the crowds, and planted their flag atop Mt.

Success. "I'll practise very hard now," she breathes, arching her neck at Tower Excelsior, searching for the top. The top is too high to see. "I'll be there *before* dawn," she decides.

The grey-uniformed supervisor approaches, strutting and huffing, his mouth set grim and ugly. His "slattern" and "piece of filth" from yesterday are still ringing in Asha's ears. Her throat tightens. She turns and half-marches, half-slides back down her section, resweeping. The supervisor watches, arms akimbo. His shadow retreats. Asha keeps her head down and sweeps on.

The physical labour mellows her anger and gives her a sudden glimpse behind Amma's anger. She pictures Amma, squatting on the narrow concrete strip between the bathroom and the kitchen door. Amma's back is craned over the washtub with the cracked lip. Her callused hands are sudsy. Her thighs tremble against her calves as she squats, and shake as she rises, one hand clutching the wall, the other stabilising her swollen knee. And Asha realises with a sudden brief threat of tears that it's for Amma's sake that she must break free of this life.

Amma's angry only because she thinks Asha will fail. But today there are opportunities Amma cannot imagine. Today, it's resignation that's folly. Next *Ganesh puja*, she'll drive home in a big, red, chauffeured car. She will conjure from it a washing-machine with many buttons, twenty bottles of hand-lotion, and an automatic wheelchair. Asha's feet already hurt from her new shoes but energy jolts through them now as she pictures herself, on Thursday, leaping high.

Ganesh puja is the day for new beginnings.

Under Tower Éclat, Nimisha's finishing her section. Her back is horizontal to maximise broom contact with the

89

ground. The leaves rattling against her broom make music in her ears. She empties her leaf-bucket into the rubbish-bin and looks around. Two hundred feet away, Asha is resweeping her section. Nimisha sits down on a bench under the boundary-wall. "Hi Kuttu!" she types into WhatsApp.

She scrutinises the exclamation-point, replaces it with a comma, then a smiley face, then a comma again, then switches to Hindi. Pausing for inspiration, she flexes her feet in her new shoes. Barely worn, the fabric white-and-baby-blue, the rubber soles intricately grooved, they're a hand-me-down from a Tower Effulgent resident whose bathrooms Nimisha cleans during her lunch-break. Nimisha, happy with her cardboard-thin slippers, accepted this gift with profuse thanks and secret scepticism. But yesterday, in these funny shoes, her feet barely hurt. She'd stopped noticing the pain, so it was with astonishment that she noticed its absence. Back home, cooking dinner, sitting was not a necessity but a luxury. I understand, now, she wants to tell Mummi, why you were the way you were: you'd stopped noticing the pain, but it was always there and you were always exhausted. It'll be different, now, when you come to live with me. But Nimisha doesn't dare text Mummi. Not again. Not yet.

Looking up, she sees Asha, under Tower Excellence, rubbing her back, then dancing a few steps. Not a care if anyone's watching! Three years ago, it was Kuttu who was mad on entering showbiz. "Katrina Kaif made it without any contacts in Bollywood," said the ten-year-old. "Why not me?"

Katrina's a British citizen, Nimisha wanted to tell her daughter. Katrina's parents are a British lawyer and a Kashmiri businessman. They gave Katrina that skin, white as a *firang*'s, and that posh accent. But she kept her mouth shut. And God granted her prayer: he freed Kuttu from her ambition. It's with mild amusement, now, that Nimisha regards Asha's ambition. Showbiz has, after all, taken people from rags to riches. Kangana, for instance, and Shah Rukh, king of Bollywood.

"I know you'll do well," Nimisha types to Kuttu. Kuttu's event was to end at 10. At posh places, things happen on time. "I know you've done well," she edits on her second-hand Blackberry's sticky buttons. No, Kuttu hates it when Nimisha presumes. What's the point of talking to me, she demands, if you already know everything? "Let me know how it went," Nimisha edits.

Prickly sweat breaks out on Nimisha's forehead in her terror of another gaffe. She arches her neck. A netting of wild-almond branches, bejewelled with leaves, some emerald, some ruby, holds up the sky's leaden locks. It's nice to still see trees somewhere. Her message can wait. The big question is what she'll make for dinner to celebrate Kuttu's win.

Nimisha mentally browses the slatted plastic boxes at the greengrocer's that stands opposite that huge new condo complex. She peeks in occasionally on her way home. "Bro-ko-li," she mouths (Rs.160/kilo). "Ju-ki-ni" (Rs.200/kilo). She'll buy something exotic, but not so exotic that she'll cook it wrong and send Kuttu skulking to her room.

Asha is still resweeping her section, her back finally horizontal. Nimisha's face softens. Asha's only fourteen years her junior, but really she's from another generation: she contributes only half her salary to the household, and her parents are only now scouting bridegrooms. Foolish child! She hates her work so much she always does it twice. Nimisha learned early that work is a terrible master, not content with your body alone.

The other maids are heading with carpet-beaters towards

the common areas. They stop for a chat. Nimisha asks after teething toddlers and ailing parents. They ask her about Kuttu. She replies loquaciously, filling the lacunae in her knowledge of her daughter's life with imaginary facts and conversations. They point their heads towards Asha the oddball, and titter. Nimisha only tsks. Her colleagues walk on.

It's 10:40. Should she go help Asha finish sweeping? She consults her cosy shoes. They tell her her day stretches long enough without doing other people's work, longer still with her secret engagement that begins this evening.

Letter-by-letter, AutoComplete an alien concept, Nimisha types out a message to Kuttu in Hindi. She tried to practise English with Kuttu. But Kuttu turned away, shuddering. The memory makes Nimisha's mouth spasm with anger. She immediately rebukes her anger. It's natural for Kuttu to dread the corruption of her own accent. She remembers the video she overheard. It was a man's voice that drew her to Kuttu's locked door. "It doesn't matter how good your English is," said the man, "if your accent is wrong." Nimisha leaned against the door, her heart sinking, listening to Kuttu repeating English phrases after the man. Then her heart bobbed back up. There was no difference between the instructor's accent and Kuttu's!

At dinner that night she searched for the words with which to tell Kuttu she was already perfect. She searched her memory for reassurances Mummi had given her. When she was getting her tetanus booster, whimpering at the big needle, she'd looked up at Mummi. Mummi was gazing with clasped hands at the doctor with his big-city Hindi and prosperous paunch. The only words Mummi said were in apology on Nimisha's behalf. So Nimisha came up empty that night. Just as well. Anything she said would've likely just irritated Kuttu.

She watches the thick green water-hose, striped white

down its length like a mythical serpent. The walkway is flooded, like the rice paddies she danced in with her sisters, weaving between the rows of toiling grown-ups in colourful saris and white dhotis. Now the water drains from the fields, the colour drains from Mummi's sari, and Mummi stands gazing alone across the wasteland. At dusk a neighbour will hobble towards the cottage, bringing a fistful of rice.

Why does Mummi prefer her lonely cottage and the charity of strangers over Nimisha's home? Hurt scurries like a hounded rat across her pleasant face. She brings up Mummi's number. Her finger hesitates. One more phone call and Mummi might swear she'll never come. Nimisha must be patient.

It wasn't till 2019, on their annual visit to Basti, that Mummi began to relent. They were sitting on the veranda, shaded from the noonday glare, peeling mangoes for pickles. Nimisha had never mastered the art of peeling with a knife. Her knife sometimes slipped over the raw mangoes' tight thin peel, sometimes sliced into the butter-yellow flesh. She studied Mummi's peeling. Mummi kept her eyes down and held her face the same. But her hands shifted a smidge to afford Nimisha a clearer view. Nimisha resumed peeling. They sat in silence still. But now the silence felt peaceful. After all these years, toiling at home for Mummi and Papa, toiling in Bangalore for husband and child – Nimisha had her reward.

And then Papa died – suddenly, at fifty-four. The doctor said a lot of long words, needing to explain. And Mummi, who'd lived by God's will, needed to understand. It must be for Nimisha's adolescent sin that God had punished the family, belatedly and inaccurately, as was his wont. Mummi has never said a word about Papa's death, but Mummi blames her. She knows it. How else to explain

Mummi's stubborn solitude, her ostentatious suffering, the snarl with which, when Nimisha asked, after the funeral, how she was doing, Mummi rose and hobbled away?

She can't live that way forever. Leave her alone. She'll come around. And when she gets here, and sees Kuttu setting forth smartly uniformed, tastes Nimisha's curries which aren't just potatoes, and eases herself down on a proper mattress, then she'll stop snarling. She will look at Nimisha and will finally consent to tell Nimisha stories of her childhood.

But you never know with Mummi. Mummi seems to have lost capacity for all pleasure except the pleasure of foiling other people's pleasure. Nimisha's waited three weeks for Mummi to answer her last text. Does silence mean consent? Mummi likes to let you think you've won a battle, only to hoist you on your own petard as you're launching your victory march.

A raven's pensive warbling recalls Nimisha to the flooded jogging-track before her. She makes a mental note to ask about the tanker. The plastic and steel buckets, salvaged paint-cans, two-litre water-bottles, and aluminium pots, which Nimisha filled with water last fortnight, and arranged in coolish spots around her shack, are almost empty. The BBMP stopped piping water to their neighbourhood years ago. They all buy water from private borewells. She must check when the next tanker's due. Which of her neighbours hasn't paid up, is trying to borrow his share, talking about funds expected, relying on the tragic generosity of the poor? She pictures the defaulters' faces, honest need cracking through their mask of lies.

"SouthRegionInterSchoolDebateChampionship,"
Nimisha mouths. Kuttu translated and explained the words; Nimisha was listening hard; but, fearful of spoiling Kuttu's good mood, she wasn't listening at all. The words'

meanings slipped between her fingers, like the fishes in the green ponds they used to have at Basti. Now the syllables run together in one brick wall.

Nimisha wanted to go watch the debate. She's got holidays to spare. But Kuttu said, "I won't inconvenience you." Nimisha took that the wrong way, swiping at wet cheeks as she walked here this morning. Now she thanks God for Kuttu's independence. Let the other children drag their parents along, costing them a half-day's wages. Kuttu is a blessing.

Nimisha's husband wanted another child. But Nimisha refused to repeat her parents' mistake. Mummi and Papa raised five children, now scattered across the country. In her twenties Nimisha gave herself several abortions, passing the sickness off as a woman's natural weariness. Her husband grumbled about their sonlessness but never hit her. Mummi and Papa had chosen well for her. Now he's stopped trying for a son. He makes Kuttu recite English poems and pilfers her report-cards to brag to his friends. Nimisha airs out the cigarette stink with her *pallu* before sneaking the report-cards back into Kuttu's satchel.

Nimisha prays he'll never hear the account Kuttu has given of herself at school: that her mother's a housewife and her father's dead and they live with their factory-manager uncle. Nimisha has had time to see the wisdom in this story. Children can be so cruel to someone who doesn't belong. Well, her husband isn't likely to hear. He's sullen with the people he drives, sullenness being how he shows customers he's as good as them – but he's never dared attend a parent-teacher meeting, to face the parents whose children actually belong at Kuttu's CBSE school. Nimisha attends the PTMs instead, in a sari specially bought: cream-coloured cotton, embroidered with tiny orange flowers. No polyester cheap and cheerful, no hot-pink lipstick. This is not, for the other parents, a special occasion.

95

Nimisha rises: Asha's almost finished resweeping her section. Thank God Kuttu outgrew her showbiz dreams. "SouthRegionInterSchoolDebateChampionship," Nimisha chants under her breath. Debating is a far safer aspiration. It will help Kuttu keep improving her English. Soon she will stop fearing her mother's corruption. Then they can converse fearlessly: Kuttu in her posh English, she in her clown's English.

SouthRegionInterSchoolDebateChampionship.

Nimisha knows exactly what the words mean: that Kuttu's becoming a big something-or-other. Soon she'll be going around India, stunning vast crowds, speaking English at 80kph, disappearing into a chauffeured black panther of a car that glides over the sand-heaps, pot-holes, and gravel-heaps that make up the roads. When she visits home, all the busybodies, who told Nimisha she was wasting money sending Kuttu to Himanshu School, will crowd her doorway to watch the celebrity eating rice with her hands, stooping to touch the feet of her grandmother who's here at last, smiling at last.

Nimisha reviews her message to Kuttu one last time, presses Send, and begins her wait.

The two women approach each other.

Tears of frustration and footache surge up Asha's throat as the reality of another workday sinks in. But her imminent celebrity demands dignity. She fights her tears. The fight convulses her face. She lets Nimisha empty her leaf-bin into the rubbish bin for her and lead her to the bench. It's Tuesday mid-morning but, three storeys overhead behind potted chrysanthemums, a girl her age daydreams over what looks like a storybook. Asha vows aloud to make one herself with her own hands, to show them all what's what.

How childish, Nimisha thinks, bawling in public, as childish as her dreams of becoming a star dancer. But then,

96

she's better off with that dream. Nimisha remembers Asha before she began watching *D.I.D.* last year: sauntering, her mouth pulled ugly, trash-talking. Now Asha mostly talks about herself. Nimisha rubs Asha's back and reasons away her own contempt. This isn't the life either of them dreamed of.

Waiting for Asha to collect herself, Nimisha scans the rich folk's balconies. When Kuttu's living somewhere like this, and begging them to move in with her, should she say yes? She pictures her husband, painfully awkward among his betters, thrusting his chin skywards, and her daughter, embarrassed afresh. But she mustn't get ahead of herself. Her feet squirm in her new-old shoes, making sure of the ground.

Asha's rainstorm clears the sky. All this will soon be over. She sits up and wipes her face and chuckles.

Nimisha smiles back sympathetically. But her eyebrows quiver, sabotaging her smile, threatening to turn it into a grimace of contempt. She bows her head. "What beautiful shoes!" After sixteen years down south, Nimisha still speaks the warm, lilting Hindi of rural Uttar Pradesh.

"Yes!" says Asha. "Aren't they chic?" Sheikh, she pronounces it.

"Very pretty," says Nimisha. She's regained control of her smile. When she was young, and heard somebody talking nonsense, she'd allow her smile to reveal her scepticism: she'd brandish her scepticism like a medal. Now her demon of envy languishes, manacled, in the dungeon. "And how's your dancing going?"

"Wonderfully!" Asha dances a little sitting jig. Asha's mother tongue is Hindi too, but Asha's Hindi has coarsened from contact with the migrants from Delhi who dominate her slum: she uses the informal "tu" with everyone, and her vowels are clipped. "I'm practising for hours every day. I'm almost ready." She falters. "Of course, there're some kinks

97

to iron out." She can imagine the crowds' roaring applause, or their derisive laughter, but nothing in between, no approving hum signifying moderate success. "For instance, these shoes. I'm still breaking them in. Should've bought them earlier."

She longs to show Nimisha her dance video from day before yesterday. She's watched it many times herself. But another person should watch her performance, another pair of eyes that she can look into. As she stares at Nimisha, her face flushes, and she opens her lips mouth. She chokes, and gabbles about *D.I.D*'s history instead.

Last year's winner was twenty-three, four years older than Asha, and from an even humbler background, daughter of *pourakarmika* street-sweepers. "And she said she had no contacts! Though, of course, people who *do* have contacts deny it. Everyone pretends they've made it on their own... Oh! Did I tell you my friend's aunt gave me one of the producers' numbers?"

Nimisha nods cautiously.

"I finally called him! I'd kept putting it off, I was terrified I guess. He was so nice! He said they'll still have to audition me – you know, for appearance sake – but I guess I'll get in." She looks away from Nimisha's encouraging face. "Then, of course, it's up to me."

Nimisha realises the girl is guilt-struck: after all her railing against people with "ins", she's using an "in" herself. "Asha, that's wonderful news!" She pictures Asha, gone away famous, and herself, gazing after Asha, like at a star, like back in the village when the night was black and you could still see stars. Nimisha beams goodwill.

Next instant her demon breaks its manacles and bellows from its dungeon. Nimisha's still waiting for Mummi to say "Yes, I'll come live with you." She's still waiting for Kuttu to answer her message, she's sick of waiting for people. If only she could run away! But they stopped her. They found out about the missing money, and she found the front door padlocked, the light came on flickering and humming in the tiny front room, her heart jumped up her throat, and there stood Mummi, Mummi mute with shock that, after all her struggling and scrimping, this was how her eldest child repaid her. Since that night Nimisha's life has been irreproachable. These seventeen years she's lived for other people. Mummi forgave her only decades later, only a little, only briefly and now Pa's dead and she blames her, and hates her again. And why should Asha, why should this foolofallpeople gettogetaway? Thisfooldoesntdeserveit.

Nimisha wrestles her demon back into submission. "That really is excellent news," she gasps. "We've got to use our contacts. We've got to use whatever we've got... Well! Shall we go?"

The two women collect their carpet-beaters and head towards the gym.

At the checkpoint, the undergrown security guards glance towards them, tittering at Asha's red stilettoes. Many of the young men doing menial jobs in Bangalore are from the north, but these two are locals. Nimisha greets them in fluent Kannada. South Indian languages have always sounded funny, but Nimisha's been determined to get people to treat her family well.

Asha stares through the guards, as befits a single-minded artiste who happens to be marriageable. Her parents can scout grooms and negotiate with neighbours all they like; she'll be gone soon. Who needs men, anyway? They just slow you down. These jackals are cackling only because they can't have her, because they've got no ambition of their own. She turns her face up and away.

But somewhere in her mind Asha knows they're not tittering because they're attracted to her. She knows everyone

99

laughs at her. As she struts past the guards on pigeon toes, she stumbles, falters, and quickly collects herself.

By the time Asha and Nimisha approach the gym, the other maids have gone, leaving a dust cloud swirling in the sun. They take up the acrylic beige-and-brown carpets from the left half of the gym floor and hang them up outside. Nimisha ties her scallop-edged handkerchief over her nose and starts beating her carpet, beating her demon of envy back down.

Asha studies her reflection, through the glass doors, in the gym mirror. Her figure's almost there: just needs a bit more work. What will she wear next Thursday? She baulks at the thought of her hot-pink-and-gold wedding-guest *churidar* set. If only she could afford a costume!

A resident approaches, a young Punjabi in a tank top with biceps bulging. He steers clear of Nimisha's dust clouds. He glances pointedly at Asha's shoes, at Asha's head as she leaves off carpet-beating and loses herself in the mirror.

Ignoring his gaze, blossoming under it, Asha stares into her own eyes. The Punjabi enters the gym and begins deadlifting, still staring at her in the mirror. She turns away and resumes her work. Her carpet-beater sways precariously, its tip barely denting the carpet as she stands ten feet off, face turned away, heel-tips lifting off with every stroke. If only she could take off her shoes! But she wouldn't be able to get them back on. She can't wait for next Thursday. She wishes next Thursday were over with. She pictures herself falling through the dusty carpet into the Punjabi's willing arms.

"Sometimes I can't stand it," says Asha. They're both on all fours, laying the carpets back down. "Maybe some people are just more sensitive. I doubt the others mind this work so much."

Sitting back on her heels, Nimisha feels contempt flooding through her into her mind's backwater where she's flung her demon. "Everyone's got troubles," she murmurs.

Asha looks sceptical but prepares to listen.

Nimisha hesitates. About herself she has no reserve; about her family she hesitates to speak to indifferent ears. Then again, who *can* she speak to? And maybe hearing someone else's troubles will give this girl perspective.

"Mummi's lived alone in Basti since Papa died, just after Dussehra. We've been begging her to come stay with us." Nimisha stretches her neck. The gym stinks of eroding rubber and the pungent sweat of polyester-clad men. "First she went to stay with my brother. But she didn't get along with my sister-in-law. She returned to the village after just three weeks. I keep telling her it'll be different here. But now she says she'll live alone till she dies. But sometimes she seems to be relenting."

Asha rises and rubs her knees, breathing freely now that her Punjabi admirer has left. Straightening a corner of the carpet with her foot, she over-balances and nearly tramples Nimisha's hand. Glossing over her gaffe, she says quickly, "If your mother moved in with you, wouldn't your husband complain about the extra mouth?"

"He would." Crawling about alone, Nimisha continues, "but I wouldn't let him spend a paisa of his own on Mummi." She hasn't told Asha about her secret engagement that begins this evening: to wash the windows in Tower Elpida's hallways and stairwells. That work pays fifty rupees an hour, an extra 1,500 a month: enough for the tiny amount of food and growing amount of medicines Mummi ingests. Just enough, just the right amount – a signal from God, Nimisha realised, and this is what persuaded her to accept the job. "My husband won't have any right to complain… And Kuttu will love having Mummi around."

"Kuttu? Ah, your daughter! Does she also love her Naani?" Asha perks up.

"Yes." Nimisha rises to her knees, clutching her waist. Children are curious creatures, forgiving in a grandparent what in a parent is a fatal flaw. Mummi doesn't speak a word of English. Doesn't even try. Yet Kuttu treats Naani as a lovable curiosity, a shrunken doll with beady hard eyes and hard gentle hands. "Come."

They fetch buckets and washcloths and start wiping down the equipment. Yes, Kuttu loves Mummi. Every year, on their visit home, Kuttu chatters nonstop to her Naani. Her Hindi is halting at first. For, in Bangalore, it's only with her own parents that Kuttu can speak Hindi, for the neighbour kids boycott her for going a fancy school, so she boycotts her parents and speaks to them seldom. But every summer, in Basti, Kuttu becomes fluent in Hindi again. Maybe when Mummi moves here, she'll mediate between Kuttu and Nimisha. Nimisha stifles the urge to ring Mummi, to send Kuttu a follow-up text. One false move and everything could come tumbling down.

"Bro-ko-li," she mutters, distracting herself. She polishes a machine's rubber-clad arm. The rich folk can afford to sit around all day. Why torture themselves with these machines? "Ju-ki-ni," she mutters.

*Bro*koli, *ju*kini. Nimisha first encountered these words while helping Kuttu with a project in first standard. She wasn't paying attention then: she was tired, hurrying through, amazed at how school had gone from one exam a year to a perennial parade of projects, from a student's responsibility to the whole family's. Now she wishes she'd paid attention. Now she thinks maybe her half-heartedness is why God ejected her from the paradise of intimacy with Kuttu.

Just wait till Mummi's here. Maybe one evening Nimisha will knock on Kuttu's door and find Mummi

102

helping Kuttu stick one colourful scrap of paper on another. Maybe they'll stiffen and draw a bedsheet over their project. Or maybe they'll offer her the glue stick and the evening will end with Nimisha braiding Kuttu's hair again, Kuttu chattering in fluent Hindi to both mother and grandmother.

Nimisha's own head sways back, her neck muscles slackening as she feels the tug, up through her own once-thick braid, on her scalp above her nape. When Nimisha was a child, Mummi was stubbornly undemonstrative, spurning Nimisha's demands for cuddles. But when Mummi braided Nimisha's hair every evening, her fingers sent into her scalp scolding little tugs. One soft word in those days, one undisguised caress when Nimisha sat between Mummi's knees, thirsting puppy-like, might've kept her from that night's misstep – which put at an end to those hair-braidings, and in which only now does she see the grudging little love that she's lost perhaps forever.

Nimisha wrings out her washcloth and moves to the next torture-machine. The mirror shows her a thirty-three-year-old prematurely haggard, eyes sun-creased, wind-cracked lips drooping from being pursed when nobody's looking. She cannot think who would despise her more: the widow of an impoverished but proud freeholder, or a child who's told her classmates they've got their own servant too.

A sleek young couple enters. Nimisha glances at Asha, who's gazing in the mirror, her washcloth mechanically caressing the arm of a torture-machine. Nimisha checks her phone. Still nothing. Why can't they at least let her know they're fine? Mummi did always enjoy punishing people with silence, hoarding old pots and pans and newspapers, hoarding information. Now, with the family scattered or dead, her duties done, her hoarding has become pathological. And Kuttu – would it kill her to send a short reply?

103

And now, if Mummi comes, and Kuttu tells Mummi about her hopes and fears, will Mummi pass that information on to Nimisha? Ha! She'll hoard it like she hoards all that junk. Besides, why should Kuttu receive Mummi's love, which leap-frogged clear over Nimisha? Even before Nimisha tried to run away, Mummi only ever had rebukes for her.

She stares at Asha, who's smirking at the mirror over her own shoulder, one leg raised, the heel angled towards her butt, clearly aware of the new young man while pretending to ignore him. Girls much cleverer than Asha, thinks Nimisha, get their heads turned by boys, their futures ruined. No: after all, she'd rather Mummi get Kuttu's confidence than a worthless boy.

She checks her phone again, as if Kuttu's having replied or not replied would settle her indecisiveness about Mummi. Kuttu hasn't replied. So Nimisha sets her jaw and makes her own decision. Life has already got between Kuttu and herself. She can't risk Mummi getting in the way too.

"You stay put, Mummi," she thinks, wiping the last machine on this side. "I took this new assignment hoping to pay for you to come live here. I was wrong. I'm already bone-tired. You never wanted to come. Now I don't want you to come, either. I know whom to spend the extra 1,500 rupees on. Thank God you never replied and thank God I didn't send a follow-up."

"Come, Asha!"

The two women refresh the water in their buckets to wash the gym's mirrors and glass walls.

The glass wall is flattening Asha's nose, undoing the hours she's spent pinching her nose to make it pointy. That golden-brown dog is passing by, its liquid eyes continually consulting its master's, a fair-skinned Tamil Brahmin speaking into a headset. Asha wills them to look back at her. Her dreams fortify her; her dreams drain her; she yearns to lay her dreams at someone's feet to be blessed or squashed.

Why doesn't the Tamilian glance at her, when the Punjabi ogled her so? *Was* the Punjabi ogling her? In Asha's chest the puppy of insecurity balls up, shivering. "You know how hard it is?" she thinks aloud. "You can't just dance. You've got to have an Instagram profile, with millions of followers." She sits down on a bench. The pain in her feet was something to fight against. Now her feet have gone numb and self-doubt yawns around them like a chasm. "It's all politics, anyway." She talks about some recent *D.I.D.* finalists. "Their costumes are so over-the-top, you can tell they grew up poor, and now they're like beggars in a sweet-shop."

"Hmm," says Nimisha.

Two hours and still no word. Has Kuttu even seen the message? Kuttu has disabled the blue "Message seen" tickmarks on her WhatsApp. Where's Kuttu's phone? A new Redmi, for which Nimisha scrimped, and which Kuttu received with a pursing of the lips. Nimisha pictures it lying on a crimson-and-gold seat in an auditorium. Kuttu is celebrating onstage with her teammates and teacher – the people whose texts she answers immediately. Then Nimisha pictures the Redmi lying under a bus. They were on their way to celebrate their win, the bus crashed, and now Kuttu's lying under the crumpled metal floor, blood dribbling down her forehead, oil dribbling onto her Redmi lying beside her. Nimisha's heart jumps up her throat as for an instant Kuttu dead would be better than Kuttu ignoring her texts.

"God forgive me," Nimisha mutters, "God take my life

and keep her safe." She stretches her shoulders. Maybe it's not work that's turning her shoulders into aching stone, but guilt. She hasn't told her husband about her new job, hasn't told him about her raise last year at her current job, about the money she's been saving because, years later, she still worries he'll start boozing again, stealing her money again. If Mummi were moving in, she'd have had to tell him about the extra 1,500. Now the money will be her secret.

A new building has shot up beside their shack, four misshapen storeys blocking the sun and wind. Nimisha can touch the new building's raw cement backside with her elbow on her own windowsill. These new neighbours fling soiled clothes and beer bottles onto the roofs of Nimisha's three miniscule rooms. Nimisha coughs over *tadka* sputtering in oil in her kitchen now unventilated. She lies in bed worrying they're just one night away from her husband losing his head, one more boiling night with the neighbours' stereo making their empty water vessels jangle on the floors. One more night and if her husband takes to driving drunk again, and has another crash, this time she won't pay the bribe to get him off, won't give everything up again just to prolong this intolerable life.

"How," Asha continues, "does anyone manage to do all that stuff while working a job?" She rubs her ankles. What if she can't get her feet out tonight without cutting open her shoes? Ten months' savings down the drain! "Though I doubt the other contestants have jobs. They're probably rich and well-connected."

"Why should you mind?" says Nimisha. She moves, with her washcloth, from bench to bench without rising from her squat – efficient, if crab-like. "You've got a contact, too."

"Ye-ah, but…" Asha reapproaches the mirror. "I need to gym!" Of course! This is why the Tamilian wouldn't glance at her: she's got a tiny tummy. "You've got to be fit

106

and fine to stand a chance." She's still got ten days. "D'you think if I asked the security guards they'd let me use this gym?"

Nimisha's running her fingertip down a wall, checking for dust.

"Maybe early morning," Asha continues, "or late night, when the gym's empty?" Her face clouds again. These rich folk could afford to sleep in – no Ammas to curse them awake – but they use the gym at God-forsaken hours. Is the gym ever empty? She glares at the resident who's doing squats, oblivious behind earphones. "No, really, how could anyone with a job rehearse *and* do gymming and Instagram and learn makeup?" She rubs her cheek. Her complexion could use work, too. But Instagram's over-lit photos and Korean skin-care regimens have obsolesced the cheap makeup Asha can afford. The show's staff will make her up, but that's if she clears the audition to begin with. "I try, I really try to keep my spirits up. But sometimes I feel like why even bother."

"Don't say that. Maybe they *will* let you use the gym." She pictures the guards guffawing at Asha's outlandish request. "How about I ask them for you?"

"Would you!" Asha squeezes Nimisha's shoulder. A wave of affection leaves a froth of guilt as she regrets not having got to know Nimisha better. All the things Asha's missing out on, rapt in her ambition, flash past her: lunchtime with colleagues, Sunday outings to a temple with cousins in tacky outfits, *samosa*s with relatives visiting from the village. "You're so nice! I do actually feel shy about speaking to the guards." She blushes, remembering the prospective grooms who darken her doorway on Sundays: young men bold-eyed even in her parents' presence.

"I'll ask them for you," Nimisha promises.

107

Asha's wave of gratitude demands release. Again she longs to show Nimisha her dance video. Again her heart hammers, choking her, telling her the time isn't right. "Also, I'll need leave-of-absence next Thursday. Please ask about that too."

"Couldn't you go to the audition after work?" says Nimisha. "Isn't it on all day?"

"I've got to reach early! Everything depends on reaching first... Like, even the first few seasons' winners are more successful than the recent winners. They've got movies, and modelling careers, and all. The recent seasons' winners are still just on Instagram." The other maids troop past towards the residential towers. She and Nimisha are late again. It's all her fault. She was born late, she's been sprinting all her life, breathless, trying to catch up but everyone else began years ago; she'll never catch up.

"Maybe," says Nimisha, "if you just dance well, the other things won't matter much."

"You're right," says Asha.

Asha's pendulum swings back from despair to hope, her left hand absent-mindedly strokes her right arm, and when Nimisha tries to locate her eyes they've drifted far away. A shiver runs up Nimisha's spine, tickling her scalp from nape to forehead as she experiences vicariously the adventure of waking up in love with the project of oneself.

Since her foiled runaway attempt, the closest Nimisha's come to adventure was when Kuttu had exams in primary school. Exams, Nimisha knew, were important. She'd stay up with her, bringing her *paratha* fried in real ghee and one boiled egg: a secret egg, towel jammed under the door so her husband wouldn't smell this sulphur-stinking breach of caste. Now the crepuscular adventure of Kuttu's future has ejected Nimisha into the flat hot sun. She would give both her little fingers to go back to two years ago, when Kuttu still spoke to her, if only to scream "I wish I'd never been born."

Surely, she thinks, Kuttu's just forgotten to respond. Why not send a follow-up? That would create another notification; this time, Kuttu might notice. She's probably just busy.

The money will fix it, Nimisha thinks, deciding against a follow-up. Surely 1,500 will be enough for those programming classes Kuttu wanted. Money fixes everything. She must just wait.

Does Kuttu want to be a software engineer, then, she wonders as they leave the gym; is public speaking just a hobby? It's mostly software engineers who live in condo complexes like these. But didn't she hear the software bubble has burst? She'll have to sit Kuttu down, tell her thirteen's old enough to pick a career. She pictures talking to Kuttu with the new-found authority of the 1,500.

Nimisha hangs back to ask the guards about Asha's leave-of-absence for next Thursday. Asha hurries on ahead.

"I could ask the supervisor," the guard tells Nimisha, smirking, "but I'd better not. They're already planning to fire her. Many residents have complained about "the lazy, staring girl"... In fact, now they want us all to wear ID cards! So they can better identify shirkers."

"Oh," says Nimisha. "I wish they'd at least give her a warning..." She trails off, remembering the supervisor's daily confrontations with Asha.

The guard talks on, inviting Nimisha to join in the trash-talking. Nimisha's demon stirs, urging her to relay Asha's request about using the gym, just to give this boy another antic to smirk at. "Fine then, please forget about her leave application." She catches up with Asha and takes her elbow. "He'll ask, he says, about both the gym and the leave."

"He has to *ask*?" Asha frowns. "Can you believe the circus we go through to get one day off?"

"It's too bad." Nimisha steers Asha towards Tower Éclat, called "Eclairs" by her colleagues after the bite-sized sticky candies which, when she was a child, sold for twenty-five paise. Those octagonal coins have become antiquities – nothing now costs less than a rupee. "Patience, my dear." She can't handle any more of Asha's mood swings just now. This evening she'll walk out with her and tell her her job's in jeopardy. She'll persuade Asha to go to the supervisor, apologise, and keep her job, just as a backup. "As for the gym, you know, just meanwhile, you could try lifting household objects." Then she'll come back and wash Elpida's windows.

"Hmph!" Asha hisses.

They collect the mops and big buckets and start climbing the stairs. Asha's phone rings. She reaches for her side-pocket, over-reaches, and pivots all the way around, giggling. Who's calling her, who's calling maybe it's the producer whom she was supposed to call, maybe her friend's aunt told *him* to call *her*?

It's only Amma.

"AmmaImbusyIlltalktoyoulater," says Asha, barely pausing long enough for Amma's "OK."

Climbing two steps behind her, Nimisha's throat tightens at this stupid girl, with her boulder-like cheeks, her acne scars, her queenly airs. Asha's got the one thing that matters and she's pushing it away with both hands. How lonely her success will be with nobody to celebrate with!

They climb slowly with their empty pails. Every residential tower has three lifts but Housekeeping aren't allowed. On the fourth floor they rest, gazing out a corridor window. The balcony of Embassy 4E opposite is strewn with

110

tricycles, Hula hoops, and a single pot with a wilted plant. Everything's dust-furred. But a small hand has swiped the lowest steel banister, leaving a dust-free swathe terminating in five little round heads. Nimisha tries to remember who works there. Who picked up her six-year-old from school and bade him wait quietly on the balcony while Amma finished working?

"Those toys are just lying there," says Nimisha. "Couldn't they give them away?" Asha raises her brows and rounds her lips: she's never heard Nimisha complaining. Asha's "ooh" knocks the sense back into Nimisha. "Oh, they're just thoughtless," she amends.

Nimisha's learned that life's hard enough without complaining about it. She used to squander hours in the noonday shade, fly-swatting drowsiness with whining. It solved nothing, only showed her how deep was her well of discontent. She struggled to stop. Then one day, in a lull between tasks, she realised that complaining was her boozing. Her husband had struggled for years to stop boozing, had almost died, and then he'd stopped. This thought struck Nimisha head-on and killed her own compulsion.

"Yeah, the rich folk are thoughtless," says Asha, invitingly.

"We'd be too, in their place." Nimisha scans the balconies. Which kind of flat Kuttu would like, she wonders: three-bedroom or four, ground floor or top, garden-facing or city-facing? Nimisha, of course, must refuse an opinion, even if she agrees to move in. As her mind wanders over the future, muttering a prayer to ward off the evil eye, the past invades it.

Four Sundays ago, she and Kuttu were walking to market. The previous night's rain was keeping the dust down without making too much mud. A cool morning, when life seemed

111

beautiful and anything possible. They stopped at the corner, waiting to cross. Nimisha looked up at the school bus looming over them, barely slowing to make the turn. A school bus on a Sunday? Full, too. Nimisha was wondering, reading the name – Oasis International – distracted. Kuttu was distracted too, watching a video on her Redmi, about to step into the street.

Nimisha pulled Kuttu back, quickly, and released her without a word of reproach. Kuttu gasped. She looked at her mother gratefully, just briefly, but Nimisha will carry that look to the grave. Any other mother would've made a scene, thought Nimisha, watching the startled smile break untidily across Kuttu's face.

Kuttu put her phone away. They crossed. At the small grocer's, redolent of stale oil and pastries stuffed with fake cream, Nimisha ordered bread and milk. Kuttu selected a chocolate bar for herself, a small bar, a treat from the saved-up pocket-money Nimisha gave her from her secret stash. Today she asked Nimisha which chocolate she liked.

"Nothing," Nimisha reacted.

"You must've liked something when you were young?" Kuttu waited. "Stop worrying about money all the time. This is my money, which I've saved." She nibbled at her Bournville bar.

Nimisha eyed the display-box sideways, scanning the prices. "Milkybar," she said.

Kuttu said Milkybar wasn't real chocolate, just milk powder and sugar and oil.

"I wasn't *that* fond of it," Nimisha lied, and insisted Kuttu buy her the smallest bar.

Compromising, they got the twenty-rupee bar, and stood on the pavement eating. Kuttu made her try her expensive Bournville, which Nimisha, to her relief, honestly disliked. Shouldn't chocolate be sweet, she wondered aloud. Kuttu smiled and shook her head, like she might with a classmate.

112

Keep calm, Nimisha told herself; don't make a big deal of our talking like this. Kuttu was spreading the chocolate around inside her mouth. Drawing it out. Nimisha longed to buy Kuttu another bar, five more bars. But that would screw everything up. She distracted herself thinking about the bus.

Oasis, she remembered – that's one of those IGCSE schools with sprawling campuses beyond the city. The people whose bathrooms she cleans send their children to schools like Oasis. Today they must be heading to Wonder-La, or maybe a workshop with scientists at Tata Institute. Many zeroes separate the fees for Oasis and the fees for Himanshu. But Kuttu, Nimisha thought, will bridge all those zeroes. She folded up her Milkybar wrapper and slipped it into her purse. A memento.

"We'll have to educate your tastebuds," said Kuttu. They walked on.

Suddenly Nimisha felt Kuttu freeze. She followed her stare to a pair approaching up the street: a woman ten years older than Nimisha, and a girl Kuttu's age. Kuttu's classmate, Nimisha realised. For one terrible moment she wondered whether Kuttu would mutter to her, spitting sideways, as Mummi had done when she'd crept up to her at Papa's funeral – "Go away."

Kuttu had never snapped at her. Outside her tantrum phase, her only cruelty had been silence. Kuttu was silent now.

Thinking quickly, Nimisha turned casually up a narrow flight of steps, between the *paan*-and-cigarette shop and the stationer's, leading to the tradespeople's homes. Kuttu didn't turn her head, say anything, or show any surprise: Nimisha knew this without looking back. On the landing she leaned out of sight, listening as Kuttu, her classmate, and the other mother chatted.

Her head against the wall, she tried to even out her breathing. Her racing heart slowed as she realised she'd done the right thing. But afterwards, as the two walked homewards, there was no more chatter.

"Aah!" Asha shrieks as a pigeon materialises and almost flies through the window into their faces.

They draw back. The pigeon, startled, settles on the windowsill below. Nimisha's eyes follow the bird mechanically. No, she decides: she'll tell Kuttu she and her husband are better off living by themselves. Kuttu will then insist on giving them money so they can move out of "that hovel". Was that her phone that beeped? I'm not coming, Mummi has texted: she can sense it. Of course I won, Kuttu has texted.

No. Her phone face is still dark.

"Heyyouknowyouwantedtoseemydance?" Asha blurts. She turns red, redder than the Punjabi or the Tamilian ever made her.

Nimisha has expressed no such desire, but Asha's already whipped out her phone. She cradles it in one hand and draws her *dupatta* over it against the glare. "I tried dancing yesterday in my new shoes, but I need practice. This video is from Sunday."

It's shot from an odd angle, the bottom edge whitish and blurry, suggesting the phone's resting on the cot. A naked incandescent bulb flickers overhead. Another cot stands against the opposite wall. The plywood desks and chairs have also been pushed against the walls. Even in this light Nimisha can see, through Asha's tight white top, her bra-straps making bulges in the flesh of her back. Her jeans are over-faded, like the jeans that the rich folk have long since turned into kitchen rags. They keep slipping down Asha's butt. She keeps pulling them back up surreptitiously. Her sequin-fronted top sheds its gilt spastically. The music is tinny and muffled and Asha, always a half-beat too early, hops around, sweaty and wild-eyed.

Asha's finger hovers over her phone. Should she pause the video and hear Nimisha's preliminary reactions, or let Nimisha finish watching?

Nimisha's head reels. Asha talks about dance all day. She practises for hours every day. And oh, how could this girl be so stupid? She's throwing this job away for a three-year-old's fantasy. The seconds tick by, long and loud, as Nimisha gropes for something to say.

"Well," she says. Asha faces her like a string pulled taut, waiting to be touched, either to rupture or to produce divine music. "You dance with so much energy!" Nimisha smiles desperately. She remembers what Asha said earlier. Relief floods her. "That producer you called, he'll be very impressed." It's all about contacts, Asha said: her contact will get her in, it'll all be fine. But, no, why would this lunatic getting on a talent show be fine? Kuttu's got more talent in her little finger. Yet Kuttu couldn't get her programming lessons when she wanted them.

Passionate, and now confident, the midday sunshine on her face, Asha looks almost beautiful. "Guess what? I never called the producer!" She drinks in Nimisha's confusion. "I was too scared! I thought maybe he would ignore a call from an unknown number. Such people must be so busy."

"You said you called him," says Nimisha slowly. Her eyes shuttle-cock over the window-ledge. "You said your audition will be only a formality." Now she remembers Asha looking guiltily away.

"Ye-ah, I kept imagining how the conversation might go... But, I mean, now I don't need to call him, right? You love my dance. I'll get in anyway."

"Oh, don't give too much weight to my opinion. I really know very little about dance. Nothing at all." Nimisha thinks of all the times Asha's chattered about her life after

115

D.I.D. Nimisha was just listening, smiling, taking a polite interest. Has she egged this girl on to a big mistake?

"But you're the first person who's seen me dance, and you love it. That's a good sign."

"I'm the only person who's seen you dance?"

Asha laughs. The string that was taut has been touched, and relaxed, and made to play music. There's no breaking it now. "Well, I could hardly show my family, could I? Amma thinks I'll hang around here always, doing this stupid job, giving her half my money, and then she'll marry me off and I'll keep working and my husband will keep *all* my money."

"No, you can keep control of your money if you're clever. And some men are quite reasonable."

"Yeah, maybe I'll find a nice guy sometime," Asha says lightly. A dog barks and her head whirls and she scans the balconies for the Tamilian and his gold-brown dog. She stamps her foot. "Later! After I've established my career. That's what people are doing these days, did you know? There are real opportunities today. But we're still crawling along, blind-folded, getting married in our teens."

Nimisha fumbles for words. Should she tell Asha her request for leave next Thursday was declined? Asha says thousands of people will be at the audition. They'll bring the roof down guffawing! The skin on Nimisha's neck crawls. But if Nimisha tells her she can't have Thursday off, then Asha might quit, and then she'd have nothing. No job, no bridegroom. Who'd want a girl who can't keep a job?

"Do you really practise for hours every day?"

Asha's eyes dance. "No. That's the funny thing! I mean, I'd like to, but where's the time? I practise, maybe, thirty minutes every evening. Except Sundays, of course. Isn't it ironic that we feel so much more tired on Sundays? It's like the tiredness builds and builds and waits to catch up with you the minute you're free. Sometimes I practise thirty minutes in the morning, too... if I manage to get up early." She chuckles.

Now it's Nimisha who can't meet Asha's eyes. A voice is shouting at her to tell Asha she's a terrible dancer. Does the voice belong to a demon or an angel? Nimisha's inching along a ridge between silence and speech, a ridge so narrow that a butterfly fluttering by would push her down on one side or another. Wouldn't the truth be better coming now, from a friend?

A latch clicks. Down the corridor a door opens three inches, then hovers as someone shoulders a bag and slips into shoes. Asha and Nimisha hurry out of sight and resume climbing the stairs with mops and pails, Asha leading, Nimisha following.

The moment for dropping the truth on Asha has passed. Nimisha will have to guide Asha there instead. "You've been practising *this* dance for thirty minutes every day? For weeks?"

"Yeah! Well." Asha laughs. "Not quite. I mean, I want to. But it gets boring, doing the same dance over and over, when I already know the steps. So sometimes I do some other dance." She giggles. "You know 'Crazy Kiya Re'?" Nimisha nods: another super-hit sexy item number. "Well, sometimes, actually, I just watch the original dance videos, again and again, you know, imagining it's me up there, as Katrina, or as Aishwarya... Then I come to my senses an hour later and feel so guilty for wasting that time."

"It's good you've got a backup dance," says Nimisha. "Have you made a video of that one, too?"

"No, not a backup, I just do that dance as a break. I mean yeah, if they wanted to see another dance, I could pull off 'Crazy Kiya Re,' I guess... God! I'm so relieved you

117

like it. You don't know what it's like when nobody believes in you. Sometimes I… I used to wish I had cancer. Yeah! There's a girl back in Nagpur, she's my age. She got sick when she was eight. She's been in and out of hospitals. God knows how her parents raise the money. Even when she's home, nobody ever expects her to *do* anything. She sits with her legs crossed and her mother brings *her* water! I used to envy her so much." She pauses on the landing and frowns out the window. "And she was so sweet-tempered: as if God had given her a blessing instead of a curse. I hated her for that. It was easy for her to be nice. She was so lucky, except for the cancer, I mean. Some people have lucky temperaments. Sometimes I think that's all I can ever really hope to do, myself: survive. It would be nice, people praising you just for surviving." She sighs and draws her shoulders back. "I know I'm awful. I'll be sweet-tempered too; I'll be an angel now that things are fine. I mean" – she chuckles – "going to be fine."

"It never hurts to have a backup plan," says Nimisha. They resume climbing.

"True!" says Asha. "I used to regret not having paid attention in school… My cousin was a good student, and now she's got a nice job. Her salary is twice mine. She just sits around talking English on the phone, putting on such airs… I used to hate sharing a room with her. Then she came home one day, all piqued, and told me she'd had a boyfriend for months. A colleague, from another caste, can you believe it? My uncle would skin her alive if he found out, and then lock her up, bye-bye to your fancy job!" She bites her lips. "But I always listen to her stupid stories. I never tell her how I really feel. I'd never betray her secret." Her frown relaxes into a smile. "I used to take comfort in other people's failures. I guess it made my own failure feel less like my own fault."

118

Asha looks back at Nimisha and beams. Here's another chance for Nimisha to speak up, to tell her Go, go to that supervisor you're always bad-mouthing, beg him for another chance. Nimisha's heart races, preparing her for confrontation. Her mouth gasps open. Then her phone beeps. Is she imagining beeps again?

Her phone says "2 unread messages."

"Here we are, eighth floor!" Asha touches Nimisha's arm. "Thank you for everything. I'll see you back downstairs later." She flashes a brilliant smile and climbs on alone.

"Yes," says Nimisha mechanically as she unlocks her phone.

One message is from her daughter, the other from her mother. Both just say "OK."

Nimisha mops her way down from the eighth floor. Stairs, corridors, stairs. Don't pause or the pain will catch up with you. Keep the mop moving, left-right. Empty your bucket on every floor, refill it, watch the stream that gushes forth so fast it's all froth. So much water in this building, sometimes the water-pressure bursts the pipes. So much water to fill your mind, to still it.

On the fourth floor, Nimisha waits for her bucket to fill, squatting in the tiny bathroom reserved for Housekeeping and service people. She takes out her phone. "OK," says Kuttu's message. She thumbs at it, trying to get Kuttu's other messages to load. Sometimes Kuttu sends several short messages. She turns off the tap and scrolls up through the conversation.

She starts rereading her message to Kuttu from yesterday. A brick wall of text. She reads half her own message, then scrolls up to Kuttu's response to her message from Saturday: "Fine." Her own message from Saturday is another wall of text, cracked in two when she prematurely

119

pressed Enter. Before that, Kuttu's response from Friday: "Hmm." Nimisha scrolls up faster. Hmm, says Kuttu. No, says Kuttu. OK, Yeah, OK, says Kuttu.

It's been forty minutes since Kuttu texted "OK." There is no other message.

A vice of steel grips Nimisha's throat. She rises and leans on the white tiles, forcing her breath through, mopping her face with her *dupatta*. Like an imploded building crumbles her vision of Kuttu shimmying out of her black panther car, introducing them at award ceremonies, sending them presents every month.

A door opens. Someone approaches. Nimisha ducks out of view further inside the bathroom.

Some of Kuttu's messages consist entirely of a single smiley-face: spelled out in punctuation, since Nimisha's phone can't display proper smiley-faces. Kuttu really is a blessing. So considerate! She must've lost the SouthRegionInterSchoolDebateChampionship. Maybe that's why she's just saying "OK." Her daughter was never one to complain. Nimisha fights her tears. The fight convulses her face.

The resident, waiting for the lift on the granite tiles, peers into the bathroom and catches Nimisha's eye. Nimisha braces herself. The resident disappears; the lift doors close. Nimisha carries her bucket out into the empty corridor and brings up Mummi's number.

This time her finger does not hesitate. There's only one question Mummi could've replied OK to. But maybe Mummi sent the text accidentally? Mummi uses only reluctantly the Nokia mobile-phone Nimisha got her when the landline in Basti died. If Nimisha rings now, Mummi might say, "I didn't text you. What's wrong with you?" or "I did text, I was going to come. But now, with you persecuting me so much, even before I've come, I've changed my mind."

It doesn't matter now whether Mummi comes. As Nimisha's phone rings in her ear, her heart beats slow and steady.

"Yes. What?" says a deep voice, quavering with disuse.

"How are you, Mummi?"

"As usual. I'm always the same. What's happened." Her phlegmatic tone is a slap in the face. What if something *had* happened? Then Mummi wouldn't be upset. Mummi's always prepared for the worst. Pessimism is Mummi's drinking, her complaining, her fantasising.

"I got your text, Mummi. I just wanted to check…"

"What else is there to say? You have worn me down. You have beaten your own mother into submission. I am booking a ticket for next Wednesday. Or have you changed your mind?"

"Of course not." She won't hear from Mummi again till she collects her from Central Railway Station, a ninety-minute bus-ride away. She must just wait. "See you soon. Happy journey."

Mummi hangs up.

Nimisha stares at her phone-face, counting the seconds till it goes black. All this while she was worried that when Mummi finally agreed to come, she would be exuberant, would repel Mummi with her exuberance, just like when she was a child, a child born to a woman who'd never wanted one, who'd been raised such that she could never articulate, even to herself, the words, "I never wanted a child." And now, finally, Mummi's coming to live with her.

You wait for something, and you wait, and when it comes it slaps you in the face with fish-scales and leaks fish-guts into your lap.

Nimisha tops off her pail with Phenyl pungently pine-scented and mops the fourth-floor corridors. There goes the 1,500. It's better so. Even with that extra money, there wasn't anything Kuttu really wanted that Nimisha could've afforded. It's been months since Kuttu asked for programming lessons. Has she found a way to get them for free, or has she reconciled herself to their station in life?

Now Nimisha understands why she needed the 1,500 to feel able to discuss with Kuttu what's expected of her. Because paying for Kuttu's tuition isn't enough, paying for Kuttu's uniforms and extracurriculars isn't enough. Kuttu is being sent to school with her betters. Kuttu is being assaulted from every screen by accents and clothes Kuttu doesn't have, may never have. It is for this that God exiled her from intimacy with Kuttu. It is for this that Kuttu never talks to Nimisha anymore.

Nimisha finishes mopping the fourth-floor corridors and mops the stairs, working downwards from the top step, her back to the bottom step. A new edifice rises over the ruins of her fantasy.

In this new fantasy, Kuttu has somehow fulfilled Nimisha's crazy ambitions. She's done this by making one great sacrifice. Sometimes Kuttu sends photos, which Nimisha pores over on the Redmi, which Kuttu returned to her as a farewell present. They're pictures of Kuttu's house, car, washing-machine, and other things Nimisha doesn't know the names of, things not yet invented. Here's Kuttu on a stage, surrounded by *firang*s tall as giants, so fair they're translucent. One *firang* hands Kuttu a medal. Kuttu bows as she receives it.

In Nimisha's new fantasy, Kuttu has ceased to be her daughter. Only by sacrificing her family could she achieve the impossible, which Nimisha dangled cruelly before her eyes. And Kuttu deserves success, and Nimisha deserves this.

Lower and lower, every storey darker as she descends

away from the light, Nimisha mops without pausing. She thinks of Asha, mopping a few storeys up, dancing a step or two when nobody's watching. She will not say another word to Asha about her dancing or her job. Let Asha keep her fantasy as long as she can. In this life, maybe that's all there is. She, too, was happy an hour ago.

Afterwards, when Asha's fired, Nimisha will get another workmate, someone not slowed down by fantasy. Nimisha can't afford to be slow. She'll adjust to this new Elpida job and then she'll ask for more work. Even if they don't pay her extra, it's fine.

Asha mops the steps down from the sixteenth floor. The proper technique is to lift the mop over the bucket, pin its long handle between shoulder and skull, stoop, wring the mop's curly cotton *rakshasi* locks, let the excess water finish dripping into the bucket, then draw the mop across the step. And rinse and repeat. Two hours a day. Every day. Who's got time for that? Asha slops the mop straight from the bucket and rubs it around on the step. It'll dry soon enough.

At the landing just below, she pauses for a break. It's not that she's lazy. When a job's this tedious, it's a sanitary measure to take frequent breaks. It's been an emotional morning. She loads the original dance-video of "Sheila ki Jawaani".

Cocooned in comfort, suspended in space-time, half the pleasure of watching something familiar is anticipating the next bit. In Asha's mind the music plays a half-beat too early and the dance-moves switch a half-second too early. But so absorbedly is she watching the over-produced video, with a cut every two seconds, so vividly does she see herself in the glamorous actress, that she never notices the fatal error in the rhythm in the music in her head. Just so, she thinks, watching Katrina. Exactly how I do it.

123

Someone approaches down the corridor. Asha glances up at a slim teenager with magenta-highlighted hair. The girl stares straight ahead, like a model inured to the world's ogling, carefully staying humble. She stalks past the lifts towards the steps. Is she going to climb down all sixteen storeys? Asha smirks. These nutsos are always inventing ways to eat more calories, burn more calories. She stares at the footprints the girl's leaving on the freshly swept floor. The girl stares at the water dripping from the steps. She clutches the banister. Her pointy-toed black suede boots click smartly. Asha barely stands aside to let her pass her on the landing.

Asha looks down at her phone. Katrina's eyes blaze with confidence. She knows she's a goddess to every man alive – and she doesn't care. She's got things to do. Asha sets her jaw. She, too, will make something of herself with her own hands. Against the world's monumental injustice she will fight bare-fisted. She gives Katrina a tiny nod and pockets her phone. She turns her back to the bottom step and mops on.

The door of the flat across from the stairs on the floor below opens noiselessly. A five-year-old pokes out his head. He adjusts his clown-hat and clutches his rainbow-coloured water-gun. He's about to step out, to go play downstairs. He looks up, sees the woman on the landing above in the shiny pointy shoes, and stands gaping.

The woman thrusts the mop into the bucket. Water jumps over the bucket's edge and dances down the steps. The woman begins mopping down the stairs, from the landing above, towards the child's doorway. Each step looks wetter and dirtier than the one above. The woman focuses on not flooding her own feet. On the second-from-bottom step she loses her balance and falls backwards, poised for a second mid-air, her back arched, her navy-blue *dupatta* flying, the mop's long neon-green stem clattering down, one lipstick-red shoe clinging to the wet marble, the other flailing mid-air like a bird startled by the child's peal of laughter.

SHIVER

The bone saw whines and buzzes through Ma's bones. All afternoon I've sat outside the operating theatre, listening. The thighbone is the strongest bone in a woman's body – it was a tour guide, showing Ma and me around the cremation ghats at Benaras, who told us this years ago. Is it true? I've never looked it up. It's one of 10,000 curiosities that've scuttled across my mind, made me glance up, then slunk away to rot on life's growing rubbish-heap. Between Ma and me stand two doors and steel-blue hospital curtains. Still my nostrils search the bleach-purged air for any hint of blood.

It must be by the backway that they've wheeled Ma out – I hear the bonesaw quieten, and then nothing. I'm peeping between the curtains when the nurse comes to say Ma's in the recovery-room. She leads me to the doorway and waddles away.

I lean against the door surveying the white-sheeted trolley-beds. Somewhere outside, a dog snarls and growls. One bed looks less flat than the others. I tiptoe across the room. Beside every bed is a chair. I stay standing. I won't be here long.

The nurse said Ma didn't need a transfusion, didn't lose too much blood during her knee-replacement surgery. Maybe they were wrong. Ma looks drained. Her skin's pleasant yellowness has deepened to jaundiced-yellow. People say it's melanin, but now I see it's blood that gives skin most of its colour.

I've no scruples left about looking at Ma when she can't look back. It's Ma's doing that I'm the only one left to look. Forty years she's lived with rheumatoid arthritis, with two busted knees, refusing surgery, praying aloud for death, pain her constant companion, twisting her face ugly, teasing her voice shrill, whetting her words into snakes hissing at everybody that their lives, too, would end in a rubbish-heap of bad choices, catastrophe, and pain.

Pain, they say, sows the seeds of compassion. Maybe if the seeds fall in the right soil.

Now I'm leaving, too. All these years I've only been awaiting the right moment.

I stare down at her. How long as she been shivering? She's shrunken into the sheets: no wonder it took me a second to spot her. Gingerly I take her hand, the left hand, free of the cannula. Her veins, bulging from forty years' housework, have flattened now into her yellow skin. The flesh of her fingers has shrunk, making the stiff knobby joints look enormous. Her hand feels too cold for the hand of a sleeper.

Only recently, after becoming bed-ridden, did Ma finally consent to surgery. Left knee now, right knee next year. The right moment to leave somebody – who's repelled your hugs at two and at twenty, who's made you, too, snap when somebody tries to hug you, who's cut you up, with a few words, into the ribbons permanently of the wrong kind of person – is after you've won the war. After they've admitted they need you. I've won, now. I wait for triumph to surge through my unflattened veins.

Rage comes instead, clutching my throat, choking me. Still I'm rubbing Ma's cold hand. How soft her skin is, at sixty-five, softer than mine. She's looked after her skin, this woman who kept praying for death. Unthinkingly I bend down and sniff. There's no whiff left of her Ponds' coldcream. I rub her hand, trying to rub out the hospital smells.

I ring for the nurse. She adjusts the anaesthetic and antibiotic drips, turns off the ceiling-fan, and says all's well. I run out of questions for her. She leaves.

Why should I be here when Ma awakens? Through all the crises of my life Ma was never there. When I dropped out of PhD, she told me I'd never get over myself, never amount to anything, never grow up – me, with all my freedom, squandering it on the wrong things. Then she set her lips and hobbled on.

Soon she'll awaken. Her surgeon will drop by. The nurses will sit her up, feed her soup to break her long fast and warm her up. Why should I be here? I've already sacrificed my workday. I deserve my evening back home with Bingo, who loves me, the only creature who ever will. Still massaging, I look out the window.

A vast raintree shades the courtyard. Powderpuff flowers, pink-and-white and heavy with yellow seed, speckle the bright-green canopy. Mynahs scold. Squirrels screech. In the abandoned lot behind the hospital, amidst lantana scrub and rubbish-heaps, preteen boys, shouting and laughing, play cricket: with a cracked bat, and a tennis ball cello-taped on one half to make it spin. The dog, which I still can't see, snarls on, hoarse and desperate.

Unbidden, images of another childhood throng my mind. Ma didn't grow up poor, not like these undergrown suntanned boys. Well, after Partition's mass displacement, everybody was poor. Ma considered it no deprivation, then, to share a bedroom with her two brothers, a study-table, and Sunday's one-egg omelette. But she fought her way into a PhD programme, while still giving tuitions, morning and evening, to help out at home. Halfway through her PhD, her ailing mother hurried her into marriage. Ma had to drop out and devote herself to Pa, my brother, and me.

The raintree shivers. I look down. How long have the tears been running down Ma's cheeks? Her eyelids flutter. How long has she been having nightmares? I'm looking down steadily and it's the world that blurs.

128

Furiously I wipe my eyes. Finally I find the screaming dog: a mutt, chained across the playground, the chain cutting into its flesh, making around its throat a collar of pink scars and raw pink flesh. Ceaselessly it snarls at the children playing cricket.

I discover your face only convulses if you fight your tears. Stop fighting, let your tears flow, and it doesn't hurt as much. I raise Ma's hand to wipe away my tears, as if I were two again and life stretching before us like a cat.

THE WHY AND THE HOW

Malini's pups are three months old, no longer nursing twelve times a day, but they're hungry first thing in the morning. She suckles the three still left to her. Then she licks them over, sniffing and assessing, while they play-yawn-scratch for fleas – multitasking, for fleas never rest. Squirming vigorously, they resist her grooming now. She's satisfied.

She leaves her three furballs to the care of her last year's daughter – who moped when Malini, pregnant again, cut her loose at nine months old. Eventually the bitch came around and made herself useful. All Malini's other children from the last six years have been picked up by vans, run over by delivery trucks speeding through the blue dawn, or exiled from the pack after developing sarcoptic mange.

She surveys her dog pack. Eyes brighten and tails wag tentatively. Malini chooses with one slight nod her companion for today. This fine spring morning she embarks on patrols trailed by the newcomer, Agastya: a young male petitioning to join the pack. Malini has decided that today is his last day on probation: today she'll decide whether he can stay. Of course she won't tell him. She's been watching him covertly. He knows his place, doesn't take any nonsense, and some yesterdays ago he broke up a fight between two of her daughters. But he's small, and food is scarce, and letting him stay will ruffle family feathers. It's time to put him through his paces and see what he's made of.

Crossing the street with attendant in trail, Malini fights the urge to peer into the cardboard box where she's deposited the other three from this litter. The first pup looked alright, but smelled wrong; sure enough, he died next morning. She picked him out of the box-of-rejects and laid him, soft-mouthed, on the rubbish dump downstreet, to give the other two in the box a chance. These two are runts. Malini's been making less milk than usual. She realised three pups was all she could hope to bring through this winter.

The mathematics of motherhood isn't easy, but it is simple.

Approaching the box-of-rejects now, she succumbs. She slows. Neck rigid, head forward, she peers sidelong. Inside the box – on the blankets which the seedy hobbling man brought three months ago, bloated with the Marie biscuits he brought last evening – her two runts sleep. Rapid heartbeats shake their tiny bodies; their kohl-rimmed eyelids flutter with dreams. Malini's nostrils quiver. They smell healthy. She hoofs it before they can smell her, awaken, meet her gaze, and muddle her mathematics.

"Thank you, seedy stranger," she thinks. "I forgive you the epithets you fling at me across the street. *Bitch*, you call me. Well, what do I look like?"

Malini and Agastya turn into the mansion-lined street. Malini braces herself.

"Hey, Bitch! Go to hell, Bitch!" The Dalmatian's rib-shaking bass roars from behind his grill gate. The mansion behind him is all sandstone and flower-potted balconies, but his people never let him indoors. His home is this tiny roofless granite yard, which he shares with the giant black mirror-shiny car radiating heat. Rage vibrates from his clipped ears through his eyes crazed with hunger, through his starved ribs to the stump of his docked tail.

"Morning, Ballfree!" says Malini. "How's it feel to be a living burglar alarm?"

"I've got people, Bitch! My people love me and need me and look after me!" The Dalmatian's lean-muscled body tenses into a spring.

Malini knows Ballfree's gate is securely locked. And Agastya's watching so, head raised, tail arched, Malini prances back and forth, just beyond reach of Ballfree's teeth. "I've seen what 'your people' feed you, Ballfree! Week-old bread."

"You infanticidal bitch! Everybody knows what you've done! Nobody likes you!" Ballfree barks himself mad.

They exchange the same greetings every day: still, this reproach needles Malini's heart. Caged up, this dog has become an astute sadist, a scorpion with a bull's-eye stinger. Malini knows she's doing right for her pups who're alive, who've got a chance to stay alive. But how does a mother ever really know? It's neither easy nor simple.

Tossing her head, she sings, "Nobody respects you, Ballfree. Bark-bark-barking away, guarding the people who'll toss you on a rubbish dump should you so much as sneeze. So long!"

"Why're you such a bitch!" he roars after her.

The other mansions are guarded by Alsatians, Weimaraners, and Rottweilers, all tied out in sun-baked yards beside Mercedes, BMWs, and Volkswagens. The only walking these foreign housedogs get is down to the corner to poop, on a five-foot lead, yanking along behind them, fit to displace his shoulder, an overworked undergrown servant boy.

Malini greets all her acquaintances. "Why're you such a bitch!" their cacophony calls after her. Poor souls: rationalising their circumstances, living to terrorise passers-by. She pities them. But they're not asking her a question, so she doesn't reply.

She looks around. Agastya is cowering at the other end of the street. She growls, beckoning, so he sprints towards her, tuck-tailed, eyes wide, the whites of his eyes showing.

She chuckles. Not bad for a first timer, with those

hammers of hatred battering your heart. "You'll get used to them."

Agastya licks his lips. "Will I?" He shakes his body vigorously head to tail: easy to shake things off that way. But not easy now, when he knows any day might be the last of his probation.

"You'd better," says his pack leader. "I can't have you cowering anymore. Here it's alright – these fools are locked in, they can't hurt us. But up ahead – if the other street dogs smell your fear, we're done for." She whirls around on him and lifts her lip. "You hear me?" Her display of dominance is uncalled for, but necessary: she needs to see how he takes correction. It's the pack versus the world and the pack cannot afford loose ends.

Agastya flattens himself, ears pressed back, teeth exposed in imbecile grin. "Yes, ma'am. I shan't disappoint you."

"Let's go." She knows she can trust him. He can't afford to be exiled from another pack.

The humans have been picking up Bangalore's street dogs and sterilising them. Ostensibly it's an "act of mercy". For many street dogs life is a barrage of fleas, shooings, dogfights, mange, stone-peltings, rabies, and starvation. Still, humans setting up to judge somebody else's "quality of life" – you can't deny we've got a killer sense of humour. After a dog is sterilised, the blue-uniformed municipal workers are supposed to return him or her to the original territory. But we don't pay the van-drivers enough to take such pains. They deposit the dogs back willy-nilly, creating strange neighbours, triggering dogfights. An ironical ending, for this whole sterilisation scheme was conceived to reduce dogfights.

Food is scarce. Street dogs fight for scraps. Occasionally one of us gets caught in the crossfire: a child walking past a rubbish dump, a motor scooter weaving past a mountain of chicken bones and feathers. That's how all this began, not concern for street dogs' "quality of life". We can't have dogs hurting us – not in our city, not on our planet. So out came our vans and catchers, our knives and verbal whitewash.

In all this picking-up and dropping-off, and dog packs getting reorganised, Agastya was displaced. He himself was never picked up: he hightailed it from the vans. That was the first thing Malini's wet black nose checked when he turned up last month, making himself flat and small.

He's intact. He'll be fighting for mates soon, climbing up the hierarchy: maybe an ally to her, maybe a rival. Already in relaxed moments, Malini has glimpsed the dog he used to be: playful but proud, defending his space and his food scraps. But she can't let him stay unless she knows she can trust him.

"Now steel yourself," she warns as they turn into the second mansion-lined street. "Keep your head up." This time she keeps Agastya in sight, compelling him to walk abreast of her. He shakes and cowers. Behind the gates the house dogs roar and snarl and a hundred pairs of jaws slaver, glitter, gnash. She nips his ear in warning. He yelps, more startled than hurt. Thereafter he holds himself reasonably upright. When a new bark from behind another locked gate joins the thunderstorm, his face flinches but his legs trot on.

They turn the corner. Agastya looks ready to vomit from the strain. His lean haunches tremble, his dirty-brown fur falls like third-class snow, and he stress-yawns wide enough to swallow his own head. "Not bad," Malini concedes. "Take a minute and collect yourself." He didn't let his emotions muddle his actions. As long as you act right, you're free to feel whatever you like.

Agastya nods back towards their passage of terror. "Why're those dogs like that?"

He really wants to know, so she thinks, and that's painful, for when you really think, you also feel. "They have people, but their people don't love them. So all they can do is make other dogs feel bad... You told me once, Agastya, that you wished you had people. That's natural – people bred us to need people. But, as bad as it is having nobody, it's worse having somebody who doesn't love you." She feels his eyes piercing her profile. She looks at him and he drops his head. "Ready?"

"Yes, ma'am."

They trot on.

Malini was born on the street. The first object in her awareness was Mother, a giant smelly creature nosing the litter indifferently. Mother only had energy enough to snap when her pups approached her dry teats and to shuffle away, shedding fur chunks. Fatless and hairless, Mother would've won a Sexiest Bitch contest had she been born in the mansions. But on the streets, skinny and hairless isn't sexy.

One evening soon afterwards, Mother crossed the street away from her pups. They huddled together to watch her big-eyed across the potholed asphalt. Next morning the glossy black ravens were picking at Mother's innards through the collapsed curtain of sparse fur. The ravens were frowning and scowling like epicures deigning to slum it.

From their open-air sewer-view eateries, the poor people threw their scraps not into dustbins but at the orphaned street pups' mouths. So Malini and her littermates survived a week. They were lucky: in a rich neighbourhood the rubbish would've been more prolific but all cast into man-high topple-resistant dog-proof rubbish bins. For civilised people, littering is the bigger sin.

A child on her way back from school found the pups. Oohing and aahing, she picked them up in turn to nestle under her sweater. When Malini, briefly warm, was put down again, panic seized her. She growled her littermates away. The child scolded her for being selfish, but laughingly, and picked her up again. She took Malini home, fed her, and tucked her into her soft bed. That was Malini's first lesson in survival.

Malini grew rapidly. She guarded her food; her mistress let her. All day she barked through her mansion-gates at street dogs. Her mistress scolded her for being savage, but laughingly. Malini turned two; her mistress turned twelve, and no longer thought a common no-breed dog cute. She bought a snow-white Pomeranian, a midget with a ridiculous haircut who snapped at Malini. Malini lifted her lip noiselessly and found herself promptly on the street.

She tried to get home. She failed. And out on the streets, no pack would accept the young human-reared bitch. She had never learned to grin and cower; she had learned only her way or the highway. So she carved out her own territory, starting with one narrow driveway. Then she had her first litter. She could barely feed herself – how would she feed a litter?

It was impossible but she did it. For becoming a mother didn't just double her appetite – it showed her she'd been right all along: it was you versus the world, and the right choice was always you. She felt the right choice in her bones, in her teats as her six pups pulled at them. Nothing but her own will stood between her and death, death seven times over.

Malini and Agastya trot up the street between the empty lots. Even last year these lots stood unwalled; people used to toss rubbish here, lots of juicy bits in amongst eggshells and tealeaves. Now these lots are walled off and rubbish-free and sprouting big buildings. Malini studies the construction site, an expert on buildings after six years in the ever-expanding suburbs. Soon there'll be people living here. People from big buildings seldom feed street dogs. But there'll be more shops now, and where there're shops, there're scraps.

The two patrolling dogs reach the eastern end of their territory. They survey the shops.

Grocery shops. Nothing for them here, unless a pack of biscuits slips from a shopper's bag, and Malini's teeth can perforate the plastic.

Greengrocery. Again nothing. Under the leafy greens, covered with burlap to keep them moist, Agastya sees a stunted adult dog gnawing a disintegrating turnip. The stranger looks up. His chin lowers in obeisance to the pavement strewn with wilted cabbage leaves. His tail wags and blurs as if rotoring for lift-off: preemptive appeasement at 180 mph, guarding his beggar's breakfast.

"Greetings, mistress!" he cries feebly. Malini casts him an imperious glance. "Off on morning rounds? Don't suppose I could join you?"

Malini looks away. She hates saying no. Has he no shame, begging her every day?

"No, I'm not worthy," the stranger sadly concludes. Malini and Agastya walk on. The stunted dog calls out, "Tell me, mistress! How can I become like you?'

Malini stops and looks back. "Suppose you're starving," she postulates, hating herself for saying "suppose". "You can either swallow a rotten piece of garbage or fight other dogs for a scrap of meat. What d'you do?"

The stranger glances at his half-gnawed turnip, then up at Malini, caught between a lie and a wrong answer. "I'd love to be brave like you, mistress—" he begins.

"Bravery has nothing to do with it." She prances on. Agastya follows her, flinging a smirk over his shoulder at the beggar-dog.

"Will you never tell me how?" the beggar-dog calls after them.

They're halfway down the road. Something's different today: maybe Malini's just tired of playing out the same old farce every day. "I couldn't stomach vegetables, not even if I were dying," she calls without looking back. "That's how." What she doesn't add is that vegetables, even when fresh, make poor milk. Let him think it's because of pride.

Agastya wonders why Malini deigns to acknowledge the beggar-dog. He'd be astonished if he knew they've had this conversation often before. He asks. She replies. Nothing changes.

Dairy booth. Smells good, and the plastic milk bags are thin – but the people are careful never to drop anything between the refrigerated truck and the cartons stacked outside the booth.

But this dairy booth-owner also makes tea. Customers stand around blowing on the tiny hot glasses, munching biscuits, dropping crumbs. Occasionally someone throws Malini half a biscuit – if she begs the right way. The morning tea crowd has gathered. Malini decides to stop by on the way home.

And here, at the end of their territory, stands the chicken shop. Malini's pack shares this shop with two other packs who've also arranged their territories wisely.

Early customers survey the dirty-white chickens stuffed into the filthy plastic crates stacked outside the shop. Dogs from the other packs are queueing, wagging furiously whenever the butcher steps outside to retrieve another chicken, skinny throat in peck-scarred fist. The queueing dogs snarl warnings at each other not to jump rank. Dogs don't queue in a line, as we do – what sensible creature would let out of sight the object it's after? Dogs queue in a

138

semicircle, but everyone knows his place though he may in desperation pretend to forget it.

The other packs' dogs greet Malini and Agastya with lifted lips. Bad timing. At that moment the butcher steps towards the door and flings out a fistful of entrails. Malini leaps to catch mid-air the liver, still hot and palpitating, blood still flowing. She sprints away, legs tucked under lean belly, Agastya in trail. The other dogs growl and bark, but can't give chase, too busy fighting over the remaining scraps.

Safely around the corner Malini stops to eat. At a respectful distance Agastya stands drooling, not daring to beg. She closes her eyes so as not to see him, pretending to close them in delectation. He must learn to fend for himself. She's not his mother. "Good thing for him I'm not," she thinks, torn between vicious joy and sorrow.

"We'll try again later," she reassures him, licking her lips. Her pups will drink good milk tonight. "You just have to dash in boldly and snatch the choicest morsel."

"But ma'am," Agastya objects, "your timing was picture-perfect. Isn't that just luck?"

"Today I did get lucky. But I snag a mouthful or two of entrails and fat even on bad days... Now, watch."

They're back at the dairy booth. Malini sits neatly on her haunches, forepaws together, head tilted, eyes as big as she can make them without popping them out of her skull. Bred to be a worker, she has no problem making herself a toy.

"Sit as I do," she mutters. "No, fool – closer to me. Out here you're allowed to sit right beside me. Act collegial. They like that."

A man in a biking jacket, wielding a helmet that swings and makes Agastya flinch, drops two white-flour, baked-brown biscuits before them. Malini signs Agastya to eat them both – he looks at her again to make sure – and, on his behalf, wags her tail gently and makes her eyes soft as butter. Their benefactor clumsily scratches her head and saunters away, chest outthrust as if he's cured cancer. The magic of human touch makes Malini's spine tingle and reaches towards her will, gentling, arguing, warring to unmake her will. She dismisses this witchcraft with a full-body shake and watches Agastya eat. His appetite whetted, he slowly approaches the tea-drinking crowd, small and wagging, and gets them four more biscuits. This time Malini consents to eat. A good manner with humans is a vital trait indeed.

As they trot homewards she's still not decided about him. He's small but strong, like her, and he learns fast. He needs confidence, but that'll come. He did well today among the house dogs – she made sure of that. Intact dogs have become rare, and she needs new blood for her children to breed with. She's nearing the end of her own breeding days: running dry, forced to abandon half her annual litter, dodging the sterilisation brigade with a game knee. If she can grow her pack, maybe someday they can confront the other two dog packs and monopolise the chicken shop.

But can she trust him?

On this street, too, big buildings are rising. People in big buildings eat fewer vegetables, more chicken. Maybe someday every pack will have its own chicken shop. Maybe someday dogs can stop fighting.

Back on home street she holds her head erect, staring straight ahead. But her eyes flit: first to her three pups, still alive, thank God; why wouldn't they be? Her heart swells with pride. They're well-fed, play-fighting with her last year's daughter. That girl's turned out alright. But she's just a teenager, not old enough to lead. And volatile – like her father, who ran out to chase trucks and split his bowels open in the night, many nights ago when Malini was carrying his litter.

Next Malini surveys the adults in her pack. Nine, all sterile bar herself and her children. Soon she'll lead them all out on feeding rounds. She always leads them herself. She's a bitch of a certain age in a world that stops for nobody. She can't afford to delegate.

Finally, her eyes flit to the card.

It's gone. The cardboard box-of-rejects with her two runts is gone. She's so shocked she almost gives herself away, dashes away to go looking for them. But all her pack up ahead are watching her. Their heads are half-raised, their eyes indolent with morning languor, but they would snap alert at the first sign of weakness. Malini keeps her eyes forward and walks on.

Agastya has dropped back from abreast of her to ten feet behind her, from collegial personal distance to savage. He murmurs, "I'm sorry for your loss, ma'am."

She doesn't reply, doesn't even flinch. Sharp eyes! He's watched her watching her runts across the street. But he won't tattle to the others. He can't afford to.

"How d'you do it, ma'am?" he says. "How can I become tough like you?"

There are two kinds of dogs.

Some dogs ask Malini why she's like this. Other dogs ask her how they can get like this. They all have one thing in common.

The dogs on the mansion-lined streets are not really asking her why she's a bitch. They're telling her she is one.

The dogs who ask her "how" aren't really seeking an answer, either. That turnip-gnawing beggar-dog chose his lifepath long ago. The "how" he directs at her now is not a request for a tutorial. It's an expression of admiration, so

141

that she won't nip at him; an expression of his fantasy of becoming in some other life gangsta like her.

But facing the humble-tongued, keen-eyed newcomer this spring morning, Malini feels communicative. From the rubbish dump up the street, the balmy breeze wafts the hundred-rainbow of rubbish fresh and stale, organic and plastic. She relaxes her pace.

"How can you become like me?" she repeats. "Live my life, Agastya, and survive it, that's how... Now tell me – how does my daughter strike your fancy? Fine bitch, I think?"

Agastya lowers his body and wriggles with gratitude. Malini indulges his stammering thanks. She allows herself one last glance at the spot across the street where she left her runts in their cardboard box. Wherever they may be now, they're better off.

A mother knows.

THE SACRIFICE

I drag my suitcase up the alley. Potholed asphalt and narrow, inclined driveways constitute an up-and-down obstacle course where a pavement should be. After Goa's endless beaches, half-empty in offseason, this treeless narrowness is disorienting. I glance up at our room. Against twilight's midnight blue, our second-storey window flickers white: the ceiling fan whirring against the fluorescent light tube. Komal sits hunched over her laptop. Her left arm is raised, fingers worrying her scalp, table lamp shining on the bald spot that's colonising the crown of her 22-year-old head.

I haul my suitcase up the dust-slippery stairs as quietly as possible, but at the landing I see Komal standing in our doorway, shifting her weight from one flat foot to another, grinning. "Hey, Pragya! How was Goa?"

I fling my arms around her. Ow, she says, comically flat. So I squeeze her some more. Discreetly I exhale from my nostrils the *bhringraj* pungency of the restorative hairoil that saturates her scalp. "Goa was splendid!" I squat to push my suitcase under my bed. Turning to rise, pivoting, I spot, under Komal's bed, at right angles to mine against the other wall, the hillock of Cheetos and Doritos, Little Hearts sugared biscuits, and 5-Star and Dairy Milk chocolates: all ten-or-twenty-rupee single-serving packets, a rainbow of neon plastic. My gut spasms and it's all I can do not to recoil. I face Komal brightly. "I'm starving. Travel tales over dinner?"

"OK!" Komal reaches for her jacket. She always wears a jacket outdoors, even in this roasting April, perhaps to conceal her breasts, which are big but not saggy.

I glance at her laptop. "Wait, you're reading a manuscript. Due tomorrow?"

"Ye-ah," Komal drawls. Her welcome-home smile

vanishes, leaving her smooth fair-skinned face, with its double chin, expressionless. "But I can finish later, ya."

"You're on page 254 of 270. Why not finish now? You must be in the climax."

A wave of irritation scurries halfway across her face before she suppresses it. My ten days' change has made me forget what date I was coming home to. It's 2008: I no longer call Komal out for failing to speak up for herself. When we became friends, I laughed at her doormattiness, and tried to train, roleplay, and bully her into assertiveness. That was three years ago. Last September, when we got this room together, I had a mirage of an even closer intimacy. All that is gone. And now I've only irritated Komal by confronting her with another minor conflict where she has failed to assert herself.

"Well, this MS is not exactly a page-turner." That's Komal-speak for "It's shitty". She'd sooner bite her tongue out than disparage someone else's work. "But, ye-ea-ah, I guess I could finish first? D'you want a snack?" She heads for her junk-food hillock.

"No, thanks!" I clear my throat and settle my voice. "No, thanks, I'm not hungry. You take your time."

I phone my parents, as I promised to do when I got home, as I did when I caught the train at Goa, and when I disembarked, and when I caught the bus at Bangalore Central. On speaker phone at their end, they ask me whether I've eaten, tell me I must be exhausted, and give me weather updates from Calcutta. Hmmm, I tell Pa and Ma, my mobile phone two inches from my ear, wondering why they'd think I'd give a damn. I lean back. These big executive swivel chairs are the only nice thing in the rooms at this paying-guest accommodation.

Komal rocks as she reads. Even hunched, she seems to have grown into her chair. Has she gained weight while I've

144

been gone? We're both 5'3", but she's 80 kilos: at least, she was in October, when I discovered that old-fashioned weighing machine with the running lights in the Sagar restaurant, that Sunday when I managed to drag her to Lalbagh for a walk. Her bald spot has grown too, unless her table lamp is playing tricks. I try not to stare. But Komal's oblivious. Whenever Komal pulls her hair out by the roots, she enters a trance, like a baby junkie suckling heroin milk. My skin creeps and I wonder whether I should look away and I wonder whether I should hang up on my parents and confront Komal.

This compulsive hair pulling is called trichotillomania. It's she who told me. She knows that she does it, but she doesn't know when she's doing it. She told me this, that evening last October, weeks after we became roomies. She never mentioned it again. I think I'm not supposed to notice it. I look away and say, "Hmm," on the phone.

It's in another world that I've been downing Kingfishers all week and dancing half-naked in bamboo shacks: with strangers, and with friends whose psychological damage is either absent or buried deep, under intact scalps, too deep for beer tears. Back in this room, with its musty smell and dusty corners, I've forgotten not to stare. Maybe it's like watching someone masturbate and I shouldn't. Or maybe it really is like watching a baby junkie and I should intervene. I picture creeping up on Komal, leaning over her, and kissing her hand away.

"Ah," I say on the phone. I'll graduate in June, move to Delhi, and start getting my scholarship from the university. My content-writing job will cover my remaining expenses. Then I can block and delete my parents' phone numbers. I've avoided accidentally memorising their phone numbers, accidentally listening to anything they tell me. Just two months to go before I'm born into a parentless new life.

And when I've finished two years at this job I'll request a reco and get a better job, and at JNU I'll have shiny new friends, who're going places, who'll spur me to go places too. "I see."

Komal glances across the room periodically, eyes bright and sympathetic, as if she knows. I smile and roll my eyes. About my parents she knows nothing, and now I'm glad I've told her nothing. It's she who decided we're no longer really friends. She shouldn't still be interested in my phone calls home.

Komal graduated last July and got a job reading manuscripts at Phoenix, a startup publisher cofounded by one of our literature professors. Phoenix gets mostly fiction manuscripts, from first-timers, low quality. Komal is self-sufficient now: she no longer needs to answer her parents' phone calls.

"And you're having your period regularly?" says Ma.

"Goddammit, Ma!"

Now I'm in for it. I sit up and rub my forehead. My parents react to a bad word as to a cat-o'-nine-tails suddenly across the face. One of the worst beatings I ever got was back home in the violet twilight after a birthday party, back in Calcutta, where I'd called another seven-year-old a "bastard" – a funny word I'd heard somewhere. I'd glanced at Pa between the balloons and streamers, and amended it to "bustard" – another funny word, funny bird. That didn't save me.

But Ma doesn't rebuke my "goddammit". She rephrases her question and vindicates her concern. After all, my periods *did*, you know, I *was*... but she can't say the word. After everything that's happened she still can't say the word. My vision blackens, my ears burn, and I picture flinging my mobile phone across the room. But that would startle Komal and let her know something's up. She doesn't deserve to know.

"Yes, Ma. I'm having my period." I open my fisted fingers. They're bleached from the pressure. Now the blood runs into them splotchy red.

"Good." Ma asks about my dinner plans and whether I'm drinking enough water – me, famous water-guzzler. Weather reports and all the wrong questions – that's my parents' conversation. In Bengali there's no word for sorry, no word that anyone in real life ever uses.

I go back to monosyllabic responses. Come to think of it, I've never actually heard Komal's parents calling, not even before she graduated. Can't be the time difference: Dubai's only ninety minutes behind. Suddenly I realise Komal's interest in my parents' phone calls has nothing to do with me.

Is it by the roots that Komal pulls out her hair? I wonder. If I went and hugged her, would her fingernails smell like hair-follicle blood, ovary-follicle blood, menstrual blood? She crunches into a Cheeto that she's sneaked out of a pack under her pillow.

When Komal and I became close, I told her that she shouldn't eat junk food, that maybe she should see a psychotherapist about that other thing. Hmmm, said Komal. A thoughtful Hmmm. Komal does have periods of self-awareness: clearly the idea of getting help had occurred to her. Why not, then, I wanted to ask her. I missed my chance to ask her. Komal hasn't really spoken to me since that drunken evening in the bathroom. She's snapped herself shut and I'm done trying to help. I've got my own life to solve.

Ma winds up. *"Bhalo thakis,"* she says. Stay well, take care.

"OK." I hang up.

Komal plucks out another hair and holds it before her eye glasses. Yes, there is blood on its root, yes, it is by the

147

roots that she plucks them out, or why would there be a bald spot? She stares at the hair. So she does know what she's been doing. So why doesn't she just stop? She's a year my senior, and whatever happened happened years ago, and how hard is it to get your act together? I did it. Nobody helped me.

Komal lids her laptop emphatically. "Done!"

"Ready when you are, Komal."

Komal puts on her denim jacket before the rust-blotched mirror nailed to our plywood cupboard. The button over her bust will no longer fasten. She fastens the buttons above and below, studies the effect, unfastens the button below, then unfastens the button above, then tries the whole placket unbuttoned. Then, feet planted wide, body pendulum-ing, she lowers her head and confronts her bald patch, left of centre near her crown. How does it feel, I wonder, to wake up and confront the corpses of the night.

I tear my eyes away. I text my tripmates banalities bouqueted with smiley faces. They're my batchmates: in two months we'll be scattered, will probably never meet again. But we promise each other, with all caps and exclamation points, to do this every year. I've watched the grown-ups, the successful ones, I mean. This is what they do.

When I first saw Komal, up on stage at the Literary Association, she was speaking about Malamud. I looked up thinking, Wow! Someone who's read an author I haven't, and not one of those junk pop authors. But these last eight months she's read only shitty manuscripts, hunched, tugging at her throat skin, and some rubbishy Mills & Boons romances. And she's written only Harry Potter fanfiction, which she knows better than to show me.

Never live with your idols. Better still, never have idols. Anyway, when push comes to shove, you'll be all alone. All

148

my life we've moved from place to place. I tried to keep people in my life. But when I was struggling the people close to me only hurt me. Life's easier when you have no idols, when you're the only person you expect anything from.

Komal turns around, hair swept stylishly sideways and backwards. I smile back brightly.

"Come." I rise and change my shoes.

"Do I look OK?" says Komal softly.

I whirl back around. Since when does Komal care how she looks? Some days I hardly recognise this person she's become. I care, too, I guess, but only in private, in decent. I'll never be one of those women who do a whole hair-and-makeup session in a public bathroom.

"'Course you do!"

I stride towards the door. My foot dislodges, from under my table, a giant white plastic bag.

"Oh," says Komal, "you can just—"

I'm kneeling over the bag. It's plain and unmarked. The loops are knotted tight, but the plastic is white and thin and I can see it's stuffed with wrappers: Cheetos and Doritos, Little Hearts, 5-Star and Dairy Milk. The wrappers have been folded small and stuffed densely and this plastic bag full of plastic is almost heavy.

"Can just put it—" says Komal. I shove the bag back under my table. "Sorry, you weren't here, so I shoved it there, ya."

"No problem! Hey, by the way, my treat tonight!" I haven't meant to say this. But why not. Let's get some real food into Komal, a goodbye meal or two.

She shuffles into the corridor. Yes, I can afford to treat Komal. I'm the only one in my batch who's got a job. I'm racing forward; soon the past will be banished from the rear-view mirror. I leap behind Komal and seize her shoulders, like last autumn when I thought we were going to be soul sisters. As she's descending the stairs I notice her right knee is locking, her right thigh is wobbling. Is she getting arthritis at 22? I dig my fingertips into her soft shoulders whistling, choo-choo-choo.

Our alley is all three-or-four-storey houses, painted hot pink or meth blue, overcrowded drawing rooms elbowing neighbours' bedrooms. Crimson and navy-blue SUVs share the sloping driveways with lounging street dogs and cows. Hybrid cows, these, black-and-white: mountains of flesh sitting statue-still, except for the shit-encrusted tails, fly-flicking, and the square jaws masticating, drooling whitey-green. Under the unquiet grey that stands, in the metropolis, for the black of night, the streetlamps cast deceptive shadows. A single blade of grass, cowering between paving stones, casts a mile-long shadow slithering snakelike over my foot. And a shallow circular shadow, which I felt sure was cast by a stray pebble, turns out to be a fresh pothole suddenly underfoot.

Ow, says Komal, as her stiff right knee buckles, and it's I who wince. I clutch her elbow and nudge my glasses up my nose, the better to see where I'm guiding her.

"Aryan Chariot OK for dinner?"

My question is perfunctory. Before she graduated, Komal stayed in the hostel, but she made no other friends. Her hostel mates ignored her all year, then sucked up to her the week before exams, so that she'd coach them. Komal's default response is yes: to me, to anyone who shows the slightest interest.

"Sure, or we could also try Anand Vihar?" says Komal. "They've finished their renovations."

"Which do *you* prefer?" I ask, suddenly annoyed, determined to make her choose.

"My butter-chicken-and-*naan* is equally good at both

places," says Komal. "But only Anand Vihar has that skin-on grilled chicken that you like, and the big salad."

I squeeze her elbow. "Anand Vihar it is." My annoyance vanishes, leaving me feeling foolish.

Of course Komal cares about me. When I come back from the golf course, which is open to non-member walkers and joggers before working hours, Komal asks how many laps I ran this morning, and whether the uncles gathering flowers for their wives' *puja*s had left one or two *shiuli* on the tree to scent the air for seculars. And now Komal, as I lead her through the back alleys, stumbles against shadows and stubs her toe against nothings. Maybe she's been working from home again, like after her breakup, forgetting to walk, to talk.

At Anand Vihar Komal shuffles up the steps – black granite, shiny and sharp-edged, powdered with cement dust from the upper storey that's still under construction. She stands hugging her tummy, pendulum-ing, staring at the table as the waiter clears up. She collapses into her seat. She looks up across the square little table at me, as if we were alone in the restaurant this Sunday evening, alone in the world. But maybe it's only because she's too shy to people-watch, to make eye contact even with the stick-thin, pimple-faced waiters, that she gives me this attention. But her bald spot is growing, her knees are going, her jacket's no longer buttoning, and it doesn't matter why she likes me: I'm all she's got. "No," I cry, "lemme see what else there is!" And I didn't ask for this revelation, and I refuse it and reason with it, fidgeting in my chair, frowning at the menu.

"What did you eat at Goa?"

"Prawns. Lots of prawns."

"Yum! Any good?"

"Huge and fresh and sweet." I survey the diners. There're some women skinnier than me, and some women

151

curvier than me, but there's no woman who's both skinnier and curvier than me. "Well, some restaurants skip degutting their prawns, so sometimes they're bitter. They sell them right at the beach, too; you can eat prawns lounging thirty feet from the water. You sit on a chair to keep the sand out of your bum crack, under an umbrella, that you've got to hire by the hour – and you do, for even at 9 a.m. the sun is broiling. You watch the fishermen beach their canoes, unravel their nets – which takes ages, somehow, you'd think they'd fold 'em up neatly – and sort their catch into piles. And you eat your prawns. For this scenery, you pay twice what you'd pay in a restaurant 200 meters away on the street. And it's worth it. Yes: good prawns, good scenery, good trip."

"Show photos!" Komal has so little practice asking for anything that she can only do it by regressing into childhood, lips pouting, eyes sparkling behind big mud-brown-framed eyeglasses. Is this how she looked, I wonder, that afternoon when she asked her parents for the most important thing. How badly did they fail her, I wonder – did they try to throw her out too, did they ask her why can't you just be normal?

"Fuck it," I say, "I'll just have my usual." We place our order.

I pass Komal my phone. I bring my own chair around – keeping her to my left, which takes a bit of calculation, for I'm bad at left and right, even worse at simulating them in my head. I've got photos from the spice plantation, the cruise boat, and the scenic old churches in Panjim but Komal's rushing through. I thumb back and offer commentary. "That tree with the cottony sprays of white flowers? It's allspice. I bought allspice powder at the plantation's shop. Have you ever tasted allspice? We grow it in India, we've been exporting it to Europe for centuries – but I've never seen it before! I'd heard of it, I'd thought it was a spice mix. Like 'all the spices'."

"Allspice." Komal mouths the word. "What's it taste like?"

"Like a combo of three other spices. Cinnamon, nutmeg, and the third note is, uh, clove," I venture.

"Ooh, that might work as gunpowder." "Gunpowders" are coarsely powdered blends of roasted spices and lentils, which resemble gunpowder not at all, unless you're as myopic as me and as colour blind as a collie. Back in Kerala, "gunpowders" are served alongside red rice, several vegetable dishes – and meat, if you're Hindu but non-vegetarian, as most Malayalis are, as Komal and I are, as, I discovered only lately, most Indians are, despite the glut of restaurants marked "pure vegetarian" – that, it turns out, is only because the hoi polloi are chasing the Brahmins' ostentatiously abstemious habits. "It'd make meals less boring," Komal adds. Here in Bangalore, when she's not bingeing junk, Komal makes a meal out of a mound of white rice and a teaspoon of gunpowder, sometimes made into a paste with a five-rupee sachet of Mother Dairy ghee.

"Yeah, that might work… And this was on the cruiseboat, which goes down Mandovi River and back. I photographed the sunset from deck. Then the boat began blasting music, and there wasn't much to see above, so we went down to the ballroom – yes, this is it. We spent the hour dancing to Bollywood hits. Rubbishy music, fit only for dancing to… And these are the casinoboats. Big as ocean liners!" Komal listens politely. I open my mouth to explain about the casinoboats, but Komal's thumbing her way forward, rushing forward. She's from Kerala but she's never been to Goa and now shows no interest, so why did she ask to see my photos?

"Ooh." Komal has found the beach photos. She pauses

153

on a photo of me and two of my tripmates. The waves lap at our heels. The sun crimsons behind us as it sinks through a cloudless, colourless sky. "Bikini?" says Komal.

"My friends are wearing bikinis, yes. They bought them there. They're expensive! I didn't know when I'd use one again, so," I chuckle, "I'm wearing my regular underwear."

"This is your regular underwear?" Komal peers at my phone.

"It's just a cotton underwired bra, unpadded," I add, trying not to emphasise "unpadded", "and cotton hipster briefs." I omit telling Komal that, in this photo and in all the others, my bra straps are clipped behind, racerback-style, with a bra clip, to shorten the bra straps and lift my breasts, which sag even minus a drenched cotton bra. "There's a reason they don't make bikinis from cotton," I add, irrelevantly.

"Wow. I could never wear my underwear as a bikini!"

Pokerfaced, I bite into a drumstick. Komal often leaves her underwear around our bathroom. She still wears white woven-cotton wireless bras of the kind our mothers bought us at twelve, which show their lacy seams through T-shirts, and which, working by compression rather than lift, squeeze your lungs uncomfortably. As for Komal's underpants, I mistook them at first for high-waisted, knee-length city-shorts.

"I don't think I've ever seen your underwear," says Komal.

"I don't like leaving mine around... Ha, it's my first year away from home. Two years in hostel during M.A., and *I'll* be leaving everything out, too." No, I won't. I'll never let myself go.

Komal's still staring at the first beach photo. Finally she thumbs forward. This one's just me: same setting, the photographer, a stranger we'd just met, kneeling for a better angle, five feet away. Looking at the photo now, through Komal's eyes, I see he knelt slightly to my left. He must've figured out my squint despite all my efforts to hide it, and find an angle where it wouldn't show as much. He saw me, I realise, and I feel furious and grateful and terrified. I press my palms to my cheeks, but the tandoori masala from the chicken on my fingers only makes my cheeks redder.

"You're hot," says Komal. I giggle, then bite into the drumstick so hard, I strike bone. "You've got an hourglass figure and perfect skin."

I masticate with exaggerated relish. "I do like my skin." Vanity's a sin. Vanity almost killed me. I change the subject. I tell Komal how my friend pulled her calf muscle on our jungle hike, and I carried her seven-kilo backpack, three hours forth, three hours back, sandwiched between two backpacks; and about the Nigerian giant my friend picked up on Tinder, who grabbed my backside instead, and I slapped him.

"You're so cool," says Komal.

"Aww, shut up." I don't tell Komal that midway through the hike my shoulders, strained by two backpacks plus my clipped bra straps, felt like they'd break into two; I don't tell Komal that the bottom-pinching pleased me, just a little, and that I considered not telling my friend. My actual behaviour remained admirable so there's no reason to mention those other irrelevancies, to sacrifice Komal's admiration.

"I've gained weight," Komal blurts, still staring at my phone. "Four kilos."

She looks up quickly but I'm even quicker; I've masked my horror. Four kilos in a week! "It happens," I say. I implore her to come to the golf course with me. She says people stare at her no matter what she wears. Fuck people, I say. I implore her to let me make her salads. Hmmm, she

155

says. Halfway through her meal, she's smashed up her neon-orange gravied chicken and crumbled her *naan* into it. She pushes her plate away and keeps thumbing through my photos. "See," I say, "if you eat real food, you're easily sated."

"Maybe," she says.

Maybe she's lost her appetite for real food. Maybe she's *trying* to uglify herself.

That Saturday last October, it was Komal who suggested that we drink. I gaped, then ran down to the liquor shop before she changed her mind. Midway through my Kingfisher, I realised Komal didn't want to drink: she wanted to get drunk. Soon she was kneeling over the toilet. But she didn't throw up. She talked. Maybe she felt better able to talk in that novel situation, sprawled on the shabby tiles with me. It was her brother, she said. He'd been ten, and she'd been four, and he'd tried his fingers first. That felt strange, but kind of good. Then he'd tried his – his thing, she said. After everything that had happened she still couldn't say the word. When he put in his thing, that no longer felt good. She cried out. He skulked away. She spent a week creeping around on tiptoes, wondering if people could tell, thinking up excuses why she'd let it happen. Finally, she told her parents. They shouted at her, shook her, almost slapped her. He's just a curious little boy, they said. No damage done, they said. And anyway she'd probably imagined the whole thing, with all those books you read, they said.

"What's your brother's name?" I'd cried, springing to my feet, looking around for my steel water flask. "Gimme his address. Somewhere in Nepal, wasn't it, in medical school? I'll catch a train and go bash his head in," I'd said.

She wouldn't tell me. She'd drained a quart of McDowell's but she wouldn't tell me her brother's name.

And Kumar is far too common a last name. I'd never find him myself. And Komal wasn't on social media. There was nothing I could look through. She wouldn't say another word and she refused to touch the second quart.

Not that evening, and not afterwards. So that was the end of our dawdling in Sagar restaurants, over *idli-sambhar* at one-legged, stand-up steel tables, watching clerks rushing through lunch, making up stories about them; of our expeditions to discover which hole-in-the-wall or overpriced Café Coffee Day outlet serves Bangalore's most rancid coffee; of our lounging in bed in the streaming Saturday sun, dreaming up outlines for our award-winning bestselling novels.

Komal has forsaken me. I thought that evening we were stepping into my mirage of soul-sisterhood. But, ever since, if I mention her brother, or her hair, or a therapist, she freezes up and then, if I don't take the hint, she replies with as close an approach to rudeness, to shortness, as she's capable of. Maybe she regrets telling me. Maybe she thinks I look at her differently now. Well, of course I do. Komal has forsaken me – but it's OK, I tell myself, scolding myself for the quick, hot sneaky tears gushing up my throat. It's OK, for when I graduate, it's I who will go away from her and make new friends.

Pa works for the bank; he keeps getting transferred. We've always moved around, a new city every couple of years. I make friends everywhere. I'll make friends in Delhi. How hard can it be to find someone who will discover, without my telling them, that I love oleanders and hate roses; that I secretly wonder what the big deal is about Shakespeare, with his odd pacing and inconsistent characterisation; that I need to have whoever I'm with always to my left, so I can see them properly, so they can't see my squint? I'm staring at Komal, silently bidding her

157

goodbye, and all this time she's been thumbing through photos, and I've been lecturing about salads and morning walks. With savage relish I picture Komal stuck in this dead-end job, hunched, red-handed with dusty Dorito guilt. I picture the Komal-shaped hole in my life and yes this is what I deserve. I don't deserve any friends, any success; I'm still just a fat fuck.

I take big swallows of water, draining my glass tumbler. "You OK?" asks Komal. I nod and attack my salad. She returns my phone and plays with her food.

Nobody knows me as Komal does. And the things that she doesn't know, there's nobody else I want to tell them to. I picture my life, a turnstile: pairs of ears cycling into my life, out of my life, always a new pair of ears, every pair of ears the same, sorry, have I already told you this, oh, sorry, I thought I'd told you. We blow our noses on each other, like tissue paper, and throw each other away, said Bernard Shaw; and when I read this I snorted and vowed I'd never succumb to this modern illness.

"So, yeah, you should come to the golf course with me. I can run, you can walk. Or I'll walk with you. Who cares what people say? People are always saying something, blah, blah."

"That's easy for you to say, Pragya," Komal murmurs. She grins placatingly, lest I take her words as an insult, or as an invitation to a real conversation.

"I guess." I open my mouth and close it again and focus on my salad.

Let her think it's been easy for me. Let her admire me under false pretences. For who would admire me if they knew the truth? Not even Komal.

Not even Komal. Revulsion breaks over me and throws me back, like that wave at Goa, that looked low, and came too fast, too high, and threw us back, sprawling on our backsides giggling, spitting out saltwater, sand wadding in our underpants. Afterwards, I got to my feet, didn't shake out the wad of sand; I thrust my butt out and squeezed the wad of sand instead, with my fingertips through my underpants, pretending it was poop, disgusting my dainty tripmates. But it was OK. I can afford to be disgusting. We all laughed together. They all think I'm hot. Komal thinks I'm hot. I'm squeezing every last drop of admiration out of Komal, squeezing her dry. She's all I've got.

And I face myself, and I long to hit out at myself, like I did at the mirror, that evening in April 2005 when I was locked in my room, shivering even though it was hot, stripped down to my cotton hipster briefs, weighing myself for the seventh time that day. I looked up into my face. Don't know why. I'd been sick a while and all I'd wanted was for my body to look thinner, all I'd wanted was never to look into my own face. I looked now but I couldn't see myself. I'd spent two years in a trance of starvation, of plotting how to starve myself without my parents noticing. Like a baby junkie suckling heroin milk. Then my vision cleared. I saw my stick-thin arms and dead eyes, my jutting ribs and sunken temples. Revulsion broke over me. I hit out at the mirror, missed, hit air, sprained my shoulder hitting air. So much weightlessness, so much admiration from friends and strangers, so dearly bought.

I spring to my feet pushing my chair back. It falls backwards. I catch it just in time. "Shall we go?"

The evening is cool. We've got two hours till curfew. So we take the long way home. Air-brushed skin and cookie-cutter features glow from backlit hoardings. Women stand oblivious mid-pavement, their shopping bags bristling like cats' whiskers, chatting with friends as strangers jostle past. Intrepid motor scooterists seek shortcuts around rubbish heaps and over pavements. An apple-red sheath dress in the Mango store window arrests me.

This mannequin has no figure at all. This dress is cut for me. I've never spent so much on a dress, but, well, every woman needs a red sheath dress. Even a writer. Look! That's me, lounging on a talk-show-host's royal-blue sofa in my apple-red sheath dress, chatting about my latest award-winning bestselling experimental-metaphysical bildungsroman.

"That'd look fantastic on you," says Komal.

I lean back from the store window, notice the oily intricate fingerprints I've left, wipe at them with my palm, and leave an oily smudge. I catch the staring eye of a shop attendant and decide I might as well try it on. Komal shuffles in after me, arms crossed over breasts, elbows pressed over tummy, bulky jacket covering everything.

Why don't they employ women assistants in a women's clothing store? I'm tired of buying everything, sports bras and underpants and contraceptives, from men. All the shop attendants are men, mostly young, and they're staring at us, and Komal's staring at her feet, and I cross my arms across my body too. After a few backs-and-forths we figure out which size I am. I almost snatch the dress from the attendant. "Won't be long," I promise Komal.

The dressing room is just big enough for the door to open into it. Ignoring the mirrors and bright lights, ignoring the chicken-and-salad food baby disfiguring me, I change. I unclip my bra clip behind. My bra straps loosen, my breasts sag in the bra cups, and instantly the tightness that's been cramping my upper back all day, sneaking up my shoulders into my neck, growing into a throbbing, raging headache, falls away. The dress turns out to be cut after all for a boyish figure – it was clipped behind the mannequin into an hourglass illusion. False advertising everywhere. It's loose in the waist, but not loose enough to hide my food baby. And it's tight over the bust, flattening my now inadequately supported breasts further downwards. I look terrible and I want to burrow underground. Suddenly I've got an idea.

I open the door a smidge. Feet planted wide, swaying left to right, fingernails digging through jacket into elbows, Komal is staring through the rows of dresses. "Komal!" I whisper. "Mind coming in here?"

She comes in and bolts the door.

"What d'you think?"

I stand sideways to her, showing off my grotesque food baby and hell-headed breasts. I stand as I do when nobody's looking: slouching, midsection not sucked in, butt not thrust out, shoulders not pinned back. My heart thumps in my ears deafening me. I stare at my feet. Komal says nothing and grows bigger and bigger in my peripheral vision.

"Woah," she says softly.

There's no admiration in her voice now. But there's nothing else, either. Quickly, afraid I'll lose my nerve, I unzip the dress, yanking on it, I free my arms, ease the dress down over my midsection, and let it hang over my hips, making my hips, I know, I know without looking, look even bigger. I stand exposed. My vision goes black. I am a rat, plague-ridden, half-bald, that was scurrying at midnight down the gutter when the sun rose, and froze me, and immortalised my hideousness. Come, merciful axe, terminate my shame and me.

"You look... different." Komal turns to the mirrors.

"No," I mutter, "don't look in the mirrors. The mirrors are slimming."

So she looks directly at my breasts, sagging and stretch-marked in my bra. I resist the urge to explain that when I starved myself, my breasts shrank. I resist the urge to explain that when I found, in running – in running for fun, in running for the love of misty mornings, shrill mynahs, and blue-gold sunrises – the beginnings of a cure for my self-hatred, ill-fitting sports-bras made my shrunken breasts sag.

"*You* get bloated after meals, too?" She pokes my tummy, startling me, making me look up at her at last. A smile creases her eyes.

Why was I dreading this? All the anger and shame, of which I've made stilts, on which to walk through the world, as over a bed of coals, melt, and my stilts incinerate instantaneously, poof, and I'm falling. It's only onto the beach that I fall. I'm lying on white sand, waves tickling the skin between my toes, and the sun is shining on me, legs spread wide, the sun is shining into me. The warmth enters the innermost part of me, and fills me, and surrounds me, and lifts me up into a place without weight.

"Jiggle-jiggle," says Komal, jiggling with two fingers the layer of fat, over my abs, or maybe in place of my abs, which survived two years of starvation. She giggles.

Now I want to tell her everything. I want to tell her how she's not the only one who hates her body. How the squint in my right eye is too slight for surgery to reliably correct, but bad enough to make crossing the road problematic, and how every time I "look to the right" before I cross, I have to turn and face the traffic head-on, to accurately judge distances, judge when I can safely step into the never-ceasing traffic. How, what bothers me, more than this danger to my life, is that someone might see I have a squint, might look at me differently, find me out in my shame, which is why I manoeuvre endlessly to keep whoever I'm with to my left. How my sagging breasts—

My phone rings. "Goddammit!" How many times a day do my parents need to hear I'm alive?

162

Pa's voice rings high. He's received another promotion, he says, another transfer. They're going to Chandigarh, he says, they'll be much closer to me when I'm in Delhi. Ah, I mutter. Pa puts Ma on speakerphone, and they interrupt each other, planning trips for us three during weekends and holidays. I can finally go hiking, says Ma. Hmmm, I say, not bothering to tell them that I'll be out of their lives soon. How little power, after all, they have!

They had all the power when I was in secondary school, when the other girls pointed and giggled, and nobody would sit beside me in class, or pick me for their team during Friday sports hour, or stand near me on the cafeteria queue. And so I began losing flesh, losing my period, my skin growing sallow, my mind going cold and dead. Sometimes, even now, when I wake up in the night, I find I've not been dreaming, I've been thinking in my sleep, wondering what else I lost in those two years. Pa's 5'11", Ma's 5'6", every generation grows taller, reaches further. I'm 5'3". When I was sick I felt my brain doing quiet. I'm no longer sick but I'm still not bright enough to do all the things I want to do. I hid how little I was eating, how much I was exercising locked in my room, I hid this shameful disease with which I was trying to cure my shameful body. But my parents noticed. They kept trying to drag me bodily to the psychiatrist, kept trying to throw me bodily out of the flat, kept pounding at my door, shouting at me. If you're going to starve yourself, you shan't do it under our eyes, they said, what are we to say when your aunts and uncles ask after you, they said, and how hard is it to eat a normal diet, be a normal person, they said.

And listen to them now, gushing all over the place. You'd think I'd imagined those two years. Fuck off, I long to shout at them. I see you.

Komal puts her arm around my shoulder. I look up at the mirror. I'm scowling and Komal's timid smile is

163

bursting into a grin. She waves at me, waves the hand that's draped around my shoulder, accidentally flicking my earlobe. And it's she who says "Ow."

"...OK then," says Pa. "We'll talk more later." He pauses. He always pauses. "*Bhalo thakis.*"

I look at Komal waving at me like an idiot. Little idiot. Big idiots. You can't get hurt like this unless you love someone and you know they love you too. "You too, Pa," I mutter. "Take care." This time I wait for him to hang up, suffer through his trail of OK then, yes, bye, OKs.

"You should buy this dress," says Komal. "Just don't wear it after a big meal." She tries to wink, and ends up blinking.

"It doesn't fit. Now fuck off so I can change."

We walk through the milling crowds, under the flickering streetlights, chattering. Finally, at 9:40 p.m. when we turn homewards, Komal says she's been thinking about seeing a psychiatrist. I hold my breath. "He'll make me talk about stuff," she says, slowly, like pulling teeth. "It'll be painful... But that's not what I'm afraid of."

"What then?" I say carefully.

She doesn't reply, and I wonder what I've done wrong this time, whether she's going to snap shut again. I picture the psychiatrist inching his chair forward, caressing her thighs, and I look around for my steel water flask, which I've left back in our room. It's just the right size for grasp, club, smash a rascal's skull, this asshole won't get away with it, this asshole can't hide from me.

"What if," she says finally, "he blames my parents, and my brother, and tells me I should cut them off, like they're toxic? Which, even if it's true, that isn't how I want to move forward." Shoppers push past. The smell of leftover chicken *alfaham*, warmed over, the bones burnt to a crisp, singes our nostril hair. Shop attendants, tense with closing-

164

hour anxiety, shout their wares down the street. "Some people might be able to choose between family and sanity. I don't want to." Her eyes are moist, her apple cheeks are bunched in a sorrowful smile, and she's looking at me as if I have all the answers.

I squeeze her hand. She asks me if I'll come along with her to the psychiatrist. I disengage my arm to roll up the sleeves of my shirtdress, it's a warm night, then roll them down again, no it's not. Why a psychiatrist, I want to ask, why not a psychotherapist? Is medication what Komal needs? Is it what I needed? Would medication have saved me and those two years of my life? Two blank years, through which I zombie-lurched, a blur of weighings and calorie-countings and boxes of sugar-free laxative gum. Would medication have saved me two inches of height, 12 IQ points, two years of my life which I'll never get back, by which I'll always be behind?

We're back in the back alleys. The street dogs' eyes are glinting gold-green. Komal is waddling along beside me, stumbling on shadows.

"Yes," I say. "I'll come. But you've got to speak up for yourself."

We trudge up the narrow darkened stairs of our paying-guest accommodation.

"Hey," says Komal behind me, "d'you think we could put allspice on salad? Make it taste, you know, less salady?"

I pause at the landing to turn on the light. "You can put anything on anything."

165

FIELD TRIP

The seventy-one seven-year-olds throng the green-painted wire fence, hooting or whistling or trying to whistle at the lions: two dark-maned, slim-waisted males, who're necking on the ten-foot-high wooden platform in a decidedly un-lionlike fashion. "Please," I want to tell my boys, "just let them enjoy themselves." Off to my left, a cacophony of jeers and cackles hangs in the heavy August air. I peer down the concrete walkway and adjust my eyeglasses at the raucous gang of youths we've finally managed to separate from. They hoot again and I look away: mustn't reinforce such behaviour. My boys, I vow, doing another headcount and peering back at the hyenas' enclosure for stragglers, will grow up nothing like that. I open my mouth to shush them. Then I see them: foreheads pressed to the chain-link fence, noses sniffing the enclosure's faintly toilet odours, fingers threaded through. It's OK – all the lions, including this possibly homosexual couple, are lounging at the opposite side of the enclosure under the camel-toed leaves of a bauhinia. My students' eyes shine. Their stunted bodies wriggle. This is what they need: memories of fun in school to propel them to college. I shut my mouth.

Another cacophony. My boys run on after the gang of hooting youths to the next exhibit. I linger, shepherding stragglers: Vikesh and one more. Some of my boys are wearing paper caps fashioned from newspaper. Tiny, pointed, perched on their crowns, they offer no shade, only fun. *Why India's Runaway Food Inflation Is a Global Problem*, reads a headline on Vikesh's paper cap. I shepherd my stragglers onwards.

In their unfenced bamboo-and-scrub enclosure, four or five bears doze under the wide canopy of a flame-of-the-forest. It's in full flower, though it isn't supposed to be –

166

the seasons have got mixed up and so have the trees. The bears lounge with their backs to us, claws scratching at coarse fur, ears flicking at flies.

"Moonbear," Raghav reads from the placard nailed to the iron balustrade. *"Ursus thibetanus."* He giggles. "Oorsoos susu!" Eyes dancing, hip thrusting, he gestures at his shorts, mimes holding his penis going susu. He glances up, looks stricken, and cries, "Sorry, Akanksha-miss!"

I treat Raghav's lapse the same way I'm treating the gang of raucous youths.

Raghav's father is a manual scavenger. His mother cleans people's homes. They both only finished primary school. They live in the kind of slum I've often driven past, picturesque from the outside. On my visit to their tin-roofed, sewer-view shack, with scavenged Amazon boxes flattened for windowpanes, I struggled to avoid inhaling. Then his mother offered me tea. How does anyone keep anything down in that place?

Raghav's a weak student, playing restless book-cricket during Maths, energetic real cricket during recess. I've arranged for a psychometrician to come evaluate everyone's aptitudes, and a cricket talent scout.

"Akanksha-miss!" Raghav demands. "Why's it called moon bear? They're just black."

"They've got white moons on their chests," says Vikesh, studying the faded illustration on the green information board.

Vikesh's parents graduated tenth standard, but his autorickshaw-driver father died when he was two. Vikesh's mother sells flowers, coconuts, and incense sticks outside a temple, scraping together enough for their meals and his modest school fees. They live with her brother, at the mercy of her banshee sister-in-law. In the sunless second-storey backroom, in the tenement with peeling walls and endless clotheslines, the fair, round face of Vikesh's mother shone lamp-like at me across the old iron trunk that served as coffee table. Vikesh has his mother's eyes, hazel in a black-coffee skin, and her voice, too, low and vibrant. When Vikesh tells a story, everyone listens. He gets bored in class when I haven't had time to create advanced assignments for him, or when I can't call on him, busy with the other seventy. But he never misbehaves.

"Bears' marks don't look like moons really," says Anmol, studying the information board. "More like a V. A stretched-out V like a pussycat in the sun… Like motorbike lights, or a Rottweiler's frown, or, or Batman's logo. Should call them Batman bears!" We're still waiting for the bears to turn around and show us their Vs.

Anmol is an attentive but middling student. In Art class he makes drawings Picasso-like in originality if not in execution. Recess he spends on the swing set, belting out Taylor Swift hits in a strong, passably tuneful soprano. Anmol's family I haven't met yet.

This is my first year at Gottigere Government School and we're only three months in. Anmol's parents are next on my list. These children's parents are too shy, or too busy, to attend parent-teacher meetings. I've been visiting them unofficially: checking for any problems with their sons' education, offering help with scholarships, encouraging them to keep their sons in school. My colleagues tell me it's no use tiring myself out; I should settle down and enjoy life. Hmm, I reply. It's no use challenging settled adults – that I know.

Vikesh embraces the balustrade. "Maybe we can see their chests later."

"Wake up, moon bears! Deaf or what?" Raghav's voice pierces my eardrums. The other boys join in, banging on the balustrade.

I resist the urge to plug my ears. Here's another chance to discipline them. I don't hesitate to on campus, when they're cramped into our eighteen-by-fifteen-foot classroom, four to a bench. Out here, there're no colleagues to witness my failure. But, out here, I should still be performing a teacher's basic function. Vikesh stands back, plugging his ears, showing neither shame at his own sensitivity nor derision at his classmates.

It's one o'clock. We're barely halfway through the zoo; my boys must be back home by three. "Come, children, let's walk on!" I can raise my voice when I have to – I've learned how very spoiled some of the tenth-graders at Oasis are, sitting fifteen to a class in their Tommy Hilfiger tees and Levi's jeans, a new outfit every week – but even now, three years into teaching, I hate having to raise my voice.

My column of colourful, first-graders rolls leftwards down the balustrade in an irregular wave: boys jumping off, running forward, jumping back on at a less-crowded spot. It's OK: the bears are 200 feet away, separated from us by a dry moat paved with weed-covered, weed-split concrete stones. The moon bears are puttering away with their backs to us: brown snouts vacuuming larvae from inside bamboo stems, long copper claws scratching at date-stuffed enrichment logs, foam-speckled mouths chomping the banana-leaves piled near their artificial cave. One of the somnolent females must be in heat. A young male, standing on his hindlegs, cranes his neck, drawing an odour into his nostrils.

I've bent rules for this field trip. Normally the boys would be in uniform; I begged the principal for an exception. It's a half day, they won't be on campus, it's dusty and they'd soil their uniforms. It was this last appeal that worked – the principal has three sons. So my boys are in their playclothes: their very best thick-checked shirts and

169

faded blue jeans. Styles and fabrics that the rich cast off in 2009, my boys sport in 2022. And we've brought no second escort. They trusted me alone with the boys: maybe because of my high-flying background, maybe because it's Saturday and my colleagues all have children at home and no help.

Today I'm letting my boys set the pace. Five-and-a-half-days a week I watch them struggling to stay awake, chins heavying on slack palms, elbows slipping across plywood desks worn smooth, droning through lessons. This, today, I want them to see, this is education. Your parents are scrimping to send you to school. Pay them back: hunker down and graduate college.

Swaying amiably, the amorous moon bear male lumbers towards the dozing female. My boys cheer. The female rises and lifts her lip and stalks away. The male stands crestfallen. My boys jeer, and clap, and resume shouting at the bears to flash us their Vs. Neighbouring bears doze on. Is it to escape the heat or my boys' racket that they've got their backs to us, paws over snouts, eyes half-closed? Again my lesson in empathy surges up my throat. I don't know what the bears would be doing minus my boys' racket, I don't know how my boys would be minus me. My lesson sticks in my throat.

The female settles down further away with her back still to us. This is no coincidence: it's my boys who are exasperating the bears. My silence exasperates me. We came here to learn empathy, and here's a teachable moment, so why can't I speak up? Raghav climbs the fence. I rebuke him a little harshly. He apologises, looking surprised, and climbs down. They've no idea what they're doing, my heart's pounding with disappointment, time's running out. I glide behind my boys, head counting. One little newspaper hat is askew. *13 Lakh Candidates Appear for UPSC Prelims; Vacancies Shrink to 605*. I push the hat back up on the boy's crown. A little head whips around. A little face flashes me a shy smile.

The hapless male lumbers away, his mythical moon mark still hidden. My boys fling pleas and taunts after him. Raghav jumps off the fence, runs down the road, then runs back, screaming, "Hey, leave these waste fellows! Next is rhino!"

The boys run on; I linger with the stragglers. I've paid the bus driver to wait: let the boys take their time. Most of them live nearby – for them there's no commuting cross-town to the vast suburban campuses of IGCSE schools. But many of them, I discovered this morning, have never visited the zoo. Why haven't your parents brought them? I asked. The entry fee is nominal. They assured me they've got better things to do: Gameboys and such.

The concrete walkways radiate heat. Paunchy young couples, in dark jeans, breezy FabIndia cotton kurtas, and wide-brimmed straw hats, stroll hand-in-hand with young children. These are the people who get Saturdays off. They're barely in their 30s, but the women have wide bottoms and the men paunches from laptopping all day, fingers conveyer-belting junk food to lips. Their sunhats are from the stalls outside the zoo gates, tarpaulins spread on pavements. I picture them bargaining with the squatting sari-clad vendors, not because the hats are overpriced – they are, but *they* wouldn't know – but from their sense of duty to themselves. I picture them finally paying, grumblingly, the asked price: the price of an ordinary weekday home-delivery dinner for one.

But their children, I admit, are behaving beautifully. Keeping their feet on the ground, discussing the animals in soft voices. Maybe it's only because they're in ones or twos, with one or two adults per child. Or maybe they simply

171

aren't tempted to mischief. The children of the wealthy don't need to heckle zoo animals. They've got iPhones, tennis, heated outdoor pools, and actual Gameboys. I stroll onwards with my stragglers.

Greed is good, they told us; wealth is a virtue. They told us about the invisible hand of the market, which aligns magically that which happens with that which should happen. I didn't quite understand, but I thought, wiser minds than mine have worked it out. I believed them. I believed that to do well materially was magically to become good. Most adults are, after all, less wantonly cruel than children. And when a people becomes civilised, they do, after all, gain more than wealth. If we have no gladiator fights in 2022, it's partly because humanity, in growing up, has become kinder; but partly, too, because modern Italians are wealthier than ancient Romans, with more fulfilling jobs.

But the teens at Oasis spent recess playing blood-and-guts videogames and bombarding the latest cancelled celebrity with hateful tweets. Their parents, when I visited them, left their Dalmatians and fox terriers tied out in hot concrete yards and made zero eye contact with the maidservants who were tiptoeing about their condos, scrubbing their toilet bowls, doing their dishes half-full of food rotting overnight in the flooded sink.

Greed is good, they said. How good, good how, if doing well doesn't make you good?

At the next enclosure two rhinos are squaring off on the small, gently sloping concrete patch that separates their cage door from their muddy pond. "Fight! Fight!" Raghav pounds his fists on the railing. The metal rings and clangs. My boys huddle and crane, shrilly betting imaginary *lakhs* on the contestants, on Pink-Spots or Uneven-Horns, running here, squeezing through there for a view.

172

"Will they hurt each other?" Vikesh looks up at me. In his black-coffee face his green-gold eyes iridesce pity.

"Probably they'll just posture a bit," I venture. "Rhinos get stressed easily... Actually, most animals don't really like fighting. It's mostly for show." What if I'm wrong? I picture a rhino horn piercing a rhino side, dust and blood flying, my boys halting mid-whoop.

"Really?" says Anmol. "They look like tanks."

"Thick skins and soft hearts," another student offers idiomatically in Kannada.

The combatants paw the ground and make a few feints. Raghav climbs the fence again; I stand behind him, holding him back. Excitement glitters in his eyes, bloodlust maybe; his voice breaks from shouting. But it's all for show. Raghav's just poking the world, hoping to feel one bit of it pushing back, letting him know he's real.

That gang of youths whoops off to our left.

They were at the ticket booth with us: ten or twelve men in their 20s, stick thin, in acid-washed jeans and gaudy shirts, climbing each other's shoulders, grinning monkey-like. I hold my breath lest one of them should turn out to be brother to one of my boys. How did *they* get Saturday off? Lousy layabouts.

Let the gang rush on far ahead – then I'll command my boys' attention and talk about empathy. Doing well in life won't automatically make them good people, I know that now. I've got to work on both separately. I rub my hands, scheduling a trip to IISc's shiny Aerospace Engineering lab, and another to Kidwai Children's Cancer Hospital. My boys will grow up good, unable to find pleasure in heckling zoo animals. And they will do well, have engaging jobs and equal marriages: they won't need to heckle anyone. I glide behind them, touching their backs, letting them know someone's watching. Vikesh stands back, ears plugged, watching maybe the rhinos, maybe his classmates.

173

Vikesh asks excellent questions in Science: his logical reasoning is at least three years advanced; he's at least moderately gifted. Physicist? Philosopher? But he's got plenty of time to choose. The real problem will be his mother. She's terrified living in that neighbourhood that erupts in the middle of the night in a shrieking woman, a yelping dog, a man blind with rage. She wants Vikesh to get a job after school. I'll help her move into an affordable place. And Anmol should be in the choir: I'll speak to the principal about letting me organise one. And Raghav has too much energy: he should be playing cricket after school, not minding his twin baby brothers. I picture his shack, his mother with the hunted eyes, his sullen father. They won't want their son risking everything for a career in sports. He can study sports medicine in college as a backup, or get a gym-trainer's certificate. Every two-penny gym has a trainer now.

It's been a long standoff, a stalemate, but now one rhino paws at the concrete floor, takes a short runup, lowers his horns, and waits. His antagonist holds his ground. My boys cheer deafeningly. Raghav climbs another rail up the fence. I tap his shoulder; he climbs down without apologising, without noticing, without interrupting his "hurrahs". Still I hesitate to discipline them. Still I don't know why. When I hesitated in demo classes during B.Ed., it was because I hoped to approach the children as equals. But I was twenty-one then, and naïve.

One rhino glances towards us. The other flicks his tiny ears. Can they see us, or are they short-sighted? Can they hear us – are my boys goading them over the edge?

A lion's roar earthquakes subsonically through our ribcages and crescendos, making my heart race, confronting me with the world's essential wildness. A chorus of whoops answers the roar. The gang of young men runs back past us,

174

past the lions' enclosure, shouting in Tamil. It's Vikesh who tells me what's up: a straggler friend has texted the other young men that the lion's roar has awoken the tigress, who's been dozing disappointingly all morning.

Raghav jumps off the fence. "Finally we can see Tigress's face!" I grab after him, too late – he's run off, taking half my class with him.

I stand stupidly, picturing the tigress, who has no mate, who has one narrow fifty-meter strip of grass to pace up and down in, pacing neurotically, dozing lethargically, isolated from the world by a grassy moat on one side, a green-painted fence on the other. Now my boys are going to hoot and whistle at her for ten minutes. I picture taking Raghav by the elbow – not roughly as my colleagues would, just roughly enough to get through to him. If you've got so much energy, Raghav, you're staying back after school to work on maths. D'you want your father cleaning toilets forever? I hurry after my boys, resolved at last to administer the lesson we've come here to learn.

A young man hastens up the concrete path towards us, peering here and there. He must be with that atrocious gang. He's in a new shirt too, a polka-dotted white shirt still shop creased.

He meets my eyes. He nods hello. It takes me a moment to recognise Prayas, the head clerk at my local mobile phone shop. I'm always disoriented, seeing someone in an unfamiliar context. But he's unmistakable, really. A scar runs up his left cheek, smooth and pale. His left eye is missing, the eye socket scarred over. Before I can return his greeting, he's jogged away towards the tigress. I must've embarrassed him by accidentally cutting him off. He's gone, now, gone before I can return his nod, he's breaking into a run, preemptively whooping, his size-zero, slim-fit jeans sagging about his bottom. He's passed close to me, leaving the stink of male sweat hybridised with the squashed-cockroach stink of cheaply dyed, unwashed cotton. This must be his first day off in months.

Prayas is always there, across the street from my second-storey window, in the street corner shop. At 8 a.m. and 8 p.m., weekday and weekend, I've watched him: fitting phones into protective cases, selling headsets, photographing for government records customers buying new SIMs, taking orders for batteries and rubber cases, going over accounts with the motorbike-helmeted supplier. I chatted with him a lot last summer, when my phone broke: first the touchscreen, then other parts. He listened to my rants with therapist-grade empathy.

As our suburban neighbourhood has grown, Yatharth Mobiles has expanded its staff. After five years there, Prayas has become head clerk. But sometimes he mans the counter alone. One evening, I found the counter unattended. Waiting, I noticed the A5 notebook. It was open to a pen-and-ink portrait. No DeviantArt hack-job, this, with cookie-cutter pretty face and Manga body, but a real woman: with jowls, flaring nostrils, eyes in which pain was maturing reluctantly into wisdom, and C-section scars over her prodigious bush. I turned the notebook around and turned the pages. Faces, life-wounded. Empty green lots, littered with plastic. Skyscrapers radiating heat, the glass shiny and opaque. All seen unflinchingly and drawn compassionately, but Prayas had signed only some of them.

Gently someone cleared their throat. I put the notebook down and faced Prayas with new pain, pain again, as I had when I'd first seen him with his scar. He helped me like always: unhurried and thorough, articulate but wasting no words.

That evening I chatted with him. He'd graduated secondary school, he told me. He'd planned to attend college, like his older brother Niraash. But Niraash failed to find a decent job, got "in trouble", and now he's clerking at the same shop. Prayas is thirty-five, still saving money to marry, already by the standards of his milieu a hopeless bachelor.

A woman brushes past me, trailing cotton voile and pungent sandalwood perfume, drowning Prayas's stink. I stare down the blazing concrete path after Prayas. Another one of my boys abandons the rhinos and runs after the gang.

And Raghav, and Anmol, and maybe even Vikesh – whatever I may do, whatever they may do, they'll be lucky even to get a job as good as Prayas's. Things aren't getting better. Uncertified colleges are mushrooming, relieving the poor of their life savings for a degree that will prove worthless. And graduating a state school is hardly better than being illiterate. And the rags-to-riches stories are becoming a billion-to-one.

What right have I, then, to take away whatever entertainment my boys have, whatever ways of prodding the world? I'd be Randle McMurphy, from *Cuckoo's Nest*, telling the insane to break their flickering incandescent lights, pointing them to the sun. I'd have glass-slitted throats on my conscience, and broken Icarus bodies.

My temples pound. The blinding midday radiance blackens. I can't breathe. Have I already done irreparable harm?

Into my hand steals another hand, small and warm. I look down into Vikesh's eyes, wide and unsmiling. And I, too, resist the urge to smile.

I remember my boys in class: struggling to stay awake, chins heavying on slack palms, elbows slipping across plywood desks worn smooth, droning through lessons. Maybe they've already realised that happiness is for the fat folks in beribboned sunhats, that crayons and cricket bats are toys that children like them must outgrow. I picture

177

them in fifteen years: idling at street corners, hooting at women, leaning over zoo railings, heckling graceless moon bears and possibly homosexual lions, all of whom are getting more sex than they perhaps will ever get, and leaning over too far.

My vision clears. The sun still shines. Let empathy come in its own time, empathy in whatever dose their life accommodates.

My stragglers are still clinging to the rhino's fence, still hoping. But the rhinos have forgotten their quarrel and stand facing each other, looking statuesque and stupid, half in the muddy pond, half on the concrete. This, now: this is the real stalemate.

"Come, children. Let's go back and see the tigress." The others run off; I put my arm around Vikesh's shoulder. An electric zoo-cart zooms past us and stops ahead, offloading a party of middle-aged women in neon-pink-and-yellow Gujarati saris.

"I pity them," says Vikesh in Kannada.

"Why?" I glance back at the rhinos. "They look healthy, and they settled their differences peacefully."

"I mean my classmates," he says gravely. I look down at him. He's a good student: he doesn't need to brown-nose me. But some of these children are prematurely wise, forging alliances with adults, approaching life with an adult's foresight. "Akanksha-miss, why don't you stop them from teasing the animals?"

The empty cart moves on, purring. The gouty women labour up the path towards us. Vikesh and I walk on. "Let them enjoy themselves," I reply, jogging his shoulder.

RETREAT

I survey my painting of the snow-covered peak of Kanchenjunga. I'll finish it this week. Gritting my teeth, I hustle into my blazer. Female faculty, but not male, must wear blazers. I fill my mind with thoughts of snow and grasp for grace to get through my day.

"Bye," I call, rushing across the drawing-room.

"It looks like rain. Have you got your raincoat, Pragya?" Pa's voice is muffled behind his PM-95 mask. He's been searching for a book. His bookshelf is slightly dusty and his nose highly rhinitis-prone.

"Cross the roads very carefully," Ma calls from the kitchen, pausing her breathing exercises. "Traffic is so crazy; these days anyone could just hit you and drive away."

"Alright," I mutter, shutting the front door. My shoes half-on, I hasten down the second-floor corridor. Sometimes my parents remember more dangers to warn me against, and call them out the door.

I stand at the corner hailing autorickshaws. Many are ferrying schoolchildren, plastic sacks full of produce, five-litre gas cylinders, or the drivers' wives holding stacked egg-trays bound for grocers. Ola and Uber now dominate the market, with prices so low that I wonder how they pay for fuel, never mind service. To make ends meet, autorickshaw drivers who're not online moonlight as tiny delivery-vans. But some drivers still can't be bothered: three empty autos pass me by, refusing to go so short a distance. They're still living in the pre-globalised Bangalore of extortionist autorickshaw prices.

Under my blazer, sweat prickles my neck. I've got my raincoat alright, but the rain's been holding off and it's phenomenally muggy. There was a power cut, and neither the flat-complex's generator nor our private inverter

179

powers the AC: I've barely slept. My temper rises with my temperature. "Cross carefully" – as if I were a child!

I thought it'd be nice to move back home, far from the mid-city bustle, but my parents are too much. It's alright for them to coddle themselves: with late breakfasts of whole wheat toast with smidgens of jam or butter, socks and mufflers if the temperature dips below 25°C, and a dust-mask habit far predating Covid. But I need to get away from this bourgeois mollycoddling. I need a little risk and new scenes to paint.

At university it's business-as-usual. When I began my teaching career in December, my colleagues advised me to enforce strict discipline: phones face down on the desk, laptops shut, pin-drop silence. But fresh from my PhD, and no fan of sitting still and listening myself, I gave my students leeway. I dreamed of demonstrating the effectiveness of democratic classrooms. Six months in, the whole back half of this class of ninety eighteen-year-olds spends all hour chattering. The students at the front, straining to hear, glance reproachfully over their shoulders at their football-hooligan classmates.

I whine a plea for silence, leavened with a smile. The noise ebbs briefly before deafening me afresh. I stumble through the hour anyhow: I figure it's my job to teach and theirs to listen. I pity these young people, away for the first time from cloistering parents and martinet teachers, overburdened with academics and extracurriculars. And sometimes, a tiny bit, I want to murder them.

I've got to find another job.

After classes, unable to work, waiting for sign-out time, I try to nap in my cabin. I'm exuding heat from every pore. The heat churns my lunch in my stomach.

These days even a cart-pushing vegetable-vendor accepts Google Pay, even for tiny sums, but the autorickshaw driver I approach to drive me home is elderly, so I ask whether he accepts online payment. He shakes his head.

"Then d'you have change for Rs.100?"

He nods.

He wants Rs.70; I tell him I pay Rs.60 every day, up from Rs.50 since the Ukraine war began. He nods at the backseat; we set off. Elderly drivers drive slower. Maybe it's because they can't see the road too well; maybe it's because they've seen too much.

I study him in the rear-view mirror. His skin is greyish under his grizzled beard and his grey eyes are restless. He looks like he lives on tea and cigarettes. His khaki uniform is mottled grey-brown. He scratches his chin with his inch-long index fingernail. I've watched television: I know what one long fingernail means. I wonder what he wanted to be when he was a child. I look away.

It's the peak of monsoon but the lake shows not a sliver of water: it's covered with water hyacinth. I wonder if the people who built these little, odd-shaped, too-bright houses knew that in ten years the lake would be dry, ringed by towering condo complexes, stinking with rubbish, covered with weeds, and patrolled by Nike-clad joggers as numerous and uniform as ants. I look away.

On my phone I scroll through Google Images photos of Kanchenjunga. I'm basing my painting on my own photos from midwinter, but it helps to have different views. Kanchenjunga still looks as though human beings never existed.

"If you don't have change, sir," I say, as we pass the streetful of shops, "we can get it here."

I call everyone "sir" – it's nice to be polite. They don't always call you "madam", but that's ignorance rather than rudeness. The younger drivers, who know smidgens of English, are more polite: but they drive down the narrow high-traffic streets like motorsport racers in a walled-off arena. I'll take grouchy over daredevil.

"I have change," the autorickshaw driver mutters.

I stop him at the private street leading to the flat-complex's gate. I never make drivers go all the way. I produce my Rs.100. He produces Rs.20. I wait for him to produce Rs.20 more. He pats his breast-pocket perfunctorily, then shrugs.

"Sir, you said you had change." I'm speaking Hindi, though I'm only fluent in English. His Hindi is broken too: his first language is probably Kannada or Tamil. He shrugs again, as if I'd asked him for a pen, holds out his Rs.20, and beckons for my Rs.100.

Is he dishonest, or atrocious at arithmetic? "I'm paying Rs.60, not Rs.80. Please give me Rs.20 more," I enunciate. Perhaps he's just senile.

"How can I give if I don't have?" he shouts.

I purse my lips and shake my head. I find Rs.50 in my purse and offer him that: Rs.50 is closer than Rs.80 to the fare we agreed on. He glares as if I've blasphemed Brahma. "You're cheating me!" he cries. "You pay full money."

"I'm trying to pay full money," I enunciate. "I told you we could stop for change."

"What stop for change, where would we have stopped?" His grey eyes blaze and his thin, tanned arms wave as he gesticulates.

"At any of the shops." He's in the wrong, and I long to thrust the Rs.50 into his hand and walk away, but that would put me in the wrong. "If you'd stopped anywh—"

"What shops? What shops would give change? Nobody gives change." He jerks his hand, fingers taut, signifying "nothing doing".

"What! I get change from shops all the time." So do autorickshaw drivers: I see them all the time. "You didn't even check if—"

182

"What check?" he shouts. "You're supposed to pay. You pay!" He gestures again at my Rs.100 note. I put it back in my wallet. He goes into a frenzy. "You pay! I brought you all the way here!"

Suddenly I'm tired of being interrupted and bullshitted and lied to and I shout with all my might, my voice instantly breaking, "What 'all the way'? It's three kilometres and you're already overcharging. I wanted to Google Pay you, everyone accepts online payment now, but you don't. Fine. I asked you before I got on if you had change for Rs.100, and you said yes. Fine. I said we could stop for change at the shops, and you said no need. Fine! Now you want me to pay Rs.80 when we agreed on Rs.60. You take this" – I hold out the Rs.50 – "or you get nothing."

My ears blaze. My fists tense for contact with his grizzled cheek. I'm radiating heat like Vesuvius ready to blow the world apart. I've been working on anger management: it's been years since I had a good rage.

The autorickshaw driver recoils. "You're crazy," he mutters. I stride away up the private street towards the front gate. "You're mad!" I'm too furious to reply. He follows me, driving a foot behind. I stride ahead, swallowing my fear. What'll he do: run me over at 5km/hour in this rickety vehicle? Engage me in fisticuffs? I go to the gym: I'll lay his rickety ass out flat. He follows me to the gate, shouting, "You're mad."

I enter. I hear the security guard stopping him. Relief floods me: I'm safe from this madman now. If he'd been civil, I would've borrowed Rs.10 from the security guard – but now screw him. He stands shouting beside his auto. I avoid the stares of the security guards, washerman, and housekeeping staff. Let him shout. Calling people mad is the only relief for people like that: a hollow, carnival relief.

I take the steps two at a time, trembling with anger. I mumble greetings to my parents, who're lounging over their late lunch, watching the news, bad news all day. I shut myself in my room and turn on the AC. The heat recedes from my mind, freeing it to think. I picture the old ass standing there making a scene. The security guards might ring us. That wouldn't be nice.

I replenish my wallet and stride downstairs. The autorickshaw driver stands silently at the gate, arms folded. The security guard watches as I hand over Rs.60 without a word or look. The driver takes it silently. I climb back one step at a time and shut myself in again. My anger has vapourised my tiredness. That fool did me a favour! Without him I would've needed a nap; now I'm wide-awake. I take another bath and lie bare skinned on the cool floor. Relief floods me. When I'm feeling human again I work on my Kanchenjunga painting.

My parents and I visited the Himalayas last winter. They took a car all the way: a chaperoned, slow-paced, swaddled affair. Our final two days I left them to their hot tea and multiple mufflers and local friends, walked up the foothills, and stood studying Kanchenjunga's snow-covered peak. I'm doing it in oils from a composite of two photographs: one of the snow at sunset, dyed a hundred oranges, another of an eagle flying just before me, blocking half the mountain. I focus on the texture of the snow.

The day's heat retreats beyond my closed windows. I go say hello to my parents.

Ma's watching the news while doing her Sudoku. She looks up; I stroke her grey hair; we chat about our day. Today's Sudoku is moderately difficult: three out of five stars are filled in. On the coffee table where Ma rests her legs sits a paper-clipped pile of Sudokus, snipped from many editions of The Hindu. Over the course of the day, in between watching the news and reading it, she revisits old Sudokus and fills in the occasional digit. She tried to teach me once, telling me Sudoku builds patience; I muffled my yawns and offered to get her a Sudoku app; she declined to have any more apps: WhatsApp was enough. I watch her studying today's Sudoku, resting her pen on the square she wants to solve. Often she can't, and the pen leaves a dot marking her failure. But she never gives up. Her pile of puzzles, filled in in red, black, and blue, grows thick.

Ma had to quit her PhD midway when Pa got transferred. And then I was born and then my brother. Decades later, she's begun doing Sudoku to sharpen her mind. Her head is bent as in prayer, her eyes are quiet, and her pen awaits divine inspiration. The life Ma has built herself, or anyway has accepted, consists of household chores, 24/7 news channels, and cooking shows. Her red velvet diary is full of recipes she's never cooked.

As I watch, her pen doesn't move at all. Perhaps the mind refuses to be sharper than it needs to be. I stroke her head and stroll away.

Pa's in the bathroom on his after-lunch long visit to the "temple". Pa calls himself an aggressive atheist in a nation mired in superstition and groupthink. But this scatological nomenclature for number two is the extent of his aggressiveness. I knock and tell Pa I enjoyed his latest article in *The Wire*.

"Thanks, Pragya." Through the door Pa tells me about his latest admirer: a professor at Salamanca University who read Pa's retrospective last month on Goya. A college communist, Pa spent forty years working for a bank; now that he's retired, he's pursuing his vocation as a cultural commentator. But forty years of abusing antacids have caught up with him: he splits his time between his laptop and his "temple".

185

Dicing vegetables for dinner, my mind turns from Kanchenjunga's tranquillity to this afternoon's incident. It seems far away, as a mountain does unless you're on it, and sometimes even then. As I strode upstairs, I worried the driver might resume his shouting match, or knock me over, when we crossed paths in the neighbourhood later. But I'm as safe in here, and going out from here, as if I were up on Kanchenjunga.

Waiting for the oil to heat up I gaze out the window. He's an old man ferrying strangers all day: he must've forgotten he didn't have enough change, felt too sullen to check, and then felt too terrified of losing Rs.10 to confess his error. Poor old man. You were furious because you knew you were wrong. I forgive you.

But I don't regret shouting. If you're always softspoken, people exploit you. As I add *methi* and *saunf* seeds to the oil, I make up my mind to do what I've been shilly-shallying about.

From tomorrow I'll enforce discipline. Any student who chatters persistently will lose their attendance. Marks and attendance are the only language the back half speaks. I've tried speaking my language; now I'll speak theirs. My colleagues tell me I have authority in my classroom. Why have I resisted exercising it?

I stir-fry the eggplant and bell peppers, wondering if the driver too has got over this afternoon. Has he got a painting to finish, memories of travel to relish, the season's best vegetables to fry up? And my job is, after all, quite nice – a cosy cabin, and young people calling me "ma'am" all day. Probably the autorickshaw driver is still longing to kill me, battering his wife instead, his wife who's even frailer than him. Too many people share his shack: nobody has a room of their own to get away to. He will not forgive me so easily and it doesn't matter.

186

I sniff the roasting eggplant. Outside the kitchen window the blazing sky darkens with thunderclouds. I bring in the clothes drying on the balcony and settle down to watch the downpour.

HOLIDAY

"Can we really stay awake for four days, Vegu?" says Manisha. "Will we even enjoy it?"

Four days, two of which we're spending on the train. We mustn't miss one minute. "Ready, set, go!" I cry. Together we empty our two-gramme sachets down our throats. Bru instant coffee face-punches us awake.

Manisha smiles deferentially at the aunty who's frowning from across the aisle: stomach-rolls sagging over *sari* waistband, bellybutton scowling at the obscenity of a boy and a girl, flank-to-flank in the semi-public place of an AC two-tiered compartment. The aunty looks away. If this moral-policing grouch knew the struggle I've had with Manisha, the struggle that still lies ahead, she'd crow in her harpy heart.

We're halfway to Gorakhpur. It's time for magic: for these four days to stretch into four years and coil up into one second.

We climb to our top berths. I sip the *bhang*, discreetly, though we're still in Uttar Pradesh and *bhang*'s legal here. The rosewater *lassi* cloaks the *bhang*'s earthy odour. I offer Manisha a cupful. She looks sceptical. Dosage is tricky with edibles. The last time Manisha tried *bhang*, at Holi in tenth standard, back in Bareilly with her cousins, she had too much and got a panic attack. As she narrated the story, in our second year of BSc, I struggled to picture her out of control. I've only ever known Manisha as the maturest person in any room: in lecture halls, in the union-room where student representatives bargain with the Vice Chancellor's people, or in the dingy hotel room in Allahabad where we've done things. Some things. Not everything. Every consent has been a hard-won victory. On this trip I, too, will finally get to see Manisha out of control. I'm doing this for her. It's only coincidence – or is it caffeine – that makes my dick somersault.

"Trust me," I whisper. "I've been careful with the mixing, and I'll track your dosing." I need her in the sweet spot.

She throws her head back and shuts her eyes. My pulse races. Surely she'll pinch her nose before she drinks. She probably won't smell it anyway. If she does I'll say it's just a different strain. Yes! She pinches and doesn't unpinch it till she's drained the cup and chased it down with water.

Four days. One day getting to Nepal, two days in Pokhara, one day getting back – back to Allahabad University, to pack up before hostels close for the summer. Then Manisha will go home to her parents in Bareilly, and I'll spend a month in Moradabad being a dutiful son before leaving for my M.S. at Caltech. This is what Manisha thinks will happen.

"My head is swimming, Avegh." She's facing me inches away. Her eyes are swimming a thousand miles away. "I'd be scared if you weren't here."

Tucked with her under the compartment's musty cream-coloured ceiling, behind cover of our backpacks, I slip an arm around her. "I'll always be here." Her neck slackens and her head drops into the crook of my neck.

Nepal is 500 kilometres from anyone we know. Our SIM cards won't work there, and Manisha's agreed not to bother with short-term SIMs. I'm holding on to our return tickets, our passports, and our money. If we'd needed visas, I'd be holding on to those too. This is my first trip abroad. Hers, too.

"Vegu," Manisha murmurs, her words slurring, her voice resonating through her skull and tickling my throat, "it's been wonderful these three years." She looks up at me, the angle strange, her eyes looking squinty as they gaze into my soul. "Whatever happens, you should know—"

"Yes, I know!" I interrupt, dusting my jeans. "Hey, why don't you tell me about prions again?"

"No-oo! No lecture." But her protest is playful and her pout is ready, willing, begging to be persuaded. This isn't the *bhang* – that'll take an hour to kick in. This is an empty stomach and a deliberate surrender of self-control. I squeeze her waist.

"Really, no lecture?" I tease.

We've never been stoned together, but whenever we drink together, she lectures. It's Manisha who's tutored me, exam after exam, these three years of BSc Zoology. It's Manisha who's made me unashamed of my own bookishness. I'm still slow to grasp a concept, and even then I need all my digits to keep hold of it, stranded on the ground, clutching at grass, squinting up at Manisha as she darts spiderlike down the gossamer line of reasoning pitched between two big-idea cliffs.

"Yes, lecture," I say, bopping her nose.

I'm watching her battling – has it already been an hour? – *bhang*'s tongue-loosening effects. Suddenly it's me who's high. You watch yourself, and watch yourself, but it's always when you're not looking that your brain flashes from ice to water vapour.

"Fine!" Wrists on ribs, she steeples her fingertips. "A prion is a misfolded protein. What do we mean by misfolding? Every protein has a correct shape..." She mouths the word. "What a weird word. Shay-pay. Shay-pee? Sshaaa-peee!" She giggles, recovers, resumes lecturing, then sinks back helplessly giggling.

She keeps sitting up and trying to lecture, giggling, falling back, and trying again. The *bhang*'s taken her memory away. Without memory standing over you, taunting you for failing, you can just keep trying. Do children have poor memory, I wonder. Is that what lets children be children? Manisha's speech fragments. I etch into my soul her voice low and vibrant. I memorise her smooth cheeks with the one black mole, her dark curls with that one white strand at the front that she won't pluck. I memorise Manisha while she's still whole.

The train rocks as it passes over a switch. *Bhang*'s knife descends again. My skin peels away and spills me all out into the world: like the seeds of a pomegranate, which no ingenuity can ever put back, neat, numerous, and nestling.

Wheat farms and mango orchards rush by. June sun glares in through the two-paned window below. Aunty glares up from her lower berth across the corridor. Poor sex-starved soul, trying to protect a fellow female from sex. Manisha's head lolls on my shoulder. Her eyes close. Her breath tickles my ear.

From down the daylit road the giant stone frog of our future stares at us, plain to Aunty, plain to anyone who's got eyes. Manisha has brought this on herself. Does she not see what's coming? How stupid can a smart person be? *Look*, I want to shout. I keep mum.

I'm a paper kite, high in the sky. My master has cut my string. Still I can feel, just barely, the ground beneath my feet. I keep mum. Soon Manisha's resistance will be gone, all awareness gone. One premature move would ruin everything.

"Open your mouth," I whisper. I close Manisha's fingers around the sachet and guide it to her lips. "Coffee."

"No! No more sucky coffee," she lisps, pouting.

"Darling, you mustn't fall asleep." That would be fatal. "You were telling me about prions!"

"No prions. I sleep!"

"Here, take this." If Aunty weren't watching, I'd open Manisha's mouth for her.

"Me pukey!" She's hamming it up, like a bad actress

191

auditioning to play a sleep talker. "Vay-goo! I've never been high like this."

"Just pinch your nose again, and don't let it touch your tongue." Her face is lax with sleepiness, strained with the frown of an impending headache. It goes like an arrow through me to have to do this to my beloved.

Women: you don't know what it's like. Your libido is like the hunger of a sofa-slouching patrician: hardly roused, easily sated. You don't know what it's like to want someone in your bones. We live in a civilised world. We don't let people die of hunger or cold. You tell us sex, too, is a human need. Then you let us go without it, sometimes our whole lives. Is a human being not entitled to fulfil a human need?

Her eyes still closed, Manisha contemplates with frowning brows and wrinkling nose a second dose of Bru. Then she opens her eyes, and without looking at the sachet or its contents, without moving her eyes from mine, she empties it on her dahlia-pink tongue, swallows hard, then shows me her tongue, coffee-crinkled and brown-black.

She does, I realise, she does see the stone frog. She's walking towards it open-eyed.

"Good girl," I whisper. The tracks rock the train, *bhang* rocks our bodies, the world darkens and slips away.

We're off the train and now this bus will take us all the way from Gorakhpur to Pokhara, but at the border they make us disembark and cross on foot. The khaki-uniformed woman checks our passports, glances at our bags, and waves us on. So this is how a national border looks: flat ground, irregularly paved; tourists streaming, coming and going; the air thick with dust and diesel from buses idling on the other side, awaiting their passengers. When we reembark the bus at 4 p.m., we've been up thirty hours.

I'm drifting, freed from the world and my body, through time, time freed from the tedium of linearity, linearity playing four-dimensional hopscotch. Finally I'm seeing everything as it is. Who knows how much of this is from sleep deprivation after exams week, how much from *bhang*, and how much from the X-ray-vision glasses my plan has wrapped around my eyes.

Up the mountain roads, top-speeding through one hairpin bend after another, climbs our little bus, with its thirty-odd passengers, plus eight sitting in the driver's glass cockpit. Our empty stomachs free-fall like, mountaineers dropping off the cliff; in this lurching hollowness, our thoughts form brilliantly and dissipate instantly, like St. Elmo's fire. Here we are, in the mountains, in another country, and we've financed our own holiday, with our stipends scrimped all year. And it's blue and green, and clear air, and a pit of nausea somewhere outside our bodies throbbing, growing, looming.

Manisha suffers in silence, hands clutching the seatback before her, forehead rolling on knuckles. She raises her head. She doesn't need to ask me – I'm already groping in my backpack. I hand her half a lime. She doesn't need to ask me how I knew. She knows. I'm not nauseous now; it isn't my nausea I was feeling, I never get nauseous except from musk-melon. But there's no longer her body and my body. There's one body, one nausea. I wedge half a lime between my own incisors and lean back and face our common nausea. Does closing your eyes help, I wonder. Note to self: when you're high to the roots of your hair, avoid hairpin bends.

Separate bodies, separate consciousnesses – *bhang* shows you that's all an illusion. Odd, isn't it, how you know that it's your experience now, when the ground under your feet is that gold-white, cloud pile over the next mountain, way over there, right here, that is the truth? *Bhang* exposes reality for a poorly wrought magic trick: one poke, and the plywood sides clatter off the saw-a-woman-in-half box.

When did dusk fall? I look up at the lights on the ceiling. They don't come on. "Mostly he'll keep them off," says my neighbour across the aisle, "to save a little diesel."

Turns out my neighbour's a Bihari. We chat. Then someone rings him. Hello, he says, hello-hello, he keeps saying for an hour. I realise I've had too much myself, trying to keep Manisha company, trying to nerve myself. Night descends. Manisha's still studiously sucking her lime.

I wait for the streetlights to come on. I peer left and right and realise there are no streetlights. The hairpin bends get tighter. The bus climbs faster. It's mostly locals on our bus: small-towners with bright clothes and eyes bright from a book-free, screen-free existence. Maybe to keep himself awake, the driver blasts the radio: a woman singing melodies sickly sweet in an ear-piercing falsetto.

Why do we subcontinentals want women to sound like infants? Manisha's got me into Skunk Anansie, Against Me, and Jinjer. Three years in and I can no longer stomach conventional music's falsetto cries-for-help from Rapunzel in the tower. These Nepalese songs, with their melodies desperately cheerful, nails on blackboard na-na-na-na-na-naahing reality, pierce my eardrums for hours, for weeks, till I'm ready to scream. My fellow passengers are chatting, napping, sitting back, finger-tapping along.

Manisha sits slumped in her window-seat to my right. I keep stroking her ear, pulling her hair, tickling her chin to keep her awake. This is a tourist country. There were lots of Europeans on the other buses. Nobody frowned at their public displays of affection. My hand rests on her flushed cheek. She puts her hand over mine. It looks like I've slapped her, made her flush, and her hand is embracing my

194

slapping hand. "You'll always have me, Vegu," she whispers, "either way."

"Hush." I take my hand away.

She raises her head. Is it the lime that's made her face so strange? Where did the lime go? I didn't see her spit it out. Her lips move. I put my ear to her mouth. "Is that one song that's playing on loop?" she mutters. "It's so loud, it's multiplying my nausea exponentially. I can't even sleep."

"Don't sleep," I plead. "You'll wake up horribly groggy."

"If the music goes on I'll throw up and then sleep."

Clutching seatbacks, swinging in the aisle like a ragdoll from the gallows, I stumble up to the driver. Nepalese only sounds like Hindi, but I manage to make him understand. He turns the volume down. Manisha's face slackens. She looks like she could sleep now. But she doesn't make me have to remind her again. Her eyes keep fluttering open.

Without warning, in the middle of nowhere, we halt. The driver turns off the engine, plunging us into pitch black. I hear him hopping out of his seat and off the bus. Do these buses have driver relays, I wonder, and it hurtles past us, missing Manisha's window by two inches, making Manisha gasp, making me throw both my arms around her as we sit – another bus, headlights dimmed, interior pitch black. The other bus speeds downhill, plunging us back into pitch-black night and pin-drop silence. I'm wide awake, still leaning across Manisha, and my heart is a fist choking my throat. What the hell is happening? And why's everyone sitting still like sheep on the final train?

The minutes pass. I squeeze my eyes. Still I can't shake off the afterimage of Manisha's face, in that half-second, in the headlights of the other bus: eyes blown open, lips clamped.

Nobody's getting on or off the bus. I can hear my own eyelids blinking. Far above us, perhaps, the stars are twinkling. The mountain air chills the sweat on my face.

Three men, muffled to their eyes, flashlights between their teeth, board the bus, throw sacks down on the floor, disembark, and fetch more. Soon the aisle is packed with plastic-netting sacks red, yellow, and blue. The Bihari has sunk into his seat. Manisha and I sit motionless with eyes down. My thighs are clammy, maybe with sweat, maybe with urine. I pass both arms around Manisha. Nobody will touch her. Not while I'm alive.

The driver leaps back into his seat. The bus engine growls to a start, deafening, right here inside my chest. We race up the mountain, round and round. I can no longer hear people breathing. Is everyone holding their breath? I huddle my feet up, away from the sacking, I want to scream and jump out the window. But what if I'm hallucinating?

I clamp my mobile-phone between both hands and turn on its flashlight. The light glowing red between my fingers is just enough to see by, to pick at the nearest yellow sack nearest my feet in the aisle. The netting is two or three layers thick. My fingers break through. Something pokes out, glowing whitish in the dark. It's tubular, soft, and hairy. A shudder runs from my fingertips up my neck, up my scalp, down my other cheek. It's not too late. I could still back away. I keep picking at the plastic netting. The soft warm thing falls into my hand. I bring it up to my face.

A radish.

Narrow as a newborn's wrist, the tail-end scant-haired as a newborn's scalp. Manisha's giggle breaks the silence. She squeezes my shoulders. "And you thought it was dead-body parts!" she whispers.

Roused by Manisha's hooting, the driver finally turns on the ceiling lights, dim blue-and-red LEDs. The bus screeches to a halt. Three passengers disembark. We hurtle on. I blink, disoriented by the lights, and by my own terror:

terror I realised had been building only after it burst in my face like a pricked balloon.

"Well, what did *you* think it was?" I growl. My shock has jolted me sober and annoyed at myself.

She shrugs. "All I thought was, if they're going to kill us, trapped here like this, then it would be wiser not to resist." Her hand rests on my shoulder, stroking my neck, the fondness in her eyes naked. She chuckles. "Silly balloon man, scared of a radish! You always made me laugh."

How did she know about the balloon that burst? Even in our shared *bhang* womb she's got no business knowing that. I lean away from her intoxicated rubbish talk.

Manisha and I never discussed getting married, but after three years I just assumed we would. We're from different castes. But we would've made it alright. After all, our parents do want us to be happy, don't they? This February, Manisha told me her parents have selected a groom and her wedding's in October.

We were lounging over lunch on the university lawn, under the peepul-tree with its glossy needle-pointy leaves rustling, when she told me. I sat gasping, like when my brother used to sneak up and punch me in the kidneys. I used to think he was a psychopath, but he's twenty-four now, a decent person, I sat there thinking, irrelevantly, gaping at Manisha.

"Tell your parents about me," I said at last, my voice floating out like a ghost from a cave. "Take me home. Introduce me. Tell them it's me you love. We'll prostrate ourselves and bathe their feet with tears. Or, better yet, let's elope."

She laughed at me. I ranted and raved. How long had she been hiding this from me? Finding a suitable groom takes time. Eligible candidates must've been dropping by for months on her weekend visits home. I stormed off and we didn't speak for a month.

I gave up. I rang her. I grovelled. "OK," she said, "I forgive you. But let's not make ourselves unhappy in what time we've got left." And I haven't said a word about it since.

So here we are. This trip abroad will wrench Manisha free from the fears of a conventional upbringing. Coffee will keep us up all four days. *Bhang* and sleep deprivation, combined, will melt time's chain-link into a steel-glittering rivulet, will make these four days run together, will open us up like two branches slashed open to graft together. And the alcohol, which I've secretly added to the *bhang lassi*, will potentiate all these effects of the THC.

Now that she's stoned, she'll want to have sex, to go all the way. Sex while stoned is transformative. But my plan transcends the physical.

Manisha's already used to being around me. Four days from now, it'll feel like we've been together for four decades, been one person always. After that there's no way she'll go marry someone else. She wants what I want. I will free her from her one fault: her cowardice. Then she will agree to take this chance with me.

And if she doesn't? My soul lurches and for one long second I feel sure that the bus has finally veered over the cliff and it's the long second before our stomachs unfurl skywards kitelike. If she doesn't, then I will at least have the memory of this trip, these four days, four decades. If that doesn't numb the pain then I'll find myself a tall bridge.

Nepalese does have some words in common with Hindi. From the chatter that starts up as passengers wake up and start gathering their belongings, I gather that these passenger-buses regularly load up with goods to ferry uphill and downhill: the drivers' not-quite-side hustle. The Bihari tells me these speeding, overloaded buses often lose

198

control. "Almost every day, on this road, there's a multi-bus pileup." He shakes his head earnestly: an Indian thrilled to be despising another country for a change. "But don't worry! The accidents mostly happen on the way down."

I picture Manisha and me, homewards bound three days from now, charred amidst a pile of metal, rubber, and salad. I bite into the radish. It's juicy and peppery. I pry open three other sacks and help Manisha and myself to a cucumber, carrot, and tomato each. Nobody bats an eyelid. Maybe it's a local custom for foreigners to carry part of this illicit, life-threatening tonnage up the mountain in their bellies. It's not when you're stoned that the world is at its craziest...

Chewing dissipates our nausea. And it'll keep Manisha awake. So, so now I can shut my own eyes. I throw my head back against my seat, I throw my head down on the bed and I'm stoned again. I'm the stranger who, four months from now, will lie beside Manisha, fingertips gliding in the dark down smooth skin, down the contours I've traced with mine: her cheeks, rounded like a child's, the bridge of her nose, sharp as a heroin-chic model's in side-profile; her knees, with their double dimples. And now Manisha's nausea, yes, now her nausea is finally also my own.

No. Closing your eyes doesn't help.

At 12:35 a.m. the bus halts outside our hotel. We unload our bags. The world spins. We stamp the ground to stamp out of our heads the giddying feeling of still moving, just for a second, world, stop spinning. The street is cobbled. The air is bracing. Potted geraniums and peace-lilies crowd the balconies of five-or-six-storeyed buildings with pastel facades.

Here, the clerk barely checks our IDs. Here, the clerk stares at us, stony-eyed, waiting for us to claim we're engaged and that's why we're requesting one room. I wonder, if we'd lived here in Pokhara, would we have been able to rendezvous more often? Maybe we wouldn't even have had to squander a month's savings on a decent hotel room, wouldn't have had to get Manisha a fake ID so she could tell the clerk she was here from another city to meet her fiancé. Maybe we'd have been able to meet openly in Manisha's hostel room or mine.

Fuck the world. My blood boils. And, high as she is, Manisha senses my rage, and rubs my arm on the clerk's desk.

In the lift, Manisha falls silent. The *bhang* is leaving her system, I explain as we're washing our hands and faces: now she'll long to sleep, but she won't be able to: her head will fall back on the pillow, she'll sink into something midway between death and locked-in syndrome, she'll wake up thinking the whole night has passed, but actually only fifteen seconds will have passed, and again, and again, till she grows sure that her brain is necrotising. "We'd be better off walking around for a bit," I conclude.

She glances at the double bed, white and tight and spotless, then at my face, then at the cupful of *bhang* I'm holding out. The flask's had a thorough shaking but it's insulated, and yoghurt doesn't spoil as fast as milk. "Hair of the dog?" I suggest.

She bolts it without pinching her nose, chases it down with another coffee sachet, shoulders her handbag, and stands by the door, ready.

All Pokhara's hotels, the nice ones at least, stand on streets like these, leading from the Lake Road. The streetlamps shine bright and unblinking. The shopfronts are dazzling. The tourists are dribbling out of the restaurants with aniseed on their breaths. I shouldn't have had that last half-cup myself. I can't tell if we're walking mid-street or crawling down the pavement hugging the buildings. Passers-by smile and I can't tell if I should smile back or scold them for jostling us. Have they jostled us? Am I already scolding them? I'm drifting down from the clouds, touching down briefly, grasping the ground with my toes, now trying to stay down, now trying to push off again. This is the worst part: being aware of the deficits in my own cognition, mistrusting everybody else because they can judge my deficits, wanting to hide but maybe it's already too late, maybe I've already committed this obscenity I'm fantasising so vividly, or maybe remembering so vividly. I've pulled down my trousers, I'm humping this water-fountain, they're dragging me off to jail; my mind lags behind loitering on the street, reality's about to catch up, the pavement's hurtling up towards my face. I swallow another cupful. Anything's better than this in-betweenness.

Manisha is studying the streets. I'm stumbling along, studying her, wondering if I've upset her. We've been together three years and I'm still a novice at interpreting her silences.

"It's so clean!" she says at last. "I could eat off the pavement. It's incredible. I mean, Nepal's a third-world country too. Or is Allahabad just that dirty?"

"This is the touristy area. Apparently the old town is quite dirty. We'll go there later if you like." She doesn't look at me. Panic seizes me. "Or d'you want to go now?"

"Avegh, I just want to sit down and eat and go to bed. I'm exhausted."

I stop mid street, or maybe mid pavement, and explain again about how *bhang* disrupts sleep. "And let's not eat, either. I mean, not just yet. Sometimes when you eat after *bhang*, you throw up. Must be a detox mechanism. If we eat now, we'll feel sleepy, but we won't be able to sleep, unless we throw the *bhang* up too, and that'll be no good." Four days on coffee and *bhang*, without sleep or food: this was the plan. And I made the plan sober, and it feels like something that should make sense now in my intoxication, but intoxication is slipping from me, still slipping, the other dose isn't kicking in, and my plan is looking ridiculous. "If we eat, and throw up, and fall asleep – then, when we wake up, it'll be tomorrow." It mustn't be tomorrow.

"Alright, Vegu." Manisha pats my arm. "Let's walk on."

And I see that if I'd been sober I wouldn't have seen this, wouldn't have felt all these other people feeling each other through my skin. Manisha halts outside a store window gaudy with silk scarves. The sample items' price tags are prominently displayed. Suspiciously cheap. Probably just polyester. I open my mouth to ask her which one she wants. But she's already walking on. In all our time together she's refused any presents. I run after her and seize her by the wrist.

"Pick one," I say, pointing back, my hand moving too fast, my eyes lagging, my hand blurring.

"I don't want one."

"Why not?" I drag her back to the window. "Look, they're beautiful. You were looking at them." I'm holding her hand awkwardly, hurting her, maybe, but her hand is lax in mine.

"They're nice to look at, Vegu, but I never meant to buy any."

"*You* don't buy! *I'll* buy." I'm all up in her face. I'm not being threatening, just assertive. Maybe this is how I should've always been. Maybe maybe this is the right distance between her and me. Maybe maybe all this while I've been standing too far off. "Say which one." She's silent. The words are welling from my chest up my throat, the words which it isn't time to speak, the words which, if I'd played my cards right, there would've been no need to speak. But I can't bear it anymore. As long as I don't know how this will end, this isn't a holiday, it's agony. "You never want anything, do you?" She thought by refusing anything from me she'd stop me getting attached. But I only kept looking for something she *would* accept, kept piling myself on top of myself. "You never meant to stay with me."

"I never said I would," she says, softly so that I can barely hear, so that I have to read her lips. Her eyes are moist and huge. But it won't work. I won't be softened anymore by the beauty that is the knife in my gut. "If you'd asked me, anytime these three years, I would've told you."

"But what's wrong with me? Tell me that." She tries to free her hand. "Tell me!"

"There's nothing wrong with you, Vegu. But you know we can't do this." I open my lips. She lays a finger on them. "I know what you want me to do. It wouldn't work. It would only lead to tears and outrage. My parents would disown me or lock me up. And then they'd come find you and kill you." I release her hand. "I could've taken this risk with you if there were some chance of winning in the end. There is none. Please be reasonable."

This was never meant to be a debate. This isn't about what's reasonable. I back away, turn away, walk away. She follows me, touching me but not quite, making my skin tingle. Her voice, which I wish I'd never heard, tickles my ear canal.

"Get away!" I lurch away from her. She's still here, I turn to face her. "You get this straight – people can change. If we reason with them, if we give them a chance, things can change. That's called history. People fight for change. People risk everything. Those are the people we admire – or at least, *I* admire. Only you will not change. You're a coward." She gasps, a quiet little gasp and the blood rushes to her face as if I'd slapped her. And now for half-a-second I do want to slap her. I shake my flask of *bhang* like a can of dice. "Well, aren't you? You're running away from our chance to be happy."

When Manisha's angry her voice drops. Her words become sharp and separate like knives. Her pupils become pinpoints. "Avegh, it's not brave to stand up against the impossible. It's idiotic. I've known my parents for 21 years. I've known the parents of my cousins, neighbours, friends, classmates." My fists are clenching, my fingernails digging into my palms. "If we did this thing, and got away with it, we'd be digging a chasm between our parents and us forever. They're our parents, Avegh, whatever they may be. And that's the best-case scenario. What country d'you live in? D'you even read the papers? They're still raping girls who enter inter-caste marriages. They're burning couples alive. They're leaving guys in muddy canals with their throats—"

"Love conquers hate!"

"Only in shitty movies."

I pound my thighs with my fist. The flask I'd forgotten I was holding crashes into my right femur. Pain breaks in slow shockwaves. We stand facing each other and yes, I can see now, now that pain has shredded with red fingernails my *bhang* haze, that it's not on the road but on the pavement we're standing. No chance of a bus, overloaded with salad, losing control, hurtling towards us, making us grab each other and stand rooted welcoming destiny. I grasp the flask in both hands and raise it over my head. Does she think I'll just let her leave me?

Manisha moves to let another couple pass. Her movement snaps me out of my spell. I stumble to the nearest rubbish bin. Big, black, sturdy wire rubbish bins they've got here. I toss in the flask. I sit slumped on the pavement's edge. From the restaurant across the street, under the gold-lettered crimson awning, stream the golden glow of lights, the silver hum of music.

Manisha's beside me, holding my flask. We're sitting near a drain. They cover the drains here, but there're little inlets, regularly spaced. I watch the viscous stream of greenish-white *bhang lassi* slop down the drain. Manisha gets up and goes away. Time goes away. Manisha comes back and holds out the flask. I put it to my lips and sip cool water, redolent of rose.

"That's good," I mutter.

"That shopkeeper with the fake-silk scarves told me it's water from the lake. There's fresh water up here in the mountains."

"Nonsense. If that was true, they'd grow their vegetables here instead of smuggling them up, risking a crash." The clouds have dropped me, but the ground has not yet landed under my feet. Here, in this grey midland are neither hills nor valleys. Here, I drift safely miles away from myself.

"Maybe the bus drivers do the smuggling just for the adrenaline." She nudges me. "You think you're the only person with a death wish?" Her smile is a chrysanthemum, the petals purple with joy, white-edged with sadness. I try to tear my eyes away. "What else was in the *bhang*, Vegu?"

That's just like her, to ask me a question when she's looking at me, when she knows I can't lie. "Nothing." I rise and dust my buttocks. I look up the street and down the street.

She takes my arm and leads me down the street. The main road runs around a lake, a vast blackness ringed with faraway lights. "Boating," she reads the noticeboard, "from 7 a.m. to 6 p.m. Oh Vegu, let's do this. It's almost 1 a.m. We'll hang around for a few hours."

"No. Let's eat and go to bed."

Here's my new plan: I'll sleep through these two days and through the journey home. That's one good thing about accumulating a sleep debt – you can use it when you need a break from consciousness. Sleep sixteen hours straight and the world goes mute and grey. I wasted three months at the beginning of BSc gathering the courage to ask her out. I wasted one month this spring angry at her. Those four months I lost wouldn't have mattered if we were going to spend our lives together. Now everything is going, it's already gone and this moment is a lie. I turn back to the hotel. She turns me back again to the lake. It doesn't matter anyway.

We stroll around the lake. Up ahead, a frangipani saturates the air with its fragrance heavy and sweet and sharp with memories. I shut my nostrils: I do that trick with my tongue in the back of my mouth, decommissioning my nostrils without having to pinch them. I breathe through my mouth, can't smell anything, can't see, don't hear anything. Sit tight! It'll all be over soon. Who knew Nepal was so dull?

"I've never been high like this," says Manisha. "I think I know what you put in it." Good for you. Stop talking, now: I'm trying to be deaf. "At this moment, Avegh, I feel like I could take in all the world's joy, all the pain of eight billion people, and it wouldn't hurt me. My lips would tremble like a child's. Tears big enough to refract a rainbow would cling to my eyelashes. But the pain would go through me cleanly, like a needle... You know, on the bus, before that dead-body scare, I had this vision – or maybe it was a memory from another life." She chuckles, as if she half-believes in that past-life bullshit.

"There's this man with a balloon," she continues. "A grown man is clinging to a sky-blue balloon. He's terrified the balloon will float away from him. He tries to kick it away. He wants to be the one that chooses the moment of parting, so that he can brace himself. He pushes the balloon away. The balloon begins floating away. Then he panics.

He runs after the balloon. He throws himself on it on all fours." She mimes, chuckling. "He never actually stops and enjoys having the balloon. So, in a sense, he never actually has the balloon. So, when the balloon does leave him, he's right, it will hurt terribly... Dimly he understands all this. His understanding only makes him more anxious. more resentful, more kicky. 'If only I could have you forever,' he says, 'then I would be so good! Then I could relax, and enjoy having you, and I'd treat you so well.' "

I look down the prospect of a life without Manisha. It's a bleak prospect – but only if I look. It's easy not to look. I never really looked at anything besides textbooks until I saw Manisha, sitting across the lecture hall in the window seat in the second row, bathed in the weeping sunshine of a morning in late January.

"I'm not a masochist." My voice sounds faraway. "If I'd known this was how you felt, I'd never have asked you out."

"Really? I wouldn't have changed any of it." She slips her arm around my waist.

"You wanted to go eat." I stop and look back the way we came. "Let's go eat."

"What I want is to go boating with you."

We walk onwards. We pass under the frangipani. It drops a flower on my shoulder, white, with a heart unbearably yellow. I try to shrug the flower off. It clings on. "I'm tired," I say. I've forgotten, after all, to keep my nostrils decommissioned. I've inhaled and my lungs are gasping, choking with frangipani's murder-sharp sweetness. "Maybe tomorrow."

She bops my nose. "Vegu, you idiot! It's already tomorrow."

AT PLAY

As our flight descended the sky closed in, rain-clouds glowered and skyscrapers glittered. I gaped at the glass towers. I'd flung Calcutta on the heap of things outgrown whose size indicated my own growth. Now, all grown-up at twelve, I pressed my oily frown into the double window, wondering whether the Calcutta I'd left behind had grown up too.

But the glitter turned out to be confined around the airport. It was one of the same old diesel-stinking, sunshine-yellow Ambassador taxis from my toddlerhood that carried my mother, brother, and me across town. The same double-decker buses held up traffic, wheezing, precariously lopsided, farting smoke at the same dingy shopfronts. Through lawless motor traffic wrinkled, skinny calves pedalled the same tiny cycle-rickshaws, with their rattling wooden frames, and their six-by-eighteen-inch passenger seats supposedly seating two.

Bombay was changing before my eyes. Back home, every week there was another movie shooting in a *dhaba* or on a vertiginous rooftop, another friend cat-walking into the mall in a mini-skirt, another flyover beginning construction. I disapproved of it all, Bollywood and American fashion and runaway urbanisation. But, all together, it constituted the world stage I was hankering for. Meanwhile Calcutta, I realised, sinking into the taxi seat, its embroidered upholstery exuding stale sweat and cheap cigarettes, had hung back. Perfect for a holiday.

Through the window Ma scrutinised the city she'd grown up in. The driver delightedly dispensed updates. Eight-year-old Mohan gazed into space, hands clasped in lap, body leaning away from me. I'd robbed him of his window-seat on the flight, and of his muffin while Ma was napping. Now my left cheek twitched with panic. I hated hurting him, I hadn't even wanted his muffin, but I couldn't help myself. Clearly this is who I was: nasty. I stared at Mohan, his big black eyes sparkling, his apple cheeks flushed in the humid heat: a teddy-bear. Some people just find it easy to be good, I thought, my panic hardening into anger.

I'd always let Mohan fill the bit-parts in my show. This summer I resolved to boot him out of the production altogether. I would confer on another party the honour of playing second fiddle and sharing my relatives' applause. My relatives always applauded generously, and I always wondered whether it was because they were nice or I was great.

"I don't want you in my show this time," I said gruffly.

"Oh." Mohan gazed at me liquid-eyed, his cheeks bunching with joy. "Thank you, *didi*."

"Huh!" I turned away. Before such a pig had I been casting my pearls.

But what show was I going to stage? Ma's relatives had already seen my adaptation of *Julius Caesar*. Chhordi, the youngest sister of my late grandmother and the social nucleus of my mother's side of the family, had hosted last year's production. Had we been staying with Pa's relatives I could've rehashed it this year, playing both Caesar and Antony. Should I adapt and memorise a new play? Well, that was a lot of work just for relatives. But then, if I put up something excellent, maybe this time I wouldn't be wondering why they were applauding.

Half-blocking the entrance to Chhordi's lane stood last year's construction site. The building was all empty eye-sockets and cobwebs velveting over rough floors. The mounds of sand and gravel destined to be the building's flesh had been trodden by many wheels, many feet into the road's eroded asphalt. I stared over my shoulder at this aborted child-of-a-city past her prime.

For our last visit before we moved to Boston, Chhordi had marshalled the tribe full-strength. Our cab crawled up the cul-de-sac. Aunts and cousins, frantically waving, leaned between the butter-yellow bars enclosing the first-storey balcony. Now they tumbled downstairs. They fought over who'd pay our driver, who'd carry our luggage upstairs. I shrank from their violent hospitality, clutching my backpack to my stomach. My everything notebook was in it, and my blue purse where I'd saved my pocket-money for years. That summer I had to spend it all. Rupees would be useless abroad. Pa, who'd been transferred to the overseas branch of the bank, had told me the exchange rate. "Spend it now," he'd advised, ruffling my hair.

We'd been sitting all day – cab, flight, cab – but Chhordi declared we must be exhausted, and hustled us off to the bathrooms. From the squeaky tap dribbled water yellow with iron and pungent with chlorine. I rubbed Chhordi's shampoo into my hair, waited for the foam, and kept rubbing. That sure was some sticky shampoo. I brought the shampoo bottle up to my myopic eyes. It was moisturiser. I rinsed it out with a mighty struggle, the dubious water further enriched with quantities of my hair. How stupid they'd think me! Maybe they wouldn't notice. Carefully I dried and arranged what remained of my hair.

At the heavy black dining-table, under the loquaciously arthritic ceiling-fan, Chhordi confronted us with mounds of *shingara* and *roshogolla*. Doctor's orders after our arduous day: deep-fried potato-stuffed dumplings and syrup-drenched milk-sweets.

It was a new maid who bustled upstairs with these snacks, and in from the kitchen with the plates – special-occasion white china plates. Chhordi's live-in maid-of-all-work changed every year or two. This one was called Maya. She looked my age. I watched for a chance to chat with her. All my cousins on my mother's side were younger than me, easy to bully into bit-parts. But I'd wearied of bullying people. I took this as a sign that it probably wasn't as a politician or CEO that I was going to become great. Waiting for my chance to vet the new maid, I examined my relatives: stomachs sagging, discreetly readjusting *sari* petticoats after four *roshogolla*, voices thick with boredom, awaiting the menfolk: respectable women having a good time.

"Poor *shona*!" Chhordi gathered my hands into the lap of her widow's *sari*, the white cotton worn soft. "Stuck with us old fogies your last summer in India." I murmured that I was enjoying myself, and that we'd still be visiting. "God grant I may witness your next visit." Chhordi massaged her arthritic knee and held forth on the likelihood of her impending death. Chhordi was in tolerable health but she had her generation's unembarrassed sentimentality. She'd lost five siblings, including my Dimma, and two brothers who'd died as children. She was one of seven who remained.

Before Pa got transferred from Calcutta to Bombay, Chhordi had been my favourite storyteller. She'd had a tomboy childhood on her father's estate in Barishal across the border. She was eleven when the Partition of Bengal scattered the family. The barrister father and head-mistress mother stayed behind to sell their property. The children fled the chaos, each wearing what gold he or she could under homespun *khadi*. Over the border, they roomed in twos and threes with relatives scattered across Calcutta. Of the Partition itself, Chhordi never spoke. It's Ma who had given me an overview once, and warned me against rehashing painful memories with Chhordi or Dimma. Now,

211

again, I sat listening to Chhordi's stories of thieving raw mangoes, nearly drowning in the village pond, and surviving snake-bites on midnight outings to the outhouse. She'd been a black sheep. Reminiscing, her eyes, no longer black behind bifocals, danced like ping-pong-balls in her round dark face. I nodded politely. I vowed that *I'd* never bore my audience with repeat performances.

Chhordi's eyes hardened. I followed them to Maya, who was stacking the empty plates high. "Take them two at a time, one in each hand," Chhordi scolded. "They're heavy. You'll drop them. Why must you be so lazy?"

"Yes, Chhordi," said Maya, addressing Chhordi, per custom, as if they were kin. She padded towards the kitchen, one plate in each hand.

"All these girls are the same," muttered Patu Mashi, Chhordi's only child, now grown. In English, my mother's cousin would be my sort-of-aunt, my something-cousin. In Bengali she was just aunt: Mashi. "Their hands are here, their minds are in the cinema-hall."

Mashi was dark and getting plump, face-first, as typical with Bengalis. But her features were good: slim nose, big eyes, plump lower lip. To "balance" her face, her eyebrows were plucked far too thin. With her pinched upper lip and sneering tone, Mashi reminded me of my favourite villain: *A Tale of Two Cities'* ice-cold Marquis St. Evremonde. Mashi's face relaxed as she turned to me. I grinned like Uriah Heep, ingratiatingly, and considered rubbing my hands and ducking my head for good measure, torn between irony and simpering.

How's Pa doing, Mashi asked. Fine, I said, he's winding up his affairs in Bombay. How d'you feel about going to Boston, Mashi said. I prevaricated. On the one hand, there'd be strangers to perform for, crystal balls to tell me if I was going to be great, great enough to make up

212

for how nasty I was to Mohan and everyone else. On the other hand, if the crystal balls' answer was no, then it'd be a great big place to be ordinary in. It's so far, I told Mashi, and the accent is so funny.

"Since the incident with that wretch," Chhordi was saying meanwhile, "we employ only village girls." The grown-ups cleared their throats and studied their gilt-edged teacups, side-eyeing us children. But I already knew this story. Three summers ago, too hot to sleep under the nylon mosquito-net, I'd listened at the door. All she'd done, this much-maligned maid, was elope with the counter-boy from the sweet-shop down the lane. "But even these simple village girls become spoiled by the metropolis. We keep having to let them go."

So went the grown-ups' evening *adda*: dissecting friends' and family's illnesses, domestic blowups, and financial troubles. Was this how I'd spend my summer? Right now there were girls riding an elephant through a spice plantation, scything through the thickets of Tolstoy, peering at nudes in Ajanta: seeing, doing, getting ahead. I struggled to keep my eyelids apart. In Chhordi's house the windows were closed at dusk against mosquitoes. July's mugginess was a rubber hammer between my eyes, tap-tapping me stupid.

I started awake to a wetness on my big toe. Peering under Chhordi's best white lace tablecloth, plastic-protected, I found another aunt's baby, who had crawled out of the bedroom, under the table, and was mapping my toes with her mouth. I tried to pull away. She clutched my foot with her tiny fists, razor nails digging in for a secure suckling grip.

An outcry. The baby, plucked from her play. Razor screams, piercing our eardrums. Peace, restored. *Adda*, resumed.

Mohan, heavy-lidded too, was quietly battling the mosquitoes. However early you shut the windows, one or two always snuck in. Mosquitoes loved Mohan. Miming the grownup mosquito-murderers, Mohan clapped his palms at his tormentors, examined his palms for signs of a kill, nil, followed the long-legged droners with his food-and-heat-drugged eyes, and jerked their whining out of his ears. I giggled inwardly, savouring Mohan's misery. Ma was right, I realised, when she'd screamed at me all those times, like when she'd found me beating Mohan up, or snatching away the bracelet, matching my own, that she'd given my best friend – I was an unlovable monster.

"What a grown-up little girl our Progga has become," said Chhordi, jogging my knee, "sitting so quietly!" "Pragya" isn't a Bengali name, so Chhordi settled for "Progga". "And how long your hair has grown! You're a regular beauty!"

I faced Chhordi, annoyed and flattered. Every summer for four weeks I heard nothing but how wonderful I was. Were my relatives lying or stupid? I longed to be really wonderful: to paint like Picasso, write like George Eliot, compose like Beethoven. And all my heroes, I'd discovered this year, browsing the school library's Biography section at my teacher's urging, had started early. And here I was, almost grown, and I didn't even know my path. My lips flew open.

Ma's eyes widened in warning. "I'm just sitting and listening, Chhordi! What's so grownup about that? These stories are *so* fascinating." I didn't like having to lie, so I hammed it up, so that Chhordi could see through my lie if she wanted to, see who I really was and decide if she still liked me.

Chhordi stroked my hair. "Aha! Your appreciation of gossip comes from your Bengali side."

This time I ignored Ma's waring glance. "No, Chhordi. Grown-ups gossip even in Bombay."

"Surely, surely," she said. The whites of Chhordi's eyes were yellow-tinged and pink-flecked. Never settling on anything, sometimes they looked wandering, but at that moment they looked dreamy and she looked happy. "But true gossip, *adda* – that is a patented Bengali skill."

I drew breath for a rebuttal. Why, if Chhordi wanted to appropriate something for Bengalis, did she want to appropriate gossip? A fit of coughing seized her. I jumped up, patted her back, fetched her inhaler, and stood by, ready for more fetching or patting, anything rather than sitting still. She took my hand, her eyes moist, probably from the coughing.

The novelty of pretending that I, the black sheep of this generation, had been domesticated wore off by dinner-time. Chhordi sat down to her meal last, after piling everyone else's plate with third helpings of a dozen dishes. It was past 11 p.m. when she licked the sweet mango chutney off her forefinger. I seized her plate and dashed kitchenwards, ignoring Patu Mashi's warnings not to "strain myself."

Maya sat on a two-inch-high wooden *pidhi* on the stone kitchen floor. Before her was a dented steel plate. On the plate were a hillock of white rice, tiny mounds of the vegetable and fish side-dishes, and no mound at all of Patu Mashi's special chili chicken. She was rising to see if I wanted anything. I waved her back down. I put Chhordi's china plate in the sink, squatted opposite Maya, and rolled my eyes back towards the fusspots. She giggled.

"How old are you?" I whispered.

"I'll be sixteen in *sharatkal*." She named the season of her birth, autumn, rather than the date.

An older friend: just what I needed. A friend whom I couldn't bully. "I'm twelve. I'm Pragya."

She tried to pronounce "Pragya." She failed. We giggled. I was touched: she was the only one here who'd tried. She made me teach her how to say it. There's no "gy" sound in Bengali but Maya managed a fair approximation. "Pragya-*di*," she said.

"Don't call me *di*! I'm younger than you. When did you start working here?"

"Thirteen weeks ago," Maya whispered. "I'm from a village near Malda, where your *mezdi* lives." Mezdi seldom visited Chhordi or her other siblings in Calcutta, but rang them often. "From the Malda bus depot, my village is fifteen kilometres away, by the bus that leaves twice a day, except Sunday, when there's only one bus a day."

"Thirteen weeks ago, that's... three months? Why d'you count weeks rather than months?"

"Because they might let me go home to visit my parents in another thirteen weeks, that's to say, twice a year."

"Oh." I thought of all the times I'd wished my parents miles away, months away. I looked away.

Maya chattered on, her whisper sibilant with suppressed excitement. "So you have only one brother, Mohan? He's very cute." She paused, smiling sparkly-eyed, as if she'd complimented *me*.

Yes, I said, only one brother.

"No sisters?"

"Ma-ya!" Chhordi's stentorian voice marched in from the drawing room and rapped on the kitchen door. "Less talking, more working!" In a softer voice she added, "Progu, *shona*, won't you come sit with us?"

I squeezed Maya's hand and rose to rejoin the drone of mosquitoes and mature humans.

Some of Ma's other relatives weekended at Chhordi's before dispersing to their own homes across Calcutta. Drowsily I listened to their *adda*, sat through meals, and trudged off to bed. It hadn't rained since a week before we landed: the

216

monsoon was playing truant. The air in my nostrils was like the steam from the steam-pot Ma made me bend over when I had a cold. The blood in my veins was sludge. Monday came. The others left, taking the baby, taking away the apprehension of another digital cartography expedition that had kept me semi-conscious.

Chhordi's three-storey house, built room by room in the '60s, was hemmed in by other three-storey houses, which shielded each other from the sun but cut off each other's breeze. All Sunday night I wrestled to seduce sleep and subdue it between my legs. Sleep proved a skittish lover, kept me spinning like a top. The bed grew bedraggled with my quest. Monday morning I trudged to the balcony. I lay down and sneaked the hem of my frock up my thighs to expose hot skin to cool stone. Heat's blanket lifted from me. The stone sent thrills up my thighs. Then it began to warm. I shifted a foot over, then rolled over to cool my front. On cue, the sun streamed right into my eyes, its heat even at 7 a.m. an assault. I trudged up to the roof.

The kitchen sink was small, so Maya had carried the sea-green plastic washtub to the roof. She was squatting, doing the dishes at the tap built into the square cement tank. From the wire clothes-lines hung cotton *saris* starched stiff, motionless in the heavy air. Maya looked grim. I'd be angry too, doing other people's dishes all day. I squatted near her, waiting. She finished. Her face relaxed. She laid the dishes out to dry. We lounged in the shadow of the tank. The air was one solid mass and the smell of Vim bar hung over our heads. But somehow, up here, the heat was bearable.

"Mashi says you put up a new show every year." Maya's voice was high-pitched and pleading. "What will it be this year?"

"I've not decided." I stretched my legs out. An idea struck me. I reoriented my legs towards Maya. "I could do

217

a play. But I did a play last year, and it's in English..." I scanned Maya's waiting face; it didn't change. "Or I could recite the first chapter of the *Iliad*. But that's in ancient Greek, which nobody understands." Maya's face was so open that I was seized by an impulse of honesty. "Actually, even I don't understand it. But it sounds divine, and my memory is excellent..." Maya looked impressed but still expectant. "Or I could write some poetry and recite it, But that's also in English. Or I could dance *katthak*—"

"Do that!"

"I don't dance very well," I explained, alarmed. "Plus they already saw my dance years ago." And I'd learned no more dance since then. They made us dance barefoot, and it hurt, so I'd quit. "Or" – I waited till she squirmed and her brows danced, stretching out the pause before my grand finale – "I could do a magic show."

"Yes." Maya clapped. "Do magic!"

"Alright!" I sat up and snapped the fingers of both hands. "Done."

"Your Chhordi and Mashi went to see P. C. Sarkar" – India's one big magician, pride of Bengal. "I couldn't go! Somebody had to stay home." Ever since Chhorda died, they'd been wary of burglars. In this houseful of women somebody always had to be home, and the lights on, to keep burglars away from gilt-edged china and plastic-protected lace tablecloths. "I was so disappointed, I wept."

"You can watch him on television."

"That's nothing like being there. But now I can see your show!"

"I'm just a beginner. Don't expect anything fancy."

"Mashi says your shows are splendid. She says you're a role-model, so talented and obedient—"

I'd been letting Maya lull me into a smug trance. "Obedient" snapped me awake. "They're silly, Chhordi and

Mashi and the others. They praise me for the silliest things. Just for sitting still and listening, or letting my hair grow out. Either they're stupid or they think I am."

"Rubbish!" Maya imitated my pose, half-lying, legs stretched out. Her off-the-racks *salwar-kameez* of flowered cotton couldn't disguise her slender, shapely figure, now that she'd put aside her *dupatta*, now that there were no men around to be corrupted by her shape. Maya had sparkling black eyes, curving cheeks, a pert chin, and a vivacity that animated her prettiness into beauty. She struck me as an Indian incarnation of George Eliot's Hetty Sorrel. "Your relatives only see you once a year. They don't know you well enough to really talk to you properly about anything. But they love you. They want you to be happy. That's why they say nice things to you, not because they're stupid, or they think you are."

"Ye-ah, I want to be happy too... I just don't know which thing to do. There're so many things."

Pursuing a new hobby was my version of falling in love. At first, every hobby felt like sprinting uphill, on wings of Hermes, feet barely touching ground. I wanted to stay up all night with it. Then a boulder loomed in my path. I tried to crawl around it, jump over it. Then I wasn't sprinting anymore, I was walking. Soon enough I was trudging. Then came the fork in the road: I could keep trudging up the mountain, or sprint downhill to try something new.

There was no end of hobbies to try: a whole vista of mountains. I had years, I'd thought, to choose which mountain would be mine, to climb all the way up, to plant my flag on its summit. Meanwhile I could keep staging a new show every summer, enjoying my relatives' uncritical applause. I had years to decide whether I ever wanted a bigger audience: strangers who'd expect one thing done, and done well.

But last year my teacher had made me read biographies of great people. And I'd realised I had no time at all, had to choose at once. But what if I chose wrong? I'd spend my life grappling with the boulders on one mountain, regretting not having chosen another. I stared up at the sun, glowering behind grey clouds. Silently I shifted closer to Maya's warm body.

"I wish I were talented," said Maya. Her eyes followed an eagle across the leaden sky. Must be a spotted eagle. My encyclopaedia said those are what we had in India. Why not become an ornithologist? What fun, going around with binoculars around my neck and my head in the sky. What boulders could possibly loom in an ornithologist's path?

"Talent isn't that important," I told Maya. I'm not talented, I wanted to add, just energetic. She looked at me. I looked away. My new friend was a new chance. The last thing I wanted was for my new friend to misappraise me too. But I was too vain to tell her that I was just a jumping-jack-of-all-trades. To change the subject, I asked, "What do *you* want to do?" Next moment I could've bitten my tongue out.

But Maya didn't mind, Maya wasn't insulted that I'd forgotten where she came from. She giggled and hid her face. I coaxed. Finally she murmured, "A beautician."

Beautician isn't a respectable occupation, I was about to jeer. Then I realised this opinion wasn't mine: I didn't know any beauticians. This opinion must've infiltrated me from the dimwits downstairs, who aspired only to a life nobody could gossip about. "That's wonderful," I declared.

"You don't think it's silly?" she said.

"'Course not! Now tell me, how does one become a beautician?"

"I don't know, really... I guess first I'll need to learn some English. And finish school. I've only finished tenth

220

standard. Then maybe there are beautician training courses. Or maybe I just practise hair-cutting and brow-plucking by myself. And then maybe clear some kind of entrance test."

"Splendid!" I jumped up. "Let's start."

"What?" Maya sat up. Lounging had undone her bun. A glossy curl straggled across her clay-brown cheek.

"I'll teach you English. That'll help you with beauticianing. And that way, you can also be my magic show assistant, if you want to. You just have to hand things about and say a few English phrases."

"Yes!" Maya was on her feet too, clasping my hands. "I'll learn English. I'll help you with your show."

I'd anticipated having to coax and manipulate her into being my assistant. Her quick agreement flooded me with gratitude. "And you can cut my hair and pluck my brows for beautician practice."

"Rubbish!" She stood back, eyes wide with fear. "Children don't get their brows plucked—"

"I don't mind—"

"And your hair's already short."

I suppressed my irritation. She was only a village girl, with the same antiquated notions about boys and girls as the fogies downstairs. "I want it even shorter… No, listen! I always cut my own hair when it drops below my shoulders. Ma scolds me every time. She says girls should have long hair. But I don't want to be girly. I want even shorter hair. What I would love is a 'boy-cut'…" Maya stared. I glared, arms akimbo. "D'you really want to become a beautician, or are you just playing?"

Maya looked excited and scared, as if she were about to jump off a cliff into a river that might or mightn't be flowing below. She looked how I felt when I was facing a new hobby. "Yes," she said. "I do."

"Well, if you want to be a professional, you can't be

old-fashioned." That's what my English teacher said, the one who'd made me read the biographies. He said the sonnets I'd written had been good practice, but I should graduate to contemporary forms. He'd also been behind my double promotion from the 4th standard. Sometimes I resented his rushing me. "If you want to be a beautician, you've gotta keep up with the trends. Short haircuts are trendy." Short haircuts were all over the *Femina*s Ma browsed, but never bought, on our grocery-shopping trips.

"D'you really want me to cut your hair?" Maya surveyed my face, moving sections of hair this way and that, mocking up haircuts. "I do think some short cuts can be nice. Even some Bollywood actresses have short cuts now..." Her cheeks flushed; she dropped her hands and sat back on her heels. "Oh, Pragya! Chhordi would scold me awfully."

"No." I squatted opposite her. I couldn't squat quite like her, steady on the balls of her feet. "You'll cut a half-centimetre every day. That's like this much—" I moved my thumb and forefinger close together, then wide apart, and then I waved my hand away. The mountain of mathematics was one I've never even tried to climb. "And you can pluck five eyebrow-hairs, per eyebrow, per day. Seriously, I'm telling you. Nobody will notice."

Maya gaped. She laughed. It ran through me then, in a cold shiver: the certainty that, if the grown-ups did find us out, it was Maya who'd get in trouble. I opened my mouth to warn her. I shut it again, vowing privately to share the blame if we were discovered.

A good person would've spoken up. And here I was, with a new friend, the chance to be a new person, and here I was, silent again, nasty again. "I'll teach you the best English in the world," I cried, and sprinted downstairs.

In my notebook, which contained among other things

my Ancient Greek alphabet, and my *Julius Caesar* adaptation, I left two pages blank to plan our magic show, then wrote out the English alphabet. Maya recited her ABCs correctly, from start to finish, at just the fourth try – though she called S "esh", V "bee" and Z "jed", for Bengali doesn't have these sounds. She also called Q "kwee", which puzzled me, for Bengali does have all the sounds to say "queue".

Then I remembered she'd probably only need spoken English. Torn between wanting to dazzle her with pagefuls of sentences and the desire to be a good friend, I shut my notebook. I taught her to say the numbers one to ten, good morning afternoon and night, hello welcome thank you, and please. These phrases precipitated unforeseen difficulties and giggles. Bengalis don't say good morning unless they're being stagey; welcome, thank you, or please unless they're being ironical; or hello except on the phone.

Maya's progress delighted me. Besides hello and ta-ta, English had been as foreign to her as ancient Greek had been to me. Yet she was learning English much faster than I'd learned the rudiments of Greek, before I'd encountered the first boulder: when to use τη vs. στη vs. στην. And Maya was older than me. She was supposed to find it harder to learn a language. And I'd got books, and she'd only got me. Envy stung me as I watched her leaning against the water-tank, warbling ABC. She was grinning over her flying start. I grinned back. Then it occurred to me: there'd been nobody to teach me ancient Greek, whereas I must be doing a phenomenal, fantastic, fabulous job teaching Maya English.

I wanted to hug her. I didn't. A teacher must maintain her dignity.

After lunch, we moved on to hair-cutting practice. The afternoon waned. The sky got heavier and fell lower. Mynahs shrilled in the guava-trees. Sparrows quarrelled on the cement parapet of the terrace. Yes: in Calcutta, the small, plump, speckled, cream-and-milk-chocolate house-sparrows, which I'd chased as a toddler, which in Bombay had long since been exterminated by smog and wires, still chirruped. The fine-toothed comb massaged my scalp. The rusted iron scissors stuck in my moisturiser-washed hair. Lounging in the woven-plastic chair we'd fished out of the attic, with Maya's fingers in my hair, I waged another battle against sleep. But this time I was battling to stay awake. This time the battle was delicious.

"Ma-ya!" Chhordi's voice close by awakened me, startled Maya, and sent the scissor-ends flying almost into my eye. "She's on the landing," Maya hissed. She dashed to the parapet and cast the hair-clippings overboard. Then she darted towards the dried laundry.

"No! Wipe your hands down first," I hissed, jumping up and brushing the hair off my shoulders. "Hair sticks to everything." She scrubbed her palms on her hips. "Not palms, wipe your fingertips!" I plucked two *saris* free, draped their starch-stiff lengths around Maya's shoulders, and bowled the scissors and comb under the water-tank. My heart raced agreeably. Are there still professional adventurers, I wondered. What's the 1999 equivalent of daredevil, musketeer, buccaneer?

Chhordi had called for Maya, but it was I who ran to help Chhordi upstairs. She had climbed one set of stairs and was resting on the landing below the terrace. She demurred at first against leaning on me, but was soon leaning heavily. At each step she paused and fetched up her left leg. Then she fetched up her right leg, trembling and stiff-kneed and arcing sideways, onto the same step. Then she paused for breath. I struggled with impatience then distracted myself by mentally reciting the *Iliad*, Chapter One.

Up on the terrace at last, Chhordi surveyed the laundry and dishes. They're just satisfactory, her expression announced, though I couldn't see any spots. She scolded Maya for forgetting to come sort food grains downstairs, to separate the grains of rice or *daal* from the tiny pebbles with which grocers made up the measure. Today had been pebble-sorting day, and "poor Lali," said Chhordi, that is to say my Ma, had had to help.

Maya hung her head. I grinned at her from behind Chhordi's back, but she looked sincerely ashamed. I pictured Ma, a house-guest bored stiff, begging to be allowed to help. Ma was always wanting a holiday but never taking one. In the hotel in Goa, she'd spent so long sweeping the bathroom floor, scolding us for leaving imaginary footprints from the bathtub to the door, that I'd confiscated the mop and generously offered to forego baths for the remainder of our stay. I watched Maya heading downstairs, half the laundry over her shoulders, her step demure. What's the fuss, I wanted to ask Chhordi. Maya isn't a slave, and you've got hands too. Sixty-three isn't so very old.

In my head I delivered a fine Marxist speech in two parts. The first part was directed at Chhordi the class oppressor, squashing the proletariat's spirit to keep her on the treadmill. The second part was directed at Maya, instilling her with the self-confidence to lead a violent revolution. Well, hopefully the violence would start on the other side of Chhordi's threshold. Both sides of my family had produced Marxist politicians – my freedom-fighter great-grandfather in the '40s, and now in the '90s a drunkard uncle who mostly just talked from his bedroom. Pa had wanted to be an activist-writer, too. Family circumstances had forced Pa to take the bank job. I'd browsed his inherited, silverfish-haunted volumes of Marx and Engels, Lenin and Terry Eagleton.

I leant beside Chhordi over the parapet: white cement rain-worn into a stripey antiquey white-and-black. The cul-de-sac that Chhordi's house fronted was middle class. But the back of the house overlooked craftsmen's cottages and kitchen-gardens. "Can you name these plants, *shona*?" "Shona" means gold: a unisex endearment. Bengali is a less gendered language than English: there isn't even a word for "he" or "she", it's all "o". But there is a word for "girl". And girls are to grow their hair long and keep it oiled and combed and beautiful but never wear it loose.

Chhordi taught me that evening to tell mango trees from jackfruit trees. She praised me for correctly identifying banana and coconut. She sounded so impressed, you'd never guess that half the trees in India were bananas, the other half coconuts.

Horticulture was one of my longest-running hobbies. On our balcony in Bombay I'd grown tomatoes in tubs. The first batch of fruit was tiny and tart, but fresh and mine. The second batch had got blossom-end rot. I'd tried various remedies in vain. So, reservations about the authenticity of Chhordi's praise notwithstanding, I relished my plant-naming lesson.

Chhordi corrected my mistakes, laughing. Her laughter escalated into a hacking cough, which she soothed with a patient, rhythmic moaning, as one might soothe a child. I prepared to run for her inhaler. "No need! I can manage." She seized my wrist and patted it to the rhythm of her moaning. Chhordi, like Ma, treated medication as a last resort. Her cough kept trying to break through. She squashed these attempted rebellions with more deep-voiced, metronomic moans.

Maya resurfaced to fetch the rest of the laundry. I turned to help her, but Chhordi reclaimed my attention. "Listen!" she said. "D'you know what bird that is?"

"A cuckoo," I said, scoffing.

The day was waning colourlessly and a cuckoo, invisible amid the greenery à la Wordsworth, had burst into a resonant solo. He warmed up his voice with rapid-fire scales, then issued one long, hopeful, wavering note of inquisition. He waited for a response from a mate. The twilight silence, briefly dispersed, regathered thick with mosquitoes and cricket. The cuckoo repeated his call. Still no answer. His short series of questioning notes raced higher and higher, faster and faster until his sweet voice cracked and he assaulted the world nonstop, no longer pausing for a reply but unable to stop asking.

Chhordi sang back at him, hooting to imitate his whistle. A poor imitation, but he fell for it, turning towards us, it sounded like, whistling at us now, his voice raucous with desperate hope. I tried whistling back. But whistling eluded me.

"We call him the mad cuckoo," said Chhordi. "Endlessly he calls for a mate he never finds... The mosquitoes are biting, *shona*; come downstairs. Maya, close the door behind you. And remember the kitchen counter needs washing. Properly. Last time you left dirt piled in the corners."

My magic show preparations didn't take long. I was no good at (didn't want to practise) sleight-of-hand. So I relied on contraptions. I fashioned the mind-reading device for my grand finale from a shoebox, paper-covered and acrylic-painted. Painting had been my first hobby. I sequenced my tricks, posted the invites with my saved-up pocket-money, scripted my patter, and finis.

I was barred from going out alone – "You'll get lost, *shona*, get sick with heatstroke, get kidnapped" – and the grown-ups were too busy to escort me. So I drifted through the stuffy house. I sneezed over Mashi's dusty college

227

textbooks. I watched Mohan, sprawled on the floor, amusing himself with Mashi's old Lego set, which I'd long outgrown. Chhordi called Mohan "ghughu", meaning dove. His apple cheeks were red, his eyes shone, and he was so slow to bore that I wondered if he was just, you know, slow. Feeling suddenly all grownup and tender, I bent to pat his curly head. Startled, he shrank from me, making me shout at him and storm off, the nasty boy.

To give me a change, Patu Mashi took me to work. In the bus we were all packed close. Smiling, Mashi whispered to me. "If your face itches," she said, "there'll be no room to extricate your hand, to scratch yourself with. So you have to scratch against a fellow passenger's back, like a cow against a post."

I scoffed at this transparent attempt at a practical joke. But, sure enough, my chin began to itch. I ignored it. The itch became unbearable. Before I knew it I was scratching on the broad bare back of a woman in a low-backed blouse, scratching like a bull massacring a red flag. The woman spun around. Where did *she* find room to move? When she saw it was just a girl, she smiled. I scowled at Mashi, who hid her grin behind her long, pointed, painted nails.

At her desk at the West Bengal Electrical Corporation, rustling with drowsy voices, and the whir of ceiling fans suspended on long rods from high ceilings, Mashi told me how her father, my Chhorda, had died, suddenly at 54, of a stroke. Chhordi and Mashi had been at Digha on holiday. Chhorda as usual hadn't been able to get away. Tears stood in Mashi's eyes. Her lips quivered and briefly she looked like a child, baffled.

Then someone brought Mashi a file. Mashi wiped her eyes, carefully to avoid smudging her *kajal*, primmed her lips, and began working on the file. Never had her overplucked eyebrows looked sharper, her upper lip more Marquis-St.-

228

Evremondey. Through my own tears, the truth flickered wetly at me. Mashi's problem was not that she was cold: it was that she was too warm. I regretted having avoided her company and resolved to do better this next fortnight. But then we had a rice-heavy lunch, and after dozing the afternoon away at Mashi's desk, I awoke at 5:30 p.m., sullen and longing to get away.

Next, Mama took his turn to amuse me. Chhoto Mama, my mother's younger brother, arrived at Chhordi's before work one morning. He was an engineer. He also worked at the Electrical Corporation, repairing the transformers that broke down like clockwork. Chhoto Mama had stayed single. He worked double shifts to support the wife and daughter of his alcoholic older armchair-politician brother, slept in a cot at work, and spoke seldom and in a gruff voice.

Mama came carrying a sunshine-yellow kite with a braided tomato-red tail. "At dawn there was a hint of breeze," he said. "Let's try our luck." We went up to the terrace.

The hint had withdrawn itself. I sprinted from end to end of the terrace, flinging the kite skywards. It refused to launch.

"Never mind." Mama mopped his brow. "Maybe another day."

I gave up seeking alternative entertainment. Ignoring my relatives' hints and sidelong questions about all the time I spent with "that silly girl", I haunted Maya.

One morning Chhordi scolded her for leaving the teapot unattended, over-brewing. But it was Chhordi who'd summoned her to mop up a spill. All morning Maya flitted about, tight lipped. As she did the dishes on the terrace, I squatted beside her, ready to abuse my dull, tyrannical relatives, waiting for an indication that Maya was just waiting for me to get the ball rolling.

Chhordi scolded often, but always composedly: not in a flash of irritation did she scold, so she never apologised afterwards. Her scoldings daunted me more than Pa's. Pa had a hair trigger, abandoning self-control at the slightest excuse. Afterwards, his consciousness of having acted foolishly eclipsed his consciousness of whatever you'd done wrong, and he tried in many mute ways to beg your forgiveness. I thanked God that I was only a visitor at Chhordi's.

Maya finished her dishes. We leaned over the parapet, chattering about Chhordi's backside neighbours. Maya's face relaxed. "This," she indicated the shack with the betelnut and mango-trees in the backyard – or was it guava-trees? – "is a potter's house."

"Oh." That explained the terracotta plant pots stacked upside-down alongside the cottage. Somehow the lives of these humbler neighbours never entered the grown-ups' *adda*. When Chhordi was teaching me to name trees, she hadn't acknowledged the houses the trees shaded, the people who'd planted them. "I wonder if he'd let us practise on his wheel?"

From the potter's two-room, tin-roofed cement cottage, a voice erupted into the midmorning. Soon the solo became a duet of two voices similar in pitch. I distinguished a man's shriek and a woman's hoarse alto. The alto monopolised the argument. The shrieker couldn't get a word in edgewise. But it all sounded gibberish.

"Are they speaking Bengali?"

Maya giggled. "Yes! Bangal." That's the dialect they spoke over the border, in Bangladesh. "Can't you understand it? Your Chhordi's family grew up in Barishal."

"Well, *I* didn't... What're they arguing about?"

230

"The potter's wife is calling him lazy, and he's inviting her to go away and stay away."

"Finally, something exciting!" I turned my head this way and that for a better listen. It was still gibberish. Why do we think, when the sounds of a language are familiar, that we've only got to listen hard and it'll make sense? When we'd visited Egypt, Ma had thought Arabic sounded like Hindi, and insisted on speaking Hindi to the Egyptians, enunciating patiently. I bent, trying to peer through into the cottage windows. "I've never witnessed a real-life breakup."

"They're not breaking up." Maya laughed. "They're always fighting, just for fun. They let their anger out and go on living happily together."

"That's silly! If they're fighting they must be unhappy. They should divorce and go their own ways and be happy."

"Ye-ah…"

But now, through Maya's ambivalence, I heard the relish in the woman's voice as she abused her good-for-nothing man, the savouring of melodrama in the husband's voice as he cursed his simple-mindedness in tying himself to a shrew.

"They're just like Chhordi and Mashi and Ma," I said. "They abuse their relatives behind their backs. But when they visit, they're all smiles and bowls of *roshogolla*. If you don't like someone, just shut up and leave them." I turned to Maya, waiting for Maya's return volley of abuse, something to let me know that she and I weren't just two misfits passing the time, that we were a team, us vs. my relatives. But Maya stayed silent.

A smile tickled her lips. I followed her gaze.

Under the papaya-trees' multi-tiered umbrella of hand-shaped leaves, stood the couple's ten-year-old, a toddler on her hip. The girl made faces at her baby brother, distracting him from the deafening duet, playing mother. Their parents paused their opera to shriek for bathwater. The girl put the

231

toddler down to fill a steel bucket at the hand-pumped borewell standing in the little courtyard. Flowing water had worn slippery-smooth the tiny cement square in which the borewell stood; stagnant water had made its edges mossy. The lip of the abandoned toddler trembled. He cry-hummed and windmilled his arms towards his mother-sister.

"I have two older sisters," said Maya suddenly. "Then it's me, then another sister. And then finally my parents got a son. He's only ten." Maya called her sisters by their names – Lokkhi, Dugga, and Moushumi – but the son of the family waded waist-deep in nicknames. *Shona, moti, chandermookh*: sun, pearl, moon-face. "Lokkhi got married three years ago. And Dugga last year. And soon it'll be my turn, and then Moushumi's."

Maya's parents were tenant farmers, growing rice and greens on one quarter-acre. To make ends meet, they also ran a tiny grocery. That barely covered their irrigation costs. All over the farm districts, said Maya, all the water in the canals and in the ground had salinified. So anyone who'd got land and money to dig borewells was digging, digging ever deeper into the good earth's bowels.

"What did your older sisters do before they got married?"

"Lokkhi helped out around the farm. She's really bright! She also took tuitions for her own classmates." Even brighter than Maya? Huh! Maybe Lokkhi would've memorised the whole *Iliad* by now. I loved my friend, and I admired her big brains, but I'd seen lots of poor people with big brains and I knew that, most likely, her big brains would never get her anywhere. This thought was a dagger of joy stabbing my envious heart. "Dugga got a job like mine, in Malda. But her family wasn't nice like this."

"Nice!" I scoffed. "You don't have to lie just because they're 'my' family."

"Yes, it's bad here, but nothing compared to how some families treat their servants."

Why did Maya refuse to abuse my relatives? Did she think I'd betray her confidence?

"When there was enough money for their dowry," said Maya, "and when my parents found a boy, then Lokkhi and Dugga came home, one by one, to get married. Now they're both settled near home. They've already got cute little kids!" I tried not to grimace. "Moushumi wants to go to college. But my parents are saving the money for my dowry and hers, and for Shona's college. Though Shona is quite lazy!" Maya chuckled indulgently: even her brother's flaws were merits. "I send all my money home. We all do. I tell them to use it for Moushumi's college. She's bright too. She would be able to get a scholarship if they let her study on."

"Your parents," I said, interrupting these biographies of people I'd never met, "are already saving money for your dowry?"

"Mm-mm."

"Do you *want* to marry?"

"Ye-es," Maya's voice wavered across an octave. "But not straight away."

"'Course not! Sixteen's much too young."

Maya's stories interested me. Village life fascinated me. Everybody had an interesting life, everybody but me. The grey afternoon yellowed into evening. The air hung still. Our body heat lingered heavy over our skins, a weighted blanket. Our sweat didn't cool us, only prickled us. Still, it was bearable up here. If only the grown-ups would let us sleep up here. No, "mosquitoes," they would say.

And malaria, and dengue. And kidnapping from the street, and the corruption of my soul by my new friend. Is there anything the grown-ups weren't terrified of? I imagined Patu Mashi confronting the streets of Bombay, where hobos stabbed needles into their arms under sleepless neon lights. I pictured Patu Mashi's over-plucked eyebrows slackening, her poised lips drooping. I scoffed.

Maya and I gathered the laundry and straightened out a *sari* that'd been starched with the water drained from boiled rice. The starch had glued the *sari*'s cotton together in big folds and in thousands of tiny creases. Standing twenty feet apart, we played tug-of-war, tugging the creases loose. I'd often watched this game and longed to play it. Now Maya kept cautioning me, coming up close, sabotaging my tugs. If we tug too hard we might rip the fabric, she said. We got through one sari. I didn't offer to help her straighten out the others. This wasn't play, it was work: best left to Maya, and Mashi when she got home from work. Tonight, after everyone was abed, and the dining room floor was cleared, Maya would sit alone, ironing out the networks of tiny creases that had survived our tug-of-war.

That morning at the grocer's, Maya had bought raw tamarind, for *tetuler* chutney to accompany fish fry for dinner. Now she produced the handful she'd smuggled up for us to eat. The deshelled brown pods are full of grit, fragments of woody shell, and strangers' fine hair. Maya tempered her tamarind with salt. "That's like milking a cow into a sieve," I said, scoffing. I popped a whole pod into my mouth, unsalted, and kept my face ironed smooth as I chewed. Maya's face scrunched up just watching me.

Acid flayed my tongue. Acid seeped into the hairline gaps between my teeth, where it would lurk and send, with the first bite of lunch, nasty shivers up my molars into my gums. But I held my eyes open and kept my expression blasé and chomped on. Maya watched me, her own salt-covered pods forgotten, her hands creeping up her face to hide her gaping. The acid flayed my palate. Had my palate always been so ridged? And what was that salty metallic taste? Surely not blood. But any agony was worth enduring for the sight of Maya's eyes bursting wide, Maya's mouth frozen agape, the deafening applause in Maya's silent stare.

I am Mark Antony, up on stage in Act III, holding the Romans spellbound. I am P.C. Sarkar, holding a darkened hall full of grown-ups spellbound. If I cannot be good, I must be great. Or else why would anyone ever speak to me?

"D'you really not find it sour?" said Maya.

I tossed my head. I drank in Maya's admiration. In this admiration there could be no blinders of kinship, no grownup politeness. "Come," I said, "time for beautician practice."

I sat with my back against the water-tank, my legs outspread. Maya knelt facing me. The smell of her sweat, piquant but not unpleasant, crept up my nostrils. First she trimmed my hair. I'd decided, that first day, that a half-centimetre was as long as my thumbnail. So Maya kept borrowing my thumb for a measure. Last week, I'd unearthed Patu Mashi's primary-school geometry ruler and discovered that my thumbnail was actually a whole centimetre long. I hadn't told Maya.

The mirror was blotched, the iron scissors all rust. Maya had worked out how to make the abandoned scissors cut. The blades were long and heavy, but she made short snips with just their middles, which had some edge left. Crisply Maya snip-snipped my hair, pausing to wipe her sweaty hands on her thighs. I pictured her hand slipping, the scissors stabbing me, giving me tetanus, sending me to hospital. The hospital might have air-conditioning! I willed Maya to stab me, just a bit, just breaking the skin. I'd been so hot, so long, that all I could think of was how to cool off for a bit.

235

Then I remembered I was vaccinated against tetanus. Bloody overprotective parents.

Next Maya mocked up some hairstyles. We'd "borrowed" some hairclips from Mashi: a motley crew of long blacks, square silvers, and rounded browns. Maya pinned my neck-length hair a la chignon, a la Madame Bovary. I shook my head. "No long hair for me, please, thank you," I said slowly in English.

Head on one side, Maya studied my lips and ventured a translation in Bengali. " 'I don't want long hair'?"

"You already knew I didn't want long hair. Give me a literal translation of what I said."

She did, almost exactly. I grunted, my admiration grudgingly, for I still couldn't decide whether Maya's fluency was to her credit or mine. Maya combed my hair back, puffed it up over my crown, and pinned it at my nape in a bouffant.

She revolved the mirror around my head, giving me a full-house tour, only the back kitchen regrettably omitted. "This hairstyle you like?" she said in English.

"Very nice work, looks good, but too stylish for me."

Maya switched to Bengali. "Shouldn't I urge my clients to be stylish?"

I didn't know. But the teacher must always have an answer. "You should do what the client wants."

Maya assessed and adjusted my bouffant with quick eyes and precise fingers. "Even if the client is as unstylish as you?"

"Someone like me would never go to a parlour. People who go to parlours want to be stylish."

Maya finished perfecting my mock-up and lay down, fingers knitted on ribcage, staring skywards. "But suppose a client wants a haircut that I know won't suit them. And I give it to them anyway. Wouldn't they blame me and never come back?"

I lay down beside Maya, on my side, looming over her, hand to head to preserve my bouffant. It did look good. I longed to run downstairs and flaunt it before the fogies. You think I'm just a kid you can imprison, you think she's just a village girl – but look, even in your doddering old Calcutta, things are happening that you can't imagine. "Well, in such cases, your supervisor, or maybe the salon owner, will tell you what to do… You know, I heard my teachers in the staffroom, one day, while I was helping them sort files, saying that parlours sell every client the most expensive services. Dyeings, straightenings, serums, and whatnots." I liked looking down at Maya this way. The sweat shone over the curve of her throat and pooled in the hollow between her collarbones. My head was on my hand, a foot above her, off to the side, swaying, play-acting like I was about to fall on her. "That's what you'll probably be doing. Like marketing."

"But that's awful," Maya cried. "Shouldn't I find out what each client actually wants?"

"Ha! You just said you wanted to override a client's choice so that she'd like yours and keep coming back."

Maya's face creased with worry. "I hadn't thought about that. Does a beautician work for the client or for the salon owner?"

I lay down on my back and stared at the clouds glowing pink-yellow. "Hard, isn't it? Picking one thing, and accepting all the good and bad about it? And all the while you're looking across at another job, thinking that looks all smooth."

"Is it?" Maya stared up at the still-heavy, still-withholding thunderclouds. "I've never felt that way about my job… I've never thought about my job at all, I've just done it I guess. Never realised I had options. The beauty parlour was just a daydream till now. You're the only person who's ever believed in me… I mean, I only ever told one other person,

237

and she scolded me." She paused. I watched her lips moving, her eyes sparkling as they searched the clouds. "Now I feel good," she said in English.

"Feel fine," I corrected, my heart soaring.

For she *was*, I'd just realised: Maya was on my team, with me against the old fogies. She wanted a different life too. Turns out I was not just an excellent teacher but an excellent coach! When Pa watched sports, he made his own running commentary for Ma's benefit. He said a coach's main task was to bulldoze through players' self-doubts. I reached out to squeeze Maya's arm. Something stopped me.

Suddenly I was glad she wasn't looking back at me. I looked away. My heart grew heavier and sank towards my gut. "We'll get you the job you want," I blurted, "don't you worry." But how exactly would I do that? Maya was so bright and this was so fun and had I made a terrible mistake?

A glossy raven settled on the parapet, tilted his intelligent head at us, and cawed in treble tones. I'd never have confessed it, people would've laughed: but of all the birds' voices, I loved a raven's best. Our visitor embarked on a cawing dissertation. It was the month of peace, the place of peace. Nothing could go wrong, not in my life, not on my team. I shut my eyes.

The mad cuckoo awoke himself with a sudden set of scales, like Pa awaking himself from sleep with a thunderclap snore. Perhaps smelling rain at last, perhaps just to drown out a rival songster, he burst into song. Higher and louder, shorter and hoarser, the cuckoo called, his voice beautiful with agony, cracking with agony. Maya hooted at him. I tried whistling. Again I failed.

One evening during the third week of my holiday Maya sat on the drawing room floor, pouring the rice out of the

238

reused-newspaper packets in which the grocer sold his wares, into the glass jars that stood on the newspaper-lined shelves of the five-foot-deep stone cupboard that occupied one corner of Chhordi's kitchen. Mohan finished his Lego house. I sprawled over the latest issue of *Tinkle*. Chhordi counted the change Maya had brought back from shopping.

"It's ten rupees short," Chhordi said.

Mashi and Ma emerged from their rooms, combs suspended over wavy locks. Mohan glanced up, then set about disassembling his house and building a new one. There were recounts, interrogations, explanations, protests, and tears. Ma stayed silent, giving me the stink-eye to get me to sit up and tuck my frock between my legs. Even Mashi contented herself with glaring at Maya from the offing.

Chhordi was in fine fettle, her baritone almost male in its resonance, her eyes not wandering now. "Try to remember where you left it," she said sternly, concluding the interrogation. From the way she glanced at Ma, I saw that she'd refrained from adding "thief!" only because we were there.

Later, on the terrace, in the starless mosquito-whining evening, I found Maya squatting, sobbing quietly, doing another mountain of dishes.

"To accuse me of stealing," she cried, "and that too a piddling ten rupees!" I put my arm around her shoulder. The gently stinking dishwater lapped our rubber-slippered feet en route to the misplaced drain. "I'll run away!" She wiped her hands vehemently down her thighs. "I'll leave your Chhordi and your Mashi. I won't go home to my parents either. I'll wait for this month's salary, I'll keep it all for myself, and I'll take a train – somewhere!"

"Yes, you should. But hush, now. We'll plan it all out later. Don't cry. Look, your snot is dribbling into your mouth. Taste it. Salty, isn't it?"

Curiously Maya licked her snot, screwed up her face, wiped her tongue on her wrist, and laughed. I laughed too. Then I remembered that it was from Chhordi I'd learned this diversionary tactic. She'd deployed it on me some years ago, after pulling out without warning a milk-tooth, dangling by a single flesh-thread, that I'd been nursing all week. Later I realised it must've been precisely to enlist Chhordi's demonic-dentist services that Ma, who'd nagged me about my tooth all week, had dragged us over here, that weekend, even though Mohan had a cold. Chhordi was a traitress, a slave-driver. But the snot-licking trick, with which she'd consoled me afterwards, worked again: Maya went to lick her salty snot again, but didn't, and laughed.

"Whom did you tell about your dream?" I said.

"Hm?"

"You said that before me, you told someone else about wanting to be a beautician, and she scolded you, so you never told anyone else till me."

"Ah. Patu Mashi."

"Why did she scold you?"

"She said it was silly. She said 'all that stuff' was vain."

"Ha!" I scoffed. "You know, I don't understand grown-ups' attitude to all this silly, girly, beauty stuff. They want me to grow my hair, and use a sandalwood-and-*besan* mask for my pimples. But I also must pretend not to care about my appearance. And I must never look at boys... until I'm, what, twenty-seven, twenty-eight? And then suddenly one day, baam! I must drape myself in brocade and splurge Rs.50,000 on a bridal makeover. Ugh! Old loons."

Here was another chance for Maya to join in abusing my relatives. She was silent. "But how did you decide to become a beautician?"

Maya giggled. I faced her steadily. She drew up her knees

and hugged them. "Back in the village, we didn't have a proper barber, like here. Only a *naapit*. He went around every morning with his strigil, shaving men's faces. The first time I saw a beauty parlour was when Mashi took me along, a week after I reached Calcutta. I'd never visited the metropolis before. Even now, sixteen weeks in, I've barely seen more than this neighbourhood… Mashi was showing me around the various shops, telling me what item I should buy where, how much to pay, introducing me to them, so they wouldn't cheat me. I was following her around, dazed. In our village, we only have one grocer, apart from our own, which is tiny. Then Mashi remembered she had to get her eyebrows threaded for a friend's wedding. So we went to a beauty parlour.

"It was different from anything I've ever seen. Big shiny mirrors, not a single rust spot or finger smudge anywhere. Lights so bright they hurt your eyes and cast no shadows. Well, except under the chairs. Scissors and spray-cans and potions and basins, all clean and shiny. And the girls working there, they were just like me. My age, and dark like me, and short and slim, clearly working their way up. But they were smartly dressed. And they chattered with their clients so confidently, in posh Bengali, with English words thrown in. And they moved around like it was their place, like they were the bosses."

Maya's face glowed. She looked at me but through me. Shivers ran up my spine. Would I ever feel about any one thing as Maya did about beauticianing? She thought I had everything. It's she who had the most important thing.

"Listen, Maya." Only when I heard myself speaking did I realise something better than my envy had won, and I wasn't exactly happy about it. "We only get one life. We've got to follow our dreams." Maya looked sceptical. "No, listen. You know what you want to do. D'you know how much I envy you that?"

"You envy me!"

"Yes. I don't know what I want to do with my life." Time was running out. My idols had reached out in infancy to grasp their vocation. Even then, in their twenties they'd produced only sophomoric symphonies, jumbled-up paintings, books you read only after exhausting their mature oeuvre. And I was on the threshold of my teens, of the New World, and I was still messing about with toddlers in the sandbox. "You should run away and do what you want... Maybe we can both run away."

"What!" Maya laughed. "But you're going abroad. You'll have so much fun!"

"Maybe I won't. America is so different, in the movies, like another planet. Maybe I won't make friends. Maybe I'll be bad at school. Maybe I won't understand the accent... The accent is so bad, like a mosquito stuck in my ear canal, fluttering around, unable to get in or get out. That happened to me once." I shook my head and got back on track. "Listen! You know all about farming, don't you?" Maya nodded tentatively. "We'll start our own farm!" I sat up. I saw it all before me. "Yes. You'll teach me farming, and I'll teach you English. English will be useful to, uh, to" – I remembered our maidservant back in Bombay, a fifty-six-year-old who, Ma had discovered, had been regularly overpaying for things – "to get better prices for seeds and irrigation water. People don't cheat you if you speak English... There'll be nobody to nag us or scold us. It'll be our place. We'll be the bosses!"

Maya hesitated. I jostled her knees cajolingly, patiently. After all, a person couldn't dive straight from a crying fit into a brand-new life plan. She needed a minute. Her eyes kept roaming from right of me to left of me.

"Well?" I demanded, rising on my knees, blocking the jaundice-yellow roof light from her face. "If you don't want to run away, then what's your plan?"

"I guess I could just stay here." Her eyes were swollen with tears but her face was peaceful, had been growing peaceful till I'd spoken. Now it looked like the sky above us. "I mean, it's all a silly misunderstanding. It's just ten rupees. They'll realise they're wrong. It was silly of me to cry. Though I do feel better; I'm glad I cried."

"No!" I pounded my thighs. "This is what you always do. You get upset, and then you weep a bit or you start planning to run away. But then you get this dreamy look. Like right now. You look happy, as if you've already got the thing you want and everything will be fine. But you haven't, and it won't, so stop it! You're like that couple who quarrel all day and then it's back to normal. I've been here three weeks and I've seen you crying seven, eight times. They make you cry. You tell yourself you don't have it so bad. But you do. You *should* get angry, you should *stay* angry, and make proper plans, and carry them out… Living here like Cinderella, slaving for these people, who accuse you falsely – you can't accept this."

"You want me to run away?" She sat up. "You really want to run away, too?"

"Why not? I've got the money." Panic rippled across her face. "No, listen! It's my money. I've been saving it, I've got to spend it. We'll take a train to some part of the state where nobody knows us, and then we'll" – I waved my hands – "work out the rest."

Farmer, I realised. *That* was the 1999 equivalent of daredevil, musketeer, buccaneer. Before Maya could protest I dashed downstairs for the railway timetable, an atlas, and my purse.

By the flickering light we searched the map for a suitable district, far from Maya's village near Malda to the north, which she could never visit again, far from Calcutta to the south, which I could never visit again. We settled on Nadia district. The map showed it all green and blue. We

243

pictured a well-watered lowland where we could buy a little plot and grow lots of rice. I'd borrow the money from Pa. Pa always said I choose whatever career I wanted. What I wanted was to create, acre by acre, the hugest, most productive, most innovative fairyland jungle of a farm this side of the Indus. And maybe, if I learned to care for plants, someday I'd learn to care for people.

I let my fancy fly. I painted a glowing picture. I'd dabbled with writing stories. Under the incandescent bulb's naked yellow glare, Maya warmed to my stories of our future.

In my notebook, in the page after the English alphabet, we designed our house. I was an early riser, so my room would face east. Maya's beauty parlour would face the street, so prospective clients could see her snip-snipping through the window. I heard a client knocking, the hinges squeaking as she shyly pushed open the door, her muddy slippers scraping on our coconut-coir doormat. We moved rooms around on my diagram, back and forth with arrows, many arrows entangled like rice stalks heavy with grain.

I produced my purse. I counted out Rs.5,620.

Maya's smile died. She sat back on her haunches. "That's more than enough for train tickets," she murmured. "We'll be able to get to Nadia, and live in some tiny hotel for a while until we figure things out, and maybe even buy some implements."

Her hands clasped each other. Her fingertips squeezed her knuckles. Her hands fell into her lap. She looked sober, unrecognisable, beautiful. My heart swelled with pride that this was my friend: this house-sparrow whom I'd freed from her cage, who'd metamorphosed into a spotted eagle.

"Hush," said Maya.

I'd made no noise. But in my eagerness I'd bumped into her back. We'd spent what felt like hours opening, inch-by-

244

inch, the squeaky little two-leaved wooden door that separated the first-storey rooms from the staircase. Now I let Maya go ahead, and peered after her, waiting for my vision to adjust. Behind us, the drawing room glimmered under the light of a half-moon sulking through the clouds. But the staircase was dark. I inched forward, bare toes probing the floor. It would've taken us another twenty minutes to pull the doors closed behind us, and they might've squeaked. So we left them open. We crept downstairs.

The retractable metal-grating door at the bottom of the stairs we pulled open quickly. Maya had secretly greased the metal hinges the day before. We squeezed through, pulled the well-greased door closed behind us, and threaded the lock back through both loops. God forbid this was the night the china-and-lace-fancying evildoers had been awaiting: the gate unlocked, the lights off, my relatives snoring. We unlocked the wooden front door, strung the lock through one loop on the inside, and shut the door behind us. We crept down the cement walkway. The iron front gate we did lock behind us. Maya reached between the bars and shoved the bunch of heavy Godrej keys, steel and brass, behind a potted marigold: out of view from the alley, visible from inside for when they stampeded downstairs shouting our names.

We were off.

The alley looked alien. The street-lamps' weepy yellow lights cast long shadows and bleached the sweet-shop's cobalt-blue shutters grey. Over the abandoned construction site, deep shadows kept watch. I adjusted the straps of my backpack, as my Nature Trek team leader had taught us, to shift the weight off my tailbone. Maya was carrying her jute bag, shoulder-slung.

"Long way to go." I handed Maya a Mango Bite to suck

on. At the main road we turned right. Maya was pretty sure this was the way the bus had brought her from the railway station thirteen weeks ago. I couldn't wait till we were sitting on the train, facing each other, and I could give Maya her real treat.

This morning, while Maya was out shopping, Chhordi had found the missing ten rupees in her own purse: which stayed locked in her wardrobe, to which only she had the key, slung through the *aanchal* of her white widow's *sari*. That's how she realised she'd never given Maya that ten-rupee note to begin with. Patu Mashi told Chhordi she was getting forgetful. And it was Mashi of the Marquis St. Evremondey sneer who'd wanted to tell Maya there'd been an error, and it was Chhordi of the mango-thieving, knee-skinning escapades who'd decided not to. For an apology would lower her dignity. An employer must maintain her dignity. I'd eavesdropped on the hushed dialogue with lips pursed. I'd wanted to run and tell Maya. Something had held me back, something small and ignoble curled up inside my stomach.

I'd tell her on the train to Nadia. How relieved Maya would be to hear her name was cleared! She was deserting the tyrants with only the clothes she'd brought from home. She'd even left behind the silky magenta *churidar* set Mashi had given her last month. We'd laugh, and look out at the platform rushing by, at the laggards in loose slippers sprinting after the train, and we'd wonder how she'd ever put up with such people.

A gang of lounging street dogs looked up at us. Following Maya's lead, I ignored their piercing stares and gazed boredly straight ahead as if I'd every right to be here. I'd wanted to bring biscuits to silence the street dogs. But Maya had said that, sometimes, offering an ambivalent street dog a biscuit confirmed his xenophobic suspicion,

246

making him follow you, broadcasting your infamy, starting a relay of barking street dogs down the road.

Wheels squeaked. We whirled around. A cycle-rickshaw sped towards us. The driver slowed down and demanded where we're going. Maya and I looked at each other. We hadn't expected rickshaws to be plying so late. This driver had a face like a leather walnut. Decades of chewing tobacco had yellowed his teeth; decades of sucking on *paan* had abraded them to nubs. In his shadowed face his eyes were the only living things.

"How much for Howrah station?" I said. "It's just us two, no luggage—"

"Don't want," Maya interrupted, throwing her arm around me and marching me away.

The cycle-rickshaw-driver trailed us for a kilometre, luridly painting the evils that awaited two girls out alone at night, bargaining about the fare, bargaining with nobody. For, following Maya's lead, I'd shut up. The rickshaw driver was still pursuing us. I turned my face away from the rotten-fruit stench of his breath. Finally he cursed us and sprinted away, his bony bottom in its blue-white *dhuti* made of thin cotton *gaamcha,* rocketing with each violent stroke off his narrow cycle-seat.

"He could've kidnapped us!" said Maya. "Listen, no vehicles. We'll walk."

"I agree. It's good practice. We'll be up and about all day on the farm."

Maya had never walked so far on her errands. The beauty parlour was quite far, but to get there you turned left from Chhordi's alley, she said. Now she said she recognised the stop where the bus from the railway station had put her down. "Yes, this is where I walked from, to Chhordi's house, with my bag." She halted and looked back. "I've never walked more than this in Calcutta."

247

"Come on. Slow and steady," I quoted my Nature Trek team-leader.

Streetlights flickered. Cabbage leaves and onion skins from vendors' carts lay rotting in the no-man's land between the asphalt and the shuttered shop fronts. Up ahead, bass began to boom. Headlights blinded us. A big black car hurtled at us. We jumped off the road. The car flashed blue and red inside, like that glimpse I'd got in Bombay through the pair of heavy doors, which Pa hurried me past, one night when he'd had to go shopping late and I'd insisted on going along. The car slowed down. The men whistled and beckoned at us. Maya gripped my arm and hurried onwards, staring straight ahead, almost sprinting. Her body tensed like a rubber band. The car backed up, following us backwards up the street. My heart pounded. I looked around for a brick, a plank, a knife.

The car stopped going in reverse, the men flung curses at us, and the car sped away. Well, I inferred from their tones, and from the rickshaw-driver's tones, that the words had been curses. I'd never really heard profanity. Maya came to a standstill and stared after the vanished car.

"Here." I produced a packet of biscuits, orange cream-flavoured, which Maya had bought for us this morning while shopping for Chhordi. "It's OK. We've got enough for a trek up Everest."

Maya stared at the package as if it were a cylinder of unknown function from an alien spaceship. Her face looked like modelling clay after it's lived a little, when the red ball is flecked with accidental bits of blue and yellow clay that you've tried to pound inwards. I shoved a biscuit into her hand.

She chewed mechanically. "We could,' she said, "have a midnight picnic up on the roof with all these things."

"In Nadia?" I said, munching. How wonderful food tastes in the middle of the night! "On the hotel roof?"

"No-o," Maya's voice wavered. "On Chhordi's terrace." My mouth full of masticated biscuit fell open. "The terrace keys are on that big bunch too, behind the potted marigold. We could go back, and go to the roof, and have a picnic, and lock all the doors again and go to bed. Nobody would know."

I laughed. I shoved the remaining biscuits into my shorts pocket. "Come." I marched on. I marched to the next street-light, dusting my hands, my heart racing. At last I looked back. Maya was standing where the taxi had left her. She'd finished her biscuit. She was rubbing the biscuit powder off her fingers, staring at her fingers – as if she were a magician, doing a trick where you rubbed a biscuit back into existence, only it wasn't working.

"Forget those idiots," I shouted. Immediately a street dog started barking somewhere. "They're gone. We're fine. Let's go!" I marched back towards her.

"She wasn't wrong," said Maya. She looked up. "When Patu Mashi told me I was a silly girl, and my dream was a silly dream? She wasn't wrong."

"Of course she was!" I seized her hand. "She just said that because they want to keep you under their thumb, underpaid and overworked and hopeless. She's a class oppressor. No, listen! There's this guy called Karl Marx—"

"She's not a bad person," said Maya, still rubbing her fingers. "She just doesn't want me to dream big and be disappointed."

"Why *should* you be disappointed?" I took her by the shoulders. "Would you stop rubbing your fingers! What did those idiots in the taxi say, anyway?"

"Nasty things… but that's not why. They just shocked me, sort of woke me up. You know when you wake up from a dream, and remember who you really are, and wonder what you're doing? I'm sorry, Pragya. It's my fault. You're just a child."

"The taxi's gone!" I turned her head and made her look at the empty street. "Forget about them! We can do anything we want to."

"No-oo," Maya drawled. "I can't."

"'Course you can!" Panic passed its clammy hand around my throat. I couldn't go on alone. I didn't know where Nadia was. I didn't even know what road we were on that minute. I'd found the thing, the thing I wanted to do for always, and Maya was taking it away. I shook her by the shoulders. "You're learning English so fast. No, listen! I've never taught anyone before, but I go to a school for bright children, and I swear you could beat half my classmates. Everything you do, you do it well and fast. Why can't you become a beautician? Lots of people do. People much stupider than you."

"People do. But I can't."

"Why on earth not?"

"I can't leave my family."

"Well, sure, your family will be upset to hear you've run away. But you can phone them and tell them this is what you're doing now, this is your dream. Soon you'll be earning money. You'll be independent. They'll be happy that you're happy."

"No, they won't. They'll be furious and then heartbroken. This is not what people like us do." She was standing stock-still, speaking as if in a dream.

I shrugged. "So, then, forget about your family. If you want something, you've got to give up something else. Like, Beethoven was always alone. He liked throwing soup in people's faces, so he had no friends. And he only fancied princesses, so he had no wife… You'll give up your family and get your dream."

Maya looked up at the sky. Mid-city, between the rows of buildings, over the haze cast by the yellow streetlights, the night sky gleamed grey. Her face convulsed. "I've got nobody but my family. I don't want this that badly. I'm really sorry, Pragya-*di*."

I glared, and backed away, and clenched my fists.

"You never meant to run away," I shouted. The street dog that'd begun barking somewhere lost his head and began howling on max volume. "You were just playing at wanting to be a beautician. And I was going to be a farmer. I was learning all those tree names. We were going to be farmers." I could not go on alone. All I'd ever grown was that batch of tomatoes, and the next batch had grown blighted. "You let a little thing like this scare you, two kilometres from home. You coward, you liar, you" – you thief, I wanted to shout. Now I wanted to shout the truth at her: that they had found the money and wouldn't tell her, that these were the people she wanted to go back to. "You were just playing, weren't you?"

Maya stood looking desolate. She shrugged.

"Then just give up your fantasy," I growled. "Tell me you'll happily be a servant all your life."

Her eyes flashed, like when she'd realised we had the money to run away. Then they clouded with tears, which stood lining her eyelids, refusing to fall.

"You want me to give it up? I'd go mad then, and do something awful." Her voice rang hollow. "If I can still pretend, sometimes, that I'm a beautician, as I'm doing the dishes – life wouldn't be so bad. Do you grudge me that?"

I was glaring so hard, I thought my eyes would pop out. My shoulders throbbed. They found the money, I wanted to shout, and they wouldn't tell you. And your family? You slave for them, send them all your money, and they can't wait to marry you off. Rage clasped my throat with hot choking hands. The tears finally fell down Maya's face.

I swallowed my own tears down my throat, where they fell on my rage, the drops hissing, the rage cooling. I wanted to hug her neck and bawl into her hair. I turned on my heels and marched homewards. My backpack sagged. Fresh tears spilled out my eyes, blinding me, shattering the streetlights into a million fragments of glass, a kaleidoscope of gold against the night sky.

On the last day of our four-week stay, Chhordi reconvened the tribe, including some out-of-towners whom Mohan and I hadn't seen in years, whom I smilingly pretended to remember. I stood in the drawing room facing the crowd. Fifty-four pairs of eyes, black and dark-brown and grey, clear and cloudy, gazed back at me: magician, showrunner, star.

For my grand finale, I requested each spectator to write the name of one famous person and drop the folded chit through the slot into my painted shoebox, which Maya was carrying around. Waiting, trying to look imposing, I gazed at the spectators, wondering: did they really not notice? Afternoon by afternoon, my brows had thinned, my hair shortened. I remembered Mark Antony, whose speech I'd declaimed in many a hotel bathtub, and Napoleon, whom I'd memorialised in many squinty-eyed charcoal portraits. And I realised this covert black-sheep-shearing had been *my* revolution. And I'd got away with it.

How foolish I'd been – I thought, standing on my makeshift stage – to expect honesty from my relatives! That wasn't what they were for.

Maya brought the shoebox back. I opened it and displayed the thirty folded chits. I selected a pale-blue chit, shut my eyes, palpated the chit, and declared, "Julius Caesar." I unfolded the chit and passed it to the nearest spectator. It was Mezdi, in town for our grand see-off, who opened the chit read out, "Julius Caesar," and held it up for

252

all to see. Scattered applause broke out. Next I selected a pale-yellow chit, shut my eyes again, declared, "Napoleon Bonaparte," and ditto. The applause became frantic.

All the pale-blue chits were Caesars, all the pale-yellows Napoleons. All the handwritings were mine, disguised: tilted left or right, letters tiny or huge. The chits that the spectators had put in the shoebox were suspended in the secret compartment under the lid.

Mohan sat in the front row, wriggling with excitement, his little palms red from applauding, his eyes shining. He was young, his applause unfakeable too. Good old Mohan! It would be him and me in America. I winked at him. His eyes sparkled with pride. Something pulled on my heart, tried to jerk it out of my chest and up my throat. Suddenly I understood why I'd been mean to him. I'd kept bullying him, and he'd kept taking it, leaving me lonely in my violence, hating the person who made me feel this way, and so I'd kept bullying him. Well, then, I decided: I just wouldn't bully him anymore. And then I wouldn't hate myself anymore.

I bowed to my thunderously applauding audience. Would strangers applaud so? Not for years. Maybe not ever. I hoarded this applause.

Afterwards, in our finest clothes, faces lip-sticked and shimmer-powdered, Maya and I wove our way through Chhordi's drawing room. Today the grown-ups had allowed us kids to dress up. Maya had made up herself and me, eager and experimental: as if she still took her dream seriously, as if it didn't hurt to play with it like this. Now Maya circulated alone with trayfuls of the hors d'oeuvre that Patu Mashi had prepared. Delicious but tiny. Our flight was at noon, and Ma had protested against a seven-course breakfast before another exhausting day of sitting still. Maya vanished into the kitchen. I continued my triumphal march alone.

It hadn't been hard to forgive Maya. Striding home alone that night, my anger had dissolved into relief. Farmers never got on talk shows. Farmers got in the news only when there was a flood, or drought, or farmer suicide. That night, I'd glimpsed the mountain towards which I'd been ambling all along, my own true dream, which I wouldn't have found but for Maya abandoning hers.

As Ma took tearful leave of her relatives, and Mohan allowed his apple-cheeks to be pinched and pulled, I bid Maya goodbye in the kitchen.

"I've decided what I'll become," I said. "A writer."

"Oh," said Maya, her face disappointingly calm. "That's good... How did you decide?"

"It's the thing I'm best at. Everyone says so."

"But the magic show was so splendid, Pragya-*di*."

"Yes, but these were all beginner's tricks. And they're other people's tricks, not mine. And what I've staged today is all the magic I know."

"And you don't want to learn more?"

"Not magic, no."

Maya studied my face, got distracted by a blob of shimmer powder which she reached out to pick off, but didn't, then remembered her own face was shimmer-powdered too. She wet her handkerchief for a washcloth, wrung it out, and stood adjusting the tricksy faucet to keep the water off. I picked the blob of powder off my face and rubbed it to bits.

"So, you'll be a writer... But you'll be writing in English."

"Yes." I gazed out the kitchen window. This too was an interesting view, it struck me: a view I'd passed over, summer after summer. Maya was still wringing her handkerchief, wringing it quite dry, as if she'd forgotten why she'd wetted it. "Every story is like a new romance. It'll be like having a

254

new hobby every month. It'll be like" – like sucking raw tamarind, untempered by salt, year after year, just to wring from people their admiration. It was time to grow up.

Slowly unfolding and refolding her wrung-out wrinkled-wet handkerchief, Maya nodded. "I won't be able to read your books, but I'll hear about them, and I'll know they're good." I wanted to remind her that she'd begun learning English, to tell her she must continue, that English would always be useful. I didn't. "I have some news, too."

"Oh?"

Hope fluttered in my stomach. Had she written to her parents about her dream, had they offered to set her free from maid-servanting? My brand-new grownup nonchalance deserted me and I pictured my pocket-money, waiting in my backpack, still mostly unspent. I could hand Maya the money, slip her downstairs, and see her off to her brand-new life. I wouldn't grudge her going off alone, now that I, too, knew where I was going.

"I had a letter," said Maya, "from home last night. They want me to go home for a week, to see some boys they've shortlisted... I expect I'll be married in October."

I didn't ask her to write to me. After our aborted escape, which we'd never talked about, we'd aborted our English lessons. I'd suggested it, once. Hmm, she'd said. Then she'd invited me to play tug-of-war with the day's starched *saris*. This time I'll let you pull hard, she said.

Now I remembered she hadn't even given me her village address. I had always only been a summer's friend.

On the rooftop next door, aloe vera showered over a pot's edge, like a bouquet a Dickensian eccentric might present to his lady-love. "I hope you'll like one of the boys you meet. And I hope he'll be good to you... At your wedding, you'll be able to do your own hair and makeup. That'll be fun."

255

"Yes."

"So you'll be out of Chhordi's grasp soon! No more Patu Mashi shouting at you."

She smiled. I watched her last chance to abuse my family drifting away. I smiled back. I watched my last chance to tell Maya about Chhordi's duplicity drift away. Why should I tell her? We'd never really been on the same team.

We embraced. Mashi's shimmering face-powder rubbed off from my chin onto the shoulder of Maya's best *salwar-kameez*: the satiny magenta that Mashi had given her, that enriched her clay-brown skin to black coffee.

"You go outside, now." Tears streaked her shimmer-powder. "Your relatives will want you." She hung back to wash her face. The party was over, and for the maid it was safest to change quickly out of play-clothes.

Chhordi and Mashi had been running around all morning. Now I sat with them and thanked them for their hospitality. Gazing, now, into Chhordi's eyes, no longer black, not black at all, cloudy and faraway – I couldn't remember any of the stories that she'd been boring me with, that I'd run away from. If I hadn't listened, how had I known they were boring?

Mashi handed Chhordi her pills. As Chhordi swallowed, a drop of water went the wrong way. She coughed and coughed. Mohan and I thumped her back. She was alright soon, waving us off, eyes twinkling. But now it was I who found myself praying, to a god we'd not been raised to believe in, that Chhordi would live to see our next visit. Next time, I vowed, I'd spend all holiday listening to her stories.

Chhordi was always sentimental at farewells. She made Ma swollen-eyed too. Poor Ma! She'd lost Dimma two years ago, and now Chhordi, her favourite aunt, was all wheezy breath and wandering eyes. I should've kept Ma better company, interrupted Chhordi's melancholy talk with fun and games. When I was ill Ma always sat with me, and here I'd shunned her all holiday.

In the sunshine-yellow taxi, I leant against Ma's well-starched, well-ironed pink-and-blue cotton *sari* and passed my arms around her. In America, I vowed, I'd stick right by her.

We watched the double-decker bus ahead veering around street-corners, almost overbalancing each time. We watched a cycle-rickshaw-driver's stick-thin legs straining, carrying uphill a large bare-backed woman. My forehead itched, but I sternly forbore from scratching. The itch faded. So that's all it takes, I thought: sitting back.

Ma passed her hand through my hair, feeling the ends. I realised the ends must feel sharp from my daily haircuts. I stiffened, preparing to defend myself against Ma's reproaches for another illicit haircut. But Ma merely stroked my hair. I hugged her close, grateful for her silence, grateful for Chhordi's forgotten old toothless scissors that had gnawed my hair off dully. Abroad, I thought, maybe Ma wouldn't mind my giving myself haircuts on the cheap.

I graciously granted Mohan the window seat. I pinched his cheek. It might take years to repair the effects of my bullying. I folded my arms in my lap in my middle seat. The sky darkened. The cabin-lights dimmed for take-off. The rain-clouds gathered dark and silent. I've missed the rain, I thought. I miss Calcutta even though we're still here. I miss Bombay even though we've got another month left there. I miss Chhordi and Mashi and all their stories that I never really listened to. My face scrunched up and snot streamed down my nose.

How awful it would be to cry before Mohan! He'd laugh at me, get even for all my bullying. I swallowed my tears down my throat.

And there, in the quiet before the storm, in the plane quiet before its take-off roar – suddenly I managed to whistle. I realised that, all these years, I'd been trying whistling wrong. I'd been exhaling. My whistle, it turned out, was an inhaler. Once I'd made the air sing instead of wheeze, the rest was easy. Deftly my lips readjusted and my tongue moved in my throat. I imitated Chhordi's mad cuckoo.

First, a short lilting melody repeated a few times. Then, a single sweet note of invitation as the storm gathered suddenly dark. Finally, as we took off into a steady shower, a rising scale of interrogation. Ma shushed me. But it was alright. At last the rain had come to cool Chhordi's roof, and downstairs they'd sleep well tonight.

THE CITY

My friend in New York City was walking her rescued mutts yesterday when she heard gunshots, screaming and running, silence, then sirens. At the school where my friend's sons study and her husband teaches, a student had begun shooting people. My friend's email described how she'd texted her family, tried to call, decide if it was safe to go get them. Her coherence amazed me. Always on television, the eyewitness – to terrorist attacks, to botched nose jobs – talks coherently. In her place I'd be a blubbering mess, repeating to the correspondent ad nauseum, "I was in the wrong place, wrong time, I'll never go any place again." But, who knows, maybe I too would be coherent. I'm a basket case, but I'm also alive. The living survive catastrophe, make meaning, live on. I sympathised with my friend, and wondered how anyone could live in that country, where every day someone picks off a baker's dozen of strangers. Here in Bangalore, I wouldn't know where to get a gun if I wanted to pick someone off, which I do sometimes – a passing thought. This morning, reading my friend's email, I wasn't in a murderous mood, so I felt smug about living in India, free from the terror of the world ending in an instant without sense.

Make me, God, a time capsule: like the paper napkin with which the artist-cum-writer wiped the gravy off her lips, painted carefully raspberry to match the stones in her silver chandelier earrings. My new friend, whom I'd met online, who I hoped would introduce me to her publisher, was an ex-fashion model. Her ears sagged from six decades of statement earrings. But her breasts sagged probably no more than mine do at thirty-four. For she'd preserved herself: no high-impact aerobics to chisel and erode the knees, to tilt the nipples towards the earth's lascivious lava bowels. She'd come to our casual lunch fully made up, a psychedelic peacock, like four decades ago, when she'd confronted the world from *Femina* covers and Satya Paul ramps. She was still svelte. Even her bum was flat, concave, really; she had only a little tummy, low and abrupt, like a bum mispositioned.

At the food court, in the mall, she regarded me with wandering eyes, smiled uncertainly, too readily, and began gabbling about her achievements. She'd held shows of her mixed-media art (only in Bangalore, ha), won copywriting awards, published books about backpacking trips with *sadhu*s and *goonda*s, been inducted into white-robed cults of Buddhism and Taoism, distilled back-balcony marijuana into canna-butter, and posed with German lovers on Greek islands, their pythonlike arms garlanding her scrawny throat. I'd expected I'd be the one who had to impress. She nodded when I spoke, but flooded any islet of silence with words, words piling into a cushion for her flat bum, the more comfortably to sit opposite me. I've achieved nothing, but I'm still young – a baby, she makes me feel – my potential prickly vast, and she kept fidgeting, as if from prickly piles, piling her achievements into the scales against my youth. Three husbands married and divorced, rave reviews received, a pantheon of paramours parodied in prose poems – still nothing would be enough. Still playing catchup, her eyes scanned my unfurrowed skin, my unsagging triceps, as she dabbed her raspberry pout, rosetted with wrinkles, and pushed away unfinished her half-portion of veg fried rice, and wiped, carefully on the paper napkin, hands already clean.

Make me, God, like the paper napkin, preserving the world's oily chins and lipstick-smeared throats, illicitly recording strangers' fingerprints, documenting – with

Sherlock Holmes eyes and Dalai Lama egolessness – lunch-hour accidents, happy-hour spills: the half-empty can of Guinness that in his Lexus after happy hour he threw at my sister's face, that smashed against the window, foaming brown like the urine of the doomed, reeking, when she told him they were done; the red spot on my best friend's white trousers during lunch when she was three months pregnant and beginning to like the idea; all the other objects featuring in all the other stories that those closest to me will never narrate to me – so that, when it's all over, the forensicists may peel apart my paper layers, sticky with beer and miscarriages and lipstick, for clues to the final mystery: the mystery of human unhappiness.

Can you make me, God, a napkin? You're not there, still sometimes I talk to you, for I wish someone were listening. It was our wishes that made you, God, back before we had words to utter our wishes, to utterly distort them – the three-year-old's wish for his mother to envelop him in her geranium-scented warmth distorted into the 56-year-old opiate-addict wife-beating superstar's wish for a mansion enveloping a whole Caribbean island. Up through Homer's wine-dark sea you broke, from the forehead of our hivemind, fully formed, as Athena broke from the forehead of Zeus. But I live in the end times. My wishes could not make you, God, could make at best on-time delivery of my plastic-bagged, laminated-boxed, fifteen-spiced chicken biryani, before-time delivery. My sea is not wine-dark but plastic-white. Each wave climaxes, and the wave crest disintegrates into a thousand white plastic particles condemned never to sink, to float weightless forevermore on the surface of their own guilt. My prayers are too corrupt to resurrect you, God, could make at best a plastic snowman, tall and white as the mountain once was, composed of all the plastic in the sea, bonded with the

261

sticky spit of cave swiftlets indentured, a thermocol plate stuffed in each hollow cheek of the snowman's skull, smiling down at the people milling around, selfying: a Buddha smile, a Chelsea grin. *That* my wishes could make. But *that* they wouldn't call God. They'd call it What.

And feeling smug that, unlike my friend – who'd narrowly escaped being murdered by What knows whom, who knows why, for I live in gun-free India – sitting, now, in the black-and-yellow autorickshaw, going home from meeting the writer-cum-artist. I'm being, yes, quite snide about her. I told her I was writing a book, and she liked my stories, but she offered no introductions. Of course I couldn't ask her. She was wriggling to impress me; to have asked would've been to forfeit the upper hand. If she'd been a man I could've asked, and paid her back in bed, and evened the score. Besides, I sniffed blood. I went prepared to be awed, but there she sat fidgeting, reciting her resumé, fiddling with her bra straps. And if not awe, then something else, for nature abhors a vacuum. Something pulls me out of my mulling, I wake up, I realise my autorickshaw driver is doing stunts.

He swings the tiny vehicle across the flyover's six lanes, races traffic lights on city streets, wedges us into the four square feet between a city-bus and a delivery-van, either of which could swallow us, a one-bite snack, spicy-sweety Lays potato crisp, *No one can eat just one*™. I perch on the centre of the narrow seat, putting between myself and the swerving, speeding traffic beyond the autorickshaw's open sides one more inch of life, an air cushion. Revving his diesel engine, hurtling down the fifty meters of clear road before the next traffic jam, the driver brakes always last-second, last-inch. And, behind him, it's me who's braking for him. I dig my toes into the floor, Bang comes this sixteen-wheeler truck's backside at my head, brake, driver, brake, for What's sake. And, voilà, he feels me braking the floor, he feels my smooth round knees coaxing, through his hard seatback, the small of his back, he yields to me, the brakes screech. We lurch. Back on these streets after Lockdown, I've lost practice. The world assaults me afresh.

Why don't I ask him to slow down?

He would obey. Briefly, before insidiously speeding up again, defying me, daring death. I could scold him, or offer to tip him if he slows down. A tip wouldn't cost me much. And auto-drivers don't make much since ride-hailing apps took over, put drivers at our beck and call again, no more rudeness or crazy rates. But I don't ask him to slow down.

You hear that music blasting on his radio? The speakers sit behind me, peeking out the auto's tiny back window that's covered in plastic scratched cloudy, scratched blind, as Oedipus the monstrous scratched his eyes. Sony speakers. The driver's splurged on these. Could've bought, say, four months of Masterclass with that money, to do what, learn from world-class, autorickshaw-drivers? The woofers throb with a percussion-pounding song opening, and then a man sings, largo, of lost love, lyrics in old-world Urdu, repeating each couplet eleven times, luxuriating in his angst, as the caricature of Big Business luxuriates with his penis-sized cigar on his human-skin sofa. Love's yearning wavers vibrato in the singer's voice, pulls at my heartstrings, pulls but how? *I* don't do love. It's 2022, love went out along with USB 2.0s. The alto insists that love is here, love is all, all will be well. I let him lullaby me, I don't ask my auto-driver to slow down. For I'm not really afraid. *I* couldn't have a road accident. Lacking courage to speak up, I survey the autorickshaw, give me, What, a sign that I'll be fine. The windshield is spiderweb-cracked. Tiny shards of glass, trapped in the cracks, glister like champagne in a flute swirling against a shock-blue sky.

263

See? This driver's just had an accident, he'll be careful. He's driving fast, but not recklessly: he does always brake last-second. He's just getting me there fast.

And who wouldn't want to get there fast? There, wherever I'm going. Look at the traffic. Saturday afternoon, half-day, get us home, this is our time. Roll us down the springboard, man overboard into the weekend, my deep end, sanity room eight feet underwater. Countdown's begun, thirty-six hours to go, every second on the road is coming out of *my* time. Cars and cars and cars and cars, weaving blurring screeching. Motorbikes and motorbikes and motorbikes and motorbikes, dancing around SUVs, shortcutting over rubble-piles, mounting with engines revving the few fragments of pavement that Bangalore's got left, broken stones yawning open over sewers, bikes veering over the median's white dashes, dashing white rabbits, to overtake traffic, dash back onto the right side before the cars rushing down the other way, honking warning at pedestrians, come. And it isn't a warning. And they wouldn't slow down. This is not a game of Chicken.

On motorbikes, and in cars, autorickshaws, and buses, we sit, uncurious as sheep on the final truck. Maybe I'll get wherever I'm going, or maybe I'll have an accident, finally get time off work, familiar faces thronging my deathbed, tears dropping from their eyes onto my fire-eaten face. Something's happening to me at last, yes, life is finally beginning. It's true that the moment of death lasts forever: I thought I had forever, so I wasn't looking but now. But death refuses us, mid-afternoon sun bakes the bikers' helmets, life stretches before us, a traffic jam stretching to the moon and back. On motorbikes, and in cars, autorickshaws, and buses, the drivers' eyes glint, watching the traffic monitor's countdown, red on black, watching the seconds tick away forever, and every second there's more to catch up on, the scale tips up, our lives weigh less, matter nothing, the scale swings skywards, the birdcage swings its door open flings its bird heavenwards. My auto-driver fidgets, shakes out his shoulders, looks left and right, looking for something to look at. I feel him. I feel the back of his neck sweating into his khaki uniform-collar. Driving all day, three traffic jams per kilometre, everybody speeding, vehicles teleporting from What knows where to fondle your fenders – you must always be on, on alert, on cocaine, just to survive.

And the dust, and the heat.

All morning the sun hacked machete-like at the dusty air, at the dust that is the air, dust from metro construction, from hillocks of burning rubbish, broken plastic chairs, wedding food, car tires still gleaming new, all swept together and set afire under What's blue sky, dust swept up by maids in the condo complexes towering over the suburbs, where last year stood a shale hill covered in scrub, scrub that had spent aeons grinding, with its roots, shale into soil, doing the work of God the Eternal Grindr. Now the hill's carcass slouches between the condo complex and the megamall. The scrub is gone, the hill's formidable topple-ready boulders are gone, the slow red soil is gone. They're carving up the hill from every side, haphazardly, like the Hinduja brothers attacking the same pot of Sankranti khichdi, for gravel and cement and blocks. What did you think your tower was made of? The half-eaten hill's grey-shale bones stand spilling red-shale guts and blood-red stone-dust. All morning the sun prince fought through the dust thicket to get to earth, Sleeping Beauty, all morning the autorickshaw-driver inhaled the dust, and while I was lunching with my new friend the sun won the battle. Now it roasts us, in our thick polyester suits and acrylic dresses, which they sent us from NYC, via China, which we donned, like good sheep, sheep in clothes made for Europe, roasting ourselves on India's rapidly revolving rotisserie.

Driving an autorickshaw all day through traffic, dust, heat, riding a motorbike all day as a Delhivery man, Swiggy food-delivery man, Urban Clap domestic-chores man, as the teacher on the city-bus who's droned all day at government primary-school students, every student Googling under the desk "Barbie makeover" or "sexy Aunties", or as the Aadhar clerk who's spent all day pushing request-forms for correcting misprinted names on government ID cards, now sitting sheeplike behind the red-eyed bus-driver, counting the rupees in the bank, *how long how lo-oo-ong* before I get a motorbike – can you blame us for wanting to get there, wherever, right now, live or die? My auto-driver has no choice. However many white marble shrines Modi may erect to his own godhood, oops-sized manhood, India's a poor country. Life's cheap, and diesel's too expensive to squander it driving slowly. On the other side of the world another war is raging, supply-chains disrupted, diesel is sprinting up the charts, up and up, weightless, breaking Usain Bolt's records. Doping is suspected. Don't stop, you can't afford to, the price of diesel is what you've got to out-race, save every second, keep your engines humming through the traffic jam. Keep it moving.

Busy bee, black-and-yellow! Heroic warrior against the impossibility of existence! To your sudden pyre, one tonne of metal crumpled in a heap on its side by the roadside, your diesel blood will raise its torch of honour with a puff and a bang.

If you want to live, there's never a choice. My theory used to be that it's because India's poor, we're feeling left behind, sprinting to catch up, that we drive suicidally. But when my American friend drives down the highway, where they've got a maximum speed limit and a minimum, the other drivers, she tells me, make her drive at the maximum. Above the maximum, look, there're no cops around, go, be a blur on the traffic cameras. She used to try to drive her

Volvo sensibly. A Dodge Challenger, one Sunday morning on the highway, rear-ended her, the driver walked up and, arms akimbo, pocket maybe bulging, chastised her through her window, stop holding us up, you such-and-such. America is rich, at least those drivers of big cars are. Life shouldn't be cheap if you're rich. So what ailment have the Americans that makes them rush, live or die, rush where to? So, I realised, wrong theory.

I've got a new theory.

This one autorickshaw trip, from one part of south Bangalore to another, restaurant to home, ten kilometres, has already taken 130 minutes, and we're not even close. The roads are a series of potholes that have their own potholes, hundreds of crores of taxpayers' money wasted, the congealed blood of the murdered hills floating free again, floating murderously into the lungs of street dogs, children, murderously speeding drivers, people too poor to be ensconced in an AC car. What with diesel racing to the skies, Uber racing to the bottom, the driver must make What knows how many trips per day. To scrape by, to fund his cigarette addiction, second-hand chain-smoke vacuumed into my lungs. Still, cigarettes are better than alcohol, the leading addiction among autorickshaw-drivers, the leading cause of their wives' deaths, their sons' road rage. My driver dropped out of school, he says. But from the way he talks and the way he steers, thinking dozens of meters ahead, anticipating the next-but-one move of the driver three cars ahead, he could give Vishwanath Anand a run for his money. On these roads nobody sees the white rabbits, these lane markings must be ornamental, my driver, too, swerves anywhere any minute, decelerates with the precision of bullet-time choreography.

An intelligent man, reaction time of a silicon chip, a crazed gunman, spending all day shuttling through truck horns hopped up on speed, through this circus of the always

267

almost dead, his gun this rickshaw enwombing him pointed at his own head entombing him. Can you blame him for driving suicidally?

So I reason, sedating myself with empathy, distracting myself from my own complicity. So I keep braking the auto's floor, that'll save me from dying when he crashes, I clutch the auto's fragile frame two-handed, I listen to the Urdu alto singing. It's a different singer, different song, the love now unrequited, voice still alto, voices raised in prayer to woman, goddess, bitch. The speakers' bass is on max and the percussion pounds, coaxing my heartbeat slow, nowhere to rush anymore. Love's here now.

On motorbikes and in cars and behind the glass windows of restaurants, sit people gossiping about their friends' failed fertility fanfare, their colleagues' woeful work wardrobe, and how many crores their own new flat cost them. They don't say "Crore," they say "Cr," modestly mis-abbreviating one-syllable "Crore" into two-syllable "see-are". It costs "one-see-are", that's ten million rupees to my American friend, to put fifty kilometres between them and their jobs, to live in peace and green. Then fifty lakhs, that's point-five-see-are, for an air-conditioned Audi to zoom back into the city for work, and fifty thousand a month on diesel. Diesel is the new gold; it's gold dust that's thickening the air, sickly sweet in our nostrils, nausea in the pit of our stomachs at day's end. So you order mint chicken, delivered to your doorstep in plastic bowls, sturdy plastic bowls, which you can reuse, well, not with us, but elsewhere, see how green we are, the bag all this plastic comes in is paper not plastic. So you order mint chicken, for your body knows mint cures nausea, and the chicken comes along for the ride, comes along on the Zomato delivery-man's speeding motorbike, for, if he's a minute late, you get your money back.

In cars and in restaurants, stuffing their faces, vomiting words, sit thin people and fat people. More fat people every day. India has the world's biggest population of malnourished humans, but watch out, USA, we're course-correcting, catching up, soon we'll overtake you in gross tonnage, no Indian left behind. Curly peri-peri fries and chili chocolate ice-cream, quarter-pounder burgers and *kaju* rolls stuffed with poppy jam, mutton *dum biryani* and fried chicken, buy five get three free, 50% off on membership for free delivery. The restaurants are air-conditioned, gotta be, for Bangalore had a paradise climate, but then everybody came and the trees went and the skyscrapers came and the forests went and the roads came, now you must have air-conditioning to get any work done, to get any sleep slept. To get ahead. If you don't get ahead you'll lose your livelihood, there's no standing still, never a choice. In these condo complexes the air-conditioning is central, twenty towers per complex, twenty floors per tower – nineteen, actually, for there's no thirteenth floor, NYC said the thirteenth was a bad teenth, teenth of meth cut with fentanyl – and only six flats per floor, so that everybody gets a good view. What's 360° of concrete-view divided by six? What view do you get from six feet under? The best views, the giant hoardings promise, and 80% open space, five-mile-long jogging track gleaming white, winding intestine-like between imported palms, heated open-air swimming pools, new-and-improved flowers, hibiscuses big as your face, pink as your rejuvenated vagina, all buffering India's one-see-are persons behind their climate-controlled windows from the traffic speeding and the dead hill's blood, Andromeda-strain power-blood, dust-blood, swirling past the 50-foot-tall boundary walls into the lungs of us others.

I pretend to despise these alienated snobs in their one-

269

see-are eagle's eyries. Truth is, if I had one-see-are, I'd wedge myself in there quicker than a rabid dog's canines in your calf. The city's become unliveable, I'll take a double order of alienation. So grind down a shale hill, build me up. No, fool, not *this* shale hill. This one's part of my penthouse view, paid for and protected, go find another. A shale stone eyrie a half-mile up is the perfect soapbox from which to lament these end times. Your voice carries further: the wind prostrates itself at your feet to tear the words from your lips.

One-see-are. See-See-are. See-see-me.

My auto weaves through and locks itself, the missing puzzle piece in a tight traffic puzzle outside a condo complex. Through the gates I watch the fat green garden pipes drenching the thick poolside turf, flooding the jogging track. The swimming pool glisters blue. I think of my maidservant. Yes, I've got a maidservant, you've got one too, fellow Indian fellow oh-I'm-just-a-humble-middle-class Indian. I hope she'll never pass this way. My maidservant has no running water. She waits every Sunday for the water-tanker, fights with her neighbours for water to fill her house with for the week, water in plastic jugs, steel jars, tin cans, water for handwashing, bathing, clothes-washing, shit-flushing, cooking, drinking. In her neighbourhood of shacks, the municipal waterpipes became in 2018 purely ornamental. The pond beside her house has long since been drained by private borewells. I hope she'll never see this swimming pool empty of people, full to the brim, the thirsty wind crouching between its legs spread open sucking noisily its sun-sweetened juices.

We're off again. I survey the delivery-men on their motorbikes, searching for my maidservant's son. He spends all day and some nights riding a motor scooter around Bangalore, delivering Amazon parcels, parcels shipped from who knows where, ordered by What knows whom, ordered not even who himself remembers why. I wonder if this is he, weaving between the eighteen-wheelers. If he goes fast enough, just a little faster, he'll get rich. There's nothing to do but work, anyway: his colleagues change every few months, rotating between Amazon, Swiggy, Zomato, seeking the perfect job, gotta get there first; it won't be perfect forever. He laughs at them, his mother taught him not to be the rolling stone. He keeps on the roads all day. For his goal waits at the end of this long straight road, out of sight, it's true, but definitely there. So he speeds, while his mother overeats. My maidservant's so fat, she barely fits with the mop and bucket through the doorways. American television tells my maidservant and her son on their smartphones that they too can go from rags to riches, tells them so confidently, voice breaking with confidence, alto with lullaby. Maybe he hears with his inner ear the false note, maybe she knows in her deepest dreams that they never will catch up. Maybe that's why he speeds, determined to get wherever, now or never, and she overeats, she's already fat. She'll never be slim again. He's had two road accidents; she sticks herself with insulin thrice a day. Work all day, eat all evening. There's nothing else to do, anyway: the rest of their family is back in the village where the gaunt farmers are hanging themselves.

Fellow Indian! Away up there in your penthouse, buffered behind fifty meters of Vanuatu palms and Dutch tulips, your tower so high, your windows so shut – what has driven you hiding away up there? When you're driving, and a motorbike parked on the street's other side suddenly wheels into your path, and you miss pancaking it by a second, you honk in protest, you lament, Look at this, India will never be civilised. But you speed along with everyone else, seat belted in your BMW. You scurry up your tower, little rat legs trembling under your bulk, rat brain so skilled at maze running, and you stuff down your throat the

271

porterhouse steak, bury your head in the Fendi cushions. What's left on Netflix? Wealth does not buffer you from the malady, any more than it does the Americans on the highway. The malady is in the air, more contagious than Covid, it finds you even though you never step into the record-breaking heat, in here it's always 25°C, that's "degrees-see", and the weather's only the numbers on your iPhone, and your jet-setting job leaves you never time to read about the war, never famine, what ice-sheets collapsing? Up in your tower, still the common malady finds you, in diabetes depression rage alcoholism social media addiction domestic violence embolic stroke anxiety deep vein thrombosis lung cancer suicide insomnia obesity drug overdose.

I told you that was a bad teenth.

The auto drops me off. Such acrobatics deserve either a medal or jail, I think as I GPay the driver. But the police would laugh if I complained about speeding, here in the world's diabetes capital, malnutrition capital, rape capital, and Ola's customer care would only assure me my feedback is valuable. I could chastise the auto-driver myself, but why bother? I'm alive, his driving is no longer my problem. I walk away, I'm fine, I never would've been hurt. But my motto rings hollow. For a second I see how my friend can live in America, I see that I, too, live a life that can end in an instant without sense. What sense is there more in suicidal driving, murderous driving than in shooting strangers? I too am alive, I'll carry on, go out again tomorrow, take my life in my hands like a bull's heart dripping blood raised to the gods in tribute. I look up.

There is a hole in the shock-blue sky. A black hole, gaping. I could've died today.

My knees buckle. I drop onto the foot-high pavement. My body is shaking but my mind is chattering, valiantly repairing the hole in the sky, I couldn't've died, no I couldn't've.

My nostrils are quivering, sniffing the *tandoori* chicken, with which the students streaming from the colleges are compensating for their day's travails: up before dawn, preening studying commuting yawning through class part-time job commuting again, and fried chicken too. If only the mass shooter had sat around, eating fried chicken, listening to languid songs of love, the alto might've persuaded him: hurry not, my friend, to your end: there's time for everything. There was time for love when the world was beautiful.

My anger at the student who threatened my friend's family dissolves into pity. Even the pity evaporates. What if it is he who is right? An American but he, too, left behind, deciding already at twenty-one, nineteen, thirteen years old that he never will catch up. Looking up, seeing the black hole gaping in the sky, and not looking away, staring steadily back, raising his arms, take me God. Not fooling himself, like my auto-driver, my Swiggy delivery man, my colleagues who do their speeding for themselves in their own Citroëns, my artist-cum-writer friend, like me – he knows the truth: it's no use speeding down the straight-and-narrow. They left us behind but they told us we could catch up, so we're speeding, not really believing we could die, accepting the risk. Heads we crash, tails we burn. But that thirteen-year-old didn't look away from the hole in the sky. He realised he never would catch up to his classmates, to all the bronzed veneered he-mans on his phone. He plugged his ears against the lies and let his gun do the talking.

I get up. I walk on. I text my new old artist-cum-writer friend: I'm home safe, are you?

I want to ask her why. Why does she rub at her wrinkles, telling me unasked that they're only down her chin, and a

273

bit in her armpits, that it's other women her age who're truly unsightly, why does she keep telling me about the special lotion that keeps her face virginal, why, when we tried on clothes from the discount racks, did she suck in her little bumtummy, why does she tell me she needs to ramp up her workout routine? She has lived, and loved, and made of her living and her loving pictures and books that move strangers to hunt up her email address, to reach out to her through the internet's mile-deep shit-sea. She has earned her years, has become interesting, as every elderly person ought to be, ought to have had the chance to become. Still she wants smooth skin, taut triceps, she wants to outrun time, still her achievements don't counterbalance her years, the scales tipping every day up and up. For on this road, down which she's rushing, other drivers began hours ago, other artists began years ago: brilliant young artists, and svelte older artists with their bums the right way around. Still always playing catchup, to do more, weigh less, to feel for one second that she has caught up with time.

Make me, God, like the paper napkin, with which the artist-cum-writer – but no, but she threw the napkin away. Napkins are fragile. You can't absorb all the world's shit and stay sane. You'll plunge into the deep end and never come back up, shoot strangers, become the hurtling matchstick in a sublime ten-car conflagration. The hole in the sky is for me to fill. Make me, then, God, like the marble disc, our tabletop, at which I sat with my friend, which under our elbows kept getting hotter, marble smooth and blind and black, to shield from myself, to shield for all humanity, the hole in the sky.

Make us, What, all blind to our own malaise. Keep dribbling into our mouths, upturned like nestlings, fast cars, slow songs, preloaded guns, food-at-your-doorstep-in-five-minutes, please-tip-your-delivery-man, three minutes, you-

274

better-coz-we-can't-afford-to-pay-him, gotta-make-a-profit, brand-new content every minute, and scrub-covered shale hills to grind down into gravel and up into Bangalore's tallest newest tower, one-see-are, see-see-are, see our heads vanishing into the storm clouds. Keep us nodding along to the music as we race down the highway, visibility zero at midday in an Indian midsummer, the sun giving up its fight, the prince has given up battling through the bramble thicket, sleep on, Sleeping Beauty. Keep away the evil prince who wants to awaken us. If we woke up for a second, stopped talking shopping eating fucking watching, woke up, looked up – we'd go mad.

Turn the corner, I'm almost home, clench those glutes, get there faster. Wherever we're going isn't worth getting there slowly, doesn't deserve one extra second, so it's alright, these hair's-breadth escapes from speeding trucks and cleareyed gunmen, it's all good, little friendly free jolts to electrocute us awake.

Barrier reefs and Bali starlings and banjo evenings: the things to love, to long for, to slow down for, are going, going, gone. This engine runs now only on fury, in top gear, the gearshift has locked. Hush, now, here's music to hum along to, a tombful of food to swallow, strangers to shoot, autorickshaws to race, a wombful of sensations in which to curl up, shut our eyes and suck our thumbs and hide away from our panic and our pain.

BETTER LATE THAN NEVER

It is a truth universally acknowledged, that every human soul, must be in want of another. Growing up, Vishrammi had this axiom drummed into her skull and never thought of challenging it. Then came puberty.

Her friends lost their wits, mooning over pimple-faced boys, doodling their married signatures on the inside covers of trigonometry books, sucking in their stomachs at recess before the bathroom mirror. The nuns who ran the school had installed tiny mirrors, rust-splotched, so the girls had to stand all the way back across the bathroom on tiptoe to see their stomachs. Vishrammi, watching, wrinkled her nose and decided romance was not for her.

It was 1991. The country was high on liberalisation. People were grasping at 100-gramme neon-green packets of Lays chips sweet and salty, at 200-millilitre bottles of Pepsi coffee-black and sugar-sweet. Marriage, which had been for millennia God's will for all mankind, had become, for people of a certain class, a matter between your wallet, your groin and yourself: a matter merely of common sense. When Vishrammi asked her parents whether she'd have to get married someday, they replied, "Everyone needs security." She heard them correctly: if she could provide for herself, she would free her parents from their duty to get her married off, settled down, dispensed with.

At 14, Vishrammi topped her class of 80. At 16, she topped the school district, graduating early. Vishrammi could've gone anywhere, become anything. Doctor, lawyer, software engineer. But she enrolled at Delhi University in English Literature. Her parents were devastated by this throwing-away of her future. "If you don't mend your ways," they warned, "we'll have a heart attack." They gathered the clan to chastise and commiserate, but Vishrammi was impervious. Next year, when she earned D.U.'s gold medal, her parents declared, "She's the smartest girl, always knew what she was doing. I told you so."

Vishrammi earned her PhD at 23. Still virginal, already matronly, she settled down to teach students to bisect the Bard's double entendres and decode Derrida's deconstruction. Her colleagues were much older, their faces creased with teething troubles and impossible in-laws, their abdomens, under their meticulously draped saris, scarred with childbirth – all female, of course: for only men too stupid for science, or women who needn't be breadwinners, choose the humanities. Every few months one of them squeezed out another baby, and stopped by Vishrammi's cabin to ask when the prodigy would settle down.

Vishrammi would smile till they left, fume afterwards, and answer them by squeezing out another paper in an international journal. On Sunday evenings, babies wailing on laps, husbands lounging with the *Statesman*, heels above head, Vishrammi's colleagues would shred her latest paper over milk coffee and sugar-studded Nice biscuits. After due deliberation they concurred that the secret of Vishrammi's prodigious paper productivity was deep dissatisfaction with her personal life – very deep, very well-concealed, consummate actress as she was. Pity was called for, and flowed freely with the tea.

Every summer vacation, Vishrammi went to the hills. From the guesthouse balcony she watched the fog leak from the lowest mountain's armpit to blanket the whole range. How peaceful to be among the clouds. The first day or two, coming from Delhi's circus traffic's nonstop honking, the silence was resounding, soporific. She'd awaken with a jolt, ideas for books ricocheting in her skull, her mind stretching and rolling in the silence like a dog in grass.

The guesthouse caretaker would smile, and bring Vishrammi tea at her paper-strewn desk, even when she forgot to ask. Vishrammi's brow would unfurrow from her literary labours, and she'd offer the old man a tip. He always refused. His neighbours called him a fool. They knew that Vishrammi was a big-city professor, too odd for an ordinary groom, but saving all her handsome salary – living on campus, dining at mess. They knew, for she'd told them, for she hid nothing. The old man could've taken her for a ride, but he didn't want her. He liked her.

Vishrammi hopscotched from success to success, publishing papers in top journals, getting foreigners to review her latest book, publishing her own book reviews into top international dailies, supervising the innovative work of doctoral students: students who hadn't yet surrendered to the banalities of finances, family, and new fridge; students whom she treated, to her colleagues' amusement, like her peers.

Vishrammi never made flesh-and-blood friends. She was content to confide in *Little Women*'s Jo, *A Dubious Battle*'s Doc, and *Buddenbrooks*'s Antonie. Between them, these three understood her rebellions and ambitions, her existential ailments, and the curious yearning that sometimes seized her. But this last generally happened after a day of being sniggered at by her colleagues, so she dismissed it as a socially constructed, therefore artificial yearning. (Vishrammi's academic work was cutting-edge, but in her personal life, her reasoning was crude: what existed only in words didn't exist at all, she thought.)

When Vishrammi was thirty-nine, her mother died of a stroke. After the funeral, Vishrammi sat in the empty house with her stunned father.

"She wanted you to marry," he mumbled, eventually. "That was her final wish." Vishrammi didn't contradict him, didn't remind him that Mumma had died in her sleep, unlikely to have handed down final wishes. "Independence is very well, but when you grow old – you will pine for a companion." Vishrammi didn't bother to remind him there were no guarantees in life, that everyone dies alone.

"Come live with me, Papa," said Vishrammi.

Papa offered the decent minimum of resistance, then packed his bags. "Alright, but don't let me get in your way. You're old enough, you pick out a man for yourself, however you judge best. I'll look the other way... Your mother always said it wasn't too late for you." Vishrammi, sweet-tempered, Vishrammi, who'd been sending money home for years, pursed her lips, dissimulating proper gratitude for Mumma's high opinion.

They went to Delhi – by flight, at Vishrammi's insistence. She hoped this new experience at age seventy would uplift Papa's spirits. But Papa just sat there, staring out the window, oblivious even to the air hostesses with smooth hair and immaculate makeup.

Decades of *de facto* celibacy, grief, age, and now transplantation had made Papa a woman. All day he shuffled around Vishrammi's bungalow on campus, tidying up, mumbling to himself. At mealtimes he'd sit across from her at the table, hesitating woman-like to eat his own meal till the (wo)man of the house had finished hers. When she addressed him, it took his mumbling lips ages to start making sound. "Your mother said," he kept mumbling, "it wasn't too late for you."

Vishrammi hadn't realised how close her parents had been. She'd never seen them touch, not even a hand to the shoulder: like all Indian parents, they were sexless bar the procreational mandate. Sometimes Vishrammi was gentle with Papa; sometimes she tried tough love, hoping to goad him into recruiting himself. But had he anything left to recruit? She began lying awake at night, staring at her bed's smooth other half. Perhaps Mumma had lain so, on her side,

279

whispering to Papa, "If I die, you tell Vishru – it's not too late for her." She'd catch herself, snap out of it, and shut her eyes.

Papa kept creeping about the house. Vishrammi began staying in bed later and later every morning, just leaving herself time to get dressed and hurry out the door. The *Hindu*, which she used to read to Papa, at morning tea after her 5-kilometre jog around campus, she began tucking under her arm, to read over lunch. She longed for someone to confide in, to tell her what to do about Papa. A grandchild running around would snap him awake. But she'd never wanted children. Had she? She was no longer sure. Anyway, it was too late. She was 43. Realising that this decision, which all her well-wishers had been thrusting at her, was safely behind her, should've produced relief. It produced only that old curious yearning.

She lunched in her cabin, the tray delivered from the mess, while her colleagues downstairs whiled away an hour or two over deep-fried *puri* and *gobi manchurian*. Vishrammi's mind strayed from *The Hindu*. One afternoon, on a whim, she visited BharatMatrimony.com.

She filled in her profile, guiltily peeking out her cabin window, her fingers on her laptop as antsy as a debutante bank-burglar's. Bharat Matrimony's algorithm presented her with a list of matches.

She opened the first profile. A man's face flashed onscreen: passport photo, white background, blue shirt, big limpid eyes. A shadow flickered outside her office. Vishrammi half-jumped from her seat and shut her Chrome, switched off her monitor, and frowned sceptically at her *Hindu*.

But the big limpid eyes haunted her dreams. They watched her toss and turn on the rumpled half of the bed. They stared up at her from the face of an undergraduate, and she flushed and stammered and turned away to dab with a chalk-stub at the blackboard. This was unacceptable. Not even at twenty-three had she felt attracted to a student. She contacted the Bharat Matrimony man. Amrit Beriwal. They discussed meeting.

Amrit suggested Chandni Chowk. Vishrammi hesitated. Everyone in Delhi knows Chandni Chowk, everyone goes there to shop for cheap sandals, brand-rip-off handbags, *lehengas* for a cousin's wedding, saris for their own wedding. Vishrammi had lived in Delhi two decades, but she'd never visited Chandni Chowk. Too noisy. Besides, she never needed anything. Now sitting at her laptop, at her desk facing her wall full of diplomas, her bedroom window opening onto the sleepy garden, she pictured Chandni Chowk. A riot of colours, loudspeakers throbbing with music, the air sweet with spicy deep-fried dough and pungent with sweat, thick with all the living she had missed. She struggled to breathe. "OK, Amrit. See you there."

But Amrit took her to a chic little café overlooking Chandni Chowk. He was about her age, neither obese nor pungent, neither lecherous nor tongue-tied. Passable. Vishrammi had bathed twice, changed five times, and tried three hairstyles, all the while shaking her head.

"Forty-three," Amrit began, "is late to start dating. Will you go first, or shall I?" Vishrammi giggled and tilted her glass of ice tea, the better to stare into it. Was he being forthright or rude? Amrit continued, "My parents have been nagging at me to get married since I got my first job."

Vishrammi asked him about his work. Intent on getting the most fun out of this dating thing, she had refrained from looking him up beforehand.

Ducking his head between his shoulders, he said, "Software engineer. But I'll try not to be boring! Please don't walk away."

"Of course not!" But Vishrammi had in fact drawn back across the table, and her face had fallen. She prided herself on her manners; she recruited her best smile. But really, what could they talk about? Everyone knows software engineers never read, never stargaze, never masticate the imponderables. "Please tell me more."

He told her about blockchain and cryptocurrency, how it worked, and what he did and how, lucidly. She nodded along eagerly. Something to do with money, she understood that much. Vishrammi knew exactly how much money she had, in what assets – nothing venturesome, all fixed and recurring deposits, and one mutual fund. But in transacting money, moving money around, in money for money's sake, she had no more interest than a pig in pearls. She beguiled the time by mentally reciting her favourite Shakespeare speeches: the tribune's tirade against *Julius Caesar*'s fickle public, deserting Pompey who'd served them well for Caesar who served only himself; Prospero telling Miranda how gullibility had cost him his kingdom; Leontes wondering whether poison can kill you if you don't know you've swallowed it. Amrit finished his narrative. Vishrammi swallowed her yawn, but not before it had squeezed out her tears. Bright-eyed, she said, "That's fascinating!"

Amrit laughed softly. Vishrammi felt exposed. It was his turn to sit back. He gazed at her: not contemptuously, only assessingly, as she gazed at her most impervious students. "In my defence," said Amrit, "a whole generation of boys were pushed into software, at least those of us who weren't hopeless in school. Doesn't mean we aren't also trying to be interesting."

"Of course not." Vishrammi bit her tongue.

A fat lot of good a lifetime's literature had done her, leaving her so closed-minded! She was as bad as her colleagues. The ghost of a smile creased Amrit's eyes. He was a perfectly balanced boat, dancing on the sea: no storm of her dunderheaded contempt could rock him. A yearning to earn his esteem seized Vishrammi. Her smile was no ghost, was full-blooded with good intentions.

Amrit worked from home, mostly nights, so Vishrammi began devoting her afternoons and weekends to him. Any guilt she felt on Papa's behalf she repressed: after all, he'd wanted this for her, and so, apparently, had Mumma. How had she ever imagined she didn't need a flesh-and-blood friend? Amrit contained a whole new world behind his forehead, whole new perspectives which weren't spelled out for her leisurely perusal in black and white, which she had to worm out in the half-sense, constantly edited imperfection of ordinary human speech. Amrit was an adventure. Rope-girdle around waist, nailed boots on her feet, Vishrammi looked up the mountain and realised that she'd never really learned to converse. To her colleagues, literature was merely a livelihood. And her students were too ignorant, too deferential, too easily excited by their brain's free-range sputterings, to engage her in real conversation. She'd learned to lecture but not to speak.

Racing to make up for lost time, to learn what she should've learned thirty years ago, Vishrammi embarked on Amrit as a full-time project. She too, was finally among the world's normal people, among the accepted.

Vishrammi had been saving for a flat, for when she retired. Just a small place: in Delhi a closet costs a crore. She'd intended to rent it out at first. Now she talked it over with Amrit, and decided it'd be better to move in now, to move away from campus, which was, like most campuses, insular and gossipy. "We don't want anyone prying," said Amrit, and she agreed.

She paid the whole sum down, but – over Amrit's protests – put both their names on the deed. She knew

Amrit would pay her back his share, bit by bit. He had recently buried both his parents after long stays in ICU. During the weeks they'd dated, he had once or twice begun speaking of those days, briefly and haltingly. Vishrammi had patted his hand and shushed his lips. She'd felt grateful that Mumma had not suffered, had left behind neither debts nor the nightmare image of herself pale and white-sheeted, plastic tubes wending their way around an antiseptic-stinking room, winding around her throat.

Vishrammi and Amrit met in March, got the flat in May, and set the date for their wedding in July. No need for a long engagement. The traditions of millennia, traditions so outdated, didn't apply in her case. News of the wedding made Papa perk up with such alacrity that she wondered if his whole malaise hadn't been put-on. But she was too happy to grudge him his subterfuges. The morning of the wedding she hugged the frail old man till he squealed. "This is all thanks to you, Papa." His throat was too full of swallowed tears to speak, but his eyes shone with mischief, like when she herself had done something mischievous. Papa had sympathised with her childhood capers, and had only ever scolded her when Mumma approached, only so that Mumma wouldn't scold him.

Vishrammi was the world's luckiest woman. Engaged at forty-four, and not one question about whether she was still fertile; not one hint that, once a woman married, it was her husband's parents she should live with. The wedding was a small Hindu ceremony, only a sister and a cousin representing Amrit's side. The women made themselves useful, but hadn't a word to say for themselves. "They're tongue tied before you, professor," Amrit whispered. He didn't seem to regret his family's absence, so Vishrammi thanked her stars she'd have him to herself.

Vishrammi, Amrit, and Papa got along well. Papa

began sitting up straight, speaking with his former booming voice, and making the young couple wait on him in state. But in a few weeks it became clear this was a prolonged lucid interval, fuelled by excitement now ebbing. His eyes grew cloudy, strayed away from faces, and stared endlessly out the window. His lips began to mumble, wondering when his wife would be home. Vishrammi took him again to the doctor, to get his medications changed again. Nothing helped much. On his excursions away from sanity, it was on Amrit that Papa focussed the distrust and ill-temper of dementia.

"Not just for our sakes," began Amrit, as Vishrammi sat clasping the mug of chamomile tea he'd made her, gazing at Papa shuffling around, looking for his eyeglasses, which were on his face, "but for his, it would be kinder to move him to an institution, under professional care."

Vishrammi gazed into the garden. March had invoked the flowers of the golden-lantern tree. *Amaltash.* It was Papa who'd taught her the Hindi names and Latin names of flowers, who'd taught her to name the things of the world. From Monday morning to Saturday midday Papa had lived for wife and daughter, colleagues and parents, but evenings and Sundays, in between naps, he'd nibble at the world via excavated albums, obscure encyclopaedias, and imported seeds which sometimes condescended to add a leaf or two to his balcony garden. Now all that, all the world as slipping from him. Vishrammi sat up and exhaled. "You're right."

All month she spent her afternoons looking up places, hunting down honest reviews, comparing facilities. A 200-acre place beyond Gurgaon topped the shortlist. Big single rooms, air-conditioned, one full-time nurse per three patients, gardening and backgammon, and as rainbow a spectrum of activities for the demented as a 21st-century social climber could want for her fame-destined toddler.

285

But on the big Sunday, Vishrammi was in hell with hot flashes, so she sent Papa with Amrit, the car stuffed full of fruit, cosy shoes, and framed photos.

At the car door, Amrit saluted her goodbye. He had the absurd habit of saluting her, as a sailor might his captain, two fingers to forehead. She teared up and to hide her tears spouted exhaustive directions. He interrupted her. "We've got GPS, we've got everything we need. Relax! He'll be fine."

Vishrammi waited all week to hear from Papa, but when he called next Saturday his voice whined and his words foundered. "What d'you mean they never feed you, Papa?" said Vishrammi. "Even here at home, you kept forgetting you'd just eaten."

"I'm pinching – my skin's hanging – they never feed me, daughter! He brought me to the wrong place. He's a bad man."

Vishrammi almost slammed the phone down. It was one thing for Papa to grasp at the scraps of reality, to stare at them, uncomprehendingly – but to shuffle the scraps into an accusation was too much. She counted to ten, then soothed him and promised to visit soon. Afterwards she wandered around the bungalow. Amrit continued lounging over the *Financial Times*.

"Let's go see Papa tomorrow," she said.

"That might be hard," he drawled. "Amma's due soon."

Vishrammi looked confused, then stunned. "What Amma? Both your parents are dead."

"Oh, you must've misunderstood. Amma's alive and well."

"I misunderstood?" Vishrammi. "No... She didn't come to the wedding. Nobody from your side came except your sister and cousin." Her head whirled. "And you told me you'd lost both your parents, that's why you couldn't pay—"

"You must've misunderstood. Why would I say that? As for my not being able to pay my half of the flat" – his voice rose, and later she realised he was nervous, that this was his first time telling so big a lie – "did I insist you pay for me, did I insist you put both our names on the deed?" He jumped up and seized Vishrammi's car-keys from the table. "I'm going to pick them up at the station."

"Station?" Vishrammi repeated, staring eyes bulging from her skull.

"Well, I didn't want to ask you for money, for a flight ticket, after everything you shelled out for your Papa." He giggled, nervous again, then composed himself. "Yes, we'll go see him sometime… Put on a nice sari and rustle up dinner, would you? They'll be famished."

"Who the hell is 'they'?"

"Amma and my sisters… You remember my youngest sister from the wedding? She's been dying to meet you again. She's a big reader, wants to study English Literature, or Comparative Literature, or something. But her marks are a little low. She'll need coaching to get into D.U." He waited. She stood leaning on a chairback, arms trembling, staring through the walls. He turned on his heel and strode out, whistling.

Vishrammi recruited her wits, searched through Amrit's drawers to try to piece together what else he'd been lying about, and met her mother-in-law in frigid silence. The spry old woman shook off her frigidity as an Arctic tern shakes off a snowflake. "I'm here to help," she chirped, taking Vishrammi's hands, gazing into her eyes. Vishrammi glimpsed the brain of the operation: the perhaps formerly good woman hardened, by who knows what hell, into Lady Macbeth's ideal: looking like the flower while being the serpent under it. A fat lot of good a lifetime's literature had done Vishrammi, leaving her so naïve, scorning the traditions of millennia, traditions so wise.

Vishrammi's mind was blank but her fingers alert as she

stood in the kitchen beside Mother-in-law, chopping *tindara* for dinner. Come to think of it, this might be nice. Amrit's sisters hovered in the doorway, studying Vishrammi big-eyed. She relented and invited them in to help.

That night Amrit tearfully explained everything to her. "I'm a gambler, Vishrammi. You've married a gambler... I got into online poker four, five years ago. I'd just been laid off from Wipro, you know during that massive restructuring." Vishrammi made the smallest possible nod. She'd seen his Wipro ID card, and he'd introduced her in May to an old colleague, and she'd looked that man up today: still at Wipro, same name, same face. "Well, I'd never been fired before. I was too embarrassed to tell anyone. But suddenly I had all this time on my hands. Of course I had to look for work, but, after the first day or two, I realised it'd be nice to take a holiday. I'd never really had a holiday. In school, holidays meant summer workshops and swimming lessons, and later internships and football and coaching... So I took my first proper holiday at 39. I discovered online poker... Well! The rest is a story you've heard often before."

Vishrammi hadn't. She knew no disreputable people whatsoever. But she could not in this crisis lose hand by confessing her ignorance. She merely nodded grimly.

Amrit continued: "That's where all my money went... Then I met you. It was my parents who'd made my Bharat Matrimony profile for me, years before all this, nagging me to get married. I'd forgotten all about it. But when you pinged me, I was blown away, I couldn't turn you down. And then I met you, and I told you lie after lie... But I vowed to clean up my act, I vowed to make it all true. I yearned to turn over a new page, and with you beside me I believed I could. That thing about my parents dying, I was so – I was at my wits' end, I didn't know how else to explain why a 43-year-old software engineer couldn't afford to make a payment on a flat... I kept waiting for something to happen, to rescue me. I never expected we'd actually get married." He cried.

Vishrammi never cried, so she thought tears a big deal, so she reserved her rebuke. They talked till dawn, or rather he talked. She found she couldn't quite hate him, this man who had, like herself, been ambushed at an advanced age by the world. "Go to sleep," she said. "We'll work things out eventually."

He told her he loved her. She turned over and went to sleep.

When she awoke that Sunday afternoon, he was gone, and her phone was beeping with notifications that the funds transfers out of her bank account had been successfully completed.

Her wits were still reeling from yesterday's twelve-round boxing-match; it took her a half-hour, and certain secret aids upon which we shan't intrude, to recruit her wits. She rang her bank's helpline, listened to canned music for forty-one minutes drip-dripping, drilling into her throbbing skull, navigated a platypus platoon of customer-care executives, who shuttlecocked her back and forth, and finally told her: it was too late.

By the time the police got involved, all her savings were gone, transferred to multiple accounts, destination accounts all cashed out. Amrit's accounts were seized, but they showed no suspicious activity.

Some days later, Amrit returned home to a wife almost hysterical, but to no legal trouble. He had merely gone to Bihar to fetch his elderly father and his two cousins, who made rather a tight fit in the Sundernagar flat. The police listened with unprofessional interest as Amrit explained himself to his wife.

Of course he'd told her he was going. She's been under

a lot of stress lately, officer, you know menopause, and some trouble at work. She's forgotten I told her. My parents are getting old, naturally they want to live with me and my dear wife, they've heard so many good things about her. Vishrammi protested till her throat cracked, till everyone was convinced she was another crazed childless middle-aged woman. The police hemmed in, looked away considerately, promised to track down the mysterious cyber-hacker, and shuffled doorwards. Suddenly Vishrammi remembered Amrit had been a software engineer. Perhaps he'd been a good one. Not good enough to hack his way to poker millions, but clearly too good for the Indian police. She stopped herself midsentence and thanked the police for their time. All fight deserted her, left her suspecting that this is what she deserved.

"I can't cook for all these people," Amrit's mother declared.

Crisis had come to Vishrammi late in life and all in a typhoon. Her mind had taken an extended leave of absence. "We'll get a maid," she mumbled.

"Where's the money for a maid?" Amrit's mother demanded. "No, you'll have to do the cooking and cleaning before work, and after work… It's not good for a woman to spend so many hours poring over books… If only you'd looked around yourself, and learned about people…" She trailed off, smiling. She wasn't a heartless woman, just adaptable.

Vishrammi rose from the crowded table. "I'm going to see Papa."

"You'll need the address." Amrit scribbled it down for her, and handed it to her, unblinking. Victory, and the company of his cool-as-a-cucumber mother, were doing wonders for him. "Tell him we'd love to have him back, only it's so crowded, and, you know, he might not get along with my folks."

Vishrammi found Papa on a shabby bed in a dingy room in an Old Delhi building, a former zero-star hotel, now run by lazy sadists. Rage made her fists clench and the blood pound behind her eyes. Papa looked up, his head nodding in battered acquiescence with the universe's mad blind logic.

She knelt before him and took his hands. He looked into her eyes. She glimpsed a human soul still flitting around back there, looking for his cue to shuffle onstage – or was it to go offstage?

She bethought herself of Portia and Viola, Cleopatra and Katherina. She couldn't decide if she was in a comedy or a tragedy. She beckoned Papa to his feet. He complied, obedient as a child, searching her face for directions. "First, let's get out of here." Of all the goods she'd sent Papa off with, he had none, and she looked for none. They shuffled into the corridor.

"Where d'you think you're going?" Vishrammi confronted a coffee-skinned, hazel-eyed man in a tan uniform, arms crossed, biceps bulging.

"Taking my father home. Checking out."

"You owe us six months' fees," said the meathead.

"He's only been here a month. And my husband paid."

"Nobody paid anything for this old fool. And that man you sent here signed our contract, which says—"

"Let us pass."

They almost came to blows. But the thug didn't dare strike them. This woman looked upper-class, spoke good English, spoke familiarly of the police superintendent. They weren't paid up, couldn't risk trifling with the wrong party. He stepped aside, growling.

"Where are we going, daughter?" said Papa, as they stood on the pavement, Vishrammi focusing the leftovers of her brain on hailing an autorickshaw.

"Don't know... Maybe back to the bungalow on campus?"

She remembered the vine-walled bungalow, her afternoons in her office cabin, the crickets chirping, her mind racing as she poured her thoughts onto paper, sipping her tea watching the warblers quarrel over the ripe *bael* fruit stinkily splattered across the grass, on the guavas, hard as stones and green as peace, clinging to the boughs. She remembered her old life, with its clock-like routines, from which she had fled as from a life-sentence. She remembered scraps of news from over the decades. "Boys burgle house, strangle residents." "Woman found raped and disembowelled in ditch." "Son and daughter-in-law turn aged mother out of ancestral house."

She chuckled. "Yes, we can go back to our bungalow. I still have my job, and my health, and you."

Crisis suited Papa. He awoke from his brain-fog. "Yes, I like our bungalow. Much better than this place where that man brought me... I don't know who he was, but he wasn't a good man. I could see that much." She turned to him, her eyes filling with tears. "But, Vishru, weren't you going to get married?"

"Yes, Papa, I was." She settled him carefully in the rickety auto, then got in herself. "Hold tight, Papa." They hadn't been in an auto in years: cabs were one of her few luxuries besides her summers in the mountains.

"Good," said Papa. "Good that you're getting married. You always were my good daughter. And your mother always says, 'Better late than never.' "

ABOUT THE AUTHOR

Amita Basu is a Pushcart-nominated writer whose fiction appears in more than eighty-five publications including *The Penn Review*, *Bamboo Ridge*, *Faultline*, *Jelly Bucket*, *Phoebe*, and *Funicular*. She's won the *Letter Review* prize and *Kelp*'s Shelter in Place contest, and been shortlisted by *Five Minute Lit*'s and *Phoebe*'s fiction contests.

Amita's favourite writers are George Eliot, Thomas Mann, and Alice Munro. Eliot, with her piercing insight into a wide range of personalities, combined with compassion, is Amita's North Star. Amita admires and envies comic writers from Aristophanes to Kingsley Amis to Wodehouse, as well as contemporary stand-up comics. She'd love to write a comic novel. She's still stuck making laboured, embarrassing dad jokes, so the comic novel will be a while coming. Meanwhile, she's working on a climate action/high-fantasy novel and her next collection of literary realist short stories.

Amita lives in Bangalore, India. She has a PhD in cognitive science. Her doctoral work examined the valuation and discounting of nonmarket goods. Climate change and environmental destruction being problems caused by human behaviour, Amita believes that solutions must focus on understanding and shifting behaviour. Amita is Senior Research Fellow at Transitions Research, a climate action thinktank. Here, she helps design and test interventions to encourage pro-environmental behaviours: e.g. the adoption of rooftop solar, the use of electric vehicles and public transport, and the segregation of waste at source. Transitions Research also works on developing behaviourally informed policy recommendations, and works with a range of stakeholders to create change.

Amita loves dogs, spending time in nature, and classical music. She blogs at http://amitabasu.com/

PUBLICATION HISTORY OF THESE STORIES

Fish**
Bandit Fiction (Feb 2022)
Kelp Journal (Summer 2020) – won the award for best
prose piece

Rebirth**
Caustic Frolic: magazine (Jan 2023)
Goat's Milk (2021)
Ligeia Issue #5 (Autumn 2020)

All Creatures Great and Small**
Kitaab (Feb 2024) – Editors' Pick of the Week
Moonlighting by Lit Pub (Mar 2024)

At Play***
Fairlight Books Short Story Portal (Winter 2021) –
refeatured as Story of the Week
Running Wild/RIZE anthology as "Last Holiday/At Play"
(upcoming, date unknown)

The City*
(alt. title: One-See-Are)
Bamboo Ridge Issue #124 (Nov 2023) (45th Anniversary
Issue)

The Sacrifice**
(alt. title: Shrimps & Gunpowder)
Rollick (Aug 2023)

The Why and the How*

Mean Pepper Vine (Winter 2022-23)

Bewildering Stories (Feb 2022) – chosen as best piece published that quarter in the magazine's Editors' Choice Awards.

Night

The Dalhousie Review's (Summer 2022)

The Chamber Magazine (Jan 2023)

Retreat

Constellations anthology Vol. 12 "Uncertainty." Website; Amazon US (Dec 2022)

Republished in *The Metaworker*; nominated for a Pushcart (Dec 2023)

Shoes***

(alt. title: The Morning After Ganesh Puja)

The flash version published in *Funicular* Issue #12 (Jul 2023)

Better Late Than Never

Contest finalist in *Phoebe* (May 2024)

Holiday***

(alt. title: First Trip)

The flash version published in *Meet Cute Press* Issue #2 (Mar 2021)

The same flash version republished in *Bull Men's Fiction* (Oct 2023)

The current version as "First Trip" *in Faultline* (upcoming in May 2025)

The current version, as "First Trip" in *Blue Press Literary* (upcoming, date unknown)

Field Trip
Flash version, called "School Trip," in *Sledgehammer*
   (Jan 2022)
Full version in *Jelly Bucket* (Sep 2024) – nominated for a
   Pushcart
Also upcoming in *El Porta*

Shiver
River and South Issue 14 (Jan 2025)
Indian Literature/Sahitya Akademi Journal #346 (March
   2025)

Audience
Unpublished

*   Revised lightly since last publication: mostly just
     some polishing

**   Revised moderately since last publication: some
     change to storyline

*** Revised heavily or beyond recognition since last
     publication: storyline totally changed

For a full portfolio of published works see
https://amitabasu.com/portfolio/

ACKNOWLEDGMENTS

In 2020 I discovered the Internet Writing Workshop (IWW). Without this community, I would never have written one decent story. In the IWW I found the community, critique, and camaraderie that are a writer's lifeblood. I'm particularly grateful to Wayne Scheer and Rod Raglin for their honest and insightful critiques. Thank you also to Phyllis Sanchez and Pamelyn Casto for your steady stream of encouragement and your own uplifting creative output. Mitchy and Mike, I'm forever in your debt for your sharp critiques, sense of humour, and friendship.

I'm grateful to Gill James for taking a risk on this book. Several agents told me they liked my writing but that short story collections by debut writers don't sell. That you decided to back my writing means more to me than I can say. I'm happy and proud to be part of the *Bridge House* family, which values literature over market considerations.

Alicia Rouverol is the best editor a writer could hope for. Her own taste is unerring, and her judgment discriminating. But she welcomes a wide range of perspectives, recognises what it is the writer is trying to do (often better than the writer herself), and allows the writer final say. The writers Alicia recommended to me have already nudged my writing in, I believe, the right directions. Conversations with Alicia showed me exactly what a story needed, and gave me the push I needed to revisit the manuscript one more time – no easy feat, when you've already spent years on a book and can't wait to see the back of it. As Commissioning Editor, I must also thank Alicia for taking on this project in the first place.

Anna Mandelbaum was my first steady critique partner. She has since become my mentor, guide, and closest friend. Thank you, Anna, for modelling grace, wisdom, and humour.

You're a world-class story doctor. You always put your finger on what ails a story. You tell me not to take your prescriptions for a cure too seriously. But they're always spot-on. So I do. Neither this book nor I would be here without you. Now I'll be on the sidelines, cheering myself hoarse as your own writing career takes off.

Jon Minton's thorough critiques of all the rubbish I sent him, the creativity, variety, and energy of his own work, and his ever-ready sympathetic ear have been my lifeline. Jon, I see right through your crusty cynicism to your good heart and impish sense of humour. Our rambling chats about books and politics, climate and films have bolstered me through hard times. Your active participation in the writing community is as admirable as your vigorous straddling of genres.

On everything I've sent him, Bill LaFond has given me critiques both honest and constructive, a harder feat than it looks. Our conversations about life, reading, and writing have broadened and deepened me. Discussions about the rapidly evolving challenges facing anyone who wants to write and publish today have helped me vent frustrations and formulate solutions. Bill, you make me wonder what I've done to deserve such fantastic friends.

I'm inspired by Mark Kline's approach to writing, thoughtful but spontaneous, and by his compassionate approach to life. Your tact in critiquing the sometimes harebrained drafts I sent you has helped me become, I hope, a more thoughtful critic partner myself. Your love of nature and music inspired me to dig myself out of the hole I'd got into while working on this book, where there was only writing, and writing had stopped being fun. Your gift for narrative efficiency and telling character detail teach me better than a guidebook. Your grace in life reminds me that writing is most fun when it's part of a well-rounded life.

Shilpi, you are my rock and my bhang buddy, my partner in hysterical giggles, painful self-examination, hope, and growth. Every day I thank God, who doesn't exist, that I met you. Your fortitude and grace in dealing with all the shit life has thrown at you, and your determination to make the world a better place, inspire me every day.

Ranjith, I admire your compassion and your resilience, your wisdom and your discretion. Whether it's spending whole days in the sea in Goa – joking how neither of us can swim – or comparing tastes in dates, every experience with you is memorable. Your good nature and your compassion present standards I can only aspire to.

I'm indebted to everyone who has ever created anything beautiful. Your books, songs, and films have helped me survive hard times and inspired me to make beautiful things myself. Artists of the world, underpaid and overworked, mocked for your crazy ideas, dismissed for your unconventional choices – you are the soul of our universe. Never stop suffering, hoping, and creating.

LIKE TO READ MORE WORK LIKE THIS?

Then sign up to our mailing list and download our free collection of short stories, *Magnetism*. Sign up now to receive this free e-book and also to find out about all of our new publications and offers.

Sign up here:
    http://eepurl.com/gbpdVz

PLEASE LEAVE A REVIEW

Reviews are so important to writers. Please take the time to review this book. A couple of lines is fine.

Reviews help the book to become more visible to buyers. Retailers will promote books with multiple reviews.

This in turn helps us to sell more books… And then we can afford to publish more books like this one.

Leaving a review is very easy.

Go to https://amzn.to/3ZbjGW5, scroll down the left-hand side of the Amazon page and click on the "Write a customer review" button.

OTHER PUBLICATIONS BY BRIDGE HOUSE

White Moon

by Mehreen Ahmed

White Moon is a collection of avant-garde short stories, micro and flash fiction.

Together they bring a stronger message than they do individually. The incidents in this book depict imaginary characters and events underpinned by dreamlike, strong surrealistic, even esoteric connections. The narratives bring together a unique blend of absorbing, entertaining and otherworldly experience.

As ever Mehreen Ahmed brings a strong and convincing voice to all of the texts. Enjoy the surreal and dreamlike quality of these stories.

Order from Amazon:

Paperback: ISBN 978-1-914199-90-5
eBook: ISBN 978-1-914199-91-2

Between Worlds
by S.Nadja Zajdman

We all inhabit multiple worlds and the real person lives in the liminal space between them.

In this fascinating collection of vignettes and creative memoir, we are invited to explore several constructs of the times and places defined by the narrator, and also envisaged by those around her. These accounts have appeared in other publications, but gathered here the whole becomes greater than its parts and tells a larger story.

S. Nadja Zajdman brings her rich and unique voice to this story: *Between Worlds*.

"This collection will not disappoint…! Bravo!" *(Amazon)*

Order from Amazon:

Paperback: ISBN 978-1-914199-84-4
eBook: ISBN 978-1-914199-85-1

Blood and Electricity
by Steven John

"We took an excursion around the sun again this year, five hundred million miles back to where we started." From *A Brief History of Time in Our House*, a story in this collection.

There are no UFOs or extra-terrestrials in this first collection of short stories and flash fiction by Steven John. Blood and Electricity is about the vital currents that flow through and around us, powering our lonely orbits of life. We are all bright stars that appear close to one another when viewed with the naked eye, but the truth is, we're separated by incomprehensible distances.

"This is a tremendous collection of flash fiction. Steven John is a master of words, but also so able to write situations and characters with which we immediately identify." *(Amazon)*

Order from Amazon:

Paperback: ISBN 978-1-914199-80-6
eBook: ISBN 978-1-914199-81-3

www.ingramcontent.com/pod-product-compliance
Lightning Source LLC
Chambersburg PA
CBHW070303260626
47160CB00003B/701